Sheila Norton lives near Chelmsford in Essex with her husband, and worked for most of her life as a medical secretary, before retiring early to concentrate on her writing. Sheila is the award-winning writer of numerous women's fiction novels and over 100 short stories, published in women's magazines.

She has three married daughters, six little grandchildren, and over the years has enjoyed the companionship of three cats and two dogs. She derived lots of inspiration for her animal books from remembering the pleasure and fun of sharing life with her own pets.

When not working on her writing Sheila enjoys spending time with her family and friends, as well as reading, walking, swimming, photography and travel. For more information please see www.sheilanorton.com

Also by Sheila Norton:

The Lonely Hearts Dog Walkers

The Pet Shop at Pennycombe Bay
The Pets at Primrose Cottage
The Vets at Hope Green
Oliver the Cat Who Saved Christmas
Charlie the Kitten That Saved a Life

Escape to Riverside Cottage

Sheila Norton

EBURY
PRESS

First published by Ebury Press in 2021

1

Ebury Press, an imprint of Ebury Publishing
20 Vauxhall Bridge Road,
London SW1V 2SA

Ebury Press is part of the Penguin Random House group of companies
whose addresses can be found at global.penguinrandomhouse.com

Penguin
Random House
UK

www.penguin.co.uk

A CIP catalogue record for this book is available from the British Library

ISBN 9781529103120

Typeset in 11.75/14.45 pt Berkeley
by Integra Software Services Pvt. Ltd, Pondicherry

Printed and bound in Great Britain by Clays Ltd, Elcograf S.p.A.

Penguin Random House is committed to a sustainable future for
our business, our readers and our planet. This book is made
from Forest Stewardship Council® certified paper.

MIX
Paper from
responsible sources
FSC® C018179

The authorised representative in the EEA is Penguin Random House Ireland,
Morrison Chambers, 32 Nassau Street, Dublin D02 YH68.

With love and thanks to my wonderful family and lovely friends, for their support and encouragement throughout all the ups and downs of my writing career. For reading, for spreading the word, and for just being there, while I'm shut away with my laptop. It's all appreciated more than I usually think to say.

PROLOGUE

In a tranquil part of south Devon, roughly midway between the outer fringes of Dartmoor and the Cornish boundary at the Tamar river, lies a tiny village set in the valley of the River Sorrel on its tidal stretch just before the estuary. The square-towered village church of Saint Peter is the biggest and most imposing building of the village, dwarfing the cottages on either side and even the squat whitewashed, crooked-walled building of the pub, the Ferryboat Inn. There's a single shop that sells everything from fresh bread, baked on the premises, to garden tools, saucepans and indigestion remedies. Outside it are trestle tables displaying fruit and vegetables supplied by local farmers, with brown paper bags – never plastic – hanging on a hook for customers to choose their own produce. Children run straight from the ancient building of the little village school down the wide, worn, stone steps to the river, where their crabbing buckets and lines are stored under the wooden jetty. There's a children's playground on the village green

1

but it doesn't get an awful lot of use. These kids grow up playing in the mud in welly boots and waders, and most of them learn to row a boat before they can ride a bike.

This is the village of Little Sorrel. If you didn't have it entered into your satnav – and probably even if you did – you'd miss it, whether you were driving east or west or just meandering around the coast and countryside looking for 'The Real Devon'. The real Devon is right here, but it's a secret. You get here by a single-track lane – one of those long, winding ones so typical of the area, with high hedges, deep ditches and very few passing places. The road doesn't even have a name, never mind a number on the map. Unsuspecting tourists who accidentally turn into the lane often panic and try to do three-point-turns in farm gateways rather than carry on. The few signposts are old, worn and unreliable. If you try to find the village in the dark or on a gloomy, rainy, winter's day, you're more than likely to turn off by mistake at one of the unmarked crossroads, believing you must surely, in time, reach a better road that way. You won't. After miles of hedges and ditches, after the possibility of a dead sheep by the side of the lane or a live flock of them being driven down the middle of it, you'll realise you've done a full circle and you'll give up and do that three-point-turn.

On the other hand, there will sometimes be an intrepid, or perhaps just bloody-minded, driver who turns onto the lane out of pure curiosity, maybe on a clear, sunny day in late spring or early summer, when the hedgerows are full of blossom, the scents through their open car windows making their nose twitch and their eyes water. And perhaps that driver might sense something different, something important, at the end of the lane and just keep on going, even when they're caught behind a tractor that takes up the full width of the road. Even if the tractor slows down to less than a walking pace to climb the unbelievably steep hill that comes a mile or two before the end of the lane, that determined driver might stick to their guns, determined to carry this thing through.

And when the tractor finally pulls into one of the only passing places – the one at the top of the hill – and waves the intrepid driver on, perhaps they won't pass him, but instead, pull off the road themselves, turn off their engine, get out of their car and stare, down the hill into the valley below, where the little river gleams silver-green in the sunlight, where the cluster of tiny cottages surrounding the church tower look like dolls' houses, all white walls and thatched roofs, and where, setting off from the wooden jetty, a little boat, from this distance resembling a child's toy, leaves a trail of seagulls in its wake as it heads for the estuary.

Perhaps, ignoring the tractor driver's signals and shrugs, that driver might stay there, in the passing place on the brow of the hill, taking in this view, for half an hour or more, before eventually continuing down the lane, down Steep Hill (yes, finally, as it enters the village, the lane has a name), and into the village of Little Sorrel, to park outside the Ferryboat Inn and buy a pint of Devon ale.

I was one such driver. The day was a beautiful, warm one halfway through May, and I can't tell you how much I appreciated that glass of beer as I sat in the little pub

3

garden, watching children crabbing in the river below me. I was travelling alone, apart from a small, scruffy brown dog called Sid.

It was just over two years ago, and like most people, I'd never heard of Little Sorrel or had any idea it existed. I had another beer, a plate of seafood salad, and ended up spending the night at the pub. And staying.

CHAPTER 1

TWO YEARS EARLIER

It was my fifty-seventh birthday, and I'd just realised I was a widow. I mean, obviously I knew my ex-husband was dead, but it wasn't until my birthday that it occurred to me how much everything had changed. We'd been separated for several years by then but hadn't got around to a divorce. If we'd been divorced, I'd have had a different status. A divorcee might have conjured up images of a feisty, independent woman of a certain age who'd shaken off the chains of marriage and emerged as her own creature, knowing what she wanted and determined to get it. Whereas now, as a widow, people would, naturally, expect me to be consumed by grief, a cloud of sadness following me wherever I went.

I knew this to be true because of the funeral.

I should explain now that I'm not actually heartless – I was, of course, really upset about Brian. I'd have been upset about anyone who died at such an unfairly young age, struck down by a massive heart attack while he was crossing the supermarket car park. Brian had once been my husband. And, however our relationship had ended up, there'd been a time, obviously, when he and I had loved each other. He'd been the most important person in my life for nearly thirty years, we'd produced two children together, and then one day he'd told me he didn't love me any more, and I was shocked to realise I didn't even mind. Our marriage had run its course. We didn't fight. Neither of us had anyone else. We simply had nothing left in common, no interest left in being together. I didn't hate him, there was no reason to, but I wasn't really sure I particularly liked him either, and it seemed the feeling was mutual.

He moved out. We sold the house and both got little places of our own. It was all very civilised. We didn't think, or talk, about a divorce at first, and even after we decided that perhaps we should, we still took a while to get on with it. And then his fatal heart attack happened, just as we'd been about to start the proceedings. So I was still his wife, in name anyway, when he died, and obviously I played a part in the funeral. Our son had taken care of most of the arrangements, and of course, he and our daughter were devastated. So devastated that they hadn't even remembered it was on my birthday, and I didn't like to tell them.

'Are you OK, Mum?' asked my red-eyed daughter, putting her arm around me, giving me a sympathetic hug as her husband supported her on the other side.

It should have been me, consoling her, but I felt too confused, too discombobulated by my own feelings, to think straight.

'Yes, I'm fine,' I said, and then shook my head quickly, realising that was hardly appropriate or even true. 'I mean, I'm OK. Sort of. How about you?'

'Oh, Mum, I still can't believe it.' She wiped away fresh tears. 'I mean, I just can't get my head around the fact that Dad's gone. I can't imagine life without him.'

And that was the whole point, really. I could. I'd been imagining it for years – but just not in the awful way it had ended up happening.

'So how *were* you imagining it?' my friend Sally asked me that evening. She'd come round to have a drink with me for my birthday, and was surprised to find me still wearing my black funeral clothes. It had felt disrespectful to change straight out of them. 'Why is it different, being without him like *this*, from being without him anyway? Or if the divorce had gone through?'

'Well, it's horrible – sad and horrible, obviously. A shock.'

'Obviously,' she agreed. 'Especially for your kids. But what was it you'd been *imagining* about being divorced?'

I sipped my wine, thinking about it. 'Well, perhaps it sounds silly, but I suppose I'd always thought of divorce as the start of a new life. I know we'd been separated for ages, but divorce is different, isn't it?'

'Yes, it is.' Sally had been divorced twice, so she should know. 'It's more final. It makes you a single woman again.' She paused. 'So what did you want to do with this new life?'

I shrugged. 'No idea, really. I mean, it's not as if I can afford to jet off on luxury holidays or buy fancy cars and a big house with a swimming pool, or anything like that. I won't be able to retire for another ten years anyway. If then.'

'And this new life you were dreaming of – did it entail meeting a new man?'

'Absolutely not!' I retorted, and we both laughed. And then I remembered again that I was a widow, not a divorcee, and I stopped laughing, feeling guilty.

'I shouldn't be joking about it,' I said. 'My children are devastated.'

'Of course they are,' she said sympathetically. 'But that doesn't mean you should have to pretend to be. You're not.'

'But I *am*,' I said. 'Honestly, I'm not that cold-hearted, of course I'm upset, of course I've found myself thinking back over our years together. I can't believe he's gone. He was a good man, Sal. I never would have wanted this to happen to him.'

'I know. I understand.' She patted my hand and changed her approach. 'Maybe the grief will take a while to come out. You had a lot of time together. A lot of memories.'

I nodded. And we drank more wine, and talked a bit more about grief, and even though she was my closest friend, I couldn't tell her that what I really felt, in my deepest, most honest, most guilty and shameful soul, was that I'd been *cheated*.

'Trust you, Brian,' I said, staring at a photo of him later that night, trying to make sense of my feelings, because I was beginning to wonder if I wasn't normal. 'Trust you to cheat me out of being a happy divorcee. Happy widow doesn't sound the same. And anyway, I'm *not* happy that you're gone. You could have been a happy divorcé too. I wouldn't have wanted you to miss out on that.'

Do mixed-up and slightly resentful count as expressions of grief?

And then, of course, there was the will. If you haven't, as a separated couple, done anything about getting divorced, you certainly won't have done anything about changing your mirror wills, written with the best of intentions when you were young parents, leaving all your goods and chattels to each other, and to your children in the eventuality of you both kicking the bucket at the same time.

'Oh, well,' I said to our solicitor. 'I suppose it should all be redirected to the children, in the circumstances. I guess that's what he would have wanted.'

'It doesn't say that here,' the solicitor said, scanning the legal document in front of him again, his glasses slipping down over his nose.

'No. But in the circumstances, he wouldn't have wanted his – well, whatever he's got – his flat, and – whatever – to go to me. I don't expect it. It wouldn't be right.'

'In that case, Mrs Finch' – even my surname hadn't been divorced from him yet – 'you'd need to make arrangements to transfer however much of Mr Finch's estate you propose to pass over to your children as a gift, bearing in mind that if you yourself were to die within seven years, this would still be subject to inheritance tax.'

I had no idea what he was talking about.

'Can't it just go straight to them? It can't be much.'

'No. I'm afraid, by law, I have to follow the terms of the deceased's will. And in fact, Mrs Finch, we're talking about a considerable amount of money.'

And there we had it. Irrefutable evidence that not only had Brian stopped loving me, but he had also stopped telling me what the hell he was doing. He'd got bank accounts I had no knowledge of, containing sums of money I'd only ever associated with other people. Rich people. Millionaires. People who lived in big houses with swimming pools, who jetted off on luxurious holidays and bought fancy, expensive cars. Not people who, when they split up from their wives, lived in a poky little apartment, still drove the same old Vauxhall and continued to work as a maths teacher at the local high school. How the hell had this happened? Had someone died – a member of his family I didn't know about – and left him a fortune? Had it happened before we split up, and he'd kept it quiet from me?

'It wasn't a relative, Clare.' Brian's closest friend Andy, a colleague from the school, fidgeted uncomfortably with his coffee cup and avoided meeting my eyes. I'd called him as soon as I got back from the solicitor's office, and he came to see me when he'd finished work. I'd spent the first ten minutes of our conversation making it clear I wanted the truth, the whole truth and nothing but the truth. 'But you're right, someone did leave him a fortune.'

'Someone – like who? Come on, Andy. I get that he might have asked you to keep it to yourself, but it can't hurt him now. Or me.'

'Well, I'm worried that it *might* actually hurt you.' He finally met my eyes. 'Why do you think he kept it quiet?'

'Presumably because it was some woman.'

'Oh.' He raised his eyebrows. 'You knew?'

'Of course I didn't bloody know, Andy! But I'm perfectly capable of putting two and two together. So he had a girlfriend, fair enough. Or he had an affair while we were still together – is that it?' I paused. 'Either way, he picked someone who had loads of money, who for reasons best known to herself decided to share it with him—'

'Not quite,' he interrupted me quietly. 'He didn't have an affair. And he hadn't had a girlfriend since you split up – not so far as I know, anyway. He dated this woman before he even met you.'

I stared at him. 'Don't be silly,' I laughed eventually. 'We got together over thirty years ago.'

'I know. And before he met you, he was dating a woman called Jacqueline Bright.'

Jacqueline Bright. Strangely enough, the name rang a bell. Perhaps Brian had mentioned her in passing, way back when we were still interested in each other's past lives.

'And she was rich?' I asked, as Andy finally sipped his coffee. 'I don't remember Brian ever saying he'd been out with a rich woman.'

'She wasn't, at the time. She became rich later in life, after they split up. She was an author. Wrote a couple of bestselling novels.'

Jacqueline Bright. Of course. That was why I recognised the name.

'*Cut You Dead*,' I said, giving a little whistle of surprise. 'I read it. And saw the film. And there was another one—'

'*Dead Ringer*.' He nodded. 'They were both international bestsellers.'

'But I don't remember seeing any more after that.'

'No. She died – a car accident, apparently. It was all over the news at the time.'

'Was it? But …' I shook my head. It didn't make sense. 'How come Brian got hold of her dosh, then? He *must* have still been seeing her!' I tried not to sound as indignant as I felt. I'd never suspected him of having an affair. But having an affair was one thing. Having it with a rich woman – a famous author – somehow felt even more disloyal. Like he had found me lacking not only as a wife, but also economically or intellectually.

'Honestly, Clare, he wasn't.' Andy shrugged, looking awkward again. 'Trust me, I'd have known. He did tell me about her, though.' I'd obviously never realised how much Brian had confided in him. 'The thing is, she was obsessed with him.'

'Really?!'

I hadn't meant to sound quite so surprised. OK, I'd have been the first to admit that Brian was a decent bloke. He'd been a good father, he'd worked hard all his life, he wasn't a drinker or a gambler, he didn't have a temper or drive like a lunatic. He was, by all reasonable standards, a nice guy. Likeable. Sensible. Dare I say it? A little bit … boring. I'd loved him, because I'd never been the type of girl to look for danger. I'd wanted to be settled, to be content, rather than to be swept off my feet. Perhaps, eventually, that was what was missing. But after so many years of knowing him, I really couldn't now reinvent Brian, in my own mind, as somebody a woman – especially a famous, bestselling one – was likely to become obsessed with.

'Yes, really,' Andy was saying. 'Apparently, she was distraught when he finished with her all those years back. To the point where she threatened to kill herself.'

'*No!*'

'He thought she was probably a bit unhinged. You know what they say, there's a fine line between brilliance and madness. He didn't want any more to do with her, but years later, she tracked him down somehow.'

'He never told *me* any of this!' I tried not to make it sound like an accusation, but honestly, how was I supposed to feel? I'd been his wife, and Andy was just his mate. 'I suppose he poured it all out to you in the pub after work?'

'Yes. Sorry.' He shrugged again. 'He thought you'd be upset. Suspicious. Well, it was rather odd, wasn't it? He told me he hadn't done anything to encourage her, far from it. She kept on messaging him and emailing him, so he decided to meet her, just once, to make it absolutely clear – tell her to her face – that he was married now and had no intention of ever seeing her again. But she still went on contacting him.' Andy sighed. 'He thought that if he told you he'd met up with her you'd think there was more to it. So he just kept quiet about it. Hoped she'd give up eventually.'

'But she didn't?'

'No. She still carried on. You and Brian had been married for years and you'd had both your kids when she died.

And in her last email, she told him she was dedicating her next novel to him. It was never published. She'd only written two chapters before she had the accident.'

'And she left him a load of her money, even though he didn't want anything to do with her?'

'Yes.' Andy gave me a very direct look. 'In fact, she left him the whole lot, Clare. It would've been even more, if she hadn't been a drinker. She'd made a fortune and had nothing to spend it on – no family, no partner, nobody – so she drank a lot of the money away. She used to tell Brian the only time in her life she was truly happy was when they were together. She spent all her time looking back to those days. It was pretty sad, really.'

'Sad?' I retorted. 'I'll tell you what was sad – my husband keeping all this a big fat secret from me, even while we were supposedly still happily married! I can't believe—'

'I know. I understand how you feel. I kept telling him he should talk to you about it. But he seemed to feel guilty. It weighed heavily on him, you know. He never touched any of that woman's money, and of course, he didn't change his will. He wasn't a selfish man, Clare. He'd have wanted you to have the money. You and the kids – he knew you'd share it with them.'

'That's supposed to make me feel better, is it?' I shot back. 'He kept her money a secret from me, in secret bank accounts, and let me find out about it after he died. I could have done with some of that at times! He could have done with it himself! What the hell was wrong with him?'

'He just didn't know how to handle it,' Andy said sadly. 'The whole *hero worship* thing.'

'Hero worship!' I scoffed crossly.

'But that's exactly what it was, you see. She was not only dedicating the new book to Brian – she told him she was writing it about him. He was going to be the hero.' He paused, giving me a little half-smile. 'It's a shame, isn't it? I'd have liked to read it.'

Oh, for God's sake! I thought to myself. I took a gulp of cold coffee and sat back in my chair, words failing me. My ex-husband, probably one of the most ordinary and self-effacing men who'd ever lived, had narrowly avoided being immortalised in fiction as some kind of romantic fantasy man.

No wonder he'd been too embarrassed to tell me.

CHAPTER 2

Not only did Brian have a secret fortune, he also had a secret dog. Well, to be fair, the dog, a scruffy little brown thing of indeterminate breed called Sid, wasn't exactly a secret, but up to this point I'd never met him. My son Daniel had been looking after him since Brian passed away, but he'd had to go back to work and didn't like leaving the little chap on his own all day.

'Can't Rachel take him?' I asked, looking down at Sid, who was looking back up at me with a suspicious expression in his eyes. 'She works from home.'

'Jason's allergic to animals.'

'What, all animals?'

Jason, my son-in-law, seemed to be allergic – in my opinion – to anything that was too much trouble. Cutting the grass (pollen), hoovering the carpets (dust), cleaning the car (something in the liquid soap). What next? Would the ironing board make him sneeze or the sight of a saucepan bring him out in hives?

Daniel shrugged. 'We thought you might like to have him, Mum. He'd be company for you.'

'Who says I need company?' I was still watching the dog carefully. His tail was down and he was growling softly at the back of his throat. 'Anyway, I can't have him. I work during the week, same as you.'

'Not such long hours, though. You're freelance, in and out all the time, aren't you? And from what you told us the other day, well ...' He paused, seeming to weigh his words. 'Maybe you can afford to retire now.'

'Retire?' I squawked. 'I'm nowhere near old enough!'

'Well, take *early* retirement. Be a lady of leisure. You're always saying you're fed up with your job.'

That was true. Being a press photographer had lost the allure it held for me when I first started work on a local newspaper as a dreamy, artistic young girl with a passion for photography and the illusion that I'd landed my perfect career. It had been a good occupation for a long time, but as we all know, things change. These days, local papers were fighting to survive. Luckily, by now I was known and trusted by the editors of the remaining newspapers and magazines in the area and still managed to eke out a living of sorts. But I was bored. Most of my jobs were photographing serious road accidents, or the outsides of houses where someone had died of an overdose, and I was finding them increasingly depressing.

'Anyway,' I said, 'as I've already told you and your sister, I don't want your dad's money. I want you to have it.'

'Mum, that's all very nice, but Rachel and I feel really uncomfortable about it. We can hardly start buying ourselves big houses, going on fancy holidays and so on while you carry on working and living … here … like this.'

'I like it here,' I said defensively, although the truth was I didn't, much. I looked around my tiny lounge. I supposed I could at least treat myself to a new carpet when the money came through.

'You deserve better,' Daniel said gently. 'It's been hard for you since you and Dad split up. He obviously wanted you to have that money—'

'Did you know about it?' I demanded, suddenly suspicious.

'Of course not! We were just as shocked as you. We never even realised Dad *had* a rich uncle in Australia.'

Well, look, I hadn't told the kids about Jacqueline Bloody Bright. I'd intended to, but when it came to it, I couldn't get the words out. How do you tell your grown-up children that their father was seen by some nutcase famous author as the man of her dreams and the hero of her novel? I still hadn't got my head around it myself.

'Anyway, it'll be ages before the probate's all tied up,' he went on. 'So please, just think about it in the meantime, yeah? I mean, sure, it'd be great to have a bit of a cash injection, but you should spend whatever you want first. Couldn't you give up working for the papers and find something part-time to keep you occupied?'

'You're only saying that because you want me to have the dog.'

I glanced at Sid again. He was sitting by Daniel's feet, still growling at me.

'You like dogs,' he said.

18

'Some dogs. That one doesn't look as if he likes me. Your father must have prejudiced him against me.'

Daniel laughed. 'Don't be daft. He's a lovely boy – aren't you, Sid?' The dog tore his malevolent gaze away from me and looked up adoringly at my son, thumping his tail energetically against the floor. 'He's no trouble, and he'll soon get used to you.' He stroked Sid's head and went on, quietly, as if he didn't want the dog to hear him. 'If you can't take him, he'll have to go to one of those dogs' homes. Someone *might* want him ...'

I sighed. I knew my son was playing on my heartstrings with his talk of dogs' homes. It was nonsense – neither of us would have let that happen. And I'm as much of a soft touch as anyone when confronted with a little brown dog who could possibly end up homeless, even if he did look as if he might bite my hand off.

'All right. I'll take him for now. But he'll have to be on his own when I'm at work. I certainly can't afford to give up until the money comes through, whatever happens afterwards.'

'Thanks, Mum. He was left on his own while Dad was at work, but Dad didn't work the sort of hours I do—'

'I know. You work too hard.'

'Yeah, well, Prisha and I are saving up to get married, aren't we?'

'Dad's money will pay for the wedding, Dan. You don't have those kinds of worries any more.'

He looked at me thoughtfully as if it really hadn't occurred to him. 'It'll take a bit of getting used to, won't it, Mum?'

'Yes, it will.'

I kissed him goodbye, risking life and limb by holding onto Sid's collar while Daniel opened the front door.

'Now, then,' I told the little dog, in the tone of voice I used on the children when they were little and needed to behave, 'I'm going to give you a nice bowl of that food Dan brought round, then I'm going to put you on your lead and take you for a walk. And you're going to stop growling at me and be a nice quiet boy. OK?'

I saw a flash of something in his eyes, but I wasn't sure whether it was agreement or hostility.

That first evening, Sid prowled my flat restlessly, continuing to eye me suspiciously, keeping his distance and giving those throaty little growls from time to time. Daniel had brought round all his familiar things – his bowls and toys, a stock of food and his bed. I put this in the kitchen and encouraged him into it when I was ready to go to bed myself.

'Settle down,' I told him. 'I'll only be in the next room.'

As soon as I turned off the light and closed the kitchen door, he began to cry.

'Shush, it's all right, go to sleep,' I called hopefully.

I went into my bedroom to get undressed, but the cries were becoming louder and more desperate. Perhaps he'd stop in a minute. I got into bed but couldn't go off to sleep. I couldn't bear it. That little dog was crying for my dead ex-husband or possibly for my son. Certainly not for me. But even if he didn't like me, I was all he had. I couldn't ignore him; it wasn't his fault he'd been sent to live with me. He must be feeling so unloved and unwanted, poor little bugger.

'All right, Sid, don't cry,' I called again. I got up, went back to the kitchen and looked down at him. He didn't look hostile now, just lonely and pathetic. 'I know, it's very sad,' I said, crouching down to give him a stroke. He didn't try to bite my hand off. 'I'm sad too. It's a sorry old situation, isn't it – Brian's dead, the nutcase author is dead, and you've got to stay here with me whether we like it or not. We'd better make the best of it, hadn't we? How about I bring your bed into my room, just for tonight? While we get used to each other. Stop making that noise, though. I've got to get some sleep if I'm going out to photograph car crashes in the morning.'

As if he'd understood every word, he promptly got up, wagging his tail slightly, and followed me as I carried his bed into my room.

'There you go,' I said, and he got back in, turned around a couple of times and settled down, yawning and curling up with his nose under his tail.

I lay down and waited. No more crying, just snuffly little doggie breathing noises. I was conscious of a strange warmth creeping into my heart, like a happy memory being reawakened.

'Night-night, boy,' I whispered, reaching out a hand to touch his head.

When I woke up, he was on my bed, lying across my feet.

*

Sid and I gradually developed a kind of grudging friend-ship. I didn't really want to admit I liked him, and I think he felt the same about me. I didn't imagine I'd be keeping him permanently. How could I, when I had to leave him on his own so much?

'I might change my line of work,' I told Sally one evening. She was a wedding and portrait photographer; we'd met when we were students and had taken slightly different paths in our careers. She'd made a massive success of hers, but we'd never let that come between us.

'Because of Brian's money?' she guessed straight away.

'Well … mainly because of the dog.'

I'd been feeling so sorry for him, listening to him crying quietly after I'd closed the front door on him every morning. Obviously, I wasn't taking Dan's talk of dogs' homes seri-ously, but I had considered paying a dog-sitter or walker. Either that or stop working – just for a while, to get Sid settled. Of course, Sally could read me like a book.

'For God's sake, Clare, give up the job! You're about to inherit a bloody fortune. You can do whatever you want.'

'Not yet, I can't. It'll take months to go through. Anyway, I'm giving it to the kids.'

She shook her head, looking exasperated.

'Think about yourself as well as your kids. You could start doing something you actually enjoy.'

I sighed. Yes, I'd had enough of my job, but what could I do instead? Even if I did use some of Brian's money for myself, I wouldn't know what to spend it on.

'Maybe I'll go away,' I said suddenly. 'Just take off some-where and do absolutely nothing.'

'And if you do,' Sally said quietly, putting her hand over mine, 'I'll miss you like crazy, but I'll be cheering you on. Do it, Clare. You'd be mad not to.'

And perhaps, I finally realised, she was absolutely right.

*

'I'm going to have a little holiday,' I told my son and daughter when Brian's money finally came through. I'd already instructed the solicitor to work out how much I could transfer to them straight away without upsetting the taxman. The rest would be theirs as soon as possible – apart from what I might need for my holiday.

'Where are you going?' Rachel looked excited for me. 'On a world cruise?'

'No.' I looked down at Sid. 'Unless either of you can look after him while I'm gone.'

The silence was deafening.

'How long will you be away for?' Daniel asked eventually, as if he might be considering it.

'I don't know. It depends what I do about work.'

In fact, I'd already decided, but I wanted to see their reaction. I felt guilty. Giving up a perfectly good job to go off and do nothing seemed almost scandalous. Not what people like us had been brought up to do.

Daniel laughed. 'Give up the work, Mum – we keep telling you.'

'You've hated it for years,' Rachel joined in.

'Well, I might just take a kind of sabbatical,' I said.

'Whatever,' Daniel said. 'Go and travel the world, Mum.'

'Who with?' I looked at them both pointedly.

They weren't going to volunteer. They had their careers, their homes, their partners, their lives. Having money wouldn't change that, *shouldn't* change that, and I wasn't going to ask it of them. Instead, I answered my own question.

'Sid.' I smiled down at the little dog. He and I were friends now. He followed me around the house, wagging his tail. 'I'm going travelling with Sid.'

'That won't be easy, will it?' Rachel said.

'Yes. Because I'm not going abroad. I'm travelling around Britain. I'll get a new car. Nothing fancy, just one that won't let me down. And I'll tour the coast of Britain, taking photos!' I added, my excitement mounting as the plan finally took shape. 'I might even buy myself a new camera.'

'Good idea, Mum.' Rachel gave me a hug. 'You can go wherever you like and take as many wonderful photographs as you want.'

I smiled. My work had become so dreary lately, I'd forgotten how much I used to enjoy photography, back when it was still an art form for me, a means of expression. I'd been taking photos of Sid and had begun to recapture something of the satisfaction of taking a good shot. Sally had even suggested, when I showed her Sid's pictures, that if I wanted a new career, I could take up pet photography.

'While you're away, you can think about what you want to do with the rest of your life,' Daniel said.

The rest of my life, I mused, after they'd left. What *did* I want to do with it? I looked down at Sid. Well, at least a dog gave life some purpose. He needed to be walked and fed, and he was good company. Thank God, after all, that this funny little creature with his scruffy coat and soulful eyes had come into my life.

*

I had farewell drinks at the pub with my colleagues from the paper where I got most of my work. Sally turned up, straight from a wedding she'd been covering, and started taking photos of me with drinks in my hands and people's arms around me.

'Leave off!' I laughed, trying to duck out of shot. Unlike Sally – who was tall, dark and willowy and still looked as if age had only had a nodding acquaintance with her – I was short, a bit thick around the middle, and a mousier shade of grey. I didn't photograph well.

'I'll miss you,' she said, grabbing me for one last hug when everyone else had gone. 'Keep in touch. Come back.'

'Of course. I might even decide to come back to work.'

'You won't. Even if you asked for work again, everyone would say no on the grounds that you must be mentally ill.'

*

The second farewell was harder. We went out for a meal – all of us slightly self-conscious in new dresses, jackets, shirts and shoes – at a posh Italian restaurant. Daniel talked to me as if he was the parent, reminding me to drive carefully, look after my bank cards and lock hotel doors at night. Rachel cried into her pasta and said it was because she was happy for me. Jason couldn't eat his fish because he was allergic to something in the sauce.

'I want you to know,' Daniel's girlfriend Prisha said at the end of the evening, 'that I think of you as a second mother.'

I felt as if I were going off to my own funeral instead of on an extended holiday.

'Cheer up, all of you!' I said. 'I will be coming back – it's not goodbye forever.'

'Oh, Mum, don't even say things like that!' Rachel cried. 'Not after ... what happened to Dad.'

OK, it had been the wrong thing to say. But on the other hand, if it wasn't for what happened to Brian, we wouldn't have been able to afford the meal in Casa Bianca. Never mind buying new cars, new handbags and having our hair done in Chez Michel (which, in my case, had finally banished the grey and turned me into a nouvelle blonde so that I jumped when I caught sight of my reflection).

'Cheers, Brian,' I muttered to myself once I was home again, emptying the last of a bottle of wine into a glass and knocking it back.

I was sorry he didn't get to enjoy his crazy author's bequest himself. But when it came down to it, that was his decision. I'd made mine. Sid and I were leaving in the morning and I had no idea when I'd be back. And despite all my previous anxieties and indecision, I was looking forward to it now. The rest of my life? Bring it on.

CHAPTER 3

'We're going on an adventure,' I told Sid as I packed my bag in the morning. He was sitting on the floor by my bed watching me, letting out little whimpers of anxiety. 'It's all right, boy. We'll be together. It'll be fun.'

It was no hardship to be saying goodbye to my poky little flat. Rachel was going to pop in every week to check for post and make sure everything was OK, but all my bills were on direct debit so there was nothing to worry about. I locked the flat door and led Sid out to my shiny new Toyota SUV, which had a dog guard fitted in readiness for our trip.

'Right, we're off!' I told him. 'Goodbye to London. Hello to the freedom of the road!'

*

The freedom of the road took us down to the coast at Brighton, where we spent the first night in a hotel on the seafront. Over the next few weeks, we headed steadily west, stopping wherever I fancied. There were so many lovely places to see, to explore and take photos. My camera was full of landscapes, seascapes, thatched cottages, dawns and sunsets, and far too many pictures of Sid running along beaches and through woods. He seemed to be having the time of his life on our new itinerant lifestyle. Me? I wasn't sure. I didn't exactly miss home, but I missed feeling *settled*. I wasn't sure I enjoyed moving from hotel to hotel, but I hadn't yet found anywhere I wanted to stay longer, either. Of course, I didn't know then that just a bit further west, Little Sorrel was waiting for me at the end of that long, narrow lane leading down to the River Sorrel. Waiting to claim me, waiting to bewitch me with its strange magic.

*

That first evening, sitting in the beer garden of the Ferryboat Inn, I was overcome by a sense of having come home, despite the fact that I'd never been to Little Sorrel before or even heard of it. I'd already arranged to take a room in the pub, and after my meal I walked Sid around the tiny village in the late twilight of mid-May, admiring the cottages along the lane, breathing in the scent of the flowers in their gardens, and wondering at the peace and quiet, so unlike the bigger, better-known places I'd stayed at so far.

'Where is everyone?' I asked Sid. 'Do they all go to bed early here?'

'It's Thursday,' the landlord said when I got back to the pub – as if that explained anything. I'd ordered myself a hot drink before going back to my room and had asked him why there didn't seem to be anyone around. He was a big, gruff man who didn't seem to smile much and certainly hadn't graduated from charm school.

'Right,' I said, as evidently there wasn't going to be any more in the way of conversation. 'Well, I'll see you in the morning, then.'

There was no TV in my room, but I didn't mind. The window looked out over the river and, as Sid settled down in his bed, I sat on the window seat and watched the light fading over the water. I could see little boats bobbing gently on the current further downstream where the river merged into the estuary. I could even see the sea in the distance, and with the window open to the warm evening air, I was sure I could smell it too.

'So peaceful,' I murmured, and Sid opened one eye to gaze at me before tucking his head back into his blanket and giving a little grunt of satisfaction.

*

I slept well, and went downstairs cheerfully in the morning, anticipating a hearty breakfast.

'Cereal or toast?' the ungracious landlord asked as I sat down at a table.

'Oh.' I was disappointed. No full English – Devon or otherwise? 'Um … nothing cooked?'

He sighed. 'Cook's not here till lunchtime. I can do you an egg, I suppose. Fried or scrambled?'

'Scrambled, please,' I said, annoyed with myself for sounding so pathetic. Wasn't this supposed to be a B&B? 'With two slices of toast,' I added, trying to be more assertive. 'And a cup of tea – strong, no sugar. Thank you.'

There was no response but he sloped off into the kitchen and returned – eventually – with a passably nice breakfast, for which I thanked him with only a hint of sarcasm.

When I'd finished, Sid and I went out again, for a longer walk this time. Next to the little school I found a footpath leading down to the river and along to the estuary. It was another lovely day, and unlike the previous evening there were plenty of people about now, working on their boats, fishing from the jetty or, like me, walking their dogs. Since I'd adopted Sid, I'd found dog walkers to be the friendliest of people. Even back in London, where such behaviour wasn't exactly the norm, we dog walkers always smiled at each other, called out 'Good morning' or 'Good afternoon', and often stopped to chat about our dogs or the weather. Since I'd been on my travels, I'd found this to be even more true. People in seaside and country places generally seemed more relaxed and sociable. So I was somewhat taken aback when, after saying a cheery 'Hello! Lovely morning, isn't it!' to the first of many dog walkers I encountered in Little Sorrel that morning, I was met with a blank stare. The elderly woman, who was accompanied by a small yappy terrier, averted her gaze and walked straight past me. I shrugged, thinking perhaps she was in a hurry, in a bad mood or hard of hearing. But the next person I met – a younger woman with a toddler and a golden retriever – behaved in exactly the same way. Puzzled, I toned down the exuberance of my greetings a little for the next few people I came across. Some of them responded to my quiet *Hello* with a quick nod of acknowledgement while others ignored me completely. Coming on top of the surliness of the landlord at the Ferryboat Inn, I was beginning to wonder what I'd done to upset people around here. If I wasn't already becoming so charmed by the village, I would probably have decided to leave straight away.

But I *was* charmed. Charmed by the tiny Fore Street, only just wide enough for one-way traffic – with nowhere to park apart from an adjacent field. Charmed by the shop, where I was served by yet another woman who ignored my attempt at conversation, but where I browsed the shelves, fascinated by the assortment of goods on offer and by the gossip going on between other customers, none of whom seemed in a hurry to leave. Charmed by the pastel-coloured cottages along the lanes, by the ancient church, and by the river itself with the views down to the estuary, where Sid and I lingered, gazing out to sea, watching little boats on their way across the bay.

I'd booked my room at the pub for two nights and that evening, after my fish and chip supper – which, surprisingly after the disappointing breakfast, was excellent – I decided to spend some time in the bar. It was a Friday night, and I reasoned that surely some of the residents of Little Sorrel would put in an appearance at their local tonight, and some of them might even be friendly. Sid, tired out by our energetic walks during the day, lay on my feet under the table, opening one eye from time to time and sighing contentedly. He might have been a funny little dog, but he looked cute when he was half asleep like that, and I couldn't believe anyone would be able to resist looking at him with a smile and asking his name.

The first couple who came in had a dog themselves. I looked up and said hello as they made their way to the bar. The woman frowned in response, and the man drew the dog closer to him as if to protect him from me. Or perhaps from Sid, which was pretty ridiculous as it was an Alsatian, more than twice Sid's size. They went to the bar, got their drinks and settled at a table. The next few people to come in were all men, who sat on stools at the bar with their backs to me, chatting to the landlord.

By nine o'clock, when I went up for another drink, there was still nobody who'd given me or Sid so much as a glance, never mind talking to us. I imagined a scenario where I suddenly turned round to face the whole miserable lot of them.

Hello everyone! – I'd say – *My name's Clare, this is my dog Sid, and we're strangers here so I'm curious to know why you're all ignoring us. Is it something I said? Something I did? Or are you all just plain bloody rude and ignorant?*

But of course, I didn't. I just went back to my table with my glass of wine and my packet of crisps and carried on looking aimlessly at my phone for something to do. A few minutes later, the pub door flew open and in came a group of people, chatting and jostling each other on their way to the bar.

'I'll get the first round!' said a tall man who looked about my own age. 'Evening, Jack!' he added to the landlord. 'Two pints of bitter, um … a lemonade, a shandy and two dry white wines, please.' He turned to see where his friends had sat down – all of them having ignored me completely, of course – and, finally catching sight of me, blinked in surprise and then nodded and said, quietly, 'Good evening.'

At last! By now I'd become so used to being cold-shouldered by the villagers that I nearly dropped my wine glass in surprise.

'Hello,' I responded. Everyone turned to look at me. I smiled. 'Hello all.'

Nobody smiled back except for the tall man, who, looking slightly awkward, asked if I was staying at the pub. I guessed it was a fairly reasonable supposition as there didn't seem to be anywhere else around here for visitors to stay. And I was quite obviously a visitor, seeing as nobody knew me. Or spoke to me!

'Yes, I am,' I said, trying to use my brightest, friendliest tone. 'I ... found the village by accident. Yesterday. Without knowing where I was going. On my travels, you know. With my dog.'

I felt myself going hot with embarrassment. I didn't seem to be able to speak in proper sentences. I wondered if I'd already lost the ability to talk to people. It was so unnerving, the way they were all just staring at me, as if I'd landed in the pub straight from outer space.

'Anyway,' I stumbled on, regardless, 'it's so lovely here. In the village, I mean, not in the pub. I mean, the pub's lovely too. It's all ... really lovely.'

I think I'll just give up and go to bed now, I thought miserably. What was wrong with these people? Didn't they speak English?

I got to my feet, dropping my phone, almost tripping over Sid's paws.

'Come on,' I whispered to him. 'Upstairs.'

Then I looked up again and the tall man was standing next to me, holding out his hand. Flustered, I dropped the phone again as I went to shake hands with him.

'Mike Samson,' he said. His voice was deep and resonant, and everyone else in the bar was watching him. 'Welcome to Little Sorrel.'

Finally, someone with some manners! 'Pleased to meet you,' I responded. 'I'm Clare Finch, and this is Sid.'

Sid wagged his tail, and Mike smiled down at him before going on, 'Are you staying in the village for long, Clare?'

'Um ... well, I was originally planning to move on again tomorrow. But I noticed a couple more footpaths today that I'd quite like to explore. One that goes through the field opposite the shop ...'

'Over the stile and into the wood. Yes, that's a nice walk, especially now, while the bluebells are out. It'll take you to the ruins of Cockscombe Castle if you follow it the whole way. Lovely views from up there.'

'Oh, right – thank you. I might stay tomorrow and do that, then. Sid and I enjoy walking. And well, as I said, it's so lovely here,' I added a little wistfully. The truth was, I didn't feel in a hurry to leave. Despite the native population.

'Have a good day, then,' Mike said. He started to turn back to join his friends, and then added as an afterthought, 'If you'd like a guided tour of the church, call in some time in the afternoon. I'll be in the church office writing my sermon for Sunday.'

'Oh! You're the vicar?' I said in surprise. No evidence of a dog collar.

He smiled. 'For my sins, yes. And that lot over there are some of my choir. We've just come from choir practice.'

'I see.' Perhaps they'd done so much singing they'd worn their voices out. But still, a smile wouldn't have hurt them, would it? 'Well, yes, I would like to see inside the church, so a guided tour would be very nice. Thank you.'

'See you tomorrow, then.' He nodded. 'Good night, Clare.'

I went up to my room and sat for a long while on the window seat, gazing out into the darkness, puzzled and confused. It had been almost as if Mike the Vicar had made a point of being polite to me, while his choir and everyone else in the village were quite obviously determined to ignore me. Was he trying to set an example to his flock? Show them how it was done? Had they all lived for so long in isolation here in the back of beyond that they'd forgotten how to talk to strangers? I couldn't understand it. If *I* lived somewhere as beautiful and peaceful as this, I was damned sure I'd be a lot happier and friendlier than this lot!

And yet … for some bizarre reason I couldn't even explain to myself … I still didn't want to leave. Not yet.

CHAPTER 4

The next morning, I asked Jack the grumpy landlord if I could stay for another couple of nights. He looked at me in surprise.

'Well, I suppose so,' he said, reluctantly.

It wasn't as if I could stay anywhere else. Surprisingly, for such a pretty village, I hadn't seen 'Bed & Breakfast' signs in any of the cottage windows. Even though it was a bit off the beaten track, I was sure if they did some advertising, they could have attracted a few visitors.

I'd called my son and my daughter the previous night to update them on my travels.

'You're staying *where*?' Daniel said. 'Never heard of it.'

'Why do you like it so much,' Rachel asked, 'if everyone's so unfriendly?'

How could I explain it to her when I couldn't even understand it myself?

'I like the countryside here,' I said.

And, 'It's just got this *feel* to it,' I told Sally, when I called her too. 'It's a beautiful place, but it's not just that. It's really peaceful, of course, because basically it's barely even a dot on the map. But it's not that, either. I'm going to have to stay a bit longer, just to try to get my head around why I feel so … comfortable here.'

'Maybe it's *because* nobody's talking to you!' she commented. 'You might be in need of some peace and quiet at the moment.'

'Time to myself. Yes. And to be fair, one person *has* chatted to me this evening. The vicar. He's offered to show me around the church.'

'Probably just desperate to get himself a congregation,' she quipped.

'Oh, he seems to have a bunch of people – they all came into the pub after choir practice. He was the only one to come over and talk to me, though.'

'Watch him, then. Maybe he wants to get you on your own in the graveyard.' I heard the smile in her voice. 'Just kidding,' she added gently, as if I didn't know her well enough by now. 'So come on – what's he like?'

'He's … well, about our age. And just ordinary. Quite nice, but just ordinary.'

*

I thought about this when I went to the church that afternoon to meet Mike for the promised guided tour. *Just ordinary*. It had been a bit insulting to refer to this rather nice guy like that. Guiltily, I remembered it was how I'd also thought of Brian, at times. But, after all, what was I if not just an ordinary woman myself? I'd been passably attractive, perhaps, when I was younger, when my hair was still naturally blonde instead of being a chemically enhanced pretence, and when my waist and hips hadn't merged together in the lumpy, unpleasant way of middle age. I'd been ambitious once, and energetic, and, you know, *excited* by life. When had that all worn off? It had been mean of me, on reflection, to call Brian ordinary. There was nothing *extra*ordinary about *me* these days. Perhaps ordinariness happened to us all, eventually.

Mike came out of his office at the side of the church to meet me as soon as he heard the heavy wooden door bang shut and my footsteps echoing on the stone floor.

'You haven't brought your dog?' he said, looking around as if he expected Sid to be hiding among the rows of pews.

'No, I didn't like to. He's back in my room at the pub. I walked him off his paws this morning, so he was happy to settle down for a nap.'

'Oh yes, how did you enjoy the walk through the woods? Did you get as far as Cockscombe Castle?'

'Yes, I did.' I was surprised he'd remembered. 'And you were right, the views from up there were amazing.'

The last part of the walk had been a steep climb, up muddy woodland paths that were narrow, slippery and full of unexpected dips and craters. Sid had bounded ahead of me, stopping now and then to look back and wait for me – panting, but not as loudly as I was. I'd had my camera trained on him when a pheasant suddenly startled us by taking off out of the gorse bushes, calling loudly as he

38

soared into the sky. I was thrilled with the picture I'd
managed to take as a result. And then, suddenly, the woods
had given way to a wide grassy plain leading to the castle
ruins at the top of the hill, where a couple of wooden
benches had been thoughtfully placed overlooking the view.
I'd spent quite a while up there, strolling around, taking
photos of the ruins and of the views down to the village,
out across the river and down to the sea.

'Have you been across the river on the ferry yet?' Mike
asked as he shepherded me through the church.

'No. I wasn't sure what time it runs.'

He laughed. 'Whenever you want. Just go along to
French's boathouse down by the jetty there and call for
Robbie. Robbie French and his son – Young Robbie – run
the service, as well as looking after people's boats around
here. They'll take you across for a couple of quid. When
you disembark at the other side, go straight through the
little gate at the end of the jetty and there's a footpath
that'll take you across the headland to Sorrel-by-Sea.'

'Thank you. I'll definitely do that tomorrow, then.' He
wasn't 'just ordinary', I realised. He was tall and slim, with
sandy-coloured hair, light blue eyes and a tanned face that
broke into a smile easily. And he was nice. Friendly. That,
in itself, made him far from *ordinary* around here! It was
this thought that finally gave me the confidence – after we'd
completed our circuit of the ancient church, of which he
was obviously so proud, admiring the stained-glass windows,
the brasses, the stonework of the pulpit and the font – to
ask him, quietly and with a smile, as if I was only half serious,
'Is it me, or are the people here a little bit, well, *quiet*?'

'Oh dear,' he said, looking embarrassed. 'I hope nobody's been rude to you.'

'Um, well, not exactly rude. But not very friendly.' I frowned. He hadn't sounded at all surprised. 'Is it me? Have I inadvertently put my foot in it, somehow? Said the wrong thing to someone?'

'No, of course it's not you.' He sighed. 'I'm sorry, Clare. People around here ... well, they're not very good with incomers. They can be a bit shy. We don't get many visitors, you see, so they're not used to seeing strangers around the village.'

'That seems such a shame, though. It's a beauty spot – I'd have thought they'd want visitors to come here.'

'We do get a few. In the high season. Usually they wind up here by accident, of course, because we're so far from any of the main routes or big towns, and nobody's heard of us.'

'I wound up here by accident myself,' I admitted. 'But I love it.'

He looked at me, almost sadly. 'I'm glad you do. And I hope you won't be put off by the villagers. They don't mean to be hostile. They're just ... a bit insular.'

'Fair enough, I suppose.'

I pondered this as I walked back to the Ferryboat Inn. Insular? Shy? Not used to strangers? No, it didn't quite explain, or excuse, the way everyone, apart from Mike, had been so pointedly ignoring me. I'd already given up trying to talk to people in the street or in the shop, but I still made a point of smiling at them. I didn't want to become just as rude, or 'shy', or whatever, as they were.

*

I took my Kindle down to the bar with me that evening so I could enjoy my glass of wine without feeling awkward about being alone and ignored. In fact, it didn't bother me quite so much now; I was getting used to it and at least I had Sid for company. He was mostly well behaved and quiet, just getting up on his feet and giving little woofs of interest when another dog was brought into the bar. I was beginning to recognise some of the regulars and a lot of them had dogs. The population of the village couldn't have been very big, and by now I'd seen most of these people either in the shop, down at the jetty or out walking their dogs. I watched them surreptitiously over the top of my wine glass or as I glanced up from my Kindle, and if they looked my way I nodded at them and smiled as if we were best mates. Without exception they quickly looked away, but not before I'd seen the shock on their faces. Shock or discomfort at being smiled at by a stranger. Perhaps Mike was right, and they were all just peculiarly shy. Well, if I stayed for a bit longer, I'd eventually stop being a stranger, wouldn't I?

If I stayed for a bit longer? I put down my glass with a thump, surprised at my own thoughts. I had another day and another night, then I'd surely have seen everything there was to see around here. I'd be moving on, wouldn't I? That was the whole point of my trip – to travel – wasn't it? But then again … there were no rules. Perhaps I was intrigued enough by Little Sorrel and its 'shy' villagers to stay here longer than other places on my trip. And why shouldn't I? I had nothing to rush home for.

*

The next day was Sunday and another bright, fine day. Just the day for taking a boat trip. Sid and I walked down to the boathouse as soon as I'd had breakfast. I'd given up asking for anything cooked, settling for a bowl of cornflakes *and* a slice of toast. I was the only person staying at the Ferryboat Inn so Jack wasn't exactly overwhelmed, but there was no point in making a fuss, if there was nowhere else to stay anyway. There didn't appear to be anyone around at the boathouse, although I could hear someone whistling inside. Remembering what Mike had told me, I cleared my throat and called out, a little nervously, 'Hello? Um … Robbie?'

The whistling stopped and a face appeared from behind a large trailer where the body of a yacht was sitting, presumably for repair or painting.

'Yes?'

I guessed this must be the older Robbie – he looked about fifty. He came out from behind the yacht wiping his hands and staring at me.

'Um … I understand you run the ferry service?' I said.

'You understand right,' he responded, in a somewhat sarcastic tone.

I straightened my shoulders. Why should I keep feeling intimidated by these ill-mannered people? Why did I let myself make excuses for them? They weren't just shy and unused to strangers. They were rude! If I was going to stay any longer (again, I wondered why I was even considering it), I was not going to put up with it!

'Well, I'd like to use the ferry, please,' I said firmly.

'Right. And when would you "like to use" it?'

'Whenever you're ready. You or your son,' I amended quickly, to show I knew what the setup was.

'My son?' he countered, the sarcasm practically dripping from him now. 'Well, he's pretty good with boats but as he's only ten, you might prefer I or my father takes you.'

'Oh.' I felt myself blush crimson. 'Sorry. I presumed you were—'

'I must look older than I am,' he said. 'I'm Young Robbie.'

I gave an awkward little laugh, but quickly smothered it when I realised he didn't appear to be the least bit amused by my mistake. He merely nodded towards the river, saying, 'Come on, then, if you want the ferry.'

And without another word, he walked past me, leading the way onto the jetty.

Little Sorrel Ferry, it turned out, was a rowing boat. I don't know why I expected more – considering how few people lived here and were likely to want to cross the river without owning their own boat – but I was amused and charmed by it.

'Is it OK to bring the dog?' I asked Young Robbie a little too late, as I followed him down the ladder precariously carrying Sid under one arm.

'Sure,' he said with a shrug.

He did at least help us into the boat. Once settled, and having watched him take the oars and pull us swiftly out into the river, I decided that, whether he bothered to respond or not, I was going to have a stab at a conversation.

'I suppose you might need a bigger boat sometimes? During the summer?'

'Why?' he replied without looking at me.

'Well, if you get visitors here, in the holiday season—'

'We don't. Not if we can help it.'

'Oh.' I sighed and shook my head. So it wasn't just that tourists didn't tend to find their way here. They were, quite definitely, not wanted! I supposed I could understand the villagers not wanting to be overrun with visitors, or to have their little village changed beyond recognition by tourism, the way some pretty coastal places were. But surely it was going too far to be so completely unwelcoming! 'Wouldn't it help your business – and other local businesses – if you were to embrace the concept of summer visitors?' I persisted.

'No. People here don't want to "embrace the concept of visitors",' he said, in that same sarcastic tone he'd used earlier. I flushed. He was taking the rise out of my London accent. If this was the way he spoke to strangers, it was a good thing he *wasn't* interested in the tourism business. We spent the rest of the short trip, across the river and down to the estuary, in silence. I decided not to care. It was so beautiful out on the river, with the sunlight dancing on the water, seabirds swooping and crying as they followed us along, and the only other sound the swish of the oars. Even Sid, held fast on my lap, seemed entranced – or perhaps he was just scared stiff.

'Thank you very much,' I said, making a point of being polite as Young Robbie helped me out of the boat.

'Welcome. That's five pounds for the return trip.' He held out his hand for the money.

'Oh.' I'd got a couple of pound coins in my hand, ready to give him – the amount Mike had suggested it was going to cost. I rummaged in my purse for more. I wasn't about to make a fuss; five pounds was cheap enough, but it appeared the Frenches had a different rate for locals!

'What time do you want taking back?' he added.

'Oh. I ... hadn't thought.' On this side of the river, there was no boathouse, no habitation at all by the look of it, just the jetty and a little shingle beach where the river met the sea, and the gate Mike had told me about, where the footpath would take me to Sorrel-by-Sea.

Robbie shrugged. 'Give me a call, then. Got your phone?' And he reeled off his number, too fast for me to enter it into my contacts without having to ask him to repeat it. 'Low tide's four fifteen this afternoon,' he added as he jumped back into the boat and took up the oars again. 'Can't navigate the river for about an hour either side.'

'Oh. Right, thanks for the warning.' I gave him a wave as he pulled back out into the river, not that he was looking at me. 'Come on, then, Sid. Let's try this footpath.'

Perhaps Sorrel-by-Sea might have a teashop or some nice little touristy shops to browse, I thought as we set off along the path. And perhaps the people there might be a little more welcoming!

CHAPTER 5

I'd brought my camera, of course. In fact, I'd already taken plenty of pictures from the boat, trying to catch the light dancing on the water, the seagulls following us, the wildflowers on the riverbanks. My camera was already so full of pictures of Little Sorrel, I knew I needed to set aside time to download the best ones onto my laptop and delete those I wasn't so happy with. I always used to save my best pictures, and sometimes had them printed for framing or mounting on canvas, but in recent years I'd lost interest. I now had hundreds of pictures from the various places I'd stopped at during my trip, including lots of Sid. But I hadn't taken as many anywhere else as I had at Little Sorrel.

The path to Sorrel-by-Sea led uphill through quite dense woodland for a mile or so. There was nobody else about, so I let Sid off his lead and he ran a little way ahead, sniffing the ground, plunging in and out of the under-growth, having the time of his life. I caught sight of the little white tail of a rabbit as it hurried away from him, and laughed as Sid came trotting back to me, looking disappointed but undeterred. The path eventually joined a lane via a kissing gate, and a signpost told me Sorrel-by-Sea lay half a mile to the right. I soon discovered I'd guessed correctly: Sorrel-by-Sea did indeed have some quaint little gift shops, and an old-fashioned tea shop. I popped my head round the door of the Singing Kettle and asked if it was OK to take Sid inside, and before long we were sitting in the window enjoying coffee and a croissant. Well, I was. Sid had to make do with a bowl of water and a dog chew that I gave him under the table.

Suitably refreshed, we set off down the main street, looking in the shop windows, and turning off down a side road to look at the church – not as old or as pretty as Little Sorrel's – and the village school, which, although small, was inevitably bigger and newer than the tiny one in Little Sorrel. I supposed they were lucky both schools had remained open. Perhaps that was because, as I'd already established from Google Maps, to get from one village to the other by road it was necessary to drive quite a long way inland: up the hazardous narrow lane I'd arrived by, and taking one of the side turnings which were equally narrow, eventually coming to a bridge across the river.

At the end of Sorrel-by-Sea's main street I came to a pleasant expanse of lawn at the top of the cliffs, where there was a pub, another café, and a couple of B&Bs. It was obvious now why the Little Sorrel 'ferry' couldn't come all the way to Sorrel-by-Sea but had to drop off its passengers back down the coast, at the estuary. The red Devon cliffs here were fenced off, and there were warning notices explaining that they had suffered recent erosion and rock-fall. So visitors to the village might come here for the sea views, or the bracing walks along the cliff top, but they wouldn't be able to access the pebble beach below.

Despite this, and despite being a small village itself, it was certainly better provided with facilities than Little Sorrel. There were more people around – a mix, as far as I could tell, of locals and tourists. And yes, most of them did smile and say hello! But having explored the whole village, taken a few photos, walked along the cliffs for a while and eventually ended up back at the pub, the Jolly Sailor, for a ploughman's lunch, I had to admit I hadn't fallen in love with the place the way I had so instantly with its smaller neighbour. I gave Young Robbie a call, saying I'd be ready to return in half an hour or so, and set off to walk back along the footpath.

*

The boat arrived almost as soon as I got back to the estuary jetty. To my surprise, as it came closer, I realised it wasn't Young Robbie at the oars but an older man who I guessed must be his father.

'You called for the ferry?' he yelled at me as he approached.

'Yes. Thank you. I presume you're Robbie Senior?' I said as he gave me his hand to help me and Sid into the boat. He was sturdy and muscular-looking but must have been about seventy.

'Aye. Most people call me Old Robbie,' he replied.

'Well, I thought that might sound a bit rude,' I said, with a smile – and to my surprise, I noticed a little twitch at the corner of his mouth, as if he'd wanted to smile back but wasn't allowing himself.

'You staying in Little Sorrel?' he asked as we headed out into the river.

'I am, yes.' I was becoming so unused to conversation with people by now, I almost forgot to add, 'I'm Clare and this is Sid.'

'You been here before, then, Clare?' he asked a little gruffly.

'No, never. And that was my first visit to Sorrel-by-Sea, too.'

He nodded. 'And I daresay you liked Sorrel-by-Sea a whole lot better than Little Sorrel. Most visitors do.'

'Well, I guess I'm not like most visitors, then. Sorrel-by-Sea's nice, but nowhere near as nice as Little Sorrel,' I retorted.

'I'd have thought you'd like those shops with all those so-called *craft* things in them. And those cafés with those so-called Devon teas and such-like nonsense.'

I flushed.

'I did like them, but even so, I still prefer Little Sorrel. It's beautiful, and peaceful, and—' I stopped, and shrugged. I could hardly say it would have been perfect if only the people weren't so unpleasant!

He nodded, seemingly satisfied – or perhaps not believing me, it was hard to tell – and went back to gazing upstream. Nothing more was said until we arrived back at the Little Sorrel jetty, where he jumped out of the boat with a surprising agility and helped me and Sid up the steps.

'Thank you,' I said. 'I paid your son this morning—'

'Aye, I know.' He nodded again. 'Thanks.'

It wasn't exactly a friendly chat, but it was more than most of the villagers had bothered to say to me. Perhaps eventually I might find someone to talk to around here other than the vicar!

The weather was still so lovely, I decided to stay by the river for a while, watching the local children making their own Sunday afternoon entertainment – paddling, playing in the mud, looking for crabs. There was a bench near the jetty and I sat there, enjoying the sunshine. Sid was happy to lie at my feet, one eye closed, the other lazily watching the kids playing. I must have closed my eyes for a few minutes too, because when I looked up again, there was only one boy left, sitting on the bank on his own, his feet in the mud. He looked around and, seeing Sid lazily wagging his tail, got up and plodded over to us in his welly boots.

'Can I stroke him?' he asked me shyly.

'Of course. He's very friendly,' I said. 'His name's Sid.'

The boy squatted down and stroked Sid gently. 'Hello, Sid,' he said. 'I'm Leo.'

'Have all your friends gone home, Leo?' I asked him.

He shrugged, his mouth turning down. 'They're not really my friends.'

'Oh.' I didn't like to ask any more. Perhaps there'd been a little bust-up between the kids – they'd probably be back on good terms again the next day. 'Well, you've made a friend here,' I said, nodding at Sid, who was now up on his feet, his tail wagging happily, sniffing around Leo's legs and making him giggle.

'I love dogs,' he said. 'But Mum won't let me have one.'

'Well, they can be hard work,' I said. 'And they cost money too – to feed and look after them.'

'That's what Mum says,' he conceded, sadly.

'Perhaps when you're grown up you'll be able to have a dog of your own.'

'I will. I'll have one like Sid,' he said, looking up at me with his big brown eyes. 'What sort of dog is he?'

'I've no idea,' I laughed. 'He's just a dog.'

'I think that's the best type there is,' Leo said firmly.

'Me too.'

We smiled at each other.

'I suppose I'd better go home,' he said, with a sigh. He straightened up. 'Bye, Sid. Bye!' he added to me.

'Bye, Leo.'

I watched him go, hands in his shorts pockets, welly boots slipping up and down slightly as he walked, kicking stones, with a dejected air about him, even from his back view. I wondered why. He'd seemed a nice kid, and the children here seemed to have such lovely little lives – running around outdoors all the time, those old enough to be trusted apparently free to play with their friends by the river, on the jetty or in the fields. There was little evidence of parental supervision. I guessed they'd grown up in this environment and from their first steps had been taught about things like the tides, and where it was safe to play. There was hardly any traffic in the village and I suppose everyone looked out for everyone else's kids.

*

I called my daughter again that evening.

'Are you still in that Sorrel place?' she said.

'Little Sorrel. Yes. It's just … so lovely here. Peaceful.' I smiled to myself. 'I'll send you some pictures. I've taken loads, although I don't know whether they'll do it justice.'

'OK, I'll look forward to seeing them. So I guess you'll be moving on soon?'

'Mm. I guess.'

'You sound like you're happy there.' She laughed. 'Don't you want to leave?'

'Maybe not quite yet,' I admitted. 'If I can persuade the miserable landlord to let me stay a few more days …'

'Are the people still being grumpy? *All* of them?'

'Apart from the vicar. He's nice. And a little boy I met today. But I'm working on the rest of them; I'm sure they'll get used to me eventually.'

There was a silence. Then, 'You really *don't* want to move on, do you? You sound … completely different. At one point, I thought you might be going to give up and come home.'

'So did I,' I admitted.

'But now you're sounding, kind of relaxed. Calmer. Settled.'

Settled, I thought to myself afterwards as I spent a while looking through my photos. Well, yes, I did seem to have fallen in love with the place. But obviously I'd have to move on at some point.

You're just too intrigued by the grumpy people there, that's your trouble – Sally messaged me later in reply to a text I'd sent her, telling her I might stay a bit longer. *You won't give up till you've made them all your friends. Then you'll leave and break all their hearts!*

I laughed. Hell would probably freeze over, I thought ruefully, before people like Jack the landlord and Young Robbie French decided to be friends with me. I wasn't going to waste too much energy on them. But equally, I couldn't explain why their attitude wasn't making me get straight in my car and head for somewhere else, somewhere where tourists were welcomed instead of being stared at resentfully. I just knew I wasn't ready to do that yet.

Jack gave me a look of pure astonishment when I said I'd like my room for another week – almost as if he couldn't believe he hadn't managed to scare me away.

'Unless you can recommend anywhere else to stay?' I said with a smile. 'If it's inconvenient for me to stay here?'

'Not inconvenient in the slightest,' he said. 'Just unusual, is all.'

'You mean you don't normally have any paying guests?'

'Not for more than a few days. That's normally enough for 'em. Not much for visitors to do around here.'

'Pity.' I wanted to persist, to ask why the hell the villagers didn't make more of an effort to attract tourists, but he was already turning away. 'Doesn't anyone else here do B&B?' I called after him. 'Just wondering!' I added as he turned back to stare at me.

'A couple of folks used to put signs up during the summer,' he said with a disdainful shrug.

'How about short-term rents? Are there any properties available?'

'Not that I know of,' he said, picking up a cloth and walking away to wipe the bar down. 'People round 'ere don't go in for that type of thing.'

'I see.' I went back upstairs, wondering why on earth I'd asked. I mean, it wasn't as if I wanted to rent a house or anything – hardly worth it for a week! I was just curious, obviously. And curiosity, around here, definitely killed the cat – or conversation, anyway – stone dead.

CHAPTER 6

The next couple of days were rainy and miserable. In a way, it was a good thing that, regardless of the weather, I still had to walk Sid, so there was no option other than to put on waterproofs and boots and head out along the towpath or through the woods. Despite the rain, it wasn't cold, and I still enjoyed being outside, the streets and footpaths of the little village becoming so familiar to me, as were the faces of the people I met, and even their dogs, most of whom I could now put together in my mind with their owners. Determined not to stop trying, I continued to greet everyone with a smile and a quiet 'Hello', and gradually I found that a few of them were, at least, nodding at me in slightly puzzled recognition. Like Jack, it seemed they couldn't understand why I was still there. I couldn't blame them.

'Aren't you getting bored here yet?' Mike said, one morning in the middle of the week. The rain had held off for a few hours, and Sid and I were on our way back from our walk, taking a shortcut through the churchyard. I'd been studying the inscriptions on some of the old grave-stones, noticing how often the same surnames were repeated. I'd seen Mike around the village loads of times–he always seemed to be out and about, calling on various people or talking with them on the street in his loud, cheerful voice. If it hadn't been for the occasional chats I'd had with him, I'd probably have lost the art of conversation by now.

I laughed. 'Why? Do you want to get rid of me? I feel as though most people around here do.'

'Oh, no, of course not,' he exclaimed at once, flushing and putting a hand on my arm to reassure me. 'Sorry, Clare, I didn't mean it to come out like that.'

'It's OK, I was joking. But you know, you *are* the only person here who's been friendly to me. Apart from a small boy I met the other day, anyway!'

He looked away, a pained expression on his face. 'I'm sorry about that, too. I have talked to the congregation about it. About being more welcoming.'

'Really?' I said, shocked. I couldn't imagine him standing in front of his flock on Sunday, delivering a sermon about being more sociable. And more to the point, it hadn't exactly worked!

'Yes. I really hope they don't drive you away. Most people *do* get bored here. There isn't anything here for people to do. They take a few photos and move on.'

'Perhaps that's what I like about it – having nothing to do,' I said thoughtfully. I looked around the churchyard, taking in the ancient yew trees where a couple of squirrels were chasing each other along the branches, the bluebells and wood anemones scattered in the grass, the old crooked gravestones with their faded inscriptions and the honeysuckle climbing up the warm stone walls of the church. 'Nothing to do except look, and ... and *digest* everything.' I couldn't explain, however easy Mike was to talk to, that I felt more alive here, in the peace and quiet with nothing to do, than I'd ever felt as part of the surge and rush of humanity back at home.

He smiled. 'You must be a country girl at heart.'

'Not at all. Born and bred in London, lived there all my life.' *And never want to live there again*, I found myself thinking. The thought shocked me. Of course I wanted to go home. My family was there. My friends were there. My *life* was there. This was just an ... interlude. An escape from reality. It couldn't last.

'You'll get fed up living in one room, though, before long,' Mike said, as if he were reading my mind.

'Yes, I'm sure I will. I must admit the menu isn't terribly inspiring, either!' I laughed. 'But there's nowhere else to stay, so it's fine. I'm not complaining.'

He put his head on one side, hesitating for a moment, and then went on, 'I don't want you to think there's been ... um ... *gossip* about you,' he said quietly, looking around him now as if to check nobody was listening, even though we were alone in the churchyard. 'But I did hear someone say you'd been asking about properties to let.'

'I'm sure there *is* gossip about me!' I laughed. 'And it's true, I asked Jack about it. I don't know why, really. I suppose I just thought ... if there were any short-term lets available, I might, perhaps, stay a bit longer. But there aren't, so never mind,' I finished quickly, embarrassed at myself. What was I saying? Why *would* I want to stay? I'd planned to leave at the end of this week.

'Actually, there is somewhere.'

'Oh. But Jack said—'

'It's very small. Just a little cottage, two bedrooms, one living room.' He shrugged. 'Been empty for a while, probably full of cobwebs, doubt you'd be interested.'

'But why ...?' I frowned. There weren't enough houses in the village for anyone living here to be unaware of a vacant one. 'Why wouldn't Jack have told me about it?'

'The owner of the cottage is living abroad. Nobody's sure how long the cottage might be available for. So it's not been advertised. It's not really suitable for anyone who might want to stay for more than a short time.'

'I see,' I said, although I didn't, at all. Jack could have explained that to me. He had no reason to think I'd want to stay for long. Or ... perhaps he was afraid I might. Perhaps *that* was why nobody had mentioned this cottage to me, despite the fact that they were all, obviously, tittle-tattling about the fact that I'd been enquiring after somewhere to stay. I felt my cheeks burn with sudden humiliation, thinking of all these people, these *unfriendly* people, discussing me, the weird woman from London who insisted on trying to engage them in conversation, who'd already outstayed her welcome and seemed to have no intention of clearing off back where she came from. 'OK, well, it's been nice talking to you,' I said quickly to Mike. 'I think I'd better take Sid back, he's getting impatient. Bye.'

'Clare—' he said, as I turned and started to walk away, pulling Sid – who, in fact, had been watching the squirrels playing, giving excited little whimpers and showing absolutely no desire to leave – behind me. 'Clare, it's not about you, I promise you, if that's what you're thinking. Don't feel pushed away, if you want to stay here. People will get used to you eventually.'

Perhaps they will, I thought, as I walked back up Fore Street to the pub, deciding for once to forget about smiling at the people I encountered. But I'm suddenly starting to think life's too short. I'd leave at the weekend, as planned. There were plenty more pretty little villages in the West Country to explore. Perhaps I'd find one where people were actually nice to outsiders, before I headed back to London.

*

I didn't calm down until I'd had my usual toasted sandwich for lunch in the pub. As I waited for it, I texted my daughter to tell her I was finally fed up with the miserable Little Sorrel villagers and would be moving on in a couple of days. A little later I walked down to the bench by the river, taking my Kindle so that I wouldn't be tempted to try to talk to anyone. Sid settled down under the bench for a doze. The sun had come out. I rolled up my sleeves, looked out at the light sparkling on the water, and sighed. What a fool I'd been to think I could settle, even for a few weeks, in such an isolated, inward-looking community. What a shame. I was going to miss it, even though I wasn't sure why. Well, no point moping about it. I opened the Kindle and started to immerse myself in the thriller I'd been reading.

'I like that song too,' said a little voice close beside me, making me jump. It was Leo, the boy I'd spoken to at the weekend. He'd sat down at the other end of the bench without me even noticing. I smiled at him, and glanced at my watch, surprised that it was already after school finishing time. I hadn't even realised I'd been humming to myself – a particularly catchy song I'd heard on the radio Jack always had playing in the pub.

'Do you like singing, Leo?' I asked him.

He nodded. 'I sing when I'm sad. It makes me feel better.' He looked up at me and added shyly, 'Is that why you were singing? Are you sad?'

'No.' I laughed. 'I've got nothing to be sad about. The sun's shining, I've got a good book to read and a nice little doggy friend ...' I trailed off, remembering that he'd told me his mum wouldn't let him have a dog. 'What have *you* got to be sad about?'

He shrugged, kicking his legs, looking out over the river. There were, I noticed, some other children out there, on what looked like a home-made raft, which the biggest boy was pushing along with a pole while the others laughed and shouted. Having fun, while young Leo sat here with such a look of misery on his face.

'Don't you like playing with the others?' I asked gently.

'They don't like me,' he said flatly.

'I'm sure that's not—' Again, I stopped myself. I should know better. It's never helpful for adults to tell children we don't believe them, that their feelings aren't legitimate, just because we don't want them to be, because they make us feel uncomfortable. 'Why do you think they don't like you?' I asked instead.

He shrugged again. 'They think I'm chicken.'

I stared out at the other boys again. 'Because you don't like playing on the river?' I suggested.

'I *do* like it!' he retorted, sounding indignant. 'I *would* like it.'

'But you can't? Why's that?'

He'd bent down now to stroke Sid under the bench. I guessed he could talk to me more easily if he didn't look at me. He was obviously embarrassed about this whole *chicken* thing. Why are kids so cruel to each other? I wondered.

'I'm not allowed,' he muttered. 'Mum won't let me. I can't go out on the raft or anything, and I can't swim unless she's with me, and she's never with me because she's always working. All I'm allowed to do is paddle. Like a baby.'

'So the others laugh at you?' I said sympathetically. 'That's tough.'

He nodded, looked up at me quickly, and back down at the dog again.

'Who's the older boy there?' I asked him. 'The one doing the punting, I mean, the one with the pole?'

'That's George,' he said darkly. 'George French. He's ten and he's a *brilliant* swimmer and *brilliant* at rowing and … and everything, really.'

French. The name rang a bell. And it came to me suddenly. Young Robbie – this must be his son. No wonder George was so confident on the river. I tried to swallow back an instinctive dislike of this unkind show-off. He was only a kid. And, of course, all the others looked up to him and of course they'd join in with his teasing of poor little Leo. That's what kids do, unfortunately.

'I don't suppose they mean to be nasty,' I said carefully. He pulled a face. 'Would your mum let you play with them if somebody older was with you all?'

'No,' he said flatly. He looked up at me. 'It's dangerous.'

'Well, I guess ...' I frowned. 'If that's the case, then fair enough.'

I stared out at the river. It moved so slowly and from here it looked quite shallow, almost as if you could wade across it. Was it really that dangerous?

'Those other boys' parents are OK about them playing in the water, though?' I asked, keeping my tone light.

'Yeah. They can't go into the estuary, though. That's *really* dangerous. They have to stay in the river.'

'Fair enough,' I said again. I didn't know what else to say. Perhaps Leo was younger than all these other children, in which case I couldn't blame his mum for keeping him on a tighter rein. But I felt sorry for him – he seemed so lonely.

'Can I take your dog for a walk?' he asked suddenly, looking up at me with a smile. It completely changed his face.

'Well ...' I didn't want to risk falling foul of his mother's rules – whichever one of the surly local women she might be! But his face had dropped when he saw me hesitate, and I really wanted to make him smile again. 'Will your mum be at home now?'

'Yes,' he said, looking at me doubtfully. 'But she'll be working. She works from home. She doesn't like being interrupted.'

'What time does she finish, Leo?'

'Teatime,' he said with a shrug.

'Then why don't I come with you when you go home for tea, and we'll ask your mum if she'll let us take Sid for a walk *together* – maybe tomorrow.'

He jumped up, grinning with excitement. 'Yeah! She'll say yes, I know she will.'

Sadly, I didn't share his confidence. After all, I was not only a stranger, but someone nobody seemed to like. Why would Leo's mother agree to me spending time with her son? But I was determined to give it a go. If she refused to talk to me, I was going to find out why. I wanted to try to help this sad little boy. After all, he seemed to be one of the only two friends I'd made here in Little Sorrel.

CHAPTER 7

Leo, apparently feeling happier, ran off to paddle in the river, looking up occasionally at the other children playing on the raft. I got my phone out of my bag and sent a message to Sally, telling her I'd decided that morning to give up at the weekend, and move on from Little Sorrel.

Although I have just made another friend here, I finished.

Perhaps I was hoping she'd try to talk me out of leaving – that she'd say, *Why go now, then, if you've started to make friends*?

But she didn't. *Sounds like the best plan. The people there sound awful. Who's the new friend?*

A lonely little boy called Leo. He's about eight or nine, I guess. He doesn't seem to have any friends and I feel sorry for him.

Oh dear, that's sad – came Sally's reply. *But don't stay just to try to help the kid, will you!*

No. She was right, of course. I shouldn't even be interfering. His mother was probably going to tell me to clear off. I went back to reading my Kindle, and at five o'clock

I called Leo and asked him if he thought it would be OK to go to his home now. He looked at his watch, seeming to struggle for a minute to read the time, muttering numbers to himself, and then called back, 'Yes! It's nearly teatime. Mum will have stopped work. Come on. Come on, Sid!'

I felt ridiculously nervous as I followed Leo back up to Fore Street and down one of the lanes leading off it. He stopped at a neat little semi-detached house with white-washed walls and a green front door.

'Come on!' he said again, leading me up the front path. He rang the doorbell, and I waited beside him on the step with Sid, mentally rehearsing what I might say to his mother.

It was a few moments before she opened the door. She was, I thought, about the same age as Rachel – late twenties – very slim and attractive, with chestnut-coloured hair and warm brown eyes like her son's. I'd seen her around the village, of course, and just like everyone else, she had ignored me too.

'Hello,' I began. 'I'm Clare. I hope you don't mind—'

'Mum, this lady says I can walk her dog,' Leo interrupted before I could go on. 'Can I? Please? He's a very friendly dog—'

The woman frowned. 'I don't know about that, Leo.' She looked up at me. 'I hope he hasn't been pestering you.'

'Not at all. We've just been chatting about my dog,' I said in a rush. 'And I realise you might not like the idea of him walking the dog on his own, not that Sid – the dog – is any trouble. But I'd be happy to walk with them, if that helps.'

She continued to frown at me as if she couldn't under-stand what I was saying. Perhaps it was my accent. Hers was a very thick Devon brogue.

'I ... er ... do realise you don't know me at all,' I went on quickly. 'I've been staying at the pub for a ... kind of holiday. I'm not sure how long I'll be here.' Where did that come from? I'd only just told Sally I was definitely leaving at the weekend! 'But, well, Leo and I seem to have become friends, so while I'm here, it's fine if he wants to walk with me and Sid. If it's fine with you,' I added.

'Do you normally make friends with little boys?' she said. She was sounding merely interested rather than accu-satory, but nevertheless I felt my face flare with heat.

'Look, if you think it's inappropriate, forget it – I quite understand. It was just that Leo asked if he could walk Sid, that's all. And I said we'd have to ask your permission. I'm sorry to have taken up your time—'

'It's all right, Clare.' Finally, she smiled. It was only a brief flicker of a smile, but it was so unexpected that I blinked in surprise. 'I'm Kerry, by the way. I've seen you and your dog around the place. I don't mind if Leo walks the dog with you—' She smiled again as Leo whooped with excitement and bent down to stroke Sid and whisper in his ear. 'Just don't let him make a nuisance of himself. He gets bored, see. Nothing much for kids to do around here.'

I was tempted to contradict her, to say it was the most wonderful place for children to live, where they had the freedom to run around traffic-free streets and enjoy the water. But because of what Leo had told me about the limitations his mother placed on him, I knew it wouldn't be wise.

'OK,' I said instead. 'Well, Leo, if you meet me after school tomorrow, at the bench where we chatted this afternoon, we can have a walk then. Thank you,' I added to Kerry. 'Nice to have met you.'

'You too,' she said. It was said without any particular warmth, but it was an improvement on the interaction I'd had with most of the villagers. 'We don't get many visitors here,' she added.

'So I've heard. But I love your village.'

I thought this might endear me to her a little, but she just shrugged, said goodbye and told Leo to go and wash ready for tea.

'See you tomorrow, Clare!' he called back joyfully as he ran inside.

*

I talked to Rachel at some length that evening.

'You sound a bit confused, Mum, to be honest,' she interrupted me eventually. 'I mean, first you said you loved it there so much, you sounded like you'd never been happier. Then you say you've had enough of the place and you're leaving this weekend, but now you're saying you've met this little boy and you feel sorry for him and you're going to be walking the dog with him. I don't get it.'

'Neither do I,' I admitted quietly. I gazed out of the window of my bedroom, watching French's ferry boat crossing the river, the evening sunlight dancing on the ripples thrown out by the oars. 'I suppose it's just … the peace, the calm …'

'Yes, you keep saying that, but surely peace and calm wear off after a while, especially if most of the population are too bloody rude to talk to you?' She sounded a bit exasperated. 'Well, look, you're the only one who can decide. But keep us updated, won't you?'

For a while, after finishing the call, I continued to stare out of the window. Rachel was right, of course. I needed to snap out of this dreamlike state I seemed to have fallen into since I'd arrived at Little Sorrel, stop finding excuses to stay where I quite obviously wasn't welcome, and do what I'd said I was going to do: move on. I picked up my Kindle and headed down to the bar with Sid. The clouds had lifted and it was now such a lovely evening, I decided I'd get a beer first and take it out into the garden to drink. Then I'd tell Jack that this Friday would be my last night.

'Ah! Hello, Clare. I'm glad I've seen you,' said a voice behind me as I settled down at a table in the garden. It was Mike, smiling as he pulled out a chair. 'Can I join you for a minute?'

'Of course.'

'Look, I wanted to apologise for this morning. I'm so sorry if you got the impression that people here are—'

I put my hand on his arm to stop him. 'Mike, you've got nothing to apologise for. You've been very kind to me, but please don't try to pretend there isn't bad feeling here from everyone else. I'm not taking it personally, exactly. I take your point: people just don't like outsiders. It doesn't matter. I'm leaving at the weekend.'

'OK.' He nodded. 'I understand. I ... was going to offer to show you round Riverside Cottage, but if your mind's made up, I won't trouble you any further.' He gave me a quick smile and started to get up. 'I'm sure I'll see you again before you leave, anyway.'

'Wait.' I frowned. 'Riverside Cottage? Is that the place you said was empty?'

'Temporarily. Available for short-term lets. It's fully furnished.' He pulled a set of keys out of his pocket. 'I'm looking after it for the owner. He's my neighbour.'

'You live next door to this cottage?'

'Yes. On Duck Lane. It's the lane off the far end of Fore Street, leading up away from the river.' He sat back down, watching me carefully. 'Clare, I'm not trying to dissuade you – as I said, if you've made up your mind to go, I do understand. And to be honest, I can't blame you. I know you were upset to think that people might be talking about you. I'm not defending them, far from it, but honestly, the gossip isn't malicious. It's just—'

'They're not used to outsiders. I know, I get that, Mike. And yes, I was upset this morning, mostly because it seemed like people are so keen to get rid of me, they won't even admit there's a vacant property.'

He sighed. 'Perhaps I should have another word with the congregation—'

'No.' I drained my glass and put it down on the table with a decisive thump. 'Perhaps you should show me this cottage. And then I can make a definite decision about leaving.'

*

Riverside Cottage was one of the first houses on Duck Lane, so it looked directly across the lane and over the river. It was even smaller than I'd imagined, dwarfed as it was by the tall brick building of the vicarage next door. The cottage walls were painted a deep cream colour, burnished to a warm gold by the evening sun. The front garden was tiny, and overgrown with weeds, through which a few flowers were struggling for existence. But there was trelliswork around the blue front door, over which a clematis was rambling, with some fronds trailing across the door, its flowers scenting the warm air. I breathed in and found myself smiling.

'Shall we go inside?' Mike asked, sounding hesitant, as if he'd expected me to be put off by the exterior.

'Of course.' No point coming here and not having a look, at least.

He put the key in the door and shoved it open, bending down to grab some post off the mat as he went inside. The door led straight into a small, square living room, brightly lit by windows on either side, the walls painted a very pale yellow, the wooden floor partly covered by a light grey rug patterned with a swirl of bright gold. There were two comfy-looking grey sofas with gold cushions, and a single picture on the wall facing me. It was large and striking, depicting a sunset over a dark sea, and in the foreground was a lone yacht with one white sail, one yellow. I stood, mesmerised, staring at it.

'Well, they have good taste – the people who own the cottage,' I said.

'It's just Harry. He's on his own. He's an artist,' Mike explained. 'That's one of his paintings.'

'Wow.'

'And that's Harry himself.' He pointed to a smaller picture hanging on one of the side walls. 'A self-portrait.'

I looked at this with interest. The man in the picture was dark and rugged-looking, his expression brooding and his eyes half-closed as if in concentration. I wondered why he didn't portray himself smiling – but there was certainly something striking about his face.

'Of course, he was younger there!' Mike said. 'He's … about my age. Now, do you want to see the rest of the house? It won't take long.'

'Of course.'

He led me through to the kitchen, which was about the same size as the living room and appeared to be used as a kitchen-diner, with a small wooden table and two chairs against one wall. A large window looked out onto a little patio garden where various tubs struggled to contain overgrown and neglected plants that were spilling sadly over the ground.

'Harry's made the best use of the space in here,' Mike said, indicating a row of units incorporating an integrated fridge-freezer and a dishwasher, a small oven and separate gas hob. 'The washing machine's through here—' He opened a slightly rickety door beside the back window, which led into a tiny and ancient-looking conservatory only half the width of the kitchen and almost empty apart from the washing-machine, some coat pegs and, leaning against the wall, a wooden easel. 'This is where he used to work,' Mike said. 'It's south-facing, so the light's good in here.'

'Used to?' I queried. I'd had the impression the owner was only abroad temporarily, but Mike made it sound very much like a past-tense occupation.

'Until he went abroad,' he corrected himself quickly, blinking and shaking his head.

'Well, it's lovely, anyway.' I looked around the conservatory, picturing a cane chair with cushions out here, perhaps a little table for a cup of tea – or glass of wine. A few nice house plants on the windowsills, another well-chosen rug … It seemed a shame that this little room appeared to have been neglected, compared with the rest of the cottage. Perhaps the owner had been too busy with his painting to bother with it.

'Want to see upstairs?' Mike said, and headed back into the living room. 'The stairs are on this side.' I followed him up the staircase, which brought us onto a little landing with three doors opening from it. He showed me into the main bedroom at the front, and the first thing I noticed was the big window overlooking the river and, in the distance, the blue of the sea and the haze of the horizon. I took a deep breath, feeling my heart lift. I loved this village. It was so beautiful, so peaceful. At that moment I couldn't have cared less about the unfriendly locals. If anything, their exclusion of me added to my feelings of peace and relief from any kind of stress or anxiety. I felt so relaxed here. The offer of this lovely cottage seemed to have fallen into my lap. Why shouldn't I give in and stay for a while?

Tearing myself away from the view to face the room, I could see again the artist's touch: the walls a pale aquamarine, the carpet thick and creamy-white. There were blue-and-white striped blinds at the windows, a matching striped duvet on the bed, and to complete the seaside feel of the décor, another large canvas hung on the wall over the bed, depicting a row of blue, white and yellow beach huts, with a line of white surf and turquoise sea just showing in the distance.

'Fitted wardrobe ... chest of drawers ...' Mike said, waving his hand around the room and sounding like an estate agent. 'And the bathroom is here.' Stepping onto the landing, he opened the door to a tiny room with a shower cubicle, sink and toilet. 'Just about enough space to swing the proverbial cat,' he joked.

'So is that another room?' I asked, pointing to the third door. 'Or a cupboard?' I pictured a walk-in wardrobe. Or maybe a storage room for the artist's paints and canvases.

'Oh yes, spare bedroom. It's not in use,' he said a little abruptly. 'Harry's locked it up. I guess he has stuff stored there while he's away.'

'Of course. Fair enough.' I was probably right about the art things. 'I only need one bedroom anyway, obviously.'

Mike looked at me in surprise. 'You're really considering renting the cottage?'

I checked myself. I had begun to take it for granted. In truth, I was already imagining myself living there. 'It, er, seems I am,' I said, with an embarrassed little laugh.

'You haven't even asked about the rent. Harry doesn't know how long he'll be gone, so he said he'd be happy with very short-term lets. He could come back any time and—'

'I'll take it for a month, if that's OK,' I said, excitement making my voice hoarse.

'But you still haven't asked about the rent!'

It's funny how inheriting a small fortune can make you forget about the most basic aspects of budgeting and start behaving as if you're to the manner born. In any case, the rent, when I finally did ask about it, was ludicrously low.

'Are you sure that's all he's asking?' I said.

'Yes. As you've probably worked out, nobody comes to this village,' Mike joked. 'I don't think Harry seriously thought anyone would want to use the cottage.' He smiled at me. 'But I'm pleased, Clare. Really pleased. It'll be good to have a neighbour again, even if only for a few weeks.'

I doubted anyone else around here would be pleased. But I didn't care. I'd fallen in love with Riverside Cottage just as I'd already fallen in love with Little Sorrel itself. And it seemed I'd stopped trying to deny it.

CHAPTER 8

It was something of a pleasure, the next morning, to be able to tell Jack the landlord I'd definitely only want my room for a couple more nights. Mike had promised me he'd have a simple rental agreement sorted out ready for me to move in on the Saturday. Harry had arranged for him to deal with his solicitor on his behalf.

'Going home, are you?' Jack asked, sounding satisfied.

'No. I'm staying. In Riverside Cottage.'

His head jerked up so sharply I swear I heard his neck crick. He stared at me across the bar, evidently lost for words.

'Talked the Reverend into letting you have it, did you?' he managed eventually.

I gave him my sweetest smile. 'Actually, I think *he* talked *me* into it. I'll have a fried egg on toast this morning, please. Thank you.'

I was humming cheerfully to myself as I came out of the village shop a little later with a supply of Sid's dog food.

I'd had the definite impression there were even more curious looks being cast in my direction that morning than usual. I was pretty sure Mike wasn't one to gossip, but I wouldn't put it past Jack to spread the word, and by now probably half the population of the village was aware that the strange woman from London would be moving into the empty cottage. I was startled to realise that I wasn't at all daunted by the fact that I'd committed myself to spending a whole month here among these people. It would sort things out, I reasoned, one way or another. I'd either be spending a very quiet month on my own, continuing to be ignored by almost everyone apart from the vicar and a little boy, or perhaps I'd start to be accepted and become one of them, for a few weeks at least.

My buoyant mood lasted all day, so that when I met young Leo, as arranged, for our afternoon walk together, I was still beaming happily.

'Sid's been looking forward to this,' I told him as we set off along the path next to the river, Leo holding Sid's lead.

He laughed. 'How do you know?'

'Oh, he talks to me, of course.' I smiled down at Leo. 'All the little barks and grunts and snuffly noises he makes are his language, and I'm the only one who understands.'

'Nooo!' he said. 'You're *so* making that up!'

I laughed. 'It's fun to make up things like that, though, isn't it?'

'Yes.' He entered into the spirit of it. 'OK, I'll talk to him too. Hello, Sid! I'm your new friend. Do you like me walking you?'

Sid, fortunately, gave one of his little snuffly grunts just at that moment, and Leo and I both burst out laughing – just as another boy, around the same age as Leo, was coming towards us, heading for the group of children gathering at the river.

'Whose dog is that?' the boy demanded, staring at Leo.

'Clare's.' Leo pointed to me. 'My friend.'

The other boy stared at me, then back at Sid.

'What's his name?'

'Sid,' said Leo proudly. 'I'm allowed to walk him.'

'Can I walk him too?'

'No,' Leo said, surprisingly firmly.

'Why not?' the boy said. 'He's not your dog. It's not up to you.' He glanced up at me again. 'Can I walk him?' he asked me.

'No.' I smiled at the boy. 'Sorry. Only Leo is allowed.' I hesitated, glancing at Leo. 'Unless Leo *wants* you to walk with us.'

The boy thought about this, scuffing the ground with his shoes.

'Let me, Leo,' he said eventually. 'Go on. Please.'

'Not yet,' Leo said, puffing out his chest a little bit. 'But I'll think about it.'

I said goodbye to the other boy and we walked on.

'What's his name?' I asked Leo.

'Reggie,' he said with a shrug. 'He's in my class.'

'Do you like him?'

'He's all right. He used to be my friend. But he's one of the ones who's started calling me a chicken.'

'I see,' I said. 'Well, he probably doesn't deserve to walk Sid with us, does he? Until he stops calling you names.'

'No.' He smiled up at me. 'That's what I think, too.'

'And so does Sid,' I said firmly.

*

We had a nice walk along the river and then down one of the footpaths around the edge of the village. I didn't want Leo to be late back for his tea, but he nodded happily when I suggested we might have a longer walk at the weekend.

'I hope he wasn't any trouble,' Kerry said when we arrived back at her house.

'Not at all,' I said. 'We had a lovely time.' I was feeling so cheerful, I failed to notice the frown of suspicion on her face and continued in the same gushing tone, 'And Leo will be welcome to keep on coming out with us whenever he wants. I've decided to stay here. Temporarily, at least. I'm renting Riverside Cottage.'

Kerry stared at me, her expression not changing.

'Oh, you are, are you?' she said at length, just as I was wondering whether she'd even heard me. 'I see.'

I resisted the temptation to ask what the hell that was supposed to mean.

'Yes,' I said, a little less cheerfully now. 'I am. I've agreed to a month's lease.'

'You have, have you?'

'Yes.'

This was getting silly. I started to pull Sid closer, ready to walk away, but just as I did, she went on, abruptly, 'I suppose you got round the vicar to let you have the place.

Everyone's seen how you've been cosying up to him. I suppose you like the idea of living next door to him. Well, just watch yourself. He's seeing someone, you know. He's not available. So don't go getting any ideas.'

'What?' I turned back to face her, my face flushing with shock. 'What on earth are you talking about? I haven't been "cosying up to him"! And I certainly haven't got any "ideas", as you put it! It was his suggestion that I looked at the cottage. I … I … can't believe people are saying things like that!'

Although, I realised with a strangled gasp, I probably should have done. After all, this was exactly what people seemed to be like around here: gossipy, suspicious, unkind. And although I'd spent a week here now, talking myself into putting up with their attitudes and their rudeness before finally deciding to stay anyway and ignore it, the unfairness of it suddenly got to me.

'If you want to know the truth,' I went on, my voice shaking but trying to keep from shouting in case Leo was listening from inside the house, 'if people have seen me *talking* to Mike – yes, that's all, just talking! – it's because he's the only person in this village who's had a single polite word to say to me since I've been here. The only person who hasn't, frankly, been bloody rude and downright ignorant! Apart from your son,' I added quietly, wondering if I'd now spoiled things for Leo and the dog walks.

But it was too late, I'd said it – and let's face it: if I was going to stay for a month it needed to be said. People needed to know how I felt about their so-called 'shyness'. About their gossiping and rumour-mongering and their spreading of ridiculous fake news about me and the vicar. I swung away, pulling Sid with me, and was halfway down the path when Kerry came after me, grabbing my arm.

'I'm sorry, Clare,' she said quietly.

I looked round at her, surprised but still too cross to respond.

'Honestly, I am sorry,' she repeated. 'I shouldn't have said that about Mike. I shouldn't have listened to the gossip. You're right, people around here *are* rude to outsiders. And you've been kind, letting Leo walk your dog. He's talked of nothing else.'

'Well, I don't want to upset Leo, of course. He seems to need a friend,' I said bluntly.

She looked down, nodding. 'Yes. Thank you. And – look, maybe we can start over again? If you want to? Why don't you come in for a cup of tea after I finish work tomorrow? After your walk?'

I let out a long breath, forcing myself to let go of the anger. She was holding out an olive branch. It seemed to be genuine.

'OK,' I said. 'Thank you. Tell Leo I'll meet him at the same place tomorrow, then.'

Who knows, I thought to myself, I may even have made a friend. Perhaps I should lose my rag with these people more often.

*

That evening I sent a message – the same one – to Rachel, Daniel and Sally. I was aware I was taking the easy way out, because I knew if I told any of them over the phone that I'd just agreed to move into a cottage in Little Sorrel for a month, despite all my complaints about the miserable people here, it would have instigated long interrogations into my sanity, whether I was sure I was doing the right thing, whether I might change my mind yet again, and what exactly I was doing. So a brief message about staying put for a bit longer sufficed, without mentioning the cottage, and it didn't generate any response other than similarly brief messages along the lines of *OK, let us know when you move on.* They were probably all despairing by now of my indecisiveness. I'd talk to them properly later, I decided, once I'd settled into the cottage.

Instead of sitting in the bar or the beer garden after dinner, I took Sid for another walk, finding myself instinctively heading towards Duck Lane. I stood by the river, on the corner of the lane, gazing at Riverside Cottage, picturing myself opening the garden gate and walking to the front door with the key in my hand. I'd always loved the idea of living in a country cottage. Well, if nothing else, I was going to make that dream come true, even if just for a month of my life.

As I watched, a little black and white cat wandered out of the entrance to the vicarage, pausing to lick its paws and wash its face, as if it had just had its dinner, and then suddenly jumped up onto the gate of Riverside Cottage and into the little front garden.

'All right, Sid, behave yourself,' I said, as he tugged at his lead, whining softly, wanting to run after it. I smiled, wondering if it was Mike's cat. I didn't even know whether he had one. But then, I didn't even know he had a girlfriend – as

Kerry had hinted – either. Let's face it, I thought to myself, I didn't know him at all. But we were going to be neighbours, for a while at least. He'd been friendly to me, and he'd told me about the cottage. That was all I cared about.

Sid and I walked on past Riverside Cottage to the end of Duck Lane, past the handful of other houses and cottages, until we came to a marshy green area where, behind a pair of weeping willow trees, I could see a small pond. A little wooden seat was set beside it, and a small wonky sign asking 'Please Do Not Feed the Ducks'. So this was where the eponymous ducks of Duck Lane hung out! There were none to be seen at the moment. Perhaps they were off flying over the fields or swimming further up the river, or maybe settled somewhere for the night. I looked forward to meeting them!

*

The next afternoon when Sid and I went to meet Leo again, he was already waiting at the bench. Another bigger boy was with him, and something about Leo's body language, even from a distance, told me he wasn't happy about it.

'So where is it – this dog?' the older boy said as I walked up behind them.

'He'll be here in a minute,' Leo said.

'Unless you've just made it up.' Now I was closer, I could see the other boy was George French, the ferryman's son. 'Your imaginary friend, is it?' he added with a sneering laugh. 'I s'pose you haven't got any real friends, so—'

I let Sid off the lead, and with an excited bark he ran straight to Leo, jumping up at him, wagging his tail, licking his legs. Leo laughed and bent down to stroke him, but

George, taken by surprise at this small furry bombshell arriving from behind, jumped out of the way and tripped over his own feet, ending up stumbling onto the bench and sitting down in an inelegant heap.

'Oops!' I said. 'Sorry about that. Sid gets so excited when he sees Leo.'

George glared at me but didn't say anything.

'See you later, George,' Leo said, taking Sid's lead from me, fastening it back on and strolling off along the path.

'Bye.' I smiled sweetly at George before following after Leo, a little way behind, to give him time to make his point.

'Thank you,' he said shyly when, round a corner in the path, I caught up with him.

'I didn't do anything,' I said. 'Sid was just pleased to see you.'

Once we were out on the footpath beyond the church-yard, away from civilisation, I suggested Leo could take Sid off his lead and practise calling him back. Luckily, he was such a good little dog, it was no problem getting him to obey. I offered up silent thanks to Brian for training him properly!

'Well done,' I said, as Leo grew more confident in his control over the dog. 'He really looks up to you.'

'I told George he was my dog,' he admitted in a little voice.

'Well, he kind of is, isn't he? Your dog friend.'

'But what he said, about me not having any other friends – that was true.'

'Maybe that's a temporary thing, though. It happens sometimes. Friends come and go. I haven't really got any around here, either. Well, only you and the vicar,' I added with a smile.

'The vicar's nice to me, too,' he said thoughtfully. 'Because I used to sing in the choir.'

'Did you? Don't you like doing it any more?'

'No.' He sighed. 'I like singing, but the other kids laughed at me for being in the choir. There aren't any kids in it now, only grown-ups.'

'That's a shame. Singing cheers us up, doesn't it?' I promptly burst into a loud rendition of 'If You're Happy and You Know It', making Sid start barking in surprise, and Leo laugh and join in with me.

We were still laughing and singing when we finally walked up to his mum's front door half an hour later. Kerry opened the door with a puzzled expression on her face.

'I thought it was the vicar bringing his choir to the door,' she joked. 'Nice to see him so happy,' she added quietly to me as Leo ran indoors. 'Come in. Don't worry about the dog. I like dogs. I'd have one myself if I could afford it.'

It was as if the hostile way she'd spoken to me the previous day had never happened. Over tea and biscuits, she talked to me about her work – she wrote advertising and PR copy for various Devon businesses' websites, blogs and social media – and her worries about Leo, her only child, who was doing well at school but 'not very good at making friends'.

I kept quiet, aware that it wouldn't be prudent to probe, however carefully, into Leo's claims that he wasn't allowed to do the things the other children did. He was outside now, playing with Sid in the garden.

'Well, I'm glad he's made friends with Sid, then,' was all I said.

'Yes. Thank you. It really is kind of you, to let him.' She sighed. 'Life is … difficult, at times.'

She didn't elaborate, and again, I felt the truce between us was too new, too fragile, to risk asking questions. But she suddenly straightened up, gave a little smile, and added, 'Still, it'll be easier next week when my mum's back. She's been away, up-country, for a couple of weeks visiting my aunt. She helps out, see, normally – looks after Leo for me, keeps him at her place to do his home-work, does his dinner too if I'm busy. Thank God she'll be back for half-term next week or I'd be going mad trying to keep him entertained.'

'You must be glad, then, that you've got your mum here. Living so close.' I thought, with a sudden pang, of my own children, and added, 'I think, if my daughter had a child, I'd want to live close by, too.'

She nodded. 'I know, I'm lucky, she's been such a support. And she deserves to be happy, too. That's why I'm glad she's settling down with someone local, you know? I know it sounds selfish, but I'm glad she won't be moving out of the village when they get married.'

'Your mum's getting married?' I said. 'That's nice.'

'Yes. Well, they've been engaged for ages.' She laughed. 'But they'll get around to it soon, I'm sure. He's just so busy, you know, organising *other people's* weddings, and funerals, and everything—' She stopped, noticing my puzzled expression. 'I told you, didn't I? Mum's engaged to Mike. The vicar.'

'Ah. I see.'

I took a sip of my tea, smiling at her. I felt as if something had fallen into place. As if Little Sorrel were a jigsaw puzzle and I'd just managed to place the very first piece in the right place. And that there were another nine hundred and ninety-nine pieces jumbled up together in the box, waiting to be sorted out.

CHAPTER 9

That evening, Mike and his choir were in the bar when I went down for my glass of wine.

'Ah, good,' he said when he saw me. 'I've got the keys for you.' He reached into his pocket and handed them to me. 'Do you need any help moving in tomorrow morning?'

I laughed. 'I've only got a suitcase.'

'What about Sid's stuff? Haven't you got a basket or a bed for him?'

'Oh, yes – and a bag full of dog food. But my car's in the pub car park.' I smiled. I hadn't even used the car since I'd arrived at Little Sorrel; I'd almost forgotten about it. 'Is there anywhere to park outside the cottage? I didn't notice.'

'Yes, you can park in the road outside, there's plenty of space. OK, well, I've opened some windows to air the rooms, and done a bit of dusting—'

'You didn't have to do that,' I protested.

He shrugged. 'It was no trouble. And I'm sure you'll want to do some shopping, but I've left you some tea bags to be going on with, and put some milk in the fridge.'

'Thank you. You've been really kind.' I looked around me, suddenly aware that it had gone very quiet in the bar. The choir members all appeared to be concentrating on their drinks but it was obvious their ears were flapping. 'I'm moving into Riverside Cottage for a month,' I said, making it an announcement to the room in general. 'I expect you've all heard about that already on the village grapevine. Mike has kindly arranged it for me. That's it – nothing else to know – so you can get on with your drinks. And I'll have a glass of Merlot, please, Jack.'

Mike was grinning widely as he went back to his flock.

I settled my bill with Jack as soon as I'd had breakfast in the morning. I was looking forward to cooking my own meals again. Sid whined, looking surprised and disappointed at being put in the car.

'Don't worry, we'll still have a walk a bit later!' I laughed.

It took all of two minutes to drive down Fore Street into Duck Lane and park outside the cottage. I don't know who was more excited as I unlocked the front door – me or Sid.

'This is home now!' I told him, as he trotted into the living room ahead of me, sniffing into all the corners, looking up at me and wagging his tail. 'For a few weeks, anyway.'

Mike had left biscuits as well as tea bags on the kitchen table. I unpacked Sid's food, putting it into an empty kitchen cupboard, put down his water bowl and his bed, and watched as he sniffed it suspiciously, as if he wasn't sure it was really his.

'And here's the garden,' I told him, opening the door to let him out. To my surprise, he bounded straight out of the door, barking – and then I saw the reason. The little black and white cat I'd seen the night before jumped swiftly up onto the back wall, staring down at Sid as he came to a stop, looking disappointed. I followed him and reached up to stroke the cat, who didn't seem at all worried – in fact, he rubbed his face against my hand as if he'd known me all his life.

'There, look, he's a nice little cat, Sid,' I said. 'He must live in one of the houses around here. He might even be Mike's. So please don't chase him again – OK?' Sid wagged his tail and I laughed. 'That's it, you can be friends.'

I sat for a while on a blue-painted wooden bench set against the wall, enjoying the warmth of the sun and imagining how I might tidy up the plant pots in time to rescue the flowers that looked like they were on their last legs. Then I went back inside, leaving Sid to explore, and carried my bag upstairs. It didn't take long to unpack the contents into the wardrobe and chest of drawers, and once I'd finished, I called Sid in, locked the back door and took him for a walk before tying him to the post outside the village shop while I bought some supplies. For the first time I could remember, shopping for food was fun. Back in London, I'd either drive to the huge supermarket on a nearby retail park and stock up with enough of everything to last as long as possible – the whole process feeling like a tiring but necessary chore – or sometimes I'd resort to ordering everything online, which I found took almost as long. Now I was going to shop like it was the 1950s – as everyone in the village seemed to do – coming here every day and buying only what I needed right away. Everything fresh. Potatoes and carrots in their natural, dirt-covered state; wonky-shaped fruit, unpolished and unwrapped; cheese cut from a huge block and wrapped in waxed paper; bread baked on the premises, still warm from the oven; meat from a local farm, weighed out in front of me and parcelled up in two layers of thick, white paper. How would I be able to bear going back to the over-packaged, sanitised produce I'd been used to? Just the smell of the bread, the cheese and the sweet, juicy tomatoes had my mouth watering, wanting to make lunch as soon as I'd carried my bags back to the cottage.

It's like starting over again, I thought as I put things away in the fridge and the cupboard. It felt like the early days of my marriage to Brian, when sharing our first home together was a novelty, and choosing mundane things like saucepans and curtains was a source of excitement. I felt a momentary pang of nostalgia, but soon talked myself out of it. Everyone starts out like that, don't they – full of happiness and enthusiasm? It tends to wear off. It certainly did for us.

*

Halfway through the afternoon there was a little tap on the front door. Assuming it to be Mike, I was surprised to find, instead, Leo standing on the doorstep, clutching a bunch of flowers.

'Mum says to tell you they're only from our garden,' he said.

'But they're lovely!' I smiled at him. 'Thank you both. Come in while I put them in a jar of water. Have a look around. It's such a nice little cottage.'

'I know,' he said.

'Oh – you've been in here before? Do you know Harry the owner?'

He nodded. I waited for him to elaborate, but instead, he asked, 'Can I play outside with Sid?'

'Of course you can.' Sid was already dancing around his legs enthusiastically. I let them both outside and watched for a while from the window as Leo found a stick and threw it for Sid to fetch. Of course, everyone in the village knew everyone else, so it shouldn't be a surprise that he knew Harry and had been in the cottage before. After I'd arranged the flowers, I took out a tray with iced water for him, a cup of tea for myself, and a packet of biscuits. We sat companionably on the little blue bench together. Leo seemed quiet, a little subdued, and I wondered if he was worried about the other boys.

'Has George said any more to you about walking with Sid?' I asked him.

'No. Haven't seen him.' It was the weekend now, and school had broken up for the May half-term. 'But I saw Reggie this morning and he asked me again about letting him walk Sid with me,' he went on, with a shy little smile. 'Next time we're down at the river, if he calls me "chicken" again, I'll tell him he's never going to be allowed.'

'Good for you.'

'Can we take Sid for his walk now?' he added, putting down his glass.

'Definitely. Come on, let's get his lead.'

*

It was almost five o'clock by the time Sid and I arrived back at the cottage, just as Mike came out of his own house.

'Settled in OK?' he asked.

'Yes. Thanks so much, again, for everything.'

He brushed this aside. 'Look, I've just got to go and call on someone – one of the parishioners who's a bit poorly – but why don't you pop in later for a glass of wine? About eight o'clock?'

'Oh. Well, OK, um, yes, that would be nice ...'

I tailed off, staring after him as he gave me a wave and dashed off on his mercy mission. It was kind of him to invite me in, another of his thoughtful gestures of friendship. A welcoming drink celebrating my moving in: it was a normal, neighbourly thing to suggest. But after what Kerry had said, I could imagine how it would look to the nosy-parker gossips in this village. I shrugged. Well, nobody was likely to be around to notice. And even if they did, why should I care?

I sang happily to myself in the kitchen as I cooked my pasta and home-made tomato sauce for dinner. It was good to feel settled, to have a home, even if only for a month. So perhaps the idea of my grand tour of the UK had been a mistake, after all. Maybe I wasn't suited to a life on the road, living out of a suitcase. Well, at least I'd given it a try. Perhaps when my month in the cottage was up, I'd go straight home and – as my children had suggested – find myself somewhere different to live. Nothing grand, just a bit nicer than my poky little flat, somewhere with a bit of character, where I could start again. Start 'the rest of my life', as the kids had referred to it.

Thinking about them reminded me that I really ought to let them know, soon, that I'd now moved into this cottage. That I was living somewhere with an address, for a definite period of time, so that they could forward anything important that might have come in the post. I'll call them tonight, after I've eaten, I decided. And almost as if I'd willed it, my phone began to trill, just as I was dishing up my dinner.

Rachel said the display.

'Hello, darling! What a coincidence! I was just thinking I'd give you a call—'

'Were you?' She didn't sound terribly happy.

'Yes. Are you OK?' I should have waited for a reply, but I was so keen to give her the news that I babbled straight on. 'Guess what? I've rented a cottage here: Riverside Cottage. It's perfect – you'd love it. I moved in today.' I paused. '*Are* you OK, Rach?'

'Well, no. To be honest, no, not really. I'm worried, Mum.'

'Worried? What about?' I sat down, holding the phone in one hand and the serving spoon I'd been using in the other.

'About *you*. I think … really, I think we should come down there and see you. Talk to you about this, face to face—'

93

'What? It's fine, honestly! Look, OK, I know I've been a bit ... indecisive. You probably think it's odd, me wanting to stay here, after all I've said about the people being so unfriendly. But I *am* starting to make friends, and I love it here. It's hard to explain—'

'You're right,' she interrupted me. 'We do find it odd, yes – and now you're *renting a cottage*. I mean – really? For how long? Are you going to *move* down there?'

'No, no,' I laughed. 'It's only for a month. I—'

But she interrupted me again. 'Anyway, that's not it. That's not the thing we're worried about.'

'Oh.' I paused. 'Go on, then, what is it?'

'Mum, Daniel has been doing some research. Online. He wanted to know more about it, you see, so he signed up to this website, where you can search various records and talk to other people, and—'

'What?' I said, bewildered. 'He wanted to know more about *what*? I'm not following you.'

'Family history. It's an ancestry website. He wanted to find out about this so-called uncle of Dad's in Australia—'

'Ah! I see.' I sighed. 'Is *that* what you're worried about?'

'Well, of course we're worried! I mean, we'd never heard of anyone in the family living in Australia. We didn't know Dad had any uncles, let alone any that were millionaires, who would have left him all this money. So—'

'Right. Well, of course, as you've now found out—'

'We've found out, Mum, that you've been lying to us. There isn't any uncle. Dad's left you this – this *fortune*, that you claimed to know nothing about—'

'I *didn't* know anything about it, Rachel. I was just as surprised as you were.'

'If that was true, why did you make up a story about where it came from? Why, Mum? Where *did* Dad get the money from? Why did he keep it a secret – was he involved in something dodgy, something illegal? Did he *steal* it? Was he, I don't know, a drug dealer or something?'

I laughed. 'Of course not! Don't be silly, it's nothing like that. It was a legacy from an ex-girlfriend, if you must know.'

'I don't believe you. You would have told us.' She sounded wretched, like she might start crying. I put down the serving spoon, suddenly not feeling like laughing any more.

'Rachel, honestly, you're letting your imagination run away with you. I'm not lying to you—'

'But you did! You told us that story about the rich uncle! I mean, why would you do that, if there was nothing dodgy about it? I'm really worried about you, Mum. Should you be spending that money? Should any of us? Where did it come from?'

'There's nothing dodgy about it! It was your dad's money, and it was all legal and above board; you're getting yourself upset about nothing. I know it was silly of me to invent the rich uncle, but it just seemed easier. I can explain—'

'Well, I hope so. You can explain it when I get there. I'm coming down to see you. I'd been thinking about it anyway, but now, now you've got yourself a *cottage* there—' She said 'cottage' as if it were something disreputable.

'Well, Dan and I were both worried already, but now I really need to see you. I think we need to sit down and talk all this over properly. Without any more lies, Mum. I'm coming tomorrow. Give me the postcode.'

'Satnavs can't find this place,' I said faintly, as if that was all that mattered. 'Rachel, honestly, there's no need. I can explain it now – it's really not a big deal. Not that it wouldn't be lovely to see you, of course,' I added quickly.

'So I'll come. Give me the postcode,' she insisted again. 'If I can't find it, I'll call you.'

'I'll wait for your call,' I said with a smile. 'Drive carefully. Is Jason coming with you?'

'No. He seems to have developed some kind of allergy to the leather car seats.'

Some things never change.

I was sorry my kids were upset with me. Sorry I'd worried them unnecessarily. But I was looking forward to seeing my daughter. Even if I was going to have to go and look for her when she failed to find her way here!

CHAPTER 10

That evening, I found myself looking around me, as if I were doing something illegal, when I rang the doorbell at the vicarage next door.

'Come in, Clare.' Mike looked at me in amusement. 'Don't look so worried.'

'Sorry.' I shook my head, laughing to myself as he ushered me inside. 'I was just thinking about my daughter. She's coming down to visit me. Tomorrow.'

'Oh, that's nice,' he said warmly. Then, seeing the look on my face, added, 'Isn't it?'

'Yes, yes, of course it is. It'll be lovely to see her.' I sat down on the sofa, gratefully accepting the glass of wine he handed me.

'But you're worried about her?

I laughed again. 'Not exactly. She's worried about *me*.'

He looked at me thoughtfully, his head on one side. 'Because you've decided to stay here for a month?'

'You're very perceptive,' I said.

'Part of the job. Being a minister is as much about being a social worker, counsellor and family therapist as anything to do with the Church.' He shrugged. 'Don't get me wrong, that's as it should be. "Take care of my sheep", and all that.'

I didn't recognise the quotation but presumed it was from the Bible, so I just smiled and asked him if he had very many *sheep* to care for.

'Oh, I treat the whole of the village as my flock,' he replied earnestly, 'regardless of whether they come to church. I care about them all, obviously.' He gave a self-deprecating little laugh. 'In fact, I sometimes struggle more with members of my congregation than I do with the ones who'd rather walk over burning coals than set foot in Saint Peter's.'

'Why's that?'

'The congregation tends to be … well, mostly my age and upwards, you see. And very traditional. I suppose it's partly a generational thing, and partly because of living in such an isolated place. I've tried to bring things up to date a bit since I've been here – introducing more modern hymns and a more informal feel to the services. But I meet a lot of resistance. It's a shame. We might appeal to younger people if we moved with the times a bit.'

'But I suppose if you insist on change, you'll risk driving the older ones away.'

'Exactly. And I wouldn't want to do that. Preaching to an empty church isn't much fun.'

We both laughed.

'Anyway,' he went on, 'tell me more about your daughter. Why is she so worried about you staying here?'

'Oh, it's my own fault.' I sighed. 'I've dithered for the whole time I've been here …' I paused. Had I *really* only been here for just over a week? It felt like much longer. 'Dithered about whether to go home, carry on travelling, or stay put for a while. And I suppose, because I've described how the people here are …'

'Being unfriendly,' he finished for me, as I hesitated awkwardly.

'Well, yes. I've complained to my kids about that, I suppose, so they must be wondering why on earth I've decided to stay for a whole month.'

'Can't blame them for that,' he said with a smile. 'I've wondered myself!'

'Me too!' I admitted, and laughed again. 'Anyway, that's not the only reason my daughter's worried. But …' I hesitated again. I'd been going to tell him about Brian, the money, the crazy author, the fictitious uncle in Australia. But suddenly it just felt like too much effort. 'It's a long story,' I finished. To say nothing of being a ridiculous one.

'Well, I can only apologise again for the attitude of the people here. I hope they'll be different now you're staying for longer.'

'It's hardly your fault! And I think I've begun to make one other friend, at least.' I told him about Leo, and he nodded, looking solemn.

'Yes, that child has had some difficulties,' he said. 'It's nice that you've befriended him, Clare.'

I considered asking about the *difficulties*, but realised Mike probably felt bound, like a doctor, by confidentiality.

And then I suddenly remembered, 'Oh, of course, you must be quite close to the family.' I blushed. 'Sorry, it wasn't that anyone was gossiping—'

'That wouldn't exactly surprise me!'

'No, I was talking to Kerry. It seems she's another friend I've acquired. And she mentioned that you were, well, you're seeing her mum.'

'Julie.' He smiled, seeming to find my discomfort mildly amusing. 'It's no secret. We're engaged.'

'Congratulations,' I said – and then burst out laughing at my own foolishness. 'Oh, sorry – Kerry did say you'd been engaged for some time. I just didn't want you to think we'd been gossiping about you.'

'Kerry's a nice girl. And Leo's a lovely little boy, as you've discovered. The family – well, they've been through a lot, that's all. Tread carefully, Clare. If Leo gets too attached to you—'

'I think it's Sid he's attached to, not me! But I take your point. I'll make sure he understands we're only here temporarily.'

I sipped my wine, resisting the urge to ask what he meant about the family going through a lot. I presumed it was something to do with Kerry being a single mum. It was none of my business, and if I was going to be accepted by the family as a friend – however temporary – I mustn't pry into their personal lives.

We talked for a while about other things – about the far more urban parish Mike had looked after in the Midlands before moving to Devon two years previously, and about my work as a press photographer.

'I had noticed you've always got your camera with you when you're walking around the village,' he said.

'Yes. I bought a new one for this trip. I've rediscovered photography as a hobby, now I'm not having to take photos every day for work. Little Sorrel is so beautiful, so photogenic. But I've also been enjoying taking pictures of Sid, and the wildlife around here too. Birds and squirrels and so on. It's a lot of fun, photographing animals.'

'You must show me some of your pictures.'

'OK, yes, of course.' I smiled. Then I stopped, looking up in alarm at a sudden loud scratching noise coming from beyond the back of the house.

'Excuse me a minute.' Mike got up and went out of the room, and I heard the back door opening. Two seconds later, the little black and white cat I'd seen in the cottage garden came trotting in, stopping to look at me in surprise before jumping up onto the other sofa.

I laughed. 'So he *is* yours! I meant to ask you. I've seen him in the garden next door.'

'She's a *she*, actually. Topsy. And no, strictly speaking she isn't mine. She's Harry's.'

'Oh! So she belongs next door? I didn't realise—'

'My fault for forgetting to tell you. I promised to look after her for Harry, and in fact a couple of other people down the lane sometimes feed her too, if I'm not around. We've sort of adopted her as a community cat while Harry's abroad,' he said with a smile. 'She's no trouble. But she still regards Riverside Cottage as her home, so if you leave the doors or windows open, she's quite likely to walk in.' He glanced at me, suddenly looking anxious.

'Oh dear, are you OK with cats? You're not allergic, or anything, are you?'

'No!' I laughed. 'I love them.'

'Thank goodness. I thought for a moment I might have to cancel the rental agreement just as you've moved in.'

'Not at all! Topsy looks such a sweet little cat. And fortunately, Sid seems OK with her – at least, he was wagging his tail while he chased her today!' I got up and went over to stroke her, smiling as she blinked up at me, purring. 'Which brand of food does she like? I'll get some to keep in the cupboard—'

'No, I'll give you some of the supplies, if you don't mind, in case she does come in and pester you to be fed. Harry set up payments for me to cover the cost of her food. But we have to be careful not to overfeed her, as she tends to wander into all the houses along the lane, pretending to be starving.'

'But of course I'd be happy to share the feeding.'

'Ah, thank you. I'm sure Topsy will be grateful. Harry was sorry not to take her with him, but he wanted – um, needed – to go quite quickly. He had a job lined up in the States. He did consider taking her with him but it takes time, you know, getting a pet passport and all that, and the regulations seemed complicated – every state has its own rules.'

'Well, it's not that easy to move cats to somewhere different, anyway, is it?' I said. 'Perhaps it was kinder to leave her where she is – especially if Harry is only abroad temporarily.'

'Yes, that's what he decided too,' Mike said.

I gave Topsy another little stroke and decided I'd make a fuss of her, at least for the month I was staying here, to make up a little for being separated from her owner.

'Well, now I'm on my feet, I think it's time I went,' I said to Mike, stretching and yawning. I suddenly felt tired after all the excitement of moving into the cottage. 'Thanks so much for the drink and the chat. I'll reciprocate another evening. And perhaps your fiancée will join us?'

'I'll ask her, of course, thank you.' Mike smiled. 'I'm sure Julie would love to meet you. She's often quite busy, though.'

I didn't like to ask what Julie was so busy with that she might not be able to spare time for a quick social drink. Much as I appreciated Mike's friendship and kindness to me, I hoped his fiancée wasn't going to feel aggrieved by him spending time with me – especially if she'd heard the gossip about us around the village that Kerry had hinted at. I'd have hated to think she might believe there was any truth in it. But I couldn't bring myself to mention that to Mike!

*

It was nice, having more space to myself, after the confinement of the room at the pub and all the previous hotel rooms before that. The cottage felt comfortable and homely already. I made myself a cup of tea, turned on the TV, put my feet up and watched the late evening news before drawing all the curtains and going to bed. The bed was comfy too, and I felt tired enough to go straight to sleep without even attempting a chapter of the book I was reading on my Kindle. But as soon as I snuggled down, I found myself tormented by anxiety about Rachel's visit the next day. Was she really upset with me for inventing the Australian uncle? Or was she more upset about the fact that I'd decided to stay here for a while? *Was* I being ridiculous? Why *did* I want to spend a whole month here? How was I going to explain it to Rachel – who was no doubt going to go home afterwards and report back to her brother? Was I being fair to them if they were really worried about me? Perhaps they actually missed me!

I tossed and turned, annoyed about being unable to sleep despite my tiredness and despite the fact that I felt so contented here in the cottage. Eventually I gave in, put on the bedside light and read a chapter of my book after all.

This is ridiculous, I told myself when I finally turned off my Kindle and settled down again. Rachel was my lovely daughter, we loved each other, it was natural that she felt concerned about me, but we'd soon sort it out between us. And if I didn't get to sleep soon, I'd still be in bed when she arrived!

CHAPTER 11

In fact, Rachel must have left London before it even got light, which was saying something at that time of year. It wasn't long after ten the next morning when she called me, sounding exasperated, to say her satnav had brought her down a 'farm track'.

'That's not a farm track,' I laughed. 'It's the main road to Little Sorrel.'

'You are bloody joking me!' she exclaimed crossly. 'I'm in a standoff with some kind of agricultural crane thing and this ... this *dirt track* is barely wide enough to drive down, never mind turning round. He won't budge. What am I supposed to do?'

'Reverse, I'm afraid, love.'

'But I don't think there were any passing places.'

'I know. You'll be able to back into a farm entrance eventually.'

'For God's sake,' she muttered as she hung up.

Five minutes later she called again.

'The satnav has now abandoned me at the top of a hill, surrounded by – well, by nothing, frankly. This can't be right.'

'Are you in a passing place now? Can you see the village down the hill? The church tower, and the river?'

'I can see a few buildings down there, yes, but it could be anywhere, Mum. This is ridiculous. There must be another route—'

'There isn't, but you're almost here. Ignore your satnav for the next bit, it won't cope. Carry on downhill and you'll come into the village in about another mile. You'll see the pub – the Ferryboat Inn – right in front of you. Turn right onto Fore Street and then right again onto Duck Lane, and you'll see my car outside Riverside Cottage.'

'Get the kettle on, then. I've fought with tractors and bloody combine harvesters or whatever and I'm shattered.'

I was singing happily as I boiled the kettle. Sid padded to the front door and back restlessly, making little breathless whining noises as if he knew we were expecting someone. When Rachel finally arrived, he went crazy with joy, jumping at her legs, barking, running to his bed to present her with his toys.

'He remembers you!' I said in surprise, giving her a hug.

'You haven't been gone *that* long, Mum.' She held me at arm's length, looking me up and down critically. 'You've lost weight! What have you been doing – starving yourself?'

'Of course not!' In fact, because of all the fresh country air, I was probably eating more than I'd ever done. But I was aware, and pleased, that I'd slimmed down quite a bit since I'd been away. 'It's all the exercise I get, taking Sid for lots of long walks.'

'Right. Well, you look well,' she conceded eventually, 'considering.'

'Considering what?' I laughed. 'I should look well, shouldn't I? I'm on holiday.'

'I meant considering you're stuck out here in the back of beyond. Honestly, I know you said it was isolated, but for God's sake – it's the middle of sodding nowhere!'

'Come on,' I soothed her. 'Sit down while I make you a coffee, and you'll feel better. What on earth was the hurry? You must have got up in the middle of the night.'

'I wanted to be out of London before the rush hour. I haven't had any breakfast, as a matter of fact. Yes, yes –' she interrupted me as I started to protest '– don't worry, I stopped halfway down the motorway and had a coffee and a break, but I wasn't hungry. I was too anxious to get here.'

'I'll make you some toast.'

She nodded. 'Thanks, Mum. Sorry for moaning. But you must admit—'

'It's a long way off the beaten track. I know. But there was no need for you to come rushing down here. As you can see, I'm fine. Absolutely fine.'

We'd gone straight through to the kitchen, where Rachel had sat at the little table with her mug of coffee and she now looked around her for the first time.

'I must say it's actually quite nice, this little place. Is it just rented out as a holiday home?'

'Kind of. For now. The owner's in America, apparently,' I said casually. I buttered two slices of toast and sat down opposite her. 'Eat up. When you've had a chance to rest, I'll show you around. You *are* staying, aren't you? For a few days at least?'

'Only today and tomorrow – is that OK? I've got to meet a client on Tuesday. In Reading, so at least it's on the way home.'

'That's good.' I remembered, suddenly, belatedly, about the locked-up spare bedroom. 'Um, we'll have to share the bed. Hope you don't mind.'

'Oh, is there only one bedroom? You didn't say.'

'It's fine. Big double bed. I promise I won't snore.' I smiled and reached across the table to squeeze her hand. 'It's so lovely to see you.'

'You too.' She smiled back, the stressed-out look finally fading. She wiped butter from her mouth and added, 'But before we do the tour of the village, we need to talk.'

'OK,' I said, leaning back in my chair. 'I know. Where do you want me to start?'

*

We started with the rich uncle in Australia.

'I know I shouldn't have made that up. But it was just so much easier to explain than the truth,' I said apologetically.

'Go on,' she said, warily. 'And the truth is …?'

I sighed. Probably best to just blurt it out. 'Your father once dated an author. Jacqueline Bright. She wrote a couple of bestsellers: *Cut You Dead* and *Dead Ringer*—'

'Never heard of her,' Rachel said dismissively. 'When was this? Last century?'

'Well, yes, the books were published in the 1980s, I think. And the first one was made into a film.'

'Right, so he went out with her, I presume before you married him, and – what? He somehow got all this money out of her and kept it quiet all these years? That doesn't make sense.'

'He went out with her before she got famous – and rich. Yes, before I met him, obviously.'

'So what has she got to do with this, then? I don't get it.'

'Nor did I, trust me, when I first heard about it,' I said. 'The thing is, you see, Jacqueline Bright died before her third book was finished. Car accident. But she was going to dedicate it to your dad.'

Rachel's mouth dropped open, then she shook her head, staring at me.

'Why?'

'Well, she never forgot him, it seems. Andy – you know, your dad's friend – told me all this. Dad apparently confided in him. It seems Jacqueline Bright was obsessed with him—'

'With who – Andy?'

'No, Rach, keep up! She was obsessed with your father, ever since he dumped her.'

'Mum, is this just another made-up story? Because if so, I think I prefer the one about the rich uncle in Australia. And it's more believable.'

'Yes, I agree, it does seem ridiculous. I know you loved your dad – so did I, obviously, before we split up. Well, even afterwards, in a way. But yes, it's hard to imagine anyone, let alone someone rich and famous, would be obsessed with him. He wasn't the type anyone would obsess over, was he?'

'No. He was just Dad,' she said, quietly, sadly. 'So did this Jacqueline author-person have psychological issues, then?'

'Probably. Apparently, she was a heavy drinker. Perhaps when she was drunk, she pictured him looking like – I don't know – Aidan Turner or someone.' I sniggered, and Rachel stared at me with a wounded look.

'Mum! Don't laugh. Dad's not here to defend himself now.'

'You're right, sorry. Well, anyway, she stayed in touch with him, even though, according to Andy, he kept trying to discourage her. And she told him she was going to dedicate that new book to him, and also –' I sniggered again. I just couldn't help it, it was so ridiculous '– she was going to base the hero of the book on him.'

Even Rachel was sniggering now. I tried my best to keep a straight face, but it was impossible, remembering how Andy had described Brian as a *romantic hero*. I struggled for a minute, then the laughter came out in a loud, undignified snort – making Rachel laugh even more. And then we were both collapsing across the table, howling, crying, with laughter.

'She wanted him to be her romantic hero!' I gasped, holding my sides.

'Oh my God! My father, the hero of a novel!' Rachel wiped her eyes. Then she suddenly sat up straight, took a few breaths to calm herself, and said, 'But I still don't understand how the money came into it. Did she *pay* him to be in this book, or what?'

I laughed. 'Of course not. She left him everything. In her will.'

'But ... *why*? Didn't she have anyone else to leave it to? Family, or friends? A favourite charity? Surely you don't leave all your worldly wealth to someone just because you've got – what? – a crush on them?'

'She was *obsessed* with him, Rach. Never got over him. And no, it seems she didn't have anyone else to leave it to. She must have just sat there on her own, drinking too much and thinking about your father all the time. Apparently, she looked back on their relationship as the happiest time of her life. I suppose she just never met anyone else or fell in love again.' We both fell quiet. I felt a lump in my throat. 'Actually, it's really bloody sad, isn't it? I never thought of it like that before. I just thought it was unbelievably stupid – daft – and I was angry, too. Angry with your father for not telling me. Not bloody well letting us spend it, when we really needed it. Letting us scrimp and save, while this big fat legacy sat in dozens of savings accounts—'

'Gaining interest,' Rachel pointed out gently. 'Probably loads of interest over the years, Mum. I bet he didn't want to benefit from that woman's madness – her obsession. Maybe he didn't think he deserved to. He was like that, wasn't he? Kind of ... humble. Unassuming. Gentle.'

'Stop it. You're going to make me cry in a minute, and I've only just stopped laughing.'

She smiled, taking hold of my hand across the table. 'I miss him, Mum.'

'Me too, in a strange, not-even-married-any more way,' I admitted quietly. 'And yes, you're most likely right. He probably did it for us. He'd made Andy his executor, maybe to save me – or either of you – the job. And he invested all that money so that it made even more – for us, not for him. Because he didn't even want it.'

We sat in silence, both of us, presumably, thinking about the unassuming, gentle man we'd lost, who didn't want his crazy author's money for himself but – as Andy had told me – always intended me and the children to have it. I felt my eyes fill with tears – and then, suddenly, I blinked them back, realisation hitting me.

'Hang on a minute! What if I'd died before him?'

'Oh. Well, maybe he didn't think that through.'

'No, and that is *exactly* like your father. He never thought things through! What an idiot! Well, I'm sorry, but it has to be said: he was a maths teacher, for God's sake, supposed to be good with numbers, and he couldn't even figure out that his grand scheme might not work, that it might have been *me* who had the heart attack, and what then? He'd still have left the money in the bank? He still wouldn't have spent it?'

'No, Mum,' Rachel said in a small voice. 'He wouldn't have. He'd have wanted me and Daniel to have it, if you … if anything had happened to you. That's why he didn't change his will, isn't it? Because everything would have come to us, if you'd already passed away.'

'Yes.' My anger dissipated again. 'Of course. Sorry. It's what I wanted, anyway, for you two to benefit from it.' I spread my hands, smiling ruefully. 'All right, I give in. You're right. He was a saint, and I didn't appreciate him.'

She managed a laugh. 'Hardly a saint, Mum. And I understand why you split up with him. But he was, at least, a good man.' She shook her head, lifting her coffee mug, staring into it, before adding, 'But a romantic hero? I really can't get over that!'

*

We'd finished our coffees, I'd put Sid on his lead, and we were just about to go out when Rachel suddenly stopped in the middle of the living room and said, 'Will there be any *more* money coming from her, then – this author woman? I mean, I know she's dead, but if her royalties kept on going to her estate – in other words, to Dad – won't they keep on coming to you, now?'

I nodded. 'In theory. But apparently there's only a trickle these days, because her books were published so long ago. There's a literary agent who handles any money that does come in. Andy had to contact her – because he was Brian's executor – to tell her Brian had passed away and I was now the literary heir. Apparently, Jacqueline Bright was popular in the States and there have been a couple of reprints over there, but the agent told Andy she doesn't expect there to be much more income now.'

'Oh well. We mustn't be greedy, must we?' Rachel said, smiling and following me to the door. 'OK, Mum. Show me what it is about this godforsaken village that has you so determined to stay here for a whole month. Or is it just that it's so bloody difficult to get in or out of the place you'd rather stay put?'

I laughed. 'Well, that might have something to do with it! Come on, Sid, let's go. We're going to show Little Sorrel off to Rachel. Let's hope the sun keeps shining.'

CHAPTER 12

Almost as soon as we'd closed the cottage door behind us, we met Mike returning from church, accompanied by a neatly dressed little woman with ash-blonde hair and startlingly blue eyes. He hailed us loudly and cheerfully and informed us he'd had a good turnout for the morning service that day.

'Nice morning, you see. People don't mind getting up early. The sunshine puts everyone in a good mood.'

'Glad to hear it,' I said, trying to keep the sarcasm from my voice – but he laughed.

'Well, OK, some of the villagers will be grumpy no matter what the weather's like.' He gave an apologetic little shrug, turning to the woman by his side. 'Julie, this is my new neighbour, Clare. Clare, this is Julie, my fiancée.'

'Oh, my daughter's told me all about you, Clare,' Julie said, giving me such a warm smile that I nearly fell over in shock; I'd become so used to hostile glares from people during the past week or so. 'You've been really kind to my grandson Leo. He loves your dog.'

She bent down to pat Sid as he sniffed around her legs, tail wagging enthusiastically.

'It's no trouble. Sid loves Leo too. It's nice to meet you, Julie,' I said. 'And this is Rachel, my daughter. She's visiting me for a couple of days. Rach – Mike is my neighbour here. And the vicar.'

'Pleased to meet you,' they both said at the same time.

'I'm just going to show Rachel the sights of Little Sorrel,' I added to Mike and Julie.

'See you back here in about five minutes, then!' he joked.

'He seems nice,' Rachel said as soon as we were out of earshot. 'You didn't tell me he lives next door.'

'I haven't had a chance yet! But yes, he is nice. He's been very kind to me.'

'Good. And his girlfriend … sorry, *fiancée* … seems nice too, doesn't she?'

'Yes, she does. She's been away, apparently, so it's the first time I've met her.' I didn't add that there'd been gossip about me being too friendly with Mike. But I was privately breathing a sigh of relief about the warmth of Julie's greeting.

We walked to the bottom of Duck Lane first. I wanted to show Rachel the little pond at the end. We were just in time to see a procession of little fluffy ducklings following their mother duck towards the water. As we watched, one of the babies tripped over his own feet and sat down inelegantly in the mud – and instantly the mother was there, picking him up in her beak and setting him back in line with the others.

'Aw, how cute!' Rachel whispered. 'Oh – did you get a picture?'

'Several,' I said with a smile as I lowered my camera. 'I'm really enjoying photographing the wildlife around here.'

'You must show me some of your pictures when we get back.'

We turned and strolled back towards Fore Street, where I pointed out the village shop.

'Is it open?' Rachel asked as we paused outside. 'I'll pop in and get some paracetamol. My head's still throbbing from driving up that ridiculous mud track.'

'I've got paracetamol at home,' I said, correcting myself quickly with, 'I mean, in the cottage. You should have said. The shop's closed. It's Sunday.'

'Closed on a Sunday?' she squawked in surprise. 'What, all day?'

I smiled. 'Yes, the whole day. Wednesday afternoons, too. And the nearest other shops are in the next village – a ferry trip plus a half-hour walk away.'

'Can't you get there by road?'

'Well, yes, you can. The same road you drove up this morning, and a turn-off that's even narrower.'

Rachel grimaced.

'And not many of the shops there open on Sundays either,' I added, 'apart from the touristy type of shops – as it's summer.'

'You're talking like a local,' she said, turning to look at me. 'I must say, you do seem different, Mum. Very calm and relaxed.'

'Well, there's nothing to get stressed about here! Come on, let me show you the church. Don't you think those little thatched cottages are pretty?'

'Yes. It is pretty here.' We walked on up the street. 'Is this the school? It's tiny!'

'I know. There are only two teachers. One takes the smaller children, the other – the head – takes the older ones. They have to go elsewhere once they're eleven, of course. A minibus picks them up from here to take them to the nearest high school.'

'Up that dreadful lane?'

'Yep! Apparently even the tractors give way to the school bus, though.'

'It does sound kind of idyllic,' she said, a little wistfully. 'But not, somehow, *real*, is it? I mean, those kids are growing up without any knowledge of how life actually is, out in the real world—'

'Well ...' I shrugged. 'Maybe that's true. But the "real world" – if you mean life in big towns and cities – isn't perfect either, is it? I guess a lot of them will want to move away when they're older, for university, work opportunities or just for a different lifestyle. But I bet they'll enjoy coming back, too.'

'For holidays; for the peace and quiet. Yes, I can see that. Oh!' We'd turned down the path towards the quay and the boathouse, and she stopped, staring around her. 'The river's much wider here.'

She'd already admired the stretch of the Sorrel River we could see across Duck Lane from Riverside Cottage, but here, where the river widened, it was a much more spectacular view. It was a perfect morning, sunlight dancing on the water, a couple of little boats making their way towards the estuary, seagulls swooping and calling up above, and the sea, in the distance, a line of azure blue. On the ramp outside French's boathouse, Old Robbie was whistling as he painted a sailing dinghy. Hearing our voices, he turned, and actually gave me a nod and a grunt of 'Morning.' I blinked in surprise as I returned the greeting.

'Well, that's three people so far who haven't been overtly rude, at least!' Rachel said quietly. She'd already noticed the unfriendly expressions and silent hostility emanating from other villagers we'd passed in the street.

We strolled along the quayside in silence, Rachel looking out at the boats.

'I had no idea it was like this,' she said eventually. 'When you said it was a little river, I imagined something green and smelly, full of mud. Not beautiful, like this.'

'Well, it is full of mud!' I conceded. 'But yes, beautiful too. I think so, anyway. The whole village is beautiful. Perhaps we'll walk up to Cockscombe Castle tomorrow. The views from up there are amazing. And it's a nice walk through the woods. Sid loves it. The woods are full of wildflowers.'

'Anyone would think you'd been born and bred here, the way you're promoting the place!' she teased me.

I shrugged and gave an embarrassed little laugh. 'I know it's daft. I've only been here just over a week. It's probably just that holiday feeling. But I feel like I've fallen in love with it.'

We strolled the rest of the way to the estuary and back, then completed our circuit of the village and ended up at the pub for lunch. Jack merely nodded at me in recognition, unsmiling, as he took our orders, giving Rachel a malevolent look.

'He probably thinks one incomer is bad enough, but two is positively worrying,' I chuckled when we were seated at a table in the beer garden. 'The village is being overrun with us.'

We both fell silent as we watched a squirrel scamper across the grass from the trees at the edge of the garden, stopping every now and then to sit up and look around him before continuing on his way.

'They're fun to watch. Sometimes they play with the magpies,' I said, 'chasing each other up and down the trees.'

Rachel smiled and leant back in her chair, face to the sun. 'I could get used to this,' she admitted. 'I can see why you're so calm, even in the face of such bloody rudeness! It's so peaceful here. It feels like nothing really matters.' She opened one eye and pulled a face, as she added, 'I bet the winters here are absolutely dreadful, though.'

*

As we walked back to the cottage later, I caught sight of Leo, walking away from the river where I could see the other children playing. He was trudging along, head down, kicking stones – but when he looked up and saw us, he broke into a smile.

'Hello, Clare! Hello, Sid!' He ran up to join us, giving Rachel a shy smile. I introduced them, and asked Leo if he'd like to take Sid's lead.

'Yes! Come on, Sid.' He grabbed the lead and ran ahead of us up the street. 'Can we go down the footpath and walk back along the quay?'

'Well, we *were* heading home.' I glanced at Rachel, who said quickly, 'That's fine with me.'

'He wants to walk Sid in front of the other kids,' I told her quietly. 'It's to make them jealous. To get back at them for giving him a hard time.'

'So the children here are as unpleasant as the adults?' she asked pointedly.

'Some of them, it seems. But you know what kids are like.' I shrugged.

Sure enough, a few minutes later as we strolled past the children who were playing in the river, there were shouts of 'Hey, Leo, whose dog?', 'What's his name?' and 'Can I walk him?' Leo walked on, his head held high, ignoring them all. Good for him, I thought. Make them beg!

'And you don't know why they pick on him?' Rachel asked.

'Apparently he's not allowed to do the things they are in the water. It seems his mum's somewhat overprotective. But she's nice enough. She's quite friendly now she knows I'm trying to help Leo a bit.'

'I'd better go home now,' Leo said regretfully, turning round to wait for us as we came out onto Fore Street again. 'Mum wants me to help her in the garden this afternoon. Bye, Clare. Bye,' he added to Rachel.

'Bye, Leo.' She smiled at him. 'Nice to meet you.'

*

By the time we were relaxing with a glass of wine in the cottage that evening, Rachel had admitted she felt reassured now she'd seen Little Sorrel for herself.

'I can understand why you love it here, even though I agree about the people. Apart from Mike and Julie, and Leo, of course. It's bizarre. What on earth's the matter with the rest of them? Still, if it doesn't put you off, fair enough. You're right, after living in London it's like a little bubble of peace and stillness here. I guess it's just what you need at the moment, Mum: an interlude of calm and quiet, to reflect on ... well, on what's happened to change your life. And what you're going to do next.'

'Yes. That's exactly it. I think I realise now that I needed this interlude, as you put it, more than I needed to travel. That wasn't really working for me. I was wondering about coming home.'

'And now? You'll stay for the month and *then* come home? Or move on again?'

I didn't answer straight away. Just as I was about to try, Sid suddenly jumped up from where he'd been lying at my feet, and rushed into the kitchen, barking.

'What's the matter?' I said, running after him. 'Oh! Hello, Topsy. Sid, stop it. Leave her alone, that's a good boy.'

It was a warm evening, so I'd left the back door open and the little cat had strolled in, presumably hoping for some food. I opened one of the packets Mike had given me and put some food down for her, holding onto Sid's collar so that he wouldn't chase her out – or eat her food himself!

'Whose cat is that?' Rachel had followed me into the kitchen and was watching with interest. 'She's sweet.'

'She's Harry's – the guy who owns the cottage. He couldn't take her when he went to the States, so Mike looks after her, but of course she still hangs around here as it's her home.' I bent down to stroke Topsy and she rubbed herself against my legs, purring. 'I feel a bit sorry for her,' I added.

Rachel watched me for a moment, then added, quietly, 'You want to stay here, don't you, Mum? You seem like you're at home here.'

'Don't be silly, I've just rented this place for a month. I couldn't stay permanently,' I pointed out, 'even if I wanted to. The cottage belongs to this Harry, and he's only gone abroad temporarily.'

I walked back through to the lounge.

'Look!' I called to Rachel. 'This is him – Harry.' I pointed to the self-portrait as she came to join me. 'He's an artist. He painted the big canvas on the other wall, too.'

'Oh! I love that big picture.' She stared at the self-portrait. 'Good-looking guy. He looks a bit … *tragic*, though, doesn't he?'

'I think that's how artists are supposed to look!' I said. 'But yes, there's something about him, isn't there – in this picture, anyway? Mike said it was done years ago though, so he's probably looking older now – like all of us! But the point is – it's his cottage. And anyway, as you said, this is just an interlude. I'm on holiday, and when the holiday's over, I'll have to pick up my life again, like everyone does.'

'OK.' Topsy had followed us into the lounge and jumped onto one of the sofas, snuggling down and beginning to purr. Rachel sat down next to her and gave her a stroke. 'If you say so, Mum.'

Rachel and I shared the double bed that night, although she did pull a face when she noticed the door to the other upstairs room and I explained that Harry had kept it locked.

'That's an odd thing to do, isn't it, if you're renting out a two-bedroom cottage?' she said.

'Well, it's his prerogative, I suppose.'

'Seems like he's as odd as the rest of the population here. Perhaps he's got something hidden in there. A stash of stolen goods. Or a couple of dead bodies.'

'Don't be so melodramatic! I'm guessing he keeps his paints and stuff in there, that's all. He wouldn't want anyone to touch them, would he, while he's away.'

'You make him sound terribly important. He's just a painter, even if he's a good one. Not God, or royalty! And anyway, you're an artist too, aren't you? Some of your photos are just as good as his paintings,' she said. I'd spent some time showing her the pictures I'd downloaded from my camera – those of Sid, and of all the wildlife around the village.

'Thank you, darling. But there's a world of difference between pressing a few buttons on a camera and painting a picture.'

'That's not true,' she said loyally. 'Both are art forms. You ought to get some of your best ones framed. I love some of the close-ups of Sid. And this one of him looking through the fence at the horses! The expression on his face!

You should specialise in animal photography. You're clearly really good at it.'

Buoyed up by Rachel's encouragement, the next day when we walked up to Cockscombe Castle together I took several more photographs of Sid and a whole series of pictures of squirrels chasing each other up and down the trees. Then to cheer myself up after she'd left on the Tuesday morning, and because it was a rainy day, I ordered prints online of some that I was most pleased with. I could decide whether to have them framed after I returned home. Whatever Rachel thinks, I will return home eventually, I told myself as I looked around at the cosy little room I'd already grown so used to. Having her here with me, even just for a couple of days, had reminded me how much I missed my family. They were fine without me, of course – they had their partners and their busy lives. But for how long would I be fine without them?

CHAPTER 13

The next time I bumped into Mike, I reminded him that I'd offered to return his hospitality one evening.

'How's Thursday for you?' I suggested. 'And you must bring Julie, of course.'

'Thursday's good for me. Thank you, I'll ask Julie, if she's free.'

'Well, if she's not, we can change it to a different evening,' I said. 'I'd like her to come. And my diary's completely empty – it's not as if I'm out boogying every night with the party animals around here!'

He laughed. 'If there *were* any party animals around here, I'd go out boogying with them myself!'

In fact, I'd been surprised to find I didn't mind the quiet and solitude in the slightest now. During my earlier travels, when I'd stayed in hotels, the evenings had felt long and empty, and when I'd been staying in the pub here, it had felt awkward, sitting in the bar being ignored by everyone. But now I had a home of my own, however temporary, it was different. On the fine, light evenings of those last few days of May, I sat outside on the bench in the little walled garden with my Kindle and a cold drink, enjoying the fresh air and birdsong for as long as possible before going indoors and turning on the TV to catch up with the news. During the day, I'd take Sid for long walks, discovering more footpaths and even venturing up Steep Hill on occasion, turning off down the lane that led to Sorrel-by-Sea, and finding footpaths along there that gave me more opportunities to photograph distant sea views across the fields and hedges, as well as some close-up photos of the gentle faces of cows and sheep feeding in the fields. On one occasion, I even managed to capture a shot of a sly old fox as he crept out from under a hedge before darting across the lane in front of me. Leo, who like all the other children was on his half-term holiday, came with me almost every time. I enjoyed his company and he shared my enthusiasm for nature, pointing out things I might well have missed without the help of his sharp eyesight.

My prints arrived, and I propped them up on the shelf in the living room, standing back to eye them critically and, encouraged by the results, I ordered more. Now that Sid was used to Topsy, she was visiting us in the cottage every day, giving me another model for my photographs. She was a pretty little cat, with her white paws, ears and tail-tip, black body and little pink nose, and she looked so cute when she was curled up on the garden bench or on one of the sofas inside. By the end of the week she'd even become brave enough to snuggle down next to Sid, giving me the opportunity for my best animal photo so far, as he turned to stare at her with indignant surprise.

On the Thursday evening, Mike arrived on his own, saying Julie had sent her apologies.

'You should have told me – we could easily have changed the day,' I said as I ushered him into the cottage. 'I'm sorry she couldn't come.'

He sighed as he took a seat on the sofa and accepted a glass of wine.

'The thing is, Clare, Julie spends such a lot of her time with Kerry and Leo. They need her support. Last week was the first break she's allowed herself since ... well, for a long time. She went to visit her sister up in the New Forest for a week. I encouraged her to go. She needed a change of scenery.' He shrugged. 'It's half-term now, and Kerry still has to work, so Julie keeps an eye on Leo during the day, gives him his dinner and takes him home at bedtime. She often looks after some of her nieces and nephews at the same time, so she's tired out by the evening.'

'You mentioned that Kerry's family had had a hard time,' I said. 'I don't want to pry, but I presume – from something Leo said about her – that Kerry's a single mum?'

He nodded. 'Yes, she is.'

'So of course, I can understand why Julie would want to help out. I'd feel the same if, God forbid, my daughter found herself in that position.'

'Yes, absolutely. Hopefully she'll be free to have a cup of tea or something with you another day soon.' He took a sip of his wine and sat for a moment, turning the glass around in his hands. 'Clare, I know you've had a hard time with some of the villagers. They're not really bad people …'

'I'm sure they're not.' I shrugged. 'And don't worry, I do understand that they're not used to visitors.'

'But you're not, are you – not just a visitor, any more.' He gave me a fleeting smile. 'You're here for a month, at least. And you're trying your best to integrate with us here. I appreciate that, even if nobody else does. Look, it's true the villagers are very insular. It's not unusual in a little community like this. Lots of people are related to each other, everyone is everyone else's friend and neighbour, so they cling together and tend to reject outsiders.'

I waited for him to go on, perhaps to explain more, but instead he put down his wine glass, got to his feet and walked over to the shelf where I'd propped up some of my photographs.

'Are these yours?' he asked in surprise.

The subject of the villagers' attitudes was obviously being dropped, even though it was Mike who had brought it up. I wondered if he felt awkward talking about it, having only recently been accepted here himself? He didn't seem to want to criticise his parishioners. Fair enough.

'Yes,' I said. 'Sorry, I forgot I promised to show you some of my pictures. Do you like them?'

'I think they're amazing.' He stood back, surveying them from a better perspective, and then turned to me, his eyebrows raised. 'You're really talented. Do you sell them?'

'Oh God, no.' I laughed, a little embarrassed by his enthusiastic praise. 'It's just a hobby. I mean, yes, I am

– or *was*, I'm not sure now – a professional photographer, but only for local newspapers.'

'You shouldn't be so apologetic about it. If you don't think you'll be going back to your work on the papers, you could set yourself up in business selling pictures like these. These ones of Sid on the beach – the way you've captured his expression – looking at you like he's laughing with excitement! And this one, here, of little Topsy! And the one of the ducklings is absolutely brilliant. Seriously, Clare, they're *really* good.'

'Oh.' I shrugged. 'Well, thank you. I must admit I do like taking pictures of animals. They're great material.'

'And there are so many animal lovers everywhere. People would love to buy pictures of their pets. You must have noticed how many people in this village are dog owners – out walking their dogs every day.'

'Yes, that's true. But I don't think I'm good enough to sell my pictures.' I laughed a little awkwardly.

'You shouldn't put yourself down,' he rebuked me gently. 'Nobody likes a show-off, but there's nothing wrong with recognising our own talents.'

'I suppose you'll say they're God-given,' I said lightly.

'They are.' He smiled at me. 'Trust me, I'm a vicar.'

'And what are *your* talents, then?'

He thought for a moment. 'Well, I was a pretty good rugby scrum-half in my day, but I'm a bit past that now. I'm not a bad singer, though. I can hold a tune. It does help with the job, you know. Nothing worse than a tone-deaf minister leading the congregation in song.'

'I can imagine!' I laughed. 'Actually, I like singing too.'

'And you've got a nice voice.'

I looked up at him in surprise and he gave an apologetic smile.

'Sorry. I couldn't help overhearing you the other day. You were singing out in the garden. I wasn't being nosy!' he added quickly. 'I was on the other side of the wall, hanging out my washing, and you happened to be singing one of my favourite songs. The one from *Cats* ...'

'"Memory"? One of my favourites too. Oh dear, I hope I wasn't deafening you with my dreadful howling. Half the time I don't even realise I'm singing out loud.'

'You're putting yourself down again,' he said with a smile. 'I wish my choir members sounded half as good – and sang with half as much gusto. Why don't you come and join us on Sunday? Or tomorrow night for choir practice?'

'Oh no, sorry, I'm not a churchgoer,' I protested quickly. 'I mean, no disrespect to you or your choir or to God or anything, but I just don't ... I've never ... it's not—'

He was laughing again now. 'OK, Clare, don't panic, I wasn't suggesting baptising you and force-feeding you communion wafers! I only thought you might enjoy giving your voice a workout. Just for future reference, though, I minister to everyone, not just those who turn up on Sundays.'

'OK. I'll bear that in mind.' I took a gulp of my wine, feeling a bit embarrassed. It was nice of him to compliment me on my pictures and my singing, but he was right: I'd panicked a bit at the suggestion that I might like to join his choir. I could just imagine how the other choir members would feel about that!

Instead, I talked to him about my children. About Daniel and his lovely fiancée Prisha; then about Rachel's husband Jason and his multiple and – I'd always suspected – psychosomatic 'allergies'.

'You're a terrible woman,' he teased me. 'Poor guy might be living his entire life in danger of a lethal reaction to something—'

'Yes, like a spot of washing-up or going to the supermarket!' I retorted, laughing. I paused. 'I take it you don't have children?'

'Me? Sadly, no. Never been married. The right woman never came along, until I came here and met Julie.'

'Then I'm glad – for you both. And I'll look forward to getting to know her.'

*

After he'd left, I sat for a long time in the lamplight in silence, feeling strangely conflicted. I'd enjoyed the evening, enjoyed Mike's company, but his admiration of my pictures, and his talk of my talents, had unsettled me. I wasn't used to being showered with praise, but on the other hand, even Sally, who was far more inclined to cynicism than enthusiasm, had suggested I could make a living from pet photography. So had my daughter. Perhaps they were right; perhaps people *would* be interested in having photos taken of their pets. But I doubted whether any of the sour-faced villagers here would be interested in doing any kind of business with me – an outsider! Perhaps I could just keep taking pictures of wildlife instead – the squirrels, deer, foxes and various birds I'd started photographing around here – and try to sell them to the gift shops in Sorrel-by-Sea. It wasn't as if I needed the money, but sooner or later I supposed I'd get bored unless I had some kind of occupation. Whether I was back in London ... or still here. And, of course, that was the real dilemma, wasn't it?

CHAPTER 14

Within a day or so, the conversation with Mike had retreated to the back of my mind and I'd settled back into my quiet, easy, holiday mood, happy to put off making any decisions about the future. Nevertheless, that weekend as I cleaned the cottage with the windows wide open, I caught myself launching into another rendition of 'Memory' at the top of my voice. I stopped mid-song, laughing to myself as I remembered his attempt to get me interested in his church choir.

That evening, Sally and I had a good long chat on the phone.

'He thought I ought to try selling some of my animal photos,' I said a little diffidently after I'd told her about my evening with Mike.

'That's exactly what I said, isn't it? You should think about it – setting yourself up with a little business as a pet photographer. You'll want something to do, won't you, when you come home? Better than going back to work on the papers.'

She paused. I hadn't responded.

'Anyway, I'm glad you've got a nice neighbour,' she went on. 'Has he talked you into going to church yet?'

'No! Although he did talk to me about his choir,' I added. 'Apparently they're hopeless, and I was telling him I like singing—'

'See!' she laughed. 'He wants you to join the choir. He won't be happy until he's converted you.'

'No, he's not like that,' I said. 'He's not pushing religion on me at all. He's just a really friendly person. His fiancée seems nice too, but I haven't had a chance to get to know her properly yet.'

'Well, hopefully she'll be another friend for you,' she said. 'If you stay there for long enough you might end up with ... well, at least four people there talking to you!'

*

Life went on, in its calm, quiet, Little Sorrel kind of way. June had brought heavy showers with it, instead of the warmer weather it should have done, but Sid still needed walking and Leo still turned up almost every day after school to walk with us, untroubled by the rain, laughing as he ran and splashed through puddles in his wellies, Sid bounding enthusiastically beside him. By now I recognised pretty much everyone we met, and while I continued to nod at people, and occasionally tried out a 'Good afternoon' to make sure I hadn't forgotten how to say it, I was still mostly being treated to stony silence and a frown. It was as if these people were pretending they'd never seen me before. I might not have been a particularly stunning sight, covered as I was from head to toe in waterproofs, but I knew perfectly well I was recognisable enough by now. And, of course, they all knew Leo. It was particularly galling to be walking with a child who was greeted with a 'Hello, lad' or an 'All right, young Leo?' by everyone we passed, while I might as well have been the invisible woman for all the attention anyone paid to me. I felt like pinching myself to make sure I was actually there and not dreaming the whole thing.

'Why don't people talk to me, do you think?' I asked Leo on impulse one afternoon.

He looked up at me in surprise. 'Don't they?' His face screwed up in concern and I wished I hadn't said anything. Why would he have noticed, after all?

'Oh, perhaps I'm just imagining it,' I said quickly, giving him a smile.

'Perhaps ...' he started, standing still in the rain and putting his head on one side. 'Perhaps they don't like you living in Grandad's cottage?'

'Grandad's ...?' I stared at him, completely taken by surprise. 'Harry – the man who owns the cottage – is he your grandad, Leo?'

'Yep,' he said with a shrug. 'He's gone to America, though.'

'I didn't realise he was your grandad. You've never said.' I paused. 'Do *you* mind that I'm staying in his cottage?'

He shrugged again. ''Course not. I like you being there.'

'Thank you. I'm glad.' Again I hesitated. We walked on, more slowly, then I asked, carefully, 'Why would other people mind, do you think?'

'I dunno.' He scowled. 'Mum says people can be horrible.'

'Does she say that when some of the children are nasty to you?' I suggested sympathetically.

'Yeah. When they call me a chicken and make cluck-cluck noises. They're stupid, Mum says. But they aren't doing it so much now.' He gave me a sudden grin. 'That's because they want to be my friend and walk Sid with me.'

I laughed, and we chatted some more about the various children who might, or might not, be allowed to walk with us eventually if they were nice enough to Leo. The moment for talking about the adult population of the village and their stony silences was gone. But when I was alone in Riverside Cottage again later that evening, I couldn't stop looking at Harry's self-portrait on the wall and thinking about him being Leo's grandad. Mike hadn't mentioned it – but then, why would he? I stared at those dark, brooding eyes and conceded that there was a resemblance to Leo when he was looking sad. I tried to imagine Harry's eyes sparkling with laughter, the way Leo's did when he was having fun – playing with Sid or singing 'If You're Happy and You Know It'. I looked at Harry's paintings on the other walls with fresh eyes too, now that I knew their creator was a close relative of the little boy who I was growing so fond of. I wondered if Leo had inherited his artistic talent. I was beginning to feel as if I understood this man – Harry, the handsome artist, living in solitude here in his beautiful cottage. I pictured him working on his paintings, looking out of the conservatory at his garden. Mike had told me he lived alone, and I wondered if he was lonely. Perhaps that was why he looked so sombre in his self-portrait. I wondered, too, if it was true that people resented me staying here in Harry's cottage – and if so, why?

*

Leo's mum, Kerry, had invited me in for a cup of tea again a couple of times, after Leo and I had been out walking, but I could tell by her slightly harassed manner that she was too busy to stop and was just being polite. While it was reassuring that somebody was prepared to be polite to me, I didn't want to be a nuisance to this busy young mum. But the next time she suggested it, she seemed less rushed.

'Are you sure you've got time?' I said.

'Yes, I've just finished a big project so I'm clocking off for today. Come in. Hasn't the weather been dreadful?'

Apart from my daughter and Mike, it was probably the most anyone had said to me for a couple of weeks. I found myself gushing with inane small talk in response, words almost falling over themselves out of my mouth, until I had to force myself to stop and, laughing, apologise.

'It's so nice to have a chat,' I admitted, deciding to be honest about it. 'People around here are so ... quiet.'

'I know.' She gave an apologetic little shrug as she put the kettle on and got out mugs and tea bags. She didn't try to elaborate, but at least she didn't start giving me the same old spiel about them being 'shy' either.

Only too mindful of what Mike had told me about her family having 'been through a lot', I kept the conversation light and neutral. We talked about Leo and how much he wanted a dog, and Kerry hinted that she might consider getting one eventually, as long as she was sure she could keep getting enough work to pay for its keep.

'It's a constant struggle to make ends meet,' she confessed with a sigh. 'But I know a dog would make Leo happy. And … make up for a lot.'

'Leo told me it's his grandad who owns Riverside Cottage,' I said when the conversation ran out. I hesitated, hoping I wasn't putting my foot in it. I wanted to ask if that meant the mysterious emigrated-to-America-without-his-cat Harry was in fact Kerry's father – presumably divorced from her mother, Julie, who was now going to marry Mike. I was intrigued enough to want to sort out their relationships in my mind, but too nervous of being thought nosy and interfering, and in the process upsetting one of the few people who was friendly to me.

Kerry sipped her tea, not answering, for a couple of minutes, before putting down her mug and saying with a sigh, 'Yes, Harry's his grandad. Leo used to go to the cottage at weekends to see him. He misses him since he's been gone, but he says he's glad you're staying there. It means he can come to the cottage and play in the garden. And see Topsy.'

'Oh yes, of course, he did tell me he knew the little cat already.'

Kerry nodded, looking down at her tea again. She looked upset, and I decided it wouldn't be right to ask any more questions. If Harry was her father, presumably she missed him too. And frankly, it wasn't any of my business.

*

A few days later, I took the ferry to Sorrel-by-Sea again. This time I gave Sid a good walk first and then left him at home. I wanted to find a present for my future daughter-in-law Prisha, whose birthday was coming up. I could have looked for something online, but I thought Prisha would appreciate a thoughtful choice from one of the touristy gift and craft shops spoken of so disparagingly by Old Robbie. As it happened, it was him, not his son, who took me across on the boat this time.

'I knew you wouldn't be able to keep away,' he muttered as we set off towards the mouth of the river.

'What do you mean?' I said, startled, as ever, by being spoken to.

'From Sorrel-by-Sea.' He spat out the name of the village so disgustedly, it might almost have burnt his tongue. 'From the bright lights and all the fancy shops.'

The idea of Sorrel-by-Sea being a shining mecca of retail opportunity was so patently ridiculous, I laughed out loud.

'I come from London,' I reminded him. 'If I wanted bright lights, as you call it, and lots of shops, I'd hardly be going over to Sorrel-by-Sea. I'd be going straight home.'

'Well, that'll come next, I daresay,' he grumbled. 'The likes of you don't stay long around here, that's for sure.'

I should have laughed it off again. After all, it wasn't as if I was surprised, any more, by the antipathy of the villagers towards me. But I snapped. I didn't deserve this. I'd been endlessly patient and polite in the face of their rudeness. They might be insular, but I didn't see why I should put up with being treated like a pariah.

'I don't know exactly what you mean by "the likes of me",' I said crossly, 'but I can assure you I am *not* about to be frightened away from this village by the stares, the gossip, or by the bloody bad-mannered deliberate wall of silence. It's no bloody wonder the majority of people don't stay here. Well, perhaps I'm just as bloody bloody-minded and bloody obstinate as the bloody lot of you.' I paused, taking a breath, the temptation to use a much stronger word than all the 'bloodys' becoming almost overwhelming. I wouldn't have wanted him to fall out of his boat with shock. 'I'm staying put,' I said more quietly, 'at least until my month's lease on the cottage is up. I'm going to Sorrel-by-Sea to buy a birthday present but, as I've already told you, I much prefer Little Sorrel. It's a lovely place, which is why I'm determined to enjoy my stay, whether people want me here or not.'

There was silence, apart from the swish of the oars and the cry of the sea birds. We'd got halfway down the river without me noticing, and were heading into the estuary. Old Robbie was nodding to himself. Probably satisfied that I've proved him right, I thought with a sigh, that I'm a stroppy, stuck-up townie who should clear off back up-country where I belong. In fact, I was considering apologising for my outburst when he broke into a smile – as broad as it was unexpected – and said, 'Good for you, my lovely. Know how to stand up for yourself, don't you?'

'I didn't mean to be rude, but—'

'No, you're right, it's people here are the rude ones, myself included. See, we're not used to—'

'To strangers. Outsiders. I know, I keep being told that. Fair enough. But there's no need for the antagonism, is there? I mean, if I've done anything wrong, anything to offend people, I'd rather be told.'

'You haven't. It's us.' He shrugged, gave me another fleeting smile, and went back to his silence. We were approaching the jetty and he concentrated on pulling the boat in and tying it to the post, before holding out his hand to help me out. 'Call us when you want bringing back,' he said, adding as I stepped onto the jetty, 'Enjoy your shopping.'

To be fair, from the start I'd always thought that Old Robbie had been less hostile to me than his son, and less hostile than most of the other villagers, come to that. But as I strode along the footpath into Sorrel-by-Sea, I found myself smiling at the thought that having finally lost my cool and had a rant, I seemed to have gained, perhaps not exactly another friend, but at least the respect of one of the most senior members of the population. Maybe I should try it more often.

I found the perfect present for Prisha in one of Sorrel-by-Sea's little shops – a raffia bag made by a local Devon company. It was just the kind of thing she liked and would be easy enough to post. I was so pleased with it, I bought one for myself. A souvenir to remind me of my time in Devon when I returned home to London, which wasn't something I wanted to think about too much just yet. Unfortunately, it was Young Robbie who was waiting at the jetty to take me back to Little Sorrel, and the most I got out of him was a grunt of 'All right?', which was better than nothing. And I wasn't going to let it spoil my mood.

CHAPTER 15

The weather had begun to improve, and the next couple of days were in fact quite suddenly hot and sunny. On the afternoon following my trip to Sorrel-by-Sea, I was sitting outside on the little bench in the cottage garden when Mike called to me over the garden wall.

'We're just having some iced lemonade. Want to join us?'

I was pleased to see Julie was with him, and she gave me a wave and insisted, 'Yes, come on round, Clare. The lemonade's freshly made.'

I'd imagined a fizzy drink from a bottle, but the reality was ten times nicer.

'Did you make this yourself?' I asked Julie. 'It's lovely.'

'Yes, I'm very old-fashioned,' she said, laughing. 'I make a lot of things that most people wouldn't dream of making. My own pastry. Fruit pies, sponge puddings, cakes, jam, stews and casseroles—'

'Stop it, you're making my mouth water!' I said. 'They all sound delicious.'

'You can see why I want to marry her, can't you?' Mike joked.

'Well, I do find it hard, these days, to find the time to do as much baking as I'd like,' Julie admitted ruefully. 'I *am* retired – I used to teach at the village school – but even so ...'

'Mike says you help out with your daughter and grandson a lot.'

'Yes.' She nodded, then looked away, not seeming to want to say any more, and Mike gave her hand a little pat as if to reassure her that it was fine to drop the subject.

'Julie used to teach the children music when she worked at the school,' he said to me, giving her a smile. 'She made it such fun for the kids – taught them to *enjoy* singing, all of them, not just the best singers.'

'Mike tells me you like singing too,' she said, smiling at me.

'Oh, I just like belting out a few songs,' I laughed. 'Nothing special.'

'But that's exactly what we need!' Julie interrupted me. 'Someone who'll *belt out*. Someone to get everyone going, rouse them up and encourage them to sing with a bit of energy.'

'You need someone ... for what?' As if I didn't know!

'For the choir, of course. Hasn't Mike told you? I lead the church choir. I do a bit of belting out myself but getting any of the others to raise more than a pathetic reedy whine is hard work.'

144

Mike had, of course, already told me as much, and frankly, it hadn't been a surprise to me. If anything, it was amazing any of the grumpy, taciturn population of Little Sorrel managed to utter a single note.

'But I did tell Mike that I'm not a churchgoer,' I said. 'Sorry, it's not my thing. And anyway, I'm probably only here for a few more weeks—'

'Oh, but Clare, couldn't you possibly join us on Friday nights, just for a week or two? It would be so helpful if I had another strong voice, besides mine, to try to get our mob to liven up a bit and raise their voices. We don't care whether you normally go to church or not – or if you have a different religion – do we, Mike?'

'Not in the slightest,' he agreed. 'Everyone's welcome at Saint Peter's. When you live somewhere as isolated as this, Clare, the church is as much a social centre as a place of worship. I doubt more than half my regular congregation have any kind of relationship with God whatsoever. Or not the God I recognise, anyway.'

'Well, it's nice that you're so inclusive.'

'You'd think so. But they still resist any deviation from traditional services and old-fashioned hymns,' Mike said with a shrug. 'More's the pity.'

'Yes, I'd love to get them all trying some of the modern choruses,' Julie enthused. 'There's nothing like singing rousing songs together with a group of friends to make you feel better.'

I nodded thoughtfully, wondering at the significance of her choice of words. The villagers of Little Sorrel certainly did seem to need something to make them feel happier

– and behave better, too, if you asked me. It was only because she seemed so nice that I said, a little half-heartedly, 'Well, perhaps I could come along one evening, if you really think it would help.'

'Oh, it would!' she said at once, beaming. 'It would be so kind of you. Even one evening would make such a difference, with the two of us trying to get some enthusiasm out of them instead of just me, flogging a dead horse, quite frankly.'

'But the problem is,' I said, slightly unnerved by her eagerness, 'I don't think they like me. I mean – not the choir, I don't even know who's in it – but everyone around here. Apart from you two, and your daughter and grandson …' I trailed off, feeling a bit pathetic now. What was I – an eight-year-old child, like Leo, whingeing about having no friends?

Mike and Julie exchanged knowing looks, but neither of them tried to deny it.

'Well, it might be a way to get to know them better,' Mike pointed out. 'It might make them warm to you more, if they see you joining in with the community.'

'In fact, that's made me think, Mike,' Julie said. 'You know what we really need around here, to lift people's spirits? A *community* choir. It could be a spin-off from the church choir, but it'd be an opportunity for people to sing something other than hymns. Other than the dreary ones our congregation favour, anyway!' she added with a smile. 'It might interest younger people, too, and those who wouldn't ever set foot inside the church.'

'And those who want to blame God for … everything,' Mike added, looking at her thoughtfully. 'It's a great idea, if we can persuade them.' He turned back to me. 'What do you think, Clare?'

'Well, yes, that does sound like an idea, if you could get one started here,' I agreed. 'There are a lot of community choirs like that springing up all over the country, especially since they featured in some TV programmes. I know of a couple in my part of London. I've been tempted to join one myself, but I was always too busy, you know, working.'

'But you're not working at the moment,' he pointed out, smiling broadly.

'No.'

'So can we count on your help? To see if we can set up something like this while you're here? We'd be so grateful.'

'We would,' Julie agreed. 'Please say you'll come along this Friday night and talk to them?'

They were both looking at me, all bright eyes and eager smiles. It flashed through my mind that to refuse to help would be like taking sweets away from a baby. I was far too cynical to believe I had a hope in hell of getting any of the truculent, miserable lot in this village to listen to a word I said – or a note I sang – but surely I couldn't make them any less amenable to me than they already were?

'OK, then,' I said, and I forced a smile. 'If you really think it would help, I'll give it a go.'

*

Julie had to leave soon afterwards. She'd promised to pick up some shopping for Kerry, who was behind schedule with her work and had needed to knuckle down all day.

'See you on Friday, then, Clare,' she said excitedly as she dashed off.

I stood up to go, too.

'She's really nice,' I said to Mike. I hesitated, then added, 'Was she … married to Harry? Leo told me about Harry being his grandad.'

'Oh – no. It's true Harry's his grandad, but on his father's side. Harry's a widower. His wife passed away many years ago.'

'Oh, right, I see.'

Mike nodded, looking down at the ground. Once again, the conversation had stalled abruptly as soon as we'd touched on Julie's family. Julie, Kerry, Leo, Harry. There was something there, something nobody wanted to talk about. Some scandal regarding Leo's parentage, no doubt. Well, these were my new friends, my only friends here, so I wasn't about to rock the boat.

'I'll see you Friday evening, then, if not before,' I said. 'I'm off to walk Sid. Leo will be waiting for us – if it's not too hot for them!'

In fact, the sun had gained even more intensity by the time I arrived at the bench by the river where Leo was already waiting, hands in his shorts pockets, swinging his legs. I sat down next to him, and Sid took advantage of the rest, crawling into the shade under the bench.

'He's feeling the heat,' I said to Leo. 'I don't think he'll want to walk too far this afternoon.'

Leo continued to swing his legs, saying nothing. I turned to look at him more closely.

'Are you OK?' I asked.

He nodded, his mouth set in a fierce pout, like he was trying not to cry. Just then, the voices of a group of children – the usual suspects, playing on the raft in the middle of the river – drifted towards us in the still, hot air, clear as bells, with a vibrancy Julie would have loved to hear from her choir members: *Leo's a chick-chick, he wears his mummy's knick-knicks.*

A single tear escaped from Leo's eye and he rubbed at it crossly as it started to trickle down his cheek.

'Don't cry,' I said, my heart almost breaking for him. 'They're idiots. Don't let them win.'

'I'm *not* crying,' he choked, as another tear followed the first. 'I'm *not* a chicken, and I don't wear knickers neither.'

Leo's a chick-chick, he wears his mummy's knick-knicks.

'It's just a stupid rhyme – they think they're clever, but they're not,' I said. 'Come on, let's get out of here.'

Leo's a chick-chick, he wears …

Leo had given up the struggle. He swiped repeatedly at his eyes but the tears were overflowing. I saw red. Kicking off my sandals, I jumped up, marched down to the river and waded straight in. It was cold, the mud squelching around my calves and sucking at my ankles, but I was too cross to care.

'She's coming in – the woman with the dog!' one of the children shouted to the others. 'She's coming to tip us off the raft!'

'Huh! She wouldn't dare. My dad would kill her!' It was George, the loudmouth son of Young Robbie. He was standing, balancing easily on the raft, staring at me across the water.

'If I wanted to tip you off your raft, I wouldn't give a toss who knew,' I shouted back. 'But actually I'm just coming to tell you –' I waded a few squelchy steps further. It was getting more difficult, the mud now halfway to my knees '– that I'm going to speak to all your parents, and your teacher, about you. Hasn't anyone taught you about bullying?'

'Yes,' one of the smaller boys said. 'It's not allowed at our school.'

'Well, I've got news for you. It's not allowed anywhere. People get arrested for it.' I was too annoyed to care how much I exaggerated or whether I might frighten them. 'So you'd better stop your stupid rhymes and your stupid name-calling, before I decide to call the police.'

'I'll tell my dad of you,' George retorted. 'Dad!' he bellowed at the top of his voice.

I swung round, almost losing my balance in the mud, just in time to see Young Robbie emerging from the boat-house, wiping his hands on a rag.

'What the—?' he shouted, staring out at me. 'What the hell are you doing? Get the hell *out* of there!'

'I need to talk to you about your son's behaviour—' I began imperiously, before wobbling again and having to throw out my arms to steady myself. The mud was clinging a little too tightly to my legs by now. I should probably wade back out of the river. In fact, I'd come a lot further than I realised, or had intended to. I managed a step, the mud sucking hungrily, and wobbled as I tried the next one. This wasn't much fun. Leo was at the water's edge, staring at me open-mouthed, and Sid was jumping around beside him, barking frenziedly. I managed another step, but it was surprisingly tiring, dragging my feet against the suction of the mud. When I looked up again, Young Robbie was in the shallows, his face contorted with anger.

'Bring the raft over!' he shouted to his son.

I looked round to see the boy, now looking a little less smug, using the pole to manoeuvre the home-made craft closer to shore.

'Hold the pole out to her!' Young Robbie yelled again, and the boy silently obeyed.

'If you stumble again,' his father called out to me, 'grab the pole. Or me,' he added gruffly as he took a step closer.

At least he has boots on, I thought as I pushed myself forward again. I doubted I'd ever get the mud out from between my toes. I hadn't realised quite how thick it was – but I didn't see the need for so much fuss. It wasn't exactly quicksand, and I hadn't been in any deeper than my knees. A couple more painstaking steps and I was almost back at the riverbank. Fortunately, I hadn't needed to grab either the pole or Young Robbie. I laughed, a little embarrassed, as I finally stumbled onto dry land.

'Not very pleasant in there!' I said cheerfully. But I wasn't in the least prepared for the response I got.

'What in God's name were you thinking, you damned idiot? If you fell over out there, you'd struggle to get up again before the tide turned.'

'What? It was little more than a paddle! The kids paddle here all the time!'

'Yes, and they've been brought up here, they know what they're bloody doing. They've got more sense than to wade out that far barefoot, wearing –' he eyed me up and down scornfully '– next to nothing.'

I drew myself up to my full, mud-soaked height. Next to nothing? I was in perfectly respectable knee-length shorts and a T-shirt. Who did he think he was talking to?

'If I hadn't had to give your son and his friends a piece of my mind—' I began.

'And who asked you to get involved? You just keep your nose out of my family's business. Bloody tourists! You're all the same. Sooner you clear off out of here, the better for everyone.'

With which he turned around and marched off back to the boathouse, leaving me staring after him.

CHAPTER 16

'Are you OK, Clare?' Leo asked in a little voice.

I looked round at him. He'd stopped crying, but he was looking almost as shell-shocked as I felt. Sid was still barking around our ankles and I bent down to give him a stroke.

'I'm fine, Leo,' I reassured him, although I wasn't, not really. I was fuming. It had been an uncomfortable moment there in the mud, but surely I wasn't in any danger – I was only a few feet from the bank. Young Robbie had obviously just been furious at me for giving his son a telling-off. George had now steered the raft the rest of the way in and was, along with his friends, watching me with a slightly guarded expression. 'You still going to the police about us?' he said.

I glared at him. 'I might do. It depends a lot on whether I ever hear that nasty little rhyme again. Or anything like it.'

'It was only a joke,' he muttered.

'A joke is only a joke if everyone's laughing,' I snapped. 'You wouldn't laugh if the joke was about you, would you?'

He shrugged. 'S'pose not.'

He started to drag the raft up the shore, helped by a couple of the others.

'See you, Leo,' one of them called back.

'See you, Reggie,' Leo said, looking surprised. We watched them go. 'Reggie's normally only mean to me when George is around,' he said quietly. He turned to me and added, quietly, 'Thank you, Clare. You shouldn't have done it, though. You got yourself all muddy and you made George's dad angry. He yells at people when he's angry.'

'Does he?' I thought about this. 'Do you think he yells at George?'

'Yes. George says he does, all the time.'

I nodded. 'People who get bullied often turn into bullies themselves, Leo. But that still doesn't make it right.'

'You won't really go to the police, though, will you?' he said anxiously.

'Probably not.' I smiled at him. 'Come on, I think we'll have to abandon our walk today, sorry. I need to go home and have a shower. Walk back with us to the cottage if you like.'

As we walked away from the river, I heard raised voices coming from the boathouse. Young Robbie, presumably berating his son, whether for teasing Leo or for talking to a *tourist*, it was difficult to guess. Just as we rounded the corner, though, another voice was raised.

'Leave the lad alone, can't you? Hasn't there been enough anger around these parts? Let's all give it a rest, son, for the love of God! Enough is enough.'

Something about the desperate plea in those last few words of Old Robbie's made me shiver inside. 'Enough is enough.' Enough of what? I thought. And why? It occurred to me for the first time to wonder whether there was a Mrs Young Robbie – mother of George. If there was, I'd never met her or heard anyone mention her. I didn't even know where the family lived, as the two Robbies seemed to spend their entire lives at the boathouse. I sighed. Perhaps this was just a sad, broken family with no female influence to keep things calm and steady. But it was still difficult to feel much sympathy with them.

*

By Friday, I was starting to regret my promise to go along to the choir practice. Why the hell had I agreed to it? I'd never thought of myself as a good singer, not really, just loud! It was true, I enjoyed belting out a few songs in the privacy of my own home and I didn't think I was tone deaf. But I was pretty sure the choir members would wonder what on earth gave me – the *incomer* they seemed to resent so much – the right to be there among them, never mind showing them how to sing more enthusiastically. Or talk to them about setting up a community choir.

'I'm not sure it's a good idea,' I said awkwardly to Mike when we chatted over the garden wall on the Friday morning.

He scratched his head, looking disappointed. 'Well, of course, if you really don't want to come, Clare, that's fair enough. I mean, it's not as if you'll be staying here long-term – why should you get involved? I'll explain to Julie.'

Put like that, though, it made me feel bad. OK, I was only going to be in the village for a couple more weeks, but Mike and Julie had been kind to me and it seemed a small thing to ask, to give up one evening and at least try to help.

'No, it's OK. I'll come and give it my best shot,' I said. 'I don't want to let Julie down. But I've a feeling I will, however hard I try.'

He shrugged and smiled. 'We'll be backing you up, Clare. We won't be throwing you to the lions.'

I laughed. 'That's good to know. OK, give me a shout when you're leaving. If we walk down to the church together, it won't feel so weird.'

*

'My nan says you're going to help her at the choir practice tonight,' Leo said when we walked Sid together after school. He gave me a shy little smile. 'She says you've got a nice voice. I liked it when we sang "If You're Happy and You Know It".'

'So did I, Leo,' I said, laughing. 'Come on, let's sing it together again now.'

We were, unfortunately, yelling out some extra words I'd added to make the song more fun – *If you're happy and you know it, scratch your bum* – together with accompanying actions and a lot of hilarity, when we were approached by some of Leo's classmates. George, who was leading the way down to the river, swinging a stick almost as big as himself, stopped and stared at us, giving a snort of derision.

'That's a baby song,' he said.

'No it's not,' I replied calmly. 'It's a *happy* song, for happy people.'

'What's he got to be happy about?' George demanded, pointing rudely at Leo, who'd fallen silent, looking down at the ground in his customary manner.

'Everything,' I said, with a shrug. 'What is there to be unhappy about?'

'Well, his dad—'

'SHUT UP!' Leo yelled, so suddenly and with such force that I stepped back in surprise. 'Shut up about my dad! *Your* dad's a bully who gets cross with everyone, and he yells at you all the time, that's why you're so horrible. Isn't it, Clare?'

'OK, Leo,' I said softly. 'Let's leave it there, come on. No point getting upset.'

'Leo's right, though,' said a little voice from behind George's back. George swung round, staring angrily at Reggie, who looked frightened out of his life but was standing his ground and looking straight at me. 'George shouldn't be talking like that about Leo's dad, should he, miss?'

'No, Reggie,' I said gently. 'And there's no need for *any* of us to be unkind about each other's family, is there? Come on, kids, it's a lovely day and Leo and I were singing about being happy and having a laugh. There's nothing babyish about that.'

'Can I walk your dog with you and Leo, please, miss?' Reggie asked, stepping away from the group.

'What do you think, Leo?' I asked him.

Leo shrugged. 'All right, then.'

Reggie shuffled over to us and stood on my other side, ostensibly avoiding looking at George, who was scowling crossly.

'OK, then, let's go,' I said. 'And you don't have to call me *miss*, Reggie. My name's Clare.'

As soon as we were away from the other children, I told Reggie he should let his mum or dad know where he was going.

'They're at work,' he said. 'But I can tell my auntie.'

He led us along the towpath to where some tiny bungalows stood right on the edge of a shingle beach beside the river. He rang the doorbell, and when the door was opened I almost fell back with surprise.

'Julie!' I said. 'I ... er ... wasn't expecting—'

'Hello, Clare.' She looked equally puzzled. 'What's the matter, Reggie?'

'Can I walk this lady's dog with her and Leo?' Reggie said. 'Please, Auntie Julie – she says it's OK and I'll be back for tea.'

Julie smiled at me. 'Of course – if you're sure you don't mind another one tagging along with you, Clare?'

'No, it's fine. I ... didn't realise Reggie is ...?'

'My nephew,' she said, nodding and raising her eyebrows ironically. 'His dad is my much-younger brother. I come from a big family and most of us – apart from the sister in the New Forest – live here in Little Sorrel. So yes, I'm auntie to quite a lot of the kids around here.'

'Oh. Right.' No wonder she sometimes felt tired! I smiled and added, 'We won't be long. I think Reggie wanted ... a change of company for a while.'

'Anything to get him away from that George French,' she muttered to me out of the side of her mouth. 'Thanks, Clare.'

I let Reggie hold Sid's lead for a while, suggesting the boys took it in turns.

'I didn't realise you two are cousins,' I said to Leo while Reggie was a little way ahead of us.

'Mum says we're *second* cousins, and *she's* Reggie's cousin.' He shrugged. 'I don't get it, really, cos me and Reggie are the same age. We normally say we're best friends. Well, we *were*.'

'And I'm sure you will be again,' I said gently. 'He stuck up for you back there, didn't he? It was brave of him to stand up to George.'

'Nobody bothers to stand up for me when George makes up his stupid rhymes about me, though. George thinks he's so hilarious,' he said wearily. 'And nobody dares to say anything.'

'Poor you,' I sympathised. 'It must be hard to keep pretending not to care.'

I wondered if it had occurred to their teacher to channel George's talent for poetry in a more useful direction. He could have a brilliant future, by the sound of it.

'George is really clever at school,' Leo said, as if he'd read my mind. 'But he's always making trouble and being mean. I'm glad he's leaving this term. He's going to be eleven during the summer holiday and he'll be going up to the comp.'

'Perhaps that will be a good thing,' I agreed. I wondered if George might find himself outsmarted at secondary school. I couldn't quite go so far as to wish for him to get on the wrong end of some bullying, by bigger kids, to teach him a lesson. But I have to say the thought did occur to me.

CHAPTER 17

That evening, when we walked to the choir practice together, I told Mike about accidentally finding myself at Julie's house.

'She bought herself that little bungalow when she divorced her previous husband,' he said. 'It's big enough for Julie on her own, but not when she has any of her many nieces and nephews staying with her.'

'Yes, she was telling me about that. I can see now why she's so busy.'

'She loves the kids. She's the eldest of a big family so she's always been used to having lots of little ones around.' He grinned at me. 'I told you – half the population of Little Sorrel is related to each other. It's very inbred around here!'

'My daughter would say that's because it's too difficult to get in and out of the village, to find anyone from elsewhere to have children with,' I joked.

'She could be right! You've seen how suspicious they are of outsiders too. Don't forget, I was an incomer myself two years ago.'

'Did it take a long while for you to be accepted?'

'A while, yes.' We'd arrived at the church so there wasn't time to say any more, but he'd hesitated for a moment, looking at me thoughtfully as if he'd considered doing so. 'Come on, Julie's here already. I can hear her on the piano,' he said instead. 'Let's go in and meet our gang of merry warblers.'

If only that description had been true. The small group who were seated in the choir stalls were chatting amicably enough among themselves as we entered. Julie was playing softly, stopping occasionally to make some comment to the others.

'Hi, everyone,' Mike called out as we walked down the aisle towards them.

'Hi, Mike!' some of them called back. But the greetings died in their throats when they saw me with him.

'Hello!' I said, as cheerfully as I could manage. I felt ridiculously nervous, like a new child on her first day at school. 'I'm Clare.'

'We know who you are,' someone muttered. And in the silence that followed, the unspoken question was quite evident: *But what the hell are you doing here?*

'I've invited Clare to join us tonight,' Julie said, getting up from behind the piano and coming to stand beside me. 'She's agreed to help us out a bit while she's here.' She turned to me. 'Thanks so much for coming, Clare.'

'You're welcome,' I said faintly. No one else was looking at me; they were all finding their hymn books terribly interesting.

'Right!' Mike said, in his usual animated way, rubbing his hands together as if he could barely control his excitement. 'Why don't we kick off tonight with a nice rousing rendition of "Onward Christian Soldiers"? OK, Julie? Come and stand next to me, Clare,' he added as Julie sounded the opening chords.

Well, at least I remembered this one from school assembly days. Mike led me to a space at the end of one of the choir stalls and handed me a hymn book, turning quickly and efficiently to the right page. Feeling as awkward and embarrassed as a fourteen-year-old trying on a bikini in front of her entire class, I mumbled along quietly with my head down, pretending to be struggling with the small print of the hymn book. But once we were into the second verse, I became aware of the voices of the others around me. To be quite frank, apart from Julie and Mike, they were awful. One or two of them were in tune, and a couple of the others were keeping time with the piano, but Mike and Julie seemed to be the only ones doing both, and were certainly the only ones singing with any degree of enthusiasm. I glanced around at the others. They all looked as miserable as sin. Without any further thought, I lifted my hymn book, raised my head and my voice and sang out loudly. I felt Mike nudge me and, out of the corner of my eye, caught his appreciative smile. By the time we'd reached the final chorus, I'd forgotten to worry about anyone else and was letting rip in my usual fashion, and actually enjoying myself. It was evoking child-hood memories of shouting out those military-sounding lyrics with my classmates in our dusty old school hall. Why had I ever thought assembly was boring? OK, it did seem pretty archaic now, singing about marching to war, but it felt great!

There were a lot more people looking at me when we sat down afterwards than there had been before.

'Thank you, everyone,' Mike said. 'Well, now that's put us all in the right mood, let's carry on with another uplifting one like that, shall we? "Amazing Grace", everyone? Up tempo, I think, Julie! Then we'll practise the hymns for Sunday.'

This time I joined in with gusto from the start, making the most of the high notes and the crescendos. With three of us now leading the way, the rest of the choir seemed to rally slightly and I began to detect one or two voices standing out from the others – good singers who hadn't wanted to be heard before. The rest of the hymns that we practised, ones Mike had chosen for his Sunday service, were mostly unfamiliar to me but easy enough to master after Julie had played the tunes through first. When we'd sat down after finishing the final hymn, Mike thanked me again and a couple of others, sounding somewhat reluctant, added their thanks too.

'OK, everyone. Before we go,' Julie said, coming round from the piano to stand in front of us, 'I want to ask you all something. Have any of you watched any of the programmes on TV about community choirs?'

Several people were nodding.

'Yes, I really enjoyed those programmes,' one woman said. 'Lovely to see how those people, who didn't have any experience before in choirs, took part and even entered competitions.'

'Me too,' said the man sitting next to her. 'It was inspiring to see how hard they worked.'

'Yes,' Julie agreed. 'But they *enjoyed* themselves too, didn't they?'

She glanced at me. I felt like something was expected of me, even though I had no prior experience of any choirs whatsoever. But I had watched the television series. I stood up, clearing my throat.

'They looked really happy,' I said. A few faces turned my way, some of them glaring. I could imagine them thinking *Who asked you?* but I tried to ignore them. 'Did you notice something earlier when we were singing "Onward Christian Soldiers"?' I went on. 'If you're singing out loud, really putting your heart and soul into it, it's almost impossible not to smile. Impossible to be miserable.' Unless you happen to be in the choir of Saint Peter's in Little Sorrel, I thought to myself, beginning to wish I hadn't started this. 'Singing is supposed to do something to your brain, apparently. It's a scientific fact that it really does cheer you up.'

I looked around at them. If this was what they looked like when they were cheered up, God help us. I gave a shaky little smile and sat down. I'd tried my best. Mike, at least, beamed at me and said, 'Thank you, Clare.'

'So what's this got to do with us?' said the woman who'd enjoyed the TV series. 'We're a church choir, not a community choir.'

'Well,' Julie said carefully, 'we had this idea – Mike and I, and Clare – that we could start one for Little Sorrel. A community choir, I mean. It could be an offshoot of this choir, but anyone in the village could join. Perhaps children too. And we'd sing all sorts of songs – whatever anyone wanted – pop songs, songs from shows, ballads, rock. Old songs, new songs – just for the pleasure of getting together and singing.'

'Sounds fun, doesn't it?' Mike put in heartily.

Nobody responded.

'Well, why don't you all give it some thought, anyway?' Julie said, sounding a little weary.

'Who's going to be in charge?' a man in the back row asked.

'Well, I'd be happy to do the piano accompaniment, of course—'

'But you'd need someone standing up the front, beating time, *being in charge*,' he insisted. 'Like that Gareth Malone on the TV.'

'I could give that a go,' Mike said with a shrug. 'But to start with, while she's here with us, we thought we might persuade Clare. As you'll have noticed tonight, she's got a lovely strong voice – she's definitely a natural!' He smiled at me, and I groaned inwardly.

'She's an outsider,' someone said at once. 'She doesn't even live here. She's just a tourist.'

'Yes, I am,' I agreed. 'It's best if someone else—'

'We don't even know why she's here tonight,' a woman in a lurid pink blouse said, giving me a hostile look. 'We've never had *tourists* coming to choir practice before.'

Poor Mike was turning puce with embarrassment, trying to shut them up, but the floodgates had been opened and others were muttering in agreement. I looked around at their stony faces, their surly looks, the way they were whispering to each other behind their hands while they fixed their suspicious glares on me, and I saw red. I jumped up to my feet again.

'I know you all think I shouldn't be here,' I said crossly. 'But I came because Mike and Julie asked me to help, to try to get you all singing more enthusiastically. And I agreed, as a favour to them, because they're almost the only people in this village who've been kind and welcoming to me. I thought it was a great idea to start a community choir, not that it's any of my business – as you say, I'll be leaving soon anyway. But because, from what I've seen since I've been here, you all need something to put a smile on your faces. I love your village, but I've never met so many inhospitable, *miserable* people in my life! I know people in little villages can be insular. Maybe you don't want the place overrun with tourists. But for God's sake! Is that any reason to show such *contempt* for anyone from outside the village? Hardly anyone finds their way here anyway, so you ought to welcome the few who do, not drive everyone away! What's the *matter* with you all?'

I spluttered to a stop, out of breath. I hadn't, obviously, meant to say any of that, but once I'd started, I couldn't stop. All the frustration I'd felt since I'd come here had poured out, and far more venomously than I would have liked. I glanced from Mike to Julie. They were both staring at me, open-mouthed with horror, and I felt my face flush with shame. How could I let them down like that? Bad enough that I hadn't set foot in a church for donkey's years, but to use God's house for an angry rant like a madwoman was unforgivable.

'I'm sorry—' I began, shakily. 'I shouldn't have—'

'You think we should be *welcoming* visitors, do you?' said the woman in the pink blouse in a sneering, sarcastic tone. She shook her head. 'You know nothing about it.'

'She don't know *nothing*,' said the man sitting behind her. He got to his feet, giving me an evil look before nodding goodbye to his companions. 'She's just another one – they're all the same. They come here, think they know it all—'

'And it's them that causes it.' Pink Blouse nodded agreement. 'Them that causes all the trouble. All the grief.' She got up too, giving me a final glare as she picked up her handbag. 'If you want to know why we don't like tourists here, well, ask your *friend* the vicar – everyone knows how you've been sucking up to him,' she added with a scowl. 'He'll tell you. Tourists don't respect our village, or the countryside. They cause damage. Worse than that, they cause accidents, serious accidents. Playing about in the river, taking risks they don't understand. They cause tragedies.' Her voice broke slightly. 'Break people's hearts.'

'I'm sorry – I didn't know. What happened?' I stammered, but she stopped me with a glare.

'This village is no place for tourists. Go back to London, *Clare*, and leave us alone. We might be miserable, but at least we're not stupid. We don't go paddling barefoot in the mud and getting ourselves stuck.'

She walked out, her head held far higher than it had been for 'Onward Christian Soldiers', and one by one, with muted mutterings of 'Goodnight, vicar', 'Goodnight, Julie', the others followed while I sat in my pew, hanging my head, my eyes filling with tears. I wasn't sure if I was crying for myself, or for Mike and Julie – who were both looking too distraught for words – or for these people, who were so full of bitterness that it seemed to have festered in them, into hatred.

CHAPTER 18

'I think she was probably right – the woman in the pink blouse,' I said, fighting back tears. 'I should go back to London, shouldn't I? I don't know why I ever thought it was a good idea to stay here any longer.'

We were back at Mike's. He'd insisted on me going in for a drink, saying we both needed one after the debacle at the church. When I'd protested that he normally went to the pub with the rest of the choir, he shook his head and said he wasn't in the mood for it.

He looked at me sadly as he poured us both a large glass of wine.

'Don't say that. You shouldn't feel pushed away by a few people who—'

'A few!' I swallowed a mouthful of wine. 'It's almost the whole village. I'm really sorry I got stroppy back there, but I've tried so hard to be patient. I've put up with their stony silences, their rudeness, and …' I sighed. 'I suppose I'd just had enough of it.'

'I don't blame you. You shouldn't have had to put up with it at all.' He hesitated. 'But it's actually my fault. I'm so sorry, I wish I'd told you the story – what happened here. The accident. I just didn't want to burden you with it when you're only here for, well, a comparatively short time. I thought it might upset you and make you leave. Julie and I would hate you to feel forced out. Stay. This … fuss … will settle down. Julie will talk to the others. She's gone to the pub with them tonight. She offered, and I thought it was a good idea. She's a Little Sorrel girl, born and bred, one of them.' He gave a little smile. 'She'll give them a piece of her mind, and they'll listen to her.'

'But they still won't accept me. I'm a "tourist", and that's enough for them, isn't it?'

I took another mouthful of wine. I was feeling rattled now, as well as upset. Mike hadn't told me about an accident that had happened here in case it made me want to leave? He hadn't exactly done me any favours, had he? If I'd known about it, I might have understood what was wrong with these people. Instead, I'd ended up making a complete prat of myself *and* feeling like I'd now have to go.

'I'm sorry,' he said again, hanging his head. 'We really hoped, if you came along to the choir practice and talked to everyone about the community choir idea, it would help get you integrated into the village.'

'And I went and blew it by getting frustrated with them and having a rant. I shouldn't have lost my temper. But I *do* wish you'd told me about this accident, whatever it was. You'd better tell me, anyway. Whether I stay or go, I think I need to know what happened.'

'Yes, of course, you deserve to know. Want a top-up, first?'

I'd knocked back the whole of that first large drink without even noticing, and held out my glass for more.

'I'm not normally such a boozer,' I said, attempting to make light of it.

'Me neither,' he said with a smile as he topped up his own glass. 'But there are times when a second glass is definitely called for.'

By the time Mike had finished relating the story of the accident, we'd both finished our second glass too – but what he'd told me had had a very sobering effect.

*

The tragedy had occurred the previous summer. Up until then, there had been two or three local people who used to offer bed and breakfast accommodation during the high season, and there had always been a small but steady stream of visitors – often people, like me, who'd found themselves in the village by accident and stayed overnight, or for a few days.

'Unlike you,' Mike said with a smile, 'most of them got bored here fairly quickly. And people here were generally glad to see the back of them, to be honest. Some visitors did cause problems. You can imagine the type of thing – antisocial behaviour. Litter, loud music, getting drunk and shouting in the street. I don't know all the details, it was mostly before I arrived, but I gather they didn't always endear themselves to the villagers, the way they behaved.'

But one group had decided to stay for a whole week. They were, Mike said, a posse of six young men who'd got lost on the way to Cornwall, where they'd planned a camping holiday. Finding themselves in Little Sorrel after dark, they managed to book themselves rooms for the night, intending to move on the next day.

'But you know what young lads are like when they're away together,' he said with a sigh. 'By the morning, they were too hungover to drive. So they pitched their tents in the field opposite the shop – without asking permission, which didn't go down very well for a start – and carried on drinking. In the end, they forgot about going on to Cornwall and stayed put.'

'I'm surprised the villagers put up with that,' I commented.

'Well, it's true they've never been particularly fond of outsiders and tourists,' Mike admitted, 'but things were different then. People did at least realise there was money to be made. Jack put up with their rowdiness in the pub because they spent so much on beer and food. The parish council decided to let them keep their tents on the field for a week if they paid a small fee – probably half what they'd pay for the site they'd booked in Cornwall – and as long as they cleared up their rubbish. The family who run the shop saw their takings practically double, so they weren't complaining either. And as for the French family ...' He tailed off, sipping his wine, gazing into the distance.

'Old and Young Robbie?' I prompted.

'Yes. They were happy enough too, although they've denied it ever since. They supplied the lads with a boat for the week. A couple of them claimed they were experienced.'

'But they weren't,' I assumed, my heart feeling heavy. I had an idea what might be coming.

'No, they weren't.'

The details were as shocking as they were predictable. The first couple of days, the boys had taken the boat into the middle of the river, scoffing at Young Robbie's warnings regarding the tide and the mud, and floated around for a while, singing and shouting drunkenly, before bringing it back to shore and wandering off to the pub. But on the third or fourth day, they were not only emboldened as usual by the alcohol they'd already consumed, but wanted to carry a box of beers on board with them to continue drinking.

'Old Robbie wasn't having it,' Mike said. 'He told them – "no alcohol on the boat, and you're not taking it out again until you've sobered up".'

'Good for him,' I said.

'Mm. But unfortunately, Young Robbie didn't back him up. He wanted the money for the week's hire, and there was no way those kids were going to stop drinking. He told his dad not to make such a fuss. "They're only sitting in the middle of the river anyway," he said. "It's not like they're capable of going any further."'

'Oh my God.' I closed my eyes. Whatever I was about to hear, I could already see that Young Robbie must have had to live with the weight of those words, that decision, ever since. I suddenly understood why he was so stern and taciturn. Why he'd been so unpleasant to me about paddling in the river.

'Father and son were still arguing about it while the boys were tumbling into the boat and heading out into the river,' Mike went on. 'At first, they just drifted out there, as before – laughing and swaying in the boat, singing, calling each other names. But after they'd had a few more of the beers out of the crate, things escalated, needless to say. They were standing up in the boat, rocking it wildly, screaming, jumping into the water – and only a couple of them had put on their lifejackets. The truth was, they were in no fit state to be in a boat at all. They hadn't been on the previous occasions either, and Old Robbie knew it.'

Mike paused and glanced up at me. 'As you know, the river isn't very deep. It's the mud and the weeds that are the problems, but it wasn't close to low tide so the danger wasn't too serious at that point. I think Old Robbie was more concerned with the nuisance they were causing. A few local people were watching from the towpath, looking exasperated, asking Old Robbie why he was allowing them to carry on like that. So he called them to bring the boat back – but they just laughed and carried on messing about. He got into his own boat, intending to bring them back in – but this is where things suddenly became more serious. They promptly headed off out into the estuary.'

'Oh no.'

'Yes. A small boat, full of drunken young men with – as we now know – no experience whatsoever, heading out into the estuary at high tide.'

'I bet Old Robbie *was* worried then.'

'Of course. If anything had happened to those boys, he knew it would be his fault – his and Young Robbie's – for allowing them to use the boat at all.'

But nothing *had* happened – not to any of the boys. As the boat carrying the out-of-control youngsters hit the waves washing into the estuary, they all suddenly sobered up, stopped laughing and larking about and began to panic and fight each other for the oars. But one of them fell out of the boat and went under the water, followed by another. And then the boat flipped over.

'Old Robbie was still a little way behind,' Mike said. 'But there was somebody closer, who was taking his own boat across to the Sorrel-by-Sea jetty at the time. He saw the wave hit the boys' boat, saw the first two boys fall in, and had already chucked them a lifebelt from his own boat. He was manoeuvring his boat closer to theirs when the remaining panicking boys turned the boat over – at which he was out of his boat and into the water in an instant. It's not easy to rescue people who are struggling,' he went on quietly. 'They thrash around and fight you. But with difficulty, he managed to get all of them into his own boat – apart from one.

'"Do something!" the other boys were screaming. "Ollie's under the boat! He can't swim! Get him out!"

'"Let me help," shouted Old Robbie, pulling his boat alongside and preparing to throw himself into the water. "It's my fault. I shouldn't have let them come out—"

'"Don't be ridiculous," panted the younger man, ducking down below the waves again and disappearing beneath the upturned boat.

175

'They were the last words he ever spoke,' Mike said. He took a deep breath and swallowed hard. 'Someone had already called the lifeboat, and the crew pulled him out of the water. We found out afterwards he'd had an undiagnosed heart defect. The strain had been too much for his heart – he died of cardiac arrest.'

'Oh my God,' I said again. 'How *awful*.' I paused. 'What about the boy? Ollie? The one who was stuck under the boat?'

'He wasn't under there at all. He'd got out on his own. He might not have been able to swim, but it's surprising what happens when someone's drunk and underwater. Instinct seems to have a way of taking over,' he said with heavy irony. 'None of the boys were any the worse for their experience, apart from being scared out of their stupid lives. There was a police investigation, of course, and although Old Robbie explained that the young men were warned about their drinking, it seems laws relating to sailing and alcohol have never been enforced for amateur boaters in control of small boats. And they were all eighteen – they were on holiday together to celebrate finishing school, in fact – so despite their behaviour, they were, by law, deemed old enough to have been responsible for their own decisions.'

'But that wasn't the point, was it? Old Robbie, and especially Young Robbie, they could have stopped them from going out. Stopped them having the boat.'

'They could have done, yes. And arguably, they should have done. But nobody around here has ever looked at it like that. They closed ranks, and refused to blame anyone other than the boys themselves.'

'And all visitors, by default.'

Mike nodded. 'Yes. Coming on top of all the other things – the litter, the noise, and so on – this terrible accident was the last straw. Bed and breakfast signs were taken down and outsiders have never been welcomed since – as you've found out. It's not fair, of course, but—'

'But understandable, I guess. And in such a small village, I can see that, as you said before, the loss of any one person must affect everyone. Who was he, anyway, the chap who died?'

'Oh, I thought I'd said.' Mike looked back up at me, his eyes full of sorrow. 'It was Paul. Harry's son.'

CHAPTER 19

'Harry's son … the Harry who owns my cottage?' I said.

'Yes. Paul was his only son. And, of course, he was also your little friend Leo's father.'

I leant back in my chair, letting out a huge breath. Suddenly, everything made sense. Not just Young Robbie's surly moods, but Harry's move away from the village to another country, presumably fleeing the loss of his son, fleeing the memories. And little Leo's angry outburst when he was teased about his father. To say nothing of his mother's reluctance to let him play in the water.

There was a little squeaky meow from the kitchen, and I looked up to see Topsy padding into the room. Harry's cat. Or perhaps she'd been Paul's.

'I get it now,' I said softly to Mike as I lifted the little cat onto my lap and began to stroke her. 'I wish I'd understood all this before. It would have helped.'

'Yes. I wish I *had* told you, Clare. But it's not easy for anyone here to talk about. I'd been here less than a year myself when the accident happened. I'd only just about been accepted by the villagers, in fact, they were still pretty suspicious of me, with my preference for modern services and uplifting choruses! And I suddenly had this terrible tragedy to deal with. A funeral of one of the best-loved young men in the village, and everyone grieving, in shock, angry. It was a difficult time for all of us. It's still difficult, to be honest; so many people were either related to Paul or were his friends. Little Sorrel is a village in mourning.'

'Of course. I can see that. It must have been awful. No wonder they stopped wanting visitors here.' I sighed, shaking my head. 'Seriously, I think it's best if I go, Mike. Apart from anything else, surely Harry wouldn't be happy that a *tourist* is living in his house? Does he know?'

Mike looked down at the floor for a moment before answering.

'Not exactly, no,' he admitted. 'But he did ask me to rent out the house for him if anyone was interested. He didn't specify whether they should be people from Little Sorrel.' He spread his hands. 'Honestly, Clare, I'm sure he'd be fine with it. He's a decent guy, normally very reasonable, not like some of the people around here—'

'But it was his *son*!'

'And you weren't even here, it was nothing to do with you, you didn't even know anything about it. It's not as if I've rented the cottage to the boys who caused the accident!'

'Even so—' I began, but I was interrupted by the doorbell, and Mike went to open the door to Julie, who'd come back from the pub to report back on the aftermath of the earlier contretemps.

'Julie, I'm so sorry,' I told her as soon as she'd come in and sat down. 'Mike's filled me in about the accident. If I'd had any idea – I mean, it all makes sense to me now, why everyone here is so anti-visitors. And, of course, I'm so sorry about your son-in-law.'

'My son-in-law?' She looked puzzled for a moment. 'Oh – no, Paul wasn't married to Kerry.' She sat down next to me, shaking her head. 'Far from it. She found herself pregnant after they'd had a short-lived relationship, one summer. She was nineteen. I wasn't amused, as you can probably imagine, but, well, Leo is the result, and he's a good kid, we wouldn't be without him, obviously.'

'Of course not.'

'Paul wasn't exactly supportive,' she said. 'He wasn't ready for fatherhood, to put it mildly.'

'So Kerry's brought Leo up on her own.'

'Yes. Unfortunately, Leo idolised Paul. He was always hanging around the cottage – Paul still lived there, with his dad – but Paul didn't really want anything to do with the boy. In fact ...' She glanced at me and stopped, shaking her head. 'No. I'd better not speak ill of the dead.'

'That's OK, it's not really any of my business,' I said, feeling awkward again. 'I was just telling Mike, I really should move out of the cottage, now that I know what happened here. And out of the village, come to that. After tonight.'

'No,' she said, surprisingly firmly. 'Not unless you want to, of course, Clare. But not because of what happened tonight. I've had a talk to the choir members, and they've asked me to apologise to you, on behalf of us all.'

I gave her a smile. 'That's kind of you, Julie. But I'm sure they're just saying that because you asked them to.'

'No. They're saying it because basically, despite how it seemed tonight, they're decent people. They might be insular, they might still be upset about what happened last year, but they know they shouldn't have treated you the way they did. The tragedy ... well, yes, it was a terrible thing to happen. But it's almost as if it gave people around here an excuse to behave even more badly to outsiders than they did before.' She raised her eyebrows at me. 'I know I'm one of them. I've lived here all my life, and I know what it's like. Some villagers were never particularly welcoming at the best of times and, well, there was a spate of problems with visitors during the couple of years before Mike arrived here.'

'Yes, Mike was just telling me there had been some antisocial behaviour.'

'Worse than just antisocial, in some cases.' She shook her head sadly. 'Of course, most visitors are decent and respectful, but you only need a few who don't bother closing gates on the footpaths crossing farmland, don't clear up after their dogs, throw their rubbish in the river, leave broken glass on the banks where the children play – and they all get a bad name. Then there were those who drove like maniacs down Fore Street.' She paused, nodding to herself. 'A child nearly got run over by one of those idiots. Car ended up on its side with its bonnet embedded in the wall of the shop. The little girl's mother pulled her out of the way just in time.'

'Oh God, that's awful.'

'Yes. It certainly hardened people's feelings towards outsiders. There had already been a lot of muttering by then about whether the visitors were more trouble than they were worth. And then those boys came.'

'So the accident just put the lid on it?'

'Yes. Even if Paul hadn't died, I think people would have been saying enough was enough, after that.'

I sighed. 'It's understandable. And I was in the wrong tonight. I lost my temper with them, said things I shouldn't have said.'

'But as I've already told you,' Mike put in, 'nobody could blame you for that. You've put up with being ignored, stared at, treated with contempt by these people for weeks now. And you came to choir practice tonight to try to *help*.'

'That's another thing,' Julie added, sitting back and giving me another smile. 'They've agreed to the idea of the community choir. If you'll get it started.'

'You're joking!' I stared at her. 'They *must* have said that just to please you.'

'Not at all. After we'd had a good heart-to-heart about it, about the fact that Mike and I think the choir would be good for the village – for all of us – to help us get over the tragedy and make us all happier, they all seemed keen to give it a try.'

'Even the woman in the pink blouse?' I said.

Julie laughed. 'That's Audrey. She's not the most diplomatic of people. But yes, she was one of the first to agree.'

'So, you see?' Mike said, grinning cheerfully as if everything were now completely hunky-dory. 'You *have* to stay now, Clare, at least until we've got this new choir up and running. Please forgive us for the way you've been treated. Give us another chance.'

'For God's sake – sorry, for *goodness'* sake –' I corrected myself awkwardly – making Mike laugh and assure me he'd never taken offence at my frequent casual misuse of God's name. 'There's nothing to forgive *you* two for. And as you know, I love it here. I don't quite know why. I think I must have taken leave of my senses the evening I first arrived here.' I got to my feet, letting Topsy jump down from my lap. I was suddenly exhausted. It had all been a bit much. 'I need to go, sorry. Sid's been on his own all evening, he'll need to go out before I go to bed. Can I think it over and let you know?'

'Of course.' Mike stood up too, following me out to the hall. 'Sleep well, Clare,' he said as he opened the front door for me. 'No doubt I'll see you tomorrow.'

*

Sleep well? I thought, as I tossed and turned and stared at the clock next to the bed. If only I could. By three o'clock in the morning, I'd only managed to doze off once, and had dreamed I was in a boat on the river, stuck in the mud, crying for help, and all the villagers were lined up along the towpath, watching me and laughing.

Did I really want to stay? Did I really care whether these people needed, or wanted, a community choir? And anyway, what did I know about setting up such a thing? How had

I got myself talked into this in the first place, just because Mike had heard me singing 'Memory' at the top of my voice? I'd always enjoyed singing, but when I thought about it, I realised it had only ever got me into trouble. As a teenager, I'd been told off at school about singing in class more times than I could count, and it had irritated the life out of my husband when I sang along to the radio. Why was I even giving this crackpot idea any consideration? Even if the villagers had been the friendliest people on the planet, why would they agree to a total outsider, a very temporary resident, trying to organise something like this?

By the time the sunshine was slanting through the curtains, Sid was whining for his breakfast and I was still wide awake, wrestling with my indecision. I'd come to the conclusion that I must either have become a masochist, enjoying the slings and arrows of unpopularity, or I must have turned into the type of person who relishes a challenge. A really far-fetched, ridiculous challenge. Because, no matter how hard I tried to tell myself to pack my bags, get in my car, drive back down that bloody lane and never come back, I couldn't seem to help it: I wanted to stay. I wasn't ready to leave. And if I wasn't going to leave, I had to grasp the olive branch being held out to me by these ... OK, bereaved but nevertheless difficult, miserable, people, and do what they apparently wanted me to do. Then perhaps I could leave, feeling that I'd achieved something here, to make sense of it all.

'Right,' I said to Mike, having knocked on his door as soon as I'd had breakfast. 'OK, I'll give it a go. I warn you,

I don't know how to do it, and I don't know why they want me to. And if anyone complains, they can do it themselves.'

'Fair enough,' he said, looking somewhat dazed. Perhaps he'd only just got up. Or perhaps he was taken aback by my new, no-nonsense manner. It was how I was going to approach this thing, I'd told myself. This way, or not at all. 'Thank you so much. I'm so glad you've agreed. I'll give you whatever help I can, so will Julie, I know.'

'Right,' I said again. 'Well, I'll see you later. Come on, Sid.' The little dog was pulling at his lead beside me. 'We're going for our walk.'

'Clare,' Mike said, softly, just as I was turning away.

'Yes?'

'I just wanted to say: they might not have realised it, but the people here need you. We all need you, especially Julie and me. We've tried our hardest to get the people of Little Sorrel back on their feet, but it's been an uphill struggle. We're so hopeful that this choir will help.'

'OK. Well, it remains to be seen.'

'You were saying last night,' he went on, 'that you wondered why you found yourself here in Little Sorrel, and why you wanted to stay, despite everything. Well, I believe I know the answer to that.'

'You do?' I was too tired to be particularly nice about it. 'What's that, then? I'm a nutcase? Or a glutton for punishment?'

'No.' He laughed, gently. 'It's obvious to me that God knew we needed someone here, someone new, someone unaffected by the tragedy, who could help to mend people's broken hearts. You were sent to us, Clare, I'm sure of it. Sent to us by God.'

I wish I could have thought of something more appropriate to say to that than 'Oh, for God's sake, Mike!'

CHAPTER 20

I was too tired to do much that day. After I'd taken Sid
for his walk, I downloaded and sorted out a few more of
my photos and then spent some time on the phone to
Sally. I needed to tell somebody the latest news, somebody
who'd laugh with me about it and not get upset and worried,
as my kids might have done.

'He said *what*?' Sally screeched when I'd finally reached
the end of my saga.

'You heard. He said he thinks I was sent here by God.'
I giggled, and then immediately felt disloyal and disrespectful to Mike. 'Just his way of saying he's grateful, I
suppose.'

'He's saying you're a bloody angel. You, an angel – that's
hilarious! He wouldn't say that if he'd known you as long
as I have!'

'All right, it's not *that* funny—'

'Yes, it is! Well ...' she paused. 'It would be, if it weren't
for the fact that you've had all that upset from the

miserable choir people. How ungrateful, when you were only trying to help! I can't understand why you didn't get straight in your car and drive hell for leather out of there for good.'

'Nor can I, to be honest,' I admitted. 'I *was* upset by it. And by losing my temper, too. It was horrible.'

'And yet you're still there, in that bloody village, aren't you? Still prepared to help those awful people despite the way they've treated you. Sorry, I don't get it. What's happened to you since you came into that money? You had a damned sight more sense when you were struggling like the rest of us! I mean, I understood you needing to get away, have a break from everything while you worked out what you wanted to do. But surely to God you could be staying in a decent hotel somewhere with a spa – treating yourself to nice meals, champagne, a view of the ocean? You can afford some luxury now instead of getting sucked into some kind of *feud* with a crowd of vengeful yokels?'

I laughed, but I sensed she was only half joking.

'I don't want to stay in posh hotels, eating posh food. What's the point when I'm on my own? I'm enjoying this, the simple life away from the rat race, the city, the traffic—'

'So you keep saying. And it does sound idyllic. I wouldn't mind giving up work and getting away from London myself, obviously, but why the hell you want to start up a choir for those miserable buggers there is beyond me. I have to hand it to your preacher man, he's hit the nail on the head – you're a frigging angel and I never even noticed.'

'Hang on, I'm just adjusting my halo,' I chuckled. 'Seriously, don't worry. I've told Mike that if anyone doesn't like this choir, they can do it themselves or go without. And then, yes, I'll clear off, leave them to get on with it.' I paused. 'It was really sad, though – the story about the guy who died.'

'Yes, I'm sure it was. And your bad-tempered boatmen *deserve* to feel guilty – it was their fault, and I must say I think it's ridiculous that the villagers didn't blame them for what happened instead of taking it out on innocent visitors.'

'The villagers stuck together over it. I suppose it's only natural, living so far from other people.'

'Of course it would've been natural in the days when it took hours in a horse and cart to get from one village to the next, but—'

'It still does, around here!' I joked. 'Sally, you must come and visit before I leave. Please say you will. I miss you.'

'I miss you too, you daft cow! I'd love to. I'd better come soon, before you lose your halo and get thrown out of the village by your own choir.'

'Any time. Soon. You can come and sing with us!'

Her reply was not at all polite. But we were both laughing when we hung up.

*

I didn't laugh for very long, though. I'd just gone into the kitchen to make a cup of tea when there was a terrible noise outside – squealing, hissing, yowling. Cat fight. Sid was up at the back door immediately, barking his head off, and I was right behind him, flinging the door open. We both dashed outside, and a large shaggy ginger cat leapt up onto the garden wall, giving us a disdainful backwards glance as he disappeared over the other side.

Topsy was sitting behind one of the flower tubs, trembling.

'Are you all right, little one?' I asked as I approached her. 'Did he hurt you?'

Even Sid had stopped barking and was looking at Topsy with his tail down, almost as if he understood the situation.

I bent to pick her up. Her eyes were wide with fright and she was meowing quietly as if in pain. I carried her indoors and put her down on her blanket on the sofa while I checked her all over. There were no obvious signs of bites, just a couple of scratches on her little pink nose.

'I think you're OK,' I muttered, stroking her gently. 'Have a nice rest there and hopefully you'll feel better. Poor little thing – what a big bully that ginger cat was, he's twice your size!'

Sid promptly lay down on the floor next to the sofa, looking like he was guarding her, and I went back to making my tea. A little later, I saw Mike in his garden, and went out to ask him if he knew who owned a big ginger cat.

'Oh, that's Archie, the French family's cat. Has he been round here again? He does wander. He seems to think the whole village is his territory.'

'He had a go at poor little Topsy earlier on. I think she's OK, but it did give her a fright.'

'Hm. I'm not surprised. He has a bit of a reputation. Hope she'll be OK.' He gave me an anxious look. 'Topsy's not being a nuisance to you, is she? She seems to spend most of her time with you since you moved in.'

'Of course she's not a nuisance! I love her, she's so sweet and affectionate. Even Sid seems to like her. Anyway, it's only to be expected that she'll spend most of her time in the cottage – it's her home. I really don't mind, it's absolutely fine.'

'Good. Well, I'll shoo that Archie away if I see him around here again.'

'Thank you.' I sighed. 'Perhaps he hasn't been neutered. That would account for him being so aggressive, and trying to take over other cats' territories, wouldn't it?'

'You're probably right. I can't imagine it would have occurred to the Frenches to get him done.' He looked down the lane, as if expecting to see Archie coming back for another fight, but then abruptly changed the subject. 'When are you thinking of having the first meeting for the new choir? Not that I want to rush you, but I think it might be good to seize the advantage, while Julie's got people feeling ashamed of the way they treated you. They're more likely to turn up.'

Julie might have read them the riot act and got them cowed into submission, but I wouldn't exactly have called it an advantage. I suspected they were still going to resent me, possibly even more now, for getting them ticked off! But if I was going to do this thing, I might as well get it over with as soon as possible.

'Well, sure, I could do it one evening this week. But I'll need to advertise it first, won't I? Perhaps put a notice up in the shop or something?'

'Leave that with me. I can mention it in church tomorrow, and I'll ask Julie to put up some notices around the village too. It's good enough of you to agree to do it.'

'OK. Let's say Tuesday, then, shall we? Seven o'clock?'

'That sounds good. The church hall's free on Tuesday evenings—'

'Actually, Mike, if you don't mind, I think it might be a good idea to keep this completely away from the church if there's anywhere else we can meet. Otherwise, people who don't go to church might feel it's not for them.'

He nodded thoughtfully. 'Good point. You're right, we don't *only* want the church choir members turning up, do we?'

'Preferably not,' I said, picturing Audrey Pink-Blouse and trying not to shudder. 'It'd be good to reach out to everyone in the village.'

'Right, I'll talk to Chris Oakley, the head teacher, and see if we can use the school. It'll be fine, I'm sure.'

'Thanks.'

I wish I could say I was looking forward to it. But I'd said I'd give it a try, so that was what I'd do. I was pretty sure I knew how it was going to turn out, though!

*

I'd thought a lot about the story of Little Sorrel's tragedy since Mike had told me what happened. I felt sad, being in Harry's cottage and understanding now the reason for his abrupt departure. How awful to have lost his only son in that way. The fact that Paul had an undiagnosed heart condition didn't alter the fact that he wouldn't have died if he hadn't gone into the water to rescue those stupid boys. I found myself staring at Harry's self-portrait, as I often did, wondering what kind of man he was. But now I tried to imagine him living here in the cottage with his son, having already lost his wife. Although he looked rather dark and forbidding in the painting, he must surely have been happy once – living here, creating his beautiful artwork – until that terrible tragedy had robbed him of his boy. I imagined him eating here in the kitchen, smiling across the table at his son, perhaps discussing their respective days or even planning a day out together. I wondered if Paul had been an artist too. Mike had referred to him as one of the most popular guys in the village but I'd got the impression Julie hadn't thought much of him. She'd said he hadn't been supportive when Kerry became pregnant, and hadn't taken much interest in Leo. Well, he'd still been Leo's father, whether he'd liked it or not. And his death must have affected Kerry, even if they weren't together.

Leo appeared at the cottage door that afternoon, as he often did at weekends, asking to play with Sid.

'Actually, let's take him for another walk. It's stopped raining.' It had been a showery day, and I grabbed my umbrella as we went out, just in case. It was too warm for raincoats.

We walked down the lane and along the river in companionable silence, Sid trotting ahead of us on his lead, sniffing the air and the ground, always happy to be outside. There were one or two children, as always, playing in the mud, but I didn't notice any of the usual crowd who hung around with George French. Perhaps they were all playing somewhere else today – without Leo, again, I thought, feeling a flash of protective anger.

'Do you know how to swim, Clare?' Leo asked me suddenly. He was gazing out across the river, a faraway look in his eyes.

'Yes, I do, Leo. I like swimming, but where I live in London, there's nowhere to swim apart from the public pool.' I paused. 'How about you? Can you swim?'

He nodded. 'We all get lessons, from Year One onwards at school. They take us to a swimming pool in a bus. It's a long way.'

I smiled. Anywhere was a long way from Little Sorrel. They must be out of school for most of the day!

'I can swim breaststroke and crawl and I can jump in the deep end,' Leo went on with pride in his voice.

'That's brilliant.'

'I can't swim in the river, though,' he went on, sadly. 'Mum doesn't let me.'

'Well ...' I hesitated, and then went on, carefully, 'It can be dangerous, can't it?'

He nodded, and then went on, suddenly and quite bluntly, 'My daddy died. In the estuary. He was a good swimmer but he still died.'

'I'm so sorry about that, Leo,' I said. 'It must be very, very sad for you. And for your mum.'

He shrugged. 'Mummy didn't like him much. But that's why she doesn't let me swim or play with the others on the raft.'

'I can understand that. But perhaps she will, in time, when things settle down.'

I was glad I'd already been told about his father's death or I don't know how I'd have managed to handle the shock of the news coming in such a matter-of-fact manner from this poor, sweet kid.

'Did you know my daddy?' he asked, looking up at me.

'No. I wasn't here when it happened. I was still in London. Did you used to see a lot of him before the accident?'

'Not really.' He sighed, and my heart gave a lurch. No wonder he was such a quiet, sad little boy. 'I wanted to. I went to the cottage quite often – you know, when he lived there, with my grandad. But Daddy was always busy. He was very clever,' he added, with a pride in his voice that almost brought tears to my eyes. 'Like my grandad. Very clever at painting and drawing and stuff. So they were always busy. Did you know my grandad lives in America now?'

'Yes, I did know that.'

'I might go and see him one day,' he said. 'I asked Mummy if I could go, but she says it costs a lot of money. I'm saving up my pocket money, though.'

I couldn't even reply, I was so choked up. Then Sid started barking at another dog and we hurried on to catch up with him and quieten him down, and the conversation was over. I'd wished before that I could do something to help young Leo, something to bring a smile to his face, and I was now wishing it more than ever. But what the hell could make up for the loss of a father, a father who didn't even seem to have reciprocated his son's obvious admiration ... and perhaps hadn't even deserved it.

CHAPTER 21

'Good luck with the choir tonight,' Mike said when I saw him on Tuesday afternoon. 'I hope plenty of people turn up.'

'Oh, aren't you coming?' I asked, surprised.

'Julie thinks it might be better if I don't. Not to start with, anyway. You're quite right about keeping it separate from the church. We wouldn't want anyone thinking that, because I'm there, they've got to sing hymns.'

'That's true, I suppose.' I felt a little nervous, though, about facing people without him there to back me up.

'Don't worry,' he said, seeming to realise what I was thinking. 'Julie will be supporting you. And playing the piano, of course.'

'Good. Well, I'll let you know how it goes.'

I set off early, wanting to be in the school hall before anyone arrived. The hall wasn't much bigger than the lounge of an average house, but at least there were some adult-sized chairs, presumably for occasions when parents came to the school, and there was a modern-looking piano in one corner, where Julie was already sitting, looking through some stacks of sheet music.

'I brought along some books of music of my own,' she said. 'But I also had a word with Mr Oakley, the head teacher, and he dug out this lot for us to borrow. Some of them are very much for young kids, though. "If You're Happy and You Know It" ...'

'Oh, I like that one!' said a voice behind me.

I turned round to see Audrey, my nemesis in the pink blouse from the Friday evening, now looking far more at ease – and considerably younger than I'd remembered – in a pair of cut-off jeans and a blue T-shirt. And she was smiling.

'Hello,' I said guardedly. Then, deciding that it was best to make no reference to what had gone before, I went on, 'Actually, I like it too. I sing it with Leo sometimes, when we walk the dog together,' I added to Julie. 'It's a cheering-up song, isn't it?'

'Well, in that case why don't we start with it tonight?' Julie suggested. 'Kerry's bringing Leo along. He'll enjoy that.'

'Oh, I'm so glad he's coming! I was hoping some of the children might be interested in joining us.'

'Probably only Leo,' Julie said, shaking her head sadly. She didn't need to elaborate. I knew Leo liked singing, but I also knew the other kids were likely to tease him about joining a choir, just as they seemed to about everything else.

'I'd have liked my Emily to come along,' Audrey said, sitting herself down with a heavy sigh. 'It'd do her good. She's at that difficult age.'

'What age is that?' I asked, picturing an awkward teenager.

'Twenty-nine,' she said. 'And still living at home, moping around every evening with those things in her ears.'

'Things?'

'Ear-things. Headphones, buds, whatever you call them. Can't have a conversation with her. My other half says we ought to kick her out. Needs to get married, if you ask me.'

By now Kerry had arrived with Leo, who was giving me shy little smiles as he sat next to his mum. And a few minutes later a couple who I recognised from the Friday evening came in, holding hands. The man smiled at us all and said hello, but it seemed his wife wanted to look anywhere else except in my direction.

'Neil and Lucy, my neighbours,' Audrey said by way of introduction. She leaned closer to me and added quietly, 'He's OK. Quiet, but that's because of how she nags him. I asked him to come, thought it'd get him out of the house, poor sod, but I might've known she'd have to come too.'

Audrey seemed to have gone from being my nemesis to my best buddy. I was beginning to wonder if she'd stop talking for long enough to sing.

'Shall we start?' Julie called over to me.

I looked at my watch and my heart sank. It was already ten past seven, and it didn't look as if anyone else was going to turn up. So much for everyone from the church choir agreeing to give it a go. But I supposed we should be grateful for small mercies.

'Yes, come on, everyone,' I said, a little weakly. 'Up on your feet, and let's have a rousing chorus of "If You're Happy and You Know It".'

'A children's song!' Lucy Long-Face muttered.

I ignored her. Julie played the opening chords and she and I led into the first line, without anyone joining in.

'Oops,' said Audrey apologetically.

'No worries. Let's try again,' I said, trying to keep the optimistic tone in my voice. 'Ready? And—'

This time, Leo joined in enthusiastically, and so did Kerry, who looked a little embarrassed. Audrey, who didn't seem to know the words despite saying she liked the song, at least had a go.

'OK,' I said, nodding to Julie to stop at the end of the first verse, 'I should have made sure you all knew the song. The first time we sing about clapping hands, then the next time we can do stamping our feet –'

'Then can we do "shouting hooray"?' asked Leo.

'Absolutely!' I smiled at him. 'And anything else anyone wants, really. Nodding our heads; shaking our bums! I know it's a song for little kids, but Leo and I have found it's very therapeutic. Cheers you up,' I translated for Audrey, who was looking puzzled. 'Makes you feel good. And we're just using it as a warm-up song.'

We tried again. Audrey got the hang of it this time, but Neil barely opened his mouth and Lucy's mouth remained firmly closed and turned down in disgust. As we finished the final verse, Audrey turned to face them.

'You might at least try, you two!' she said. 'Seeing as how you've bothered to come. Seeing as how *Clare* has bothered to come, especially after the way we've all behaved towards her—'

'Oh, Audrey, please, there's no need—' I started, but she held up a hand to stop me.

'No, it needs saying and, to be fair, I'm the one who needs to say it the most. You were quite right the other night. We've been very rude to you. Julie explained that you didn't know about the accident, and anyway you're right, this has gone on long enough – blaming everyone from up-country who sets foot in this village, just because of … what happened. We need to move on. And this choir is our opportunity to come together and do just that – right?'

'Well, I hope so, yes,' I agreed.

'So come on, everyone, let's give it our best shot. And let's encourage a few more people to turn up next time. Sitting at home feeling miserable isn't going to help any of us. Let's sing another song. What's it to be?'

I was almost too stunned by this speech to think of anything, but Julie came to my rescue, asking if anyone had a favourite song. There was silence for a moment, then she added, 'Who knows any songs about friendship? That's what we need, isn't it? We need to come together as a group of friends. It would be good to sing about that.'

'I've always liked "Lean on Me",' Kerry said. 'It's how I used to think about us all, here in Little Sorrel. We were always good at caring about each other and looking out for each other.'

I noted the past tense and wondered whether that was a general feeling here: that since the tragedy, people had perhaps drawn into themselves and stopped bonding together.

'That's a lovely song,' I agreed. 'Have you got the music for it, Julie?'

'Yep.' She found it in one of her books and played through the melody for us.

'Thanks, Julie,' I said as she finished. 'Well, maybe Julie and I could sing through the first part for you, then we'll do it again together,' I suggested. 'It's not hard.'

I went to stand behind Julie at the piano, and after the introductory chords we began to sing. It was only then that I realised it might not be the best choice, after all. The words, about having pain and sorrow in our lives and being a friend for each other, were perhaps just a little bit too close to the mark for these grieving people. But Kerry had chosen it, so presumably she must have been aware. We stopped singing after the first refrain and I walked back to join the others. Audrey had looked down at the floor, and when she raised her eyes again, there were tears in them.

'I'm sorry,' I began. 'It's probably not—'

'It's perfect,' she retorted firmly. 'We *need* this.' She turned to include the others. 'We need to open up about how the accident affected us, share our feelings, stop shutting ourselves off.' She looked back at me and added softly, 'Paul was my nephew. I'm Harry's sister.'

'Oh my God, I'm so sorry,' I said again. 'I didn't realise ...'

'Paul was my second cousin,' said Lucy. It was the first time she'd spoken.

'He was my daddy,' Leo piped up, and Kerry gave him a hug, kissing the top of his head.

'He was my best friend when we were at school together,' Neil said. 'He was something to everybody around here,' he summed up.

'And I can see why it's affected you all so much. Honestly, if I'd known, I'd never have said all that stuff the other night,' I said miserably.

'But Clare, this is what we need,' Julie insisted, standing up at the piano. 'Come on, everyone: let's sing this song, let's sing it and really mean it. The words are so true: we *have* still got each other to lean on, haven't we?'

She sat back down and played the opening chords again, pausing to see if we were going to join in. She was right, I realised, taking a deep breath. This *was* exactly the kind of song these people needed. I caught Kerry's eye, and she nodded at me.

'OK,' I said, and gave them the first line of the lyrics. This time, everyone sang. Julie, Kerry, little Leo in his sweet piping voice, Audrey coming in loud and strong, Neil booming deeply and confidently beneath us all and finally, a tremulous little high-pitched voice from Lucy. I continued to feed them the lyrics line by line, and as we went into the second verse the weaker voices were becoming a little stronger, the more confident singers really getting into it. By the time we repeated the chorus, most of them remembered the words and I was moved, as well as pleased, by the amount of feeling they were putting into them.

'OK, let's leave it there for now,' I suggested. 'We need some more copies of the words, don't we? We'll get that organised. But well done, everyone, that was terrific for our first attempt, wasn't it?'

'Can't we sing it again?' Audrey said. 'I was … kind of enjoying that.'

'Me too, actually,' Neil said, looking around him at the others, sounding a little awkward.

'Yes, let's do it again, Clare! I think I can remember the words now,' Leo piped up.

I looked back at the little group. They were all smiling at me, nodding enthusiastically. Even Lucy. I felt a lump in my throat. This song had been a good choice, after all – a perfect choice. And it was working already: the music, the singing, was working its magic, taking people out of themselves, making them open up. I'd been right to suggest this choir. I just needed to persuade more people to turn up!

'OK, everyone. One more time then, from the top!' I said, smiling back around at them. 'Let's see if we can raise the roof this time. Don't worry if you don't remember the words – sing *la la* instead!'

And they did. They *la la*'d their hearts out, lifting their heads, smiling at each other as they sang, looking like a completely different group of people from those who'd come into the hall earlier.

'Well!' I gasped after we'd finished, almost out of breath from the energy I'd put into the singing myself. 'Wasn't that something?'

'It certainly was,' Julie said, laughing. 'Who knew we had such talent here in Little Sorrel?'

'Oh, I'm not a very good singer,' Lucy protested, her smile faltering. 'I haven't got any *talent*.'

'It doesn't matter whether you – or any of us – have or not,' I said quickly. 'The important thing is having the enthusiasm. We're doing this for *fun*. For what we get out of it, as individuals and as a group.' I smiled around at them again. 'I've always believed it's impossible to sing and be miserable at the same time.'

'You're right,' Audrey said, nodding. 'That song didn't feel sad, after all, did it? Despite the words at the beginning. It felt … uplifting.'

'So what would you like to sing now?' I looked at my watch. Ten to eight. Hard to believe it was almost time to finish. Perhaps I'd suggest we go on for longer next time. For the benefit of those in the church choir, I suggested, 'Do you want to end with a hymn?'

'No, we don't!' Audrey retorted at once. She glanced at her neighbours. 'We get enough of that on Friday nights and Sundays, don't we?'

Neil laughed, and Lucy gave a little grin. 'Yes. It's nice to sing something different.'

'What about that Beatles' song "Good Night, Sleep Tight"?' Julie suggested. 'That's quite appropriate, isn't it? And there are hardly any words to learn.'

She started to sing the simple little song without the piano, and when I recognised it, I joined in, encouraging the others to sing along with the repeated line.

'That's nice,' Kerry commented. 'I've never heard it before.'

'You're too young,' I laughed.

Now that everyone had the tune, we sang it through again, and Julie promised to find the music for us for the next time.

'Same time next week?' I asked, and was pleased to hear them all agreeing. And I was quite surprised when, as she was about to leave, Audrey turned, came back and gave me a hug.

'Thanks for doing this for us,' she said. 'We don't deserve it.'

'Oh, I think you do,' I said. 'I doubt there's a village anywhere that deserves a little bit of cheering up as much as you do here.'

'You're an angel,' Kerry said lightly as she too gave me a hug goodbye. 'We'll try to get more people here next week.'

An angel, again! I smiled to myself as Julie and I put the chairs away. I could just imagine what Sally would say about that! Well, the turnout that night might have been small, but it had gone better than I'd dared to hope, and I was bursting with pride as I walked home. But you know what they say, don't you? Pride comes before a fall. And if I'd seen the fall coming, it definitely would have wiped the smile clean off my face.

CHAPTER 22

The next morning, I was still on a high, dancing around the cottage and singing to Sid and Topsy as I thought about which other songs we might try out the following week.

'I'm *so* pleased it went well,' Mike said, having invited me to join him for coffee in his garden when he heard me singing as I took in the washing. 'What a shame so few people turned up, though. I'd got the impression there were a lot more than that who were interested.'

'Well, maybe they'll turn up next time, especially if Audrey and the others encourage them.'

'Funny how Audrey's turned out to be your biggest fan,' he said, laughing. 'Well, biggest apart from me, of course.'

I tried to ignore this, but felt my cheeks burning. Even though I was certain he was only being friendly, that he loved Julie and wasn't interested in me in that way, I still found his habit of gushing overt praise quite disconcerting. But at least the gossip about us in the village seemed to have died down. Everyone was far more interested in the story of my outburst at the choir practice!

'I had no idea Audrey was Harry's sister,' I said.

'No. Again, perhaps I should have told you. But it would take forever to explain all the complexities of relationships between the villagers here. I doubt there's a single person – apart from me! – who isn't related to several people from other village families in several different ways.'

'From what you've told me about Julie's family, you'll be related to a lot of them yourself once you and she are married,' I said.

'Of course, that's true. Not that we've got around to setting a date yet. We're both so busy. But anyway, I'm sure you're right that singing will help make people happier again. As you're realising, Paul was important to just about all of them in one way or another. As the whole village was affected, it made it hard for anyone to help each other in their grief.'

'The whole village ... perhaps apart from Kerry?' I said carefully. 'I mean, of course it's understandable, as she and Paul weren't together, and even young Leo told me his mummy didn't much like his daddy. In fact, I got the impression Julie wasn't very keen on him either.'

'No.' He sighed. 'From what Julie's told me, Paul and Kerry weren't together for long. You're right: Julie didn't like him. He was a typical young man, it seems – more interested in his drinking mates, his work, his own life, than settling down with a girlfriend. Julie says Kerry felt like he was using her, so she – Julie – discouraged the relationship, as I guess most mothers would. She was glad when Kerry finished with him, but then she found out she was pregnant. Paul didn't want the baby at all. Apparently, he even suggested she should have an abortion.' Mike shook his head, sadly. 'Kerry was determined to have the baby, though, and she's brought Leo up on her own, with Julie's help, of course. Paul contributed financially and felt that was all he needed to do. They often argued about it. Poor Leo – he hero-worshipped Paul from a distance, making a kind of fantasy dad out of him. The real version didn't want to know.'

'That's so sad.'

'Yes. But the saddest part, in my view, is the fact that now Paul's gone, both Julie and Kerry feel guilty. Julie, because she'd made no secret of disliking him, and Kerry, because she now wonders whether, if she'd stayed with him back then, things might have turned out differently. He might have become a good husband and father in the end.'

'But, good father or not, he'd still have been the guy who jumped in the river to try to save those teenagers. He'd still have had the heart attack.'

'Of course. But she thinks they might have been reconciled before he died.'

'Oh. Poor Kerry.' I said. 'It sounds like she might actually have loved him, despite everything.'

'Possibly. Julie finds it difficult to talk to Kerry about it, and perhaps Kerry blames her mum for encouraging her to break up with Paul. That's the problem, you see, around here. Nobody talks to each other about this stuff. Look at Harry's reaction – Paul's own father. Taking himself off abroad, rather than staying here and trying to come to terms with his loss. He told me *he* couldn't bear the guilt of not knowing his son had a heart defect.'

'But how could he have known? It's quite a common phenomenon, isn't it – undiagnosed heart conditions in young adults?'

'Apparently so. But ...' He gave me a sad little smile. 'Put yourself in his shoes, Clare.'

I swallowed hard. The thought of something dreadful happening to either of my own children was too much to contemplate.

'Yes, I take your point,' I muttered.

'Then, of course, there's the Frenches,' Mike added. 'There, in one family, is the worst example of unresolved guilt you can imagine.'

'I agree they were guilty – or Young Robbie was, at least – of letting the kids use the boat when they were drunk. But nobody else seems to think so, do they?'

'Oh, I'm sure they do, in fact – or they would, if they started being honest with themselves. But Young Robbie became so pig-headed and bad-tempered after the accident, nobody wanted to cross him.'

'Leo told me he thinks Young Robbie shouts at George a lot.'

'Yes. And you've presumably noticed the effect that has had on George. He's turning into a little thug. The French family has acquired a terrible reputation. Nobody dares say a word to them.'

'I keep meaning to ask you: is there a Mrs French? I mean, is Young Robbie a single father – did they split up?'

'No, not at all.' He smiled. 'Justine – his wife – is a nice woman. You probably haven't met her. She's a nurse and works long shifts at the hospital in Plymouth, so what with the commute, she's seldom around. That's why George spends most of his time after school with his dad and grandad at the boathouse. To be honest, I often wonder whether Justine works more than she needs to. I can't imagine it being much fun, living with that husband of hers.'

'Old Robbie seems less aggressive, though.'

'Yes. If only he could talk some sense into his son. Being in a foul temper isn't going to change what happened last summer any more than the way the whole village has been treating visitors is going to change it.'

'Maybe time is the only thing that will heal all these wounds,' I said.

'Or maybe your choir might do it, Clare.'

Gosh. I couldn't help thinking it was a heavy burden to place on the shoulders of a newcomer. Even one sent from heaven!

*

After school that day, Leo and I were walking along the towpath with Sid, singing together as we often did, when we came upon George, sitting on his own outside the Frenches' boathouse, whittling a piece of wood.

'What you making, George?' Leo asked. I was surprised and pleased at his friendly tone. Perhaps George was less intimidating without his cohort of hangers-on, I thought.

'What's it got to do with you, chicken-boy?' George snarled without looking up. As he spoke, he kicked a stone from in front of his feet, aiming it towards us and presumably intending it to hit Leo on the shin. Instead, it collided with my ankle, making me yelp with a sharp 'Ouch!' and a furious look in George's direction.

What happened next was so sudden and unexpected that both Leo and I nearly fell backwards in shock. Sid – who was off his lead, having been walking in his normal calm and well-behaved manner between me and Leo, and had been sitting next to my feet waiting to move on again – flew at George, his hackles up, growling, and as George tried to scrabble to his feet, dropping his knife and piece of wood, Sid jumped up and down in front of him, barking angrily.

'Sid! Leave him! Here, Sid – quiet!' I yelled. Sid slunk back towards me, looking back at George over his shoulder and growling deep in his throat. 'Sit!' I told him, and fastened his lead back to his collar while he continued to growl menacingly.

Meanwhile, George was crying like a baby – sobs punctuated by big gulps of air, tears streaming down his face. And wouldn't you know it – at the sound of his son crying, out of the boathouse, with a face like thunder, came Young Robbie.

'What's going on?' he demanded. 'What happened, George?'

'That dog attacked me!' he blubbered, pointing at Sid, who'd finally quietened down and had reluctantly sat down at my feet. I was pretty sure nobody else could hear the low rumble of his frustrated anger still emanating from deep in his chest.

'Actually, he didn't,' I said, trying to stay calm. 'He barked at you, that's all. And would you like me to tell your father *why* he barked at you?'

'I didn't do *nothing*!' George said. 'I didn't do *nothing*, Dad! She's making it up.'

'Making what up?' I said.

He stared at me, confused, but then just carried on, whining, and looking up at his father pathetically. 'Honest, Dad, I didn't do *nothing*, the dog just came at me, he was going to bite me.'

Young Robbie looked from George to Sid and back again, and then turned to me. 'Is that right?' he demanded. 'Did the dog attack him?'

'Of course he didn't,' I said wearily. 'But he *was* barking at him angrily. And George knows why.'

'He kicked a stone,' Leo said. I turned to tell him not to get involved, but it was too late. His face was pink with indignation. He bent down and stroked Sid's head. 'Sid's never been angry before, has he, Clare? He's a really good dog, but it was George's fault. He kicked a stone at me, but it missed and hit Clare. She didn't even tell him off, but Sid was angry with him, and I don't blame him, so there!'

'Shut up, chicken-boy!' George shouted, starting to cry again. 'He's lying, Dad. I told you, I didn't do nothing!'

'Get inside, George,' Young Robbie said. 'I'll sort this out.' He turned to me as George, still blubbing and complaining, ran into the boathouse. 'My son's not perfect,' he said, 'but he's not a liar.'

'Yes, he is!' shouted Leo. 'He kicked the stone at us, it hurt Clare, she went "ouch" but she never even told him off!'

'OK, that's enough, Leo,' I said gently. I looked back at Young Robbie. 'I'm not going to stand here and argue with you about this. As you can see, my dog is perfectly well behaved now, as usual. He was merely defending me, exactly as Leo described. I suspect your son won't want to admit to what he did in case you're angry with him.'

He stared at me. 'It's none of your damned business whether I get angry with my son.'

'Quite. So let's just leave it there, shall we? Sid's frightened him quite enough as a punishment this time. But if he kicks stones at other people again, he might find himself in a bit more trouble.'

'Are you threatening my boy?' he demanded aggressively. 'You want to keep your bloody dog under control, before you start having a go at innocent kids! Coming here with your airs and graces, talking like you own the place – why don't you just clear off back to London?'

'Because we don't want her to!' Leo shouted back, ignoring the warning pressure of my hand on his arm. 'Me and my mum and my nan and the vicar and everyone – we want her to stay here, so there!'

For a moment, Young Robbie looked nonplussed. I was pretty amazed myself. I'd never have imagined Leo had it in him to stand up to anyone like this, especially not the bully boy's even worse bully of a father.

'Just keep the bloody dog under control,' he growled at me eventually. 'If it bothers my kid again, I'm warning you, it'll feel my boot up its backside.'

'Come on, Leo,' I said, seeing his face redden even more with anger at the appalling suggestion of his little doggy friend being kicked. 'We don't need to listen to this. We know what happened, that's all that matters.'

I took his arm and led him and Sid away, quickly, not looking back until we were around the corner. Then I stopped and gave them both a hug.

'Thank you,' I said to Leo. 'I'm very proud of you for standing up for me. That was brave of you. But you could have got into trouble, you know. Really, you should let the grown-ups sort out these things between us.'

'But it wasn't *fair*!' he retorted, his face reddening again. 'That George French is a pig and a liar. I hate him!'

'I know he lied, Leo, and I know he's very, very mean to you. There's no excuse for it. But I don't think he's a very happy boy.'

'Nor am I!' he shot back. '*I'm* not happy! My daddy's dead and my mummy's always busy and I'm not allowed on the river and I'm not allowed a dog, and I've got no friends and *I hate my life*. But I'm still not a pig and a liar like George French, am I? It's just not *fair*!'

To my absolute horror and distress, he burst into furious tears and ran off down the towpath. And I couldn't remember when I'd last felt so much like crying myself.

CHAPTER 23

'I'm really sorry,' I said to Kerry. I was beginning to feel that I now spent half my time in Little Sorrel apologising to people. 'I obviously didn't mean to upset him—'

'Of course you didn't, Clare,' she said soothingly, putting a cup of tea down in front of me on the table. 'You've been so kind to Leo. He's just feeling particularly sensitive at the moment.'

I'd caught up with Leo at the end of the towpath and we'd walked back to his home together, but although he'd stopped crying, he wouldn't talk to me, and had gone straight up to his room without a word to his mum.

'I told him it was brilliant, the way he'd stuck up for me, and for Sid,' I went on miserably. 'But I don't want him to get into a row with George French or his father. I said it's best to try to ignore them.'

'And that's exactly what I tell him, too.' She sighed. 'He was happier when he and Reggie hung around together all the time. It's really hit him hard, Reggie getting sucked into George's gang. He does feel like he's got no friends at all now.'

'I thought, recently, though, Reggie had been supporting Leo.'

'He tries to. But like most of the kids around here, he's scared of George and feels safer being with him than against him. I'm sure *he* was happier when he was friends with Leo too. Mum and I keep trying to encourage them back together. When Reggie walked Sid with you that time, I really thought we'd turned a corner, but apparently Reggie got called names afterwards because of it. It's hard to fight back against stuff like that when you're only eight. Nearly nine in Leo's case,' she corrected herself with a little smile.

'Oh, is it Leo's birthday soon?'

'Yes. This Saturday. That's why he's particularly upset right now. He says he doesn't even want a birthday, there's no point, he can't have a party because nobody will come, nobody likes him ...' She trailed off, swallowing. 'It's heartrending.'

'Oh, Kerry, I'm so sorry. Yes, it's so sad, and so unfair. Poor Leo. Surely there are *some* kids he could invite?'

'Huh! How many children do you think live in this village? Primary school age, anyway?'

I shook my head. 'I don't know. Not many.'

'There are fifteen at the village school this year. Quite a few of them related to each other.'

I smiled. 'You'd think that would make them get along better, wouldn't you?'

'Not at all, unfortunately. Eight of the kids are currently in the little ones' class – the "infants", so that's a grand total of seven, including Leo, in the juniors' class. And when one of the oldest boys is someone like George, it's very difficult, in such a small group, for the other children not to side with him.'

'Doesn't their teacher realise what's going on?' I said.

'Yes, of course, and he doesn't tolerate any bullying at school. But outside school it's a different matter.' She sighed. 'Being teased is so hurtful, isn't it? And being ignored and left out is another form of bullying in itself.'

I instinctively took hold of her hand and squeezed it. She was, naturally, so upset for her son, but I didn't really know what to suggest. It obviously wouldn't help to question her refusal to let him join the others in the river. I understood her reasons, even if they did seem a little bit over the top. In the circumstances, who could blame her for being overprotective?

After I'd called up goodbye to Leo, and thanked Kerry for the tea, I took Sid back down to the bench by the river and sat there for a while, thinking things over. It seemed like every time I'd begun to hope things were moving in the right direction – that I was making a few friends, starting to be accepted – something went wrong and I felt as if I was back where I started. I felt so sad and upset for young Leo, and for his mum. Kerry was a nice person and her life was difficult enough without the added worry about her son being so unhappy. I questioned myself, too, all over again: why was I getting so involved with these people? Why, when I was only here on an extended holiday, was

I letting their problems, their life stories and their moods affect me so much?

I stared out over the river where a small fishing boat was making its way back from the estuary, gulls swooping and calling as they followed it, and a couple of children were paddling in the mud, laughing as they splashed each other. There was a flash of colour on the far side of the river, and in a blink, a kingfisher had dived for a fish and carried it away to safety further upstream. The sun came out from behind a cloud and suddenly the river was sparkling with patterns of dancing light – blues, greens and silvers constantly moving and changing – as the giggles and squeals of the two children rang out in the still summer air.

I loved this place. I'd never be able to explain it properly, but there it was: I just loved it. And, I finally admitted to myself, I even loved the people. Yes, even when they were being grumpy and rude and unfair, even when it was aimed at me, I felt a sympathy for them, for their loss and their pain, their pride and their bloody inward-looking stubbornness. They had issues, they were damaged and hurt, but their lives were real and intense in a way that those of us who lived in cities in crowded urban communities where nobody knew each other would probably never come close to.

'I want to stay here,' I whispered to Sid, and he looked up at me trustingly, wagging his tail as if he completely agreed, making me laugh out loud.

When I looked back up, the two children I'd been watching were wading out of the river and I recognised one of them now as Leo's ex-friend Reggie.

'Hello, Clare! Hello, Sid!' he said, crouching down to stroke the dog. 'This is my sister, Daisy,' he added, nudging the little girl towards me.

'Hello, Daisy,' I smiled. 'I haven't seen you down here before.'

'She's only allowed if I'm with her,' Reggie explained importantly. 'She's only six.'

'And I don't like it down here if George and the others are around,' Daisy said in a shy little voice.

Reggie stood up and glanced around him, looking uncomfortable. 'They're not around today,' he said.

'No,' I said. 'Sometimes I imagine it's nicer when there are just a couple of you.'

He looked down, giving a little nod but not saying anything.

'I like your doggy,' Daisy said. 'Reggie says you let him walk him, before.'

'Can we walk him again now?' Reggie asked at once. 'Please, Clare?'

'Well, I think that depends on Leo,' I said, pretending to think seriously about it. 'As he kind of shares Sid with me. What do you think Leo would say? Would he agree?'

Reggie dropped his eyes again. 'I don't know. I ... *think* he'd say yes, wouldn't he?'

'You're supposed to be his best friend,' Daisy said accusingly. 'But you keep going off with George.'

'I don't even *like* George!' Reggie retorted crossly to his sister. 'I just don't want to get beaten up!'

'Is that what you think George would do if you didn't hang around with him?' I said.

'He's a bully. He's beat up other people before. And he calls everyone names and makes up rhymes about them.'

'Hmm, well, I don't think *I'd* want to be friends with him either, if he behaves like that,' I said, shaking my head. 'I think I'd much rather be friends with Leo.'

'Me too,' Reggie said regretfully. 'But he probably hates me now, cos sometimes I don't stick up for him.'

I nodded thoughtfully. 'What if you were to do something nice for Leo ... for his birthday, maybe?' I suggested. 'That would show him you still want to be his friend.'

'I know, it's his birthday on Saturday,' Reggie said. 'And he's not having a party, or nothing.'

'Maybe we could have a little party for him on our own?' I said. 'If his mum agrees, of course. We could make it a surprise.'

'Can I come too?' Daisy asked. 'I like Leo. He's nice to me. We're second cousins.'

'So I've heard.' I smiled at her. 'That's pretty special.'

'Can we really have a party, Clare?' Reggie said. 'Will it be at your house? Will Sid be there?'

'Let me ask Leo's mum, first,' I said firmly. 'Then I'll let you know.'

*

Kerry was surprised to see me back on her doorstep again. Leo was still upstairs on his own. I ran the idea past her, adding that of course she and her mother would be welcome to join us. 'And I'll ask Mike too,' I added. 'And anyone else you think Leo might like to be there.'

'This is so nice of you, Clare,' she said, her eyes filling up. 'I ... just can't get over how kind you've been to us all, since you've been here.'

'We're not all monsters, from up-country!' I said with a wink – and she laughed.

'I know. Perhaps that's why you were sent to us. To teach that fact to some of the old miseries here!'

First, I was an angel sent from heaven. Now I was an example sent to teach everyone a lesson. I wasn't sure which was the most scary!

I had several ideas already for how to make Leo's birthday special. Because he'd always shown such interest in my pictures, and he loved Sid so much, the obvious thing for a present was a framed portrait of him with the dog. Just the previous week he'd posed for a series of pictures with Sid for me, so I chose the best one and ordered a fast delivery of an eight-by-six glossy photo, including the online company's own plastic frame, which actually looked quite smart.

On Friday morning, while I waited for the delivery, I set to work making a cake. When the photo arrived, I walked Sid round to the village shop to buy a birthday card, wrapping paper and candles for the cake.

'Do you sell banners or balloons?' I asked the grumpy woman behind the counter.

'What for?' she replied, staring at me.

'For a birthday.' I gave her a smile. 'For a child.'

'Whose child?'

I thought I'd got beyond being shocked by the rudeness of people here, but it seemed they could still surprise me.

I shook my head, trying to imagine anyone in a London shop having the effrontery to be so personal and nosy. But then I remembered how few children lived in Little Sorrel, and I took a deep breath, giving her another smile and saying as calmly as I could manage, 'Young Leo, Kerry's boy. He'll be nine tomorrow.'

'Will he?' She continued to stare at me for a moment, and then to my further surprise, simply added, 'That's nice, then. Doing him a party, are you?'

'Yes, I am, in fact. Just a little one.'

'Kerry will be right pleased, then. Worries about that boy no end, she does.'

I nodded, not wanting to get into any gossip about the family.

'So do you have any? Balloons? Or banners?' I repeated.

'No. You'd have to go to Sorrel-by-Sea for that kind of thing.'

'Oh, OK. Thanks, I will.'

To be honest, I felt less than enthusiastic about going down to French's boathouse and asking for the ferry – but on the other hand I didn't see why I should be put off from taking a simple trip to the next village just because of the unpleasant attitude of the ferrymen.

'Come on, Sid,' I said. 'It's for Leo, after all.' And he looked up at me and wagged his tail, for all the world as if he understood.

Luckily, it was Old Robbie who appeared from the boathouse in response to my call. He nodded and grunted a 'hello' and helped me into the boat, informing me of the tide times. In fact, I'd been in the village long enough by now to work out for myself when the river wasn't navigable but I thanked him anyway and sat down with Sid at my feet, prepared for a silent journey. But halfway down the river he gave a little cough and said, 'I reckon I should apologise to you on behalf of my son.'

'Oh.' I blinked in surprise. 'Well, it's not really for you to have to—'

'Yes, it is,' he said quite fiercely. 'Because he's too damned stubborn to say it himself, and too damned pig-headed to admit when he's wrong. I love my grandson, that goes without saying, but I'm not blind, I know what goes on. I don't doubt he kicked that stone at you, or at young Leo. He's a big lad and he's made all the other kids around here terrified of him. It's not right, but yelling and cursing at him isn't the answer.'

'No, it's not,' I said softly. 'And thank you, I think you're right – the other children are scared of him. I get the impression he can be a bit mean to them. Perhaps he's not feeling very happy, himself?'

'Huh! You can say that again. And—' He gave me a look. 'Since you seem to be the amateur psychologist around here, you'll probably know exactly why. Unhappy father, unhappy son; angry father, angry son. Justine works all the hours God sends, so she's never around for the boy, but who can blame her? The atmosphere's so bad at home. I keep telling Young Robbie it's time to let the anger go. Before my grandson gets himself into real trouble.'

'Well, I'm sorry your family's having such a difficult time,' I said. 'I hope things start to improve for you soon.'

He nodded again and went back to staring out across the river. I followed his gaze, watching two cormorants circling and landing on some distant rocks beyond the estuary. There was a gentle breeze coming off the sea, bringing with it the smell of seaweed and the tang of salt in the air. I lifted my face up to the sun, closing my eyes and letting the wind tousle my hair.

We didn't speak again until we reached the Sorrel-by-Sea jetty, but after he'd held out his hand to help me off the boat, Old Robbie patted my shoulder in an almost fatherly way and said, 'You've done well to last this long, Clare. Don't let my son – or anyone else – get to you. You're good for us. Good for the village.' He coughed and looked at his watch. 'Call me when you're done.'

CHAPTER 24

When I arrived back at Little Sorrel with my banners and balloons from one of Sorrel-by-Sea's 'touristy' shops, there was another surprise waiting for me. As I passed the village shop, the door flew open and the woman who'd served me earlier rushed after me, stopping me with a hand on my arm and almost tripping over Sid.

'Glad I've seen you,' she said. 'Been watching out for you. Here.' She handed me a small wrapped package and an envelope. 'It's just some sweets, that's all. And a card. For young Leo, if you wouldn't mind passing it on.'

'Oh, that's nice of you. Of course I will. Who shall I say—'

'I'm Hazel. Audrey's sister. And Harry's too, of course.' She gave me such a beaming smile, I found myself stepping backwards in surprise. Was this the same surly woman who'd always served me so silently and reluctantly? 'Audrey told me about this singing group you've started. I might come myself next time.'

226

'That'd be great! I'll look forward to seeing you. And thanks for thinking of Leo,' I added.

'He's a nice lad. I don't like the way the other kids leave him out. After what happened to his father,' she said, shaking her head.

'Yes, I've heard,' I said.

'Nice of you to try and cheer him up a bit. He always talks about your dog when he comes in the shop.' She nodded, briskly. 'Well, good to talk to you, Clare.'

Unbelievable. I might have enough friends here now to actually have to count them!

*

I called at the vicarage before going home. Mike answered the door with a book in one hand and a pen in the other.

'Just choosing which hymns to practise tonight,' he said. 'Come in!'

'No, I won't hold you up. I just wanted to ask if you'd come in for tea tomorrow afternoon. I'm having a little birthday party for Leo.'

'Lovely idea. Of course I will.'

'Kerry's agreed to it, and she'll tell Julie, of course – or maybe you will, at choir practice. And – unless I see them myself – perhaps she wouldn't mind telling Reggie and Daisy. I said I'd let them know, but I don't know where they live.'

'That's no trouble, Clare. Those two spend as much time at their Auntie Julie's as they do at home. She'll probably bring them round herself tomorrow.'

I spent the afternoon icing and decorating the birthday cake, half expecting to have to hide it at any moment if

227

Leo turned up after school wanting to take Sid for a walk, but he didn't come at all. I wondered if he was still moping, and hoped Kerry would be able to persuade him to come to the party the next day. In the evening, I downloaded some music that I thought he and his friends might like. Then on the Saturday morning I put up the banners and balloons, and finally prepared a selection of sandwiches, sausage rolls and nibbles. There wasn't much else I could do, except hope the birthday boy would come.

As it happened, there were even more guests than I'd hoped. On the dot of four o'clock, Julie arrived with Reggie and Daisy, and also an older boy who she explained was another nephew – the twelve-year-old son of one of her sisters.

'Alex is staying with me today while his mum and older sister are out shopping,' she said with a smile. 'I hope it was OK to bring him?'

'Of course! Hello, Alex,' I said. 'Come in, everyone. Help yourself to squash, I've made up a couple of jugs in the kitchen.'

Next to arrive was Mike, who was carrying a large parcel, which he told me was from himself and Julie. I kept watching out of the window, keeping my fingers crossed, until – thank goodness – I saw Kerry shepherding Leo along the road, and holding the hand of a little girl who looked about the same age as Daisy.

'Oh, that's nice, Kerry's brought Evie along,' said Julie, looking over my shoulder. 'She's the little girl who lives next door to them. Evie's an only child, and she doesn't have any cousins around here either – quite a rarity in

Little Sorrel,' she added with a chuckle. 'She and Daisy are good friends.'

'Lovely.' I hoped I'd made enough sandwiches. 'Right, everyone, quickly: into the kitchen, please – and you can all come out and shout "Surprise" when you hear me say "Happy birthday". OK?'

I felt ridiculously nervous as I opened the front door. It would be so disappointing if this went badly wrong.

'Hello.' I winked at Kerry. 'Have you come to play with Sid, Leo?'

'No.' He shuffled his feet, looking awkward. 'I just came to say sorry for running off the other day. And for sulking.'

This was obviously Kerry's idea, and she must have schooled him in his little speech!

'Oh, Leo.' I gave him a hug. 'You don't need to apologise. Come in, all of you. As it happens, I think it's a special day for you today, isn't it?' I raised my voice. 'Happy birthday, Leo!'

The kitchen door immediately flew open and the others all rushed out, yelling 'Surprise!' and 'Happy Birthday' and fighting each other to give Leo a happy birthday hug. He stood rooted to the spot, his eyes wide with shock, his face turning pink.

'Some of your friends wanted to give you a little party,' I told him carefully. 'We hope that's OK with you?'

'Oh.' He blinked several times, looking around at us all, at the balloons and the Happy Birthday banners. 'Oh, um … thank you.' Finally, a little smile. 'I didn't think anyone knew it was my birthday.'

'Of course we did!' Reggie said, handing Leo a present.

I showed him where the other presents were piled up on the table.

'Come on, open them, then!' Julie said, ruffling his hair. 'We all want to see what you've got!'

And at last – like at any proper children's party – there was the rustle of paper, the whoops of excitement, the smiles and laughter that should always happen when a person becomes nine years old. When he opened my present, he sat in silence for a moment, holding the picture and smiling.

'Thank you, Clare,' he said eventually. 'I'm going to put it in my bedroom. I can look at it when I feel sad, it'll cheer me up.'

'I'm glad you like it,' I said lightly. I didn't want any further talk about feeling sad, today of all days.

'It's a lovely picture, Clare,' Julie said warmly, adding to her daughter, 'Did you know she was a professional photographer?'

'No, I didn't.' Kerry said. 'Do you advertise?' she asked me.

'No. I'm – well, I *was* – a press photographer. This is just a hobby,' I explained.

'I've told her she ought to take it up as a business,' Mike intervened. 'Pet photography. It could be a real money spinner – people love having good pictures of their pets, don't they?'

'Well, maybe ...' I said, feeling a bit embarrassed by all the attention. 'But look, Leo's opened some more of his presents. What have you got there, Leo?'

When he'd unwrapped all the sweets, books, and pens from the other children, they went out into the garden to play with Sid while Kerry helped me lay out the food on the table.

'This is so good of you, Clare,' she said again. 'I can't thank you enough: it's really helped to cheer Leo up—'

She didn't get any further before there was a sudden loud knocking on the door.

'Oh. I wonder who else has turned up?' I said, going to the door while thinking I'd definitely have to make a few more sandwiches. I couldn't think who else might have heard about the birthday gathering, unless it was someone like Audrey, or Neil and Lucy from the choir meeting. But it wasn't any of them. It was George, glowering at me as he stood on the doorstep, demanding to know if Leo was having his birthday party in my house.

'It's just Leo and some of his friends, George,' I said quietly.

'I can hear him out the back!' he said accusingly. 'And the other kids out there. I could hear them shouting about his birthday.'

'Well, as I say, I'm sorry, but it's just a small group of Leo's friends—'

'Is everything all right, Clare?' Kerry said, following me to the front door. 'Oh. It's you, George. What do you want?'

'Are all the other kids here?' George shot back rudely. 'Is Reggie out there?'

I had to struggle to remember that I was an adult, and this was merely a rather badly behaved ten-year-old – otherwise I'd have been tempted to tell him to clear off and shut the door in his face. It felt like the Bad Fairy had arrived to put an evil spell on the party.

'Sorry, George,' I said. 'But this isn't anything to do with you.'

'That's not fair!' He was red in the face, and looked more like his father than ever. 'I want to come to the party. Why have they left me out?'

'Because that's what you do to Leo!' said a surprisingly loud little voice from behind me. 'That's what you always do, you're mean and horrible to him and you're not his friend, so you're not invited!'

I looked round at Reggie, giving him a nod. 'OK, Reggie. Go back and play with the others.'

'Well, make him clear off!' he said fiercely. 'It's his fault Leo gets upset and thinks nobody likes him. Don't let him come and spoil his birthday like he spoils everything else.'

'Shut up, Reggie!' George said, glaring at him. 'You're supposed to be on my side.'

'Boys, that's enough,' Kerry said. 'George, you need to go home, please. You don't want me to call your dad, do you?'

'What's going on?' We all looked round to see Alex – who was even taller than George and two years older – staring down at him, a frown on his face. 'What's the matter, George? You haven't come round here to wreck Leo's birthday party, have you?'

For once, George seemed to be lost for words. Confronted by the older boy, he suddenly wasn't so sure of himself. Still glowering, he turned and walked away, kicking the ground as he went.

'Don't tell Leo he came,' Reggie said quietly.

'No, we won't,' I agreed. I closed the door and patted Reggie's shoulder. 'Well done for what you said.'

'I should have said it lots of other times,' he admitted. 'But he scares me.'

'He's an idiot,' Alex said dismissively.

'Thank you, too, Alex,' I said. I was glad he came, extra sandwiches or not.

'He needs to grow up,' he said with a shrug. 'If he carries on like that when he starts at my school, he'll get beaten up by some of the older boys.'

I sighed. George might be a bully, he was certainly a pain in the neck, and he'd very nearly been the Bad Fairy at our party, but I didn't like to hear talk about him being beaten up.

'I don't want him to get hurt,' I said. 'He's probably quite an unhappy boy.'

'Serves him right,' Alex said with a shrug as he followed Reggie back outside.

Was childhood always so difficult? I was glad I couldn't remember.

The rest of the party went with a swing. We played games, had tea – just about enough sandwiches, thank goodness – sang 'Happy Birthday' as Leo blew out the nine candles on his cake, and were giving him three cheers when there was another knock on the door.

'I hope You-Know-Who hasn't come back,' I whispered to Mike as I got up.

'With or without the heavy mob,' he replied, raising his eyebrows at me warningly.

I opened the door cautiously, half expecting to see Young Robbie on the doorstep, prepared to do battle on behalf of his son. And I nearly fell over in surprise.

'*Sally*?' I screamed – and, laughing and almost crying at the same time, threw myself into her arms.

'Get off, you daft moo!' she laughed back. 'What the hell's the matter with you? Didn't you get my message? Or my phone call? What's going on here?' she added, looking past me into the room, where several curious children were staring back at her. 'Have you started a crèche or something?'

'No, it's a party… oh, it's a long story – come in, for God's sake! No, I didn't get your message, or your call. I'm sorry, I've been busy, I didn't hear my phone … I didn't know you were coming, or I'd have –' I glanced back indoors, where Julie was just beginning to slice up the birthday cake '– I'd have baked another cake!'

Both of us were laughing now, holding onto each other's arms. I led her indoors and announced to everyone that this was my oldest and dearest friend from London.

'Sorry it's so sudden,' she said after everyone had finished greeting her. 'I got a wedding booking cancelled at short notice and realised I had a complete week free. God knows when that might happen again, so I made a spontaneous decision to take you up on your offer to come and stay. I presume you haven't changed your mind—'

'Of course I haven't!' I laughed.

Sally had three children of her own from her two marriages – as well as two stepsons – but they were all grown up, relocated to various parts of the UK and Europe, with

234

no sign yet of any grandchildren. Her only tie in recent years had been her job, with weddings booked nearly every week throughout the year, so I could understand why she took the chance to get away whenever the opportunity presented itself.

'I can't believe you haven't looked at your emails or checked your phone,' she said, shaking her head at me and adding accusingly, 'I've had the devil's own job to find this place.'

Everyone laughed now.

'If I had a penny for everyone who's ever said that about Little Sorrel,' Julie told her, 'I'd be filthy rich by now. I'm Julie,' she added, holding out her hand to Sally. 'And this is Mike, my fiancé. We're – I hope – Clare's friends here in the village.'

'And I'm Kerry, Julie's daughter, and this is Leo, my son – Clare's biggest fan,' Kerry said. 'It's his birthday today, and this party has all been Clare's doing.'

'Good grief, woman,' Sally said, turning to me, 'you've only been away from London for a couple of months and you've turned into Mother Teresa. What have you guys done to my friend?' she added jokingly to the others. 'She was never this nice before. Or this slim!' she added, looking me up and down in surprise. 'Living off the land, are you? No food shops around here?'

'Give her a piece of cake, can you, Julie, to shut her up?' I joked. 'I'll put the kettle on. Look at me! You've given me such a surprise, I'm actually shaking!' I turned back and gave her another hug. 'But it's a lovely surprise. I'm *so* glad you're here.'

'OK, OK, enough of the fuss. Tell me where to put my bag and I'll get it out of your way. Which room is mine?'

'Oh.' My smile dropped for a moment. 'Don't you remember me telling you?' I glanced awkwardly at Mike. 'There are only two bedrooms. And one is ... kept locked. But don't worry, the bed's a big double. Or I'll sleep on the sofa if you don't like me hogging the bedclothes.'

Mike followed me out to the kitchen. 'You don't have to sleep on the sofa,' he said quietly. 'It's silly. Harry left me the key to the other bedroom.' He paused, and shrugged. 'It was Paul's.'

'Well, I guessed that, to be honest. At first, I thought it was where Harry stored his painting things, or something like that, but after you told me about Paul, it was pretty obvious. He wouldn't want his son's room to be touched, Mike. Thanks, but it wouldn't be right.'

'I could call him, in the States. Ask him—'

'No. Please don't do that. I wouldn't feel comfortable using Paul's room. Harry's locked it for a reason, and I respect that. Sally and I will share.'

I was pretty sure that Harry would have a blue fit at the thought of someone from up-country using his son's bedroom – especially as I wasn't sure Mike had told him about me!

CHAPTER 25

Neither Sally nor I slept very much that first night, and it wasn't because we were uncomfortable or lacked enough space, sleeping together in the double bed. It was because of the amount of talking we needed to do to catch up on each other's lives. Phone calls and emails are great, but there's nothing like being with a friend in person for getting to the nitty-gritty, easing out all the little details you've missed, teasing each other and laughing your heads off together.

'I was looking forward to meeting all the people you've been telling me about,' Sally had said as soon as the party had ended and a seriously happy nine-year-old and his friends had been shepherded off the premises. 'But I didn't expect to meet them all in one go the moment I arrived!'

'Don't worry, there are still a lot more to meet. You only missed George French by half an hour or so.'

'Not George the nasty bully? Surely he didn't come to the party?'

Sheila Norton

'No.' I explained what had happened, and how Reggie and Alex had both stood up to him, and she nodded approvingly. 'I'll show you around the village in the morning,' I went on, yawning. 'I'm too knackered now.'

'I'm not surprised. Hosting a children's birthday party at your age,' she teased. 'Anyone would think you're rehearsing for grandmother-hood.'

'Oh God, no thank you!' I joked. 'Not ready for that.'

She gave me a strange look. 'But surely, if—'

'If it happened, I guess I'd get over it,' I said flippantly. 'Right now, it's enough that my kids have foisted the dog off on me, never mind babies.'

Sally bent down to stroke Sid, who was lying contentedly by her feet.

'I don't see you being too upset about having him. In fact, you seem pretty besotted.'

'Well, you know how it is.' I smiled. 'You get used to things when they're thrust upon you.'

'And what about this little cat you've been telling me about? I haven't seen her yet. Is that her, in the picture next to the one of Sid?' She picked up the photo, turning it to the light and giving it the critical appraisal of a fellow professional. 'These are really good, by the way, Clare. Even by your standards!'

'Thank you, I'm sure!' I laughed. 'I've been nagged by a couple of my friends here today about setting myself up as a pet photographer. As if I need the hassle of it.'

'Hassle?' She raised her eyebrows at me. 'Surely you'd be doing something you love and getting paid for it? Not that you're desperate for money now, I suppose.'

I shrugged. I had to admit, the thought of taking pet photography up as a serious concern had piqued my interest, but I'd been ignoring it because – well, what was the point? As Sally had said, I was no longer desperate for money, and although I'd want an occupation of sorts when I went back to London – I couldn't simply spend the rest of my life sitting around at home and taking Sid for walks – I wasn't sure it would appeal to me to start a small business back there. It might work somewhere smaller, like Little Sorrel – especially if it was the type of village that welcomed visitors! – but not so much in the city.

'Anyway, no,' I said, changing the subject. 'Topsy hasn't come in yet today. I guess all the music and noise from the kids have scared her off.' I frowned. 'Actually, thinking about it, I haven't seen her for a couple of days. Maybe she's gone back to spending more time next door with Mike. Cats can be so fickle, can't they?'

*

The following day, Sunday, after our late night, we slept in for as long as Sid would allow us.

'Oh, God,' I groaned eventually. 'I'll have to get up and feed him, poor little devil. I suppose it's only reasonable that he should want to eat.'

Still no sign of Topsy. I'd have to ask Mike, when he got back from church, whether he'd been feeding her again.

We had a leisurely breakfast and then took Sid for a slow stroll around the village. Once again, as I'd done with my daughter, I acted the tour guide and pointed out the few notable sights of Little Sorrel.

'And that's about it,' I said when we finally came to a rest at my usual bench beside the river.

'Well, it is very picturesque, I'll give you that,' Sally said. 'And very quiet. Almost a ghost town … I mean village.'

I laughed. 'That's because you've only just left London. It's a culture shock. And also, to be fair, it's Sunday. Not so many people around. Quite a few of the villagers go to church.'

'To practise their singing? To please the new *teacher*?' she teased.

'No!' I nudged her, laughing. 'I think they go to church because it's one of the few social opportunities around here. A chance to gossip with everyone after the service. If the church choir practice was anything to go by, they certainly don't seem very fired up about the worship aspect of it. Half of them sung as if they were barely awake.'

'And you're trying to get some life out of them for *your* choir?'

I shrugged. 'Hopefully. The few who came along last week became quite enthusiastic once we finally got started. You will come on Tuesday, won't you?'

'If I must,' she sighed, and then nudged me and laughed. 'Of course I will, you silly moo! I can't wait to see how they react to you bringing another *outsider* along. They'll probably accuse you of trying to stage a takeover.'

'It's all very well for you to laugh,' I said, but couldn't help joining in myself. I'd had to watch what I said so carefully with everyone around here that I'd almost forgotten the pleasure of joking around like this, and Sally was a breath of fresh air, with her sarcasm and irreverent little jibes.

We strolled on to the pub for a coffee, partly because Sally wanted to meet Jack the landlord, having dined out back at home on my stories about his grumpy moods and derisory breakfasts.

'*So* pleased to meet you,' she said, holding out her hand to him across the bar, making me snigger and have to turn away. 'Clare's told me so much about your hospitality.'

'You are terrible,' I giggled as we took our coffees to a corner of the bar where the window overlooked the river. It had started to rain – a fine, soft drizzle that turned the view of the opposite bank and the river beyond into a watercolour wash of greys and greens.

She smiled as she stirred her frothy coffee – we'd already agreed that it didn't look as if it could qualify for the title of cappuccino. 'You used to be pretty terrible yourself, Clare Finch, before you became Mother Teresa. Joking aside, I can't argue that it's obviously very peaceful here. I can see that it's a good place for a spell of breathing space. But—'

'But you can't see why the hell anyone would want to stay here?' I finished for her.

'Not yet. But I'm open to being persuaded.' She sipped the coffee and flinched. 'The first thing I'd do, if I were you, would be to open a decent coffee shop.'

We headed home during a break in the rain and met Mike on his way back from church.

'Has Topsy come back to live with you?' I asked him when we'd exhausted the topic of the successful birthday party. 'I can't think when I last saw her.'

'No.' He frowned. 'She hasn't been in to my place at all. I presumed you were still feeding her.'

'I was – but not in the last couple of days. I hope she's OK.'

'You know what cats are like,' he said, although he was frowning a little anxiously. 'Always wandering off somewhere. And before you moved in, she used to hang around several other houses down the lane and get fed by various people. Perhaps I should call at some of their homes and ask if they've seen her. In fact, I'll do it now. No time like the present.'

'I'll come with you,' I said. 'Do you mind, Sally?'

'Of course not.' She smiled. 'I want to meet as many people here as possible. I'm writing a book about the village and its inhabitants.'

Mike blinked in surprise and glanced from one of us to the other, a look of consternation on his face. 'Really?' he stammered.

'No, not really!' She laughed. 'Sorry – just teasing.'

'I apologise for my friend,' I said, raising my eyebrows to Mike. 'She thinks she's funny.'

'Phew!' He grinned. 'I was picturing the scenes in the county court when everyone sues for defamation of character!'

We strolled down Duck Lane together, calling at each house in turn – there were only seven apart from the vicarage and Riverside Cottage. Most were owned by people

I recognised but didn't yet know, although they all seemed to know who I was. I got the impression that if Mike hadn't been with me, they wouldn't have greeted me with the reluctant politeness that they did. But one cottage at the end of the lane turned out to belong to Hazel from the shop – Audrey's sister – who seemed pleased to see me and wanted to know how Leo's party had gone. The end result, however, was that nobody had seen Topsy recently. In fact, it transpired that since I'd moved in, the other residents had hardly seen her at all. In most cases, this was made to sound like an accusation, as if I'd stolen or kidnapped their communal cat.

'I see what you mean, now,' Sally said when we were finally back in the cottage on our own. We'd stopped off at the duck pond at the end of the lane so that I could show Sally the ducklings, now living close to their mother on the pond but not yet ready to fly.

'About what?' I asked.

'About people not liking you,' she said bluntly. 'I was beginning to think you were being paranoid and imagining it all – everyone apart from Grumpy Jack had been so nice to you up till now.'

'That's because you'd only met the select and very small proportion of villagers who've actually bothered to get to know me before dismissing me as just a visitor from up-country.'

'Well, it's interesting to see both sides of the debate,' she said.

'What debate?'

Sheila Norton

'The question of whether you're an angel sent from heaven or whether you are, indeed, just an annoying visitor from up-country who won't take the hint and clear off.'

I swiped at her with a cushion, missed, and we both laughed.

'I'm an angel, of course. That's been overwhelmingly agreed by one or two people.'

'OK, if you say so. I'd be interested in the opinion of your friend the ferryman, though. You haven't introduced me to *him* yet.'

'Huh.' I scowled. 'Young Robbie? You haven't missed much.'

'Let me be the judge of that,' she responded calmly. 'You never know, I might decide he's misunderstood. I might awaken his good nature.'

'If only it were just asleep. I think it died, sadly, on the day of the tragedy here.'

'Yes. I suppose we shouldn't joke about it.' She sighed. 'Well, it's all quite interesting, anyway, Clare. I really think I might seriously consider writing that book. I could always change everyone's names, and call the village something different – Little Sorrow? Great Sorrows? After all, look how much money that mad author friend of yours made with just two books.'

'Shut up, you nutcase! And she wasn't a friend of mine, as you well know. She was a "friend" of Brian's.'

'He was her muse. Her inspiration. Her *hero*,' she teased.

But I found that a bit harder to laugh about. Even now, the very idea of Brian being a romantic hero sounded absolutely ridiculous. And ... still quite sad, somehow.

*

The following day, I introduced Sally to the Little Sorrel ferry. She didn't get her wish – to meet Young Robbie – because he wasn't around that day, and it was his father who took us across to the jetty for Sorrel-by-Sea.

'He seems OK,' she pronounced as we ploughed through the overgrown footpath at the other end, Sid rushing ahead of us, exploring every thicket and dense patch of under-growth and, once again, narrowly missing the tail of a rabbit as it disappeared into its burrow. 'I mean, he's quiet, but not passively aggressive with it.'

'What are you now?' I teased. 'Amateur psychoanalyst for the village population?'

'Actually, it's not a bad idea. Perhaps that's what they all need. A few sessions on the couch. Professionally speaking, of course.'

'You're a wedding photographer, love, not a marriage guidance counsellor – or any kind of counsellor, couch or no couch. Now, look: we're just coming into Sorrel-by-Sea. I want your unbiased opinion on the village. Nicer than Little Sorrel or nastier?'

'Will I get thrown out of Little Sorrel if I vote against it?'

'Chances are you'll get thrown out anyway. Let's start at this tea room. Sid likes it in here.'

We spent a pleasant couple of hours mooching around the village. I could tell Sally was trying to hide her enthu-siasm for the little arty and crafty shops and those selling touristy knick-knacks.

'Not a patch on Little Sorrel, obviously,' she said drily, as we stood on the windswept cliffs, looking out to sea. 'No fascinatingly grumpy locals for a start.'

'OK, I knew you'd prefer it here. Typical London tourist,' I said with a shrug. 'Just don't tell Old Robbie or he'll tip you out of the boat on the way back.'

She didn't need to say anything – the fact that she was carrying a bag from one of the touristy shops, containing 'tacky' souvenirs for people at home, said it all – and Old Robbie sniffed disapproval as he helped us back into the boat. No mention was made of his grandson being turned away from the birthday party, though, and I was grateful that it was him and not Young Robbie on ferry duty that day.

We stopped off at the village shop when we arrived back in Little Sorrel to buy dinner for the evening, and I was served by Hazel who, now that she'd added herself to the small but growing list of my friends, seemed to have become almost effusive in her conversations with me.

'I was thinking, what you were saying about not seeing Harry's cat recently,' she said. 'I hope that bloody cat of the Frenches hasn't been around here again. Archie, his name is – big ginger tom, nasty thing, thinks he owns the village. Only I'm just saying, look out for it, won't you? It attacked my Pussy Willow some months back, left her with a nasty ear. Just saying, that's all.'

'Oh, right – thank you, Hazel.' I ignored Sally trying not to snigger about Pussy Willow's name. 'In fact, I *did* see that cat in the garden, about a week ago. Mike told me whose it was.' I frowned, suddenly feeling a bit sick. 'I chased it away – or rather, my dog did – because it had frightened Topsy. She had a little scratch on her nose but she seemed OK.'

Had I seen her since that day? Surely I'd have noticed if she hadn't been in at all.

'Well, I'm just saying,' she repeated again. 'He's a nasty piece of work, watch out for him.'

'I will.'

I was quiet as we walked back to the cottage, hoping against hope that Topsy would suddenly appear, winding herself around my legs the way she always did, butting me with her little head and meowing to be fed. But there was still no sign of her.

'You're worried now, aren't you?' Sally sympathised. 'I'm sure she'll turn up.'

'I hope so,' I said fervently. 'I can't imagine how awful it would be if Harry found out that – on top of everything else – an *outsider* has been living in his cottage *and* let something happen to his cat while he's away.'

'He couldn't blame you for it!' she protested.

'Oh yes he could.' I didn't know the guy, of course. But – on top of my personal worry about the little cat, who I'd already grown to love – I knew enough about Little Sorrel now to understand exactly how Harry would feel about it.

CHAPTER 26

We were into July now. The time had flown by, and I'd already renewed my temporary tenancy of Riverside Cottage for another month, telling myself that I needed to be here for a few more weeks to help with the choir until it was fully established. The weather had turned hot again, and Sally asked if we could go swimming, but I was concerned about the reaction of the locals. I asked Mike if there was somewhere not too far away that we could drive to, with a safe swimming beach.

'Of course,' he said. 'Tuffey Bay has a fabulous beach. A mile of soft sand, safe bathing, surf on good days, a lifeguard—'

'Sounds great,' I enthused. 'How far is that?'

'Not far, as the crow flies,' he said, laughing. 'But by road, from here? It'll take you over an hour. As does everywhere, pretty much.'

'Oh well. It'd be worth it, wouldn't it? To have a day at the beach, and a swim in the sea?' I asked Sally. 'It would be quite exciting. I haven't driven anywhere since I arrived here.'

She shook her head at me in amazement. 'Unbelievable! Well, it's about time you found out whether your car still works, isn't it? Or have you forgotten how to drive? Want me to take you?'

I laughed. 'No, I agree, it's time I went somewhere. We'll do it tomorrow. Thanks, Mike.'

'I'm just relieved you're not going to try swimming near the estuary here,' he said seriously.

'I wouldn't be that silly. I know it would be insensitive—'

'And dangerous. You can swim further up in the river, away from the estuary, if you don't mind the mud. And if you don't mind being stared at by the locals. But absolutely not near the estuary.'

'Don't worry, we won't,' I said. 'We'll go to Tuffey Bay. We'll set off early in the morning and make sure we're home in plenty of time for the choir meeting.'

'Oh yes, of course. I hope more people turn up this time, Clare. And have a good time at the seaside, if I don't see you before.'

We spent much of the day relaxing in the little garden of Riverside Cottage, and after school, Leo came round to play with Sid.

'I'm going out to play with Reggie now,' he said as he was leaving.

'Are you two good friends again?' I asked hopefully.

'Yeah. He played with me instead of George at lunchtime. Maybe because of coming to my party?' he said shyly.

I smiled. I hadn't told him about George turning up at the party and Reggie's part in sending him packing. But to my surprise, Leo went on, 'George knew about the party, I don't know how. He came up to me and said he wouldn't have come to my "stupid party" even if he'd been invited.' He laughed. 'I think he was jealous.'

'You're probably right, Leo,' I said.

It was nice to see him happier. I just hoped it lasted.

*

I was more worried than ever now about Topsy. I reckoned it must have been nearly a week since I'd seen her, and I knew Mike was worried too.

'Probably someone else in the village has been feeding her,' Sally said, after I'd delayed our departure for Tuffey Bay the next morning by calling for her fruitlessly in the garden and out in the street. 'You did say the whole community was looking after her.'

'I suppose so. But since I've been here, she'd gone back to mostly hanging around the cottage. It's her home. She was sleeping here every night.' I shook my head, sighing. 'If she's not back tonight, I think I'll put some posters up around the place. I do feel responsible.'

Having made that decision, I tried not to let my growing anxiety about the little cat spoil my day out with my old friend. We took Sid with us, as Mike had assured me that part of the beach was pet-friendly. Sid jumped into the back of the car with such enthusiasm, I felt almost guilty for not taking him anywhere different for so long. Sally and I laughed and sang together for most of the drive, which, as Mike had predicted, took just over an hour and involved another long narrow lane down to the coast after we'd negotiated our own lane to take us inland to the main road. It was worth it, though, for the view of the sea which suddenly came into sight near the end of the lane. The car park was busy, but the beach was so wide it didn't seem crowded, despite the number of people taking advantage of the good weather. We ran straight into the sea, squealing like kids as we jumped over the waves and splashed each other, Sid paddling in the shallows behind us.

'I haven't had that much fun for ages,' Sally said when we finally stretched out on the sand to dry off in the sun.

'Me neither.' I smiled at her. 'I wish you could stay for longer.'

'But you'll be coming home before too long.' She gave me a very direct look. 'Won't you?'

'I suppose so.' I hadn't mentioned renewing my lease to Sally, but she presumably must have realised I'd been living in the cottage for longer than a month now.

We were silent for a moment. I closed my eyes and began to think about it: going home, back to London, to my flat, to . . . what? To work, again? Or to take an unearned early retirement, and do nothing? This holiday was supposed to be giving me a chance to think about all this, all the decisions I needed to make about what to do with my life now that I didn't have to struggle financially any more. But I hadn't made any decisions at all. I'd deliberately closed my mind to the situation. I'd hardly even spent any money. There was nothing to spend it on in Little Sorrel!

'Clare,' Sally said quietly, sitting up and staring at the sea instead of looking at me. 'There's something I should probably tell you.'

'Oh God.' I didn't like the serious tone of her voice. 'What?'

'Well, it's not anything definite, really. It's just a feeling I got when I spoke to Rachel before I came down here.'

'What sort of feeling?' I asked, alarmed. 'Is she OK? And why did you speak to her?'

'Don't panic. I only called her to let her know I was coming in case there was anything she wanted me to bring down for you – post or whatever.'

'She's been forwarding my mail. But what was this feeling you got?' I persisted.

'Just that she seemed a bit ... I don't know ... *different*. I can't explain it. There was something in her tone, something that made me ask her if everything was all right – and she immediately said yes, of course.' Sally frowned. 'I was probably just imagining it. You obviously speak to her yourself, don't you? She'd have told you if anything was wrong.'

I ran through the last couple of conversations I'd had with my daughter. She'd sounded OK, hadn't she? She always told me if anything was wrong. Even if she'd had an argument with Jason, we normally ended up laughing about it together.

'What I'm trying to say, Clare,' Sally went on, sounding firmer now, 'is that I think she misses you.'

'Oh. Well, of course – I miss her, too. And Daniel. Obviously! But, well, they're grown up now, they've got their own lives, their work, their partners – and we call and text each other all the time—'

'Yes, of course.'

'And Rachel came to stay with me for a few days. She could come again – any time she likes – I keep telling her that!'

'That's fine, then, Clare,' she said, soothingly. 'I didn't mean to worry you. I just thought I should say something.'

She thought I should go home. I lay back again, staring at the sky, watching the seagulls swooping and diving. That's what this was all about. Without actually saying it, Sally obviously thought I should go back where I belonged – with my family. That I was a bad mother, neglecting them, not caring if they missed me, while I was indulging myself in the back of beyond, pretending I lived here, pretending it was my real life when really it was just – what? An escape. An escape from reality, from the decisions I needed to make, the changes Brian's money had brought, which I hadn't asked for and didn't really want.

But I'm happy here, I said inside my head. Was it selfish to be happy? Was it *odd* to be happy in a strange little village so far from home and from all the people I loved? Perhaps that was it: I'd become odd. The shock of the money had made me lose my mind.

'I'll call Rachel again tonight,' I said out loud. 'I'll be able to tell if there's anything worrying her.'

'Yes. Of course you will,' she said. 'Now – are we going back in for another swim? I'll race you! Come on, Sid!'

*

We spent the whole day at the beach, hiring a parasol when the sun became too intense, and only moving as far as the café at the top, where we had a sandwich and a beer at lunchtime.

'It's lovely here, isn't it?' Sally said, looking back over the sea when we finally gathered up our things and headed back to the car. 'If I was you, I'd stay here rather than Little Sorrel.'

'Oh. Well, yes, it's lovely – to visit for a day. But I think I'd get bored if I stayed here all the time. It's just a beach. It'd be awful in bad weather. And it's a tourist place, really, somewhere people come for holidays, whereas Little Sorrel is, well, a real village with real people – even if most of them still don't talk to me!' I laughed, aware that I was being defensive, desperately trying to rationalise what Sally must see as my inexplicable preference for the little village I'd come to love.

'Fair enough,' she said, shrugging. 'Whatever floats your boat.'

We stopped off at a pub on the main road back towards Little Sorrel to have a quick meal so that I wouldn't have to rush around cooking dinner before going to the choir meeting.

'I'd forgotten about that,' Sally admitted.

'You don't have to come—'

'Yes I do! I want to meet the rest of these weird people you've been telling me about.'

'They're not weird!' I protested, and then stopped. Here I was, being defensive again. Anyone would think I was part of the community myself.

*

When we arrived at the school that evening for the choir practice, I was delighted to see that Julie and Kerry had brought Reggie along with Leo.

'He wanted to come,' Leo told me, grinning with pleasure. 'I told him it was good. He's got a nice voice.'

'That's excellent!' I said. 'You're very welcome, Reggie.'

Of course, I was pleased for Leo as well as for the choir. It was good to see the two boys laughing and chatting together. But I was wondering how the adults – my newer acquaintances at the choir – would feel about me bringing Sally, another outsider. I needn't have worried. As soon as I began to introduce her, Audrey interrupted me to say that Julie had already told them I'd be bringing a friend who was staying with me for the week – and proceeded to make a rather nice little speech to Sally on behalf of the group.

'I know we've got a bit of a reputation here for being unfriendly to visitors,' she said. 'And to be honest, it's true, and we need to change that. I was just as guilty as everyone else, but I think Julie and the Reverend have got the right idea, that this choir will be good for us all, and we should be grateful to Clare for helping us with it. So any friend of Clare's is a friend of mine – of all of us – right, everyone?'

There was a chorus of agreement.

'Oh, well, thank you,' Sally said, naturally sounding somewhat surprised. 'I've heard so much about you all—'

'Most of it probably bad!' Audrey laughed.

Fortunately, before Sally could manage to respond to that, the door was flung open and in came Hazel from the shop, accompanied by a timid-looking man she introduced as her husband Dave, and their two teenage children.

'My sister,' Audrey told me.

'Yes, we've already met. Glad you could come, Hazel,' I said. 'And you've brought your family.'

'I told them it would do them good,' she said firmly, shepherding her husband and kids into some seats. 'And I've been telling everyone who comes into the shop that they should join, too. But you know what they're like around here.'

I smiled. It seemed unnecessary to say that yes, I certainly did know what people were like around here. But I was beginning to hope now that gradually, one or two people at a time, perhaps the ice was melting.

CHAPTER 27

This time, nobody complained in the slightest about warming up with a couple of verses of 'If You're Happy and You Know It'. Even Neil and Lucy joined in quite energetically. We'd now got copies of the words to 'Lean on Me', and when I suggested we sung this next, I was touched by how enthusiastically they all agreed. I was aware that Hazel, like Audrey, was a sister of Harry's and therefore equally affected by the loss of her nephew Paul. Her children had lost a cousin. The more people I met here in Little Sorrel, the more I understood that the tragedy had indeed affected everyone in the village. They were so interwoven by family and friendship, just as most communities would have been in times long past. A throwback to a different way of life.

'I've told Hazel why we're singing this song,' Audrey said as Julie played the opening chords. 'Listen to the words, sis. It's like they were written for us.'

This time we practised it several times over, everyone's voices becoming stronger and more confident as they mastered the tune and began to memorise the words. At one point, Julie introduced a descant, her lovely voice floating high above the melody and then returning to join it.

'That was beautiful,' I said, adding thoughtfully that if there were more of us, we could work on more harmonies, especially perhaps a bass part for the men.

'But it's quite hard for everyone else to keep to the melody while the different parts are being sung, unless there are enough of us,' Julie agreed. 'We try it in the church choir, especially with Christmas carols, and they do find it difficult.'

'We need to get more of our miserable lot involved in this,' Audrey said at once.

It was almost impossible now to believe that she was, in the beginning, the biggest critic of both me and the choir!

'It would be great if a few more turned up,' I agreed. 'Anyone got any ideas how to encourage people?'

'Well, I have, actually,' Neil responded, to my surprise. He glanced at Lucy as if to apologise for speaking up. 'See, a lot of people in the village have got dogs. We've got a new puppy, and we don't really like leaving him for long. Normally, one or other of us stays at home in the evening, but when Audrey told us about this choir, we both wanted to come.'

'That's true,' Lucy interrupted him. 'Neil wanted me to stay at home with Cuddles – that's our puppy. But I didn't want him having a night out on his own without me.'

I tried to hide a smile as I remembered Audrey telling me about Neil being 'henpecked'.

'And there are other people who don't like leaving their dogs on their own at night because they bark, and upset all their neighbours,' she went on.

'So what do you suggest?' Audrey demanded. 'We can't provide dog-sitters for them, can we?'

'No,' Neil said. 'But could we say dogs are welcome?'

'Oh!' Julie said. She looked at me in surprise. 'That's all very well, but wouldn't it be chaos? Surely the dogs would start howling when we're singing, and they'd bark and run around—'

'I don't know about other dogs, but Sid's used to me singing,' I said with a smile. 'He ignores me. I suppose we could try it, couldn't we, if it might get more people involved? As long as dogs are kept on their leads, and are good and quiet.'

'And house-trained!' Julie put in with a smile. 'We don't want to lose the support of the headmaster by leaving any little accidents in the hall.'

'We need to make it clear that any dog that causes a problem, or makes a noise, will have to be taken outside,' I agreed.

'OK.' Julie nodded. She turned to the others. 'Let your friends know, then: from next week for a trial period, quiet, well-behaved dogs will be allowed to come to our community choir.'

'Great!' Neil nodded enthusiastically. 'Cuddles will love it.'

*

259

We'd agreed to make our meetings a little longer, so we paused for a short break halfway through the evening. As it had been such a warm day, Julie had asked John, the school caretaker, if we could use the little kitchen to get ourselves glasses of water – at the same time, asking for permission for dogs to be allowed.

'He said he'll check with Chris Oakley, the head, but as Chris has dogs himself, he'll probably be fine about it. John also said we could use the staffroom kettle and make ourselves tea and coffee in future,' she said with a smile. 'I know him pretty well, he's been here years. And of course, I know Chris pretty well too.'

'Oh yes, you used to work here, didn't you?' I remembered. 'Teaching music to the children.'

'Yes. There were more kids here back then, and I used to come in twice a week, once to teach the little ones, and once for the older ones. I loved it,' she said wistfully. 'But, of course, now there are so few children at the school, the budget doesn't allow for paid staff apart from the two full-time teachers. I do still come in occasionally as a volunteer, though, when they want a bit of help – learning songs for special occasions.'

'That's nice. And anyway you're busy a lot of the time with your grandson, and nieces and nephews, aren't you?'

'Yes. Luckily I love kids,' she said, laughing.

I sipped my water, listening to the others chatting together, including Sally in their conversations, and smiled to myself, feeling relieved and happy about how the choir had taken off.

'I meant to ask you earlier, Clare,' Julie continued. 'Has there been any sign of Topsy?'

'No.' My smile dropped. How could I have let the little cat slip from my mind? 'In fact, I meant to ask if anyone here had any ideas. Thanks for the reminder.' I stood up and coughed to get everyone's attention. 'Sorry to interrupt you all. I just wondered if anyone happened to have seen Topsy recently – Harry's cat? She'd been spending most of her time with me at the cottage since I moved in there, but I haven't seen her now for about a week, nor has Mike. I've asked all our neighbours, too, as apparently some of them used to feed her occasionally before I came – but nobody's seen her and I'm getting worried.'

'Ah, don't worry, Clare,' Audrey said. 'She's quite a wanderer, that cat. Even when Harry was there, she spent a lot of time with other people – she's such a friendly girl. I bet she's just hanging around someone else for a while.'

'Yes, she even hangs around the pub sometimes,' Neil agreed. 'Although Jack doesn't particularly encourage it!'

'Yes, but like I've told Clare, she needs to watch out for that Archie, the Frenches' cat,' Hazel put in. 'Nasty thing. And apparently he's already had a go at Topsy – you said so, didn't you, Clare?'

'Yes, he did, but she seemed fine afterwards,' I said. 'I wondered if you knew whether Harry had her microchipped,' I added, 'in case she *has* strayed and got lost.'

'Don't rightly remember,' she said, shaking her head. 'She used to be Paul's cat, really. Do you think he'd have done that, Audrey?' she added to her sister.

'I don't recall him mentioning it. You have to take them to the vet's for that, don't you?' Audrey said. 'And that's a pain, to be quite honest, being as there's no vets around here. Well, there's one in Sorrel-by-Sea, but it's way out on the outskirts, so you'd have to drive there.'

Which would take about an hour, no doubt, as it did to anywhere else!

'OK,' I said. 'Well, I'll just have to keep looking for her. And I'll put up some posters around the village. That might help too.'

'We'll all look out for her, won't we, guys?' Neil said. 'I'll ask at the pub whether she's been there.'

'Thanks.' I was grateful for their help, of course. But the happy mood of the evening had dimmed somewhat. I had a horrible feeling Topsy would have come home by now if she was OK.

I asked the group for suggestions for another couple of songs to try after the break, and between us we came up with my personal favourite, and Mike's – 'Memory' – and then, to liven things up a little, and as it had been such a hot, sunny day, we finished with 'Good Day Sunshine'. Everyone was smiling as we parted company.

'Well done, Clare,' Julie said, giving me a hug as we tidied up the room. 'It's working, isn't it? People are getting something from this. They're relaxing and cheering up. It's what we needed here.'

'If only a few more would join,' I said.

'They will. Give it time.'

*

As soon as Sally and I were back at the cottage, I poured us both a glass of wine, and Sally took hers out into the garden, where it was only just beginning to get dark. I stayed inside to call Rachel. I hadn't stopped thinking about what Sally had said earlier, and I wanted to make sure she was OK.

'I'm fine,' she responded as soon as I asked her. But she didn't sound it.

'Come on – you're not. What is it? Has something happened? An argument with Jason?'

She gave a snort, as if she wanted to laugh but couldn't quite bring herself to do so.

'Huh! That wouldn't be anything unusual, would it?' Then she added quickly, 'But it's never serious, Mum, you know that. Honestly, there's nothing to worry about.'

'Everything all right with your work?'

'Yes, fine. Please stop worrying. I don't know what Sally meant. I was probably busy when she called. Everything's fine.'

I knew my daughter too well. I could hear the effort she was putting into her voice, trying to make it sound bright and breezy. Everything was *not* fine.

'Maybe I should come home,' I said.

Silence.

'Maybe I should—' I began to repeat, thinking she hadn't heard me, but she cut me short. 'Mum, you should only come home if it's what you actually want – not for any other reason. When you've had enough, not before.'

It wasn't until a little while after we'd said goodbye that, re-running the conversation in my head, I admitted to myself that when I'd offered to go home, I'd hoped she'd talk me out of it. And she hadn't, had she? Not really.

*

263

The next morning Sally helped me design some posters, using my own photos of Topsy, and we printed these off, covered them in plastic and took them around the village, tying them to lampposts.

'There are people stopping to look at them already,' Sally pointed out. 'Hopefully someone will have seen her.'

'I do hope so,' I said, sighing.

But I soon realised not everyone was going to be as helpful as the members of the choir.

'What's this got to do with you?' demanded a cross-looking woman who read one of our posters over my shoulder while I was attempting to tie it to a lamppost near the pub. 'This cat doesn't belong to you. It was Paul Baker's cat and his father left it in the Reverend's care when he went abroad.'

'I know,' I said, trying to stay calm and not to rise to the bait. 'But as you probably know, I'm staying in Riverside Cottage and Topsy has been living with me. I've been feeding her.'

'And you've gone and lost her already, I suppose,' she said, raising her eyes. She turned away, muttering something under her breath.

I instantly forgot about staying calm and not rising to the bait.

'What did you say?' I demanded.

She swung back to face me. 'I said "bloody tourists". Can't even be trusted to look after a bloody cat.'

'I love that little cat, if you must know!' I said. Stupidly, I felt like crying. It was just too much, being rounded on like this and blamed for something that wasn't my fault when I'd been worrying about Topsy all week. 'I'm doing my best to find her, and *most* people around here are trying to help.'

'And there's really no need to be so rude and unpleasant, is there?' Sally added in a deceptively silky tone.

'Who the hell are you?' retorted the woman. 'Another one from up-country, I suppose, coming here to interfere and throw your weight around?'

'If helping to start a lovely choir here to make everyone feel happier is interfering and throwing her weight around, then my friend has done a great job of it,' Sally replied in the same pleasant manner. 'So it might be nice if you just –' her tone changed abruptly '– buggered off and let her get on with finding the cat.'

'Oh!' The woman reared away from us in shock. 'Well!'

I tried, and failed, to keep the grin off my face.

'Thanks, Sal,' I giggled as Mrs Misery-Guts strutted away. 'That'll be all round the village by lunchtime!'

'Yeah, but they can say what they like about me, can't they?' she laughed, linking her arm through mine. 'I'm only here for a week. Whereas you've got to put up with them for … however long you decide to stay.'

I didn't comment on the hint explicit in that last remark. Mostly because I didn't want to worry – any more than I was already doing – about my daughter and her ambiguous response the previous night when I'd offered to go straight home. We continued on our circuit of the village until we'd used up all our posters. Hazel let us put one in the shop window and, apart from that one rude woman, everyone who stopped to read the posters as we were putting them up gave us, if nothing else, a sympathetic look.

'Let's go to the pub for lunch,' Sally suggested, trying to cheer me up. 'Someone there might have seen her.'

'OK,' I agreed.

Jack was wiping down the bar in his usual indolent manner when we walked in.

'Oh, it's you,' he said without any warmth. 'I've heard you've been insulting Margaret Manners this morning.'

'Is that her name? Really?' Sally laughed. 'How funny! It should be Margaret No-Manners. She was bloody rude to my friend, so I was rude back. Two of your finest lager shandies, please, landlord,' she said sarcastically. 'And your food menu, if it's not too much trouble.'

'Menu's on the blackboard,' he said. 'Sausages are off.'

'We'll just have a sandwich,' I said, giving Sally a warning look. 'Ham and tomato OK for you, Sal?'

'Perfect,' she smiled sweetly.

'White bread or granary?' Jack asked with a sniff.

'Granary, please,' I said.

'Oh, I forgot. Granary's off.'

*

'He's *such* a charmer!' Sally laughed as we settled at a table in the pub garden. 'You know what? I'm finally beginning to understand your fascination with these people. You really could write a book about them!'

'Nobody would want to buy it,' I replied, wearily. 'People like to read *happy* stories.'

I'd felt so optimistic the previous evening, seeing the smiles on the faces of the choir members. I'd been beginning to believe I was making friends here, and maybe even making a difference. Who was I kidding? They were only a small number of the villagers. Most people around here probably still wanted to see the back of me. Nothing had changed.

'Come on, Clare.' Sally laid a hand on mine. 'I'm joking with you. It's obvious Jack's just a miserable so-and-so by nature. Totally the wrong type of person to be a pub landlord. Cheer up. Don't let them grind you down.'

'Sorry. I don't normally let it get to me. I'm just so worried … about Topsy.'

And about my daughter, of course. But I didn't want to talk about that.

We'd just had our sandwiches brought to us – or to be more accurate, plonked on the table in front of us by Jack without a word – and were looking at them critically and wondering if they were safe to eat when there was a loud yell from across the pub garden.

'There you are! Been looking for you. Saw you from outside. Come on, come quickly!'

Sally and I stared at each other.

'What the hell?' Sally muttered. 'It's that awful woman!'

Margaret Manners was waving her arms at us, red in the face and looking very agitated.

'What?' I said, less than graciously. 'What do you want?'

'For God's sake!' she panted, 'I've been *looking* for you. Come on! She don't look too good. I didn't want to touch her.'

'Touch who?' I said. Was the woman mad? What was she talking about?

'The cat! Paul Baker's cat. I've found her. She's in the woods, by the footpath. Hurry up, come with me, I'll show you where she is.'

Sally and I stared at each other. I dropped my sandwich – it was as hard as cardboard anyway – and got to my feet.

'You've found Topsy?' I said.

'My dog sniffed her out.' She indicated the black Labrador sitting obediently by her feet. 'Come on, for the love of God, what are you waiting for? The cat looks half dead already, poor bloody thing.'

She turned, pulling the dog with her, and ran out of the garden. We ran after her. We ran all the way to the footpath, and all the way to the woods. And if anyone looked half dead by the time we reached poor Topsy, it was Mrs Margaret Manners – who had certainly surprised us with her athleticism. Perhaps Sally had done the right thing in telling her off. It seemed to have brought about a miraculous change in her!

CHAPTER 28

Topsy was lying very still, her breathing too fast and too shallow. She looked up at us with dull, expressionless eyes and gave a soft, pitiful little meow.

'Topsy!' I knelt down beside her, cradling her very gently. She felt thin. Most worryingly, although the scratch on her nose had healed, there were other wounds I could see – one on her neck, one on the top of her head – which were bright red, inflamed and angry-looking. 'We need to get her to a vet,' I said, blinking back tears, 'as an emergency. She must have been in another fight – and she looks really poorly.'

'No vets around here, my lovely,' Mrs Manners said. 'Get the poor thing home and feed her up a bit, she'll be all right, won't she?'

'I don't think so,' I said. I swallowed, hard. Had Topsy made her way into the middle of the woods because instinctively she knew her life was ebbing away? I'd heard of animals doing that.

'Come on,' Sally said, rounding on Mrs Manners. 'There surely must be a vet somewhere.'

'Not in this village, there isn't.' The bloody woman sounded almost proud of the fact. 'Nearest one is a mile or so the other side of Sorrel-by-Sea.'

'Then that's where we're going,' I said resolutely. I stripped off my cardigan, laid it on the ground and, with Sally's help, carefully moved poor Topsy onto it, wrapping it around her, and lifted her in it, like a hammock. She weighed next to nothing. 'I'm going to run back to the cottage and bring my car to where the footpath meets the road,' I said to Sally. 'Do you think you could carry Topsy and wait for me there?'

'Of course.' She took the pathetic little bundle from me and I sprinted, even faster than I'd run earlier, back to my car. I was still out of breath when I pulled up at the footpath ten minutes later. It was the most exercise I'd done for years.

Neither Sally nor I spoke much on the journey to the vet's. She'd found the place on Google Maps and I followed the directions, up Steep Hill out of the village, turning down several further narrow lanes and finally coming into a road that would eventually lead to the other side of Sorrel-by-Sea. We found the vet's down a small track beside a farm. Sally had managed to google their phone number while holding poor Topsy on the back seat, and phoned ahead to let them know we were bringing in an emergency.

'Very nasty wounds,' the vet pronounced. 'Good job you've brought her in. She's going to need IV antibiotics and fluids. This bite wound on her neck should heal, once the infection has settled, but the one on her head has turned into an abscess. It'll need draining and cleaning. Does she often get into fights?'

'Not as far as I know. She's not my cat.' I explained whose cat she was and why I was caring for her, and his eyes widened with surprise.

'Oh, I see. Didn't know Harry Baker had a cat.'

'She was his son's, apparently.'

He nodded. 'Well, we've never seen the cat here before. I'm going to have to keep her in for a few days. Is she insured?'

'Er ... I don't know.' I looked at poor little Topsy, lying there looking so weak and poorly. 'But it doesn't matter what it costs. Just make her better, please.'

'Don't worry, she should make a full recovery now we've got her here,' he assured me.

'Thank goodness.' I swallowed. 'Just one other thing: once she's feeling better, could you check her to see if she has a microchip?'

'Sure. If not, would you like me to put one in?'

'Yes please,' I said. 'It would save any worry, wouldn't it, if she were to go missing again?'

I was aware that perhaps it wasn't my decision to make. But surely, Harry, like any cat owner, would be relieved, when he came back, to know his cat had been cared for properly and not allowed to stray? And for the rest of the time I was here, looking after her, I would certainly be relieved!

*

We took the drive home more slowly, having said goodbye to Topsy and feeling reassured by the vet's promise to call me later with an update. By the time we arrived back in Little Sorrel, the place was already buzzing with gossip.

'I hear that darn cat of the Frenches attacked poor Topsy again,' said Hazel, having seen us pass the village shop and run up the lane to meet us as we got out of the car. 'Will she live? Margaret Manners has been telling everyone she was as good as dead.'

'She's got an abscess from a bite wound and a bad infection,' I said. 'But she should start to recover once that's been treated.' I frowned. 'Who said anything about the Frenches' cat being responsible?'

'Well, stands to reason, doesn't it? That Archie's well known for being aggressive to all the other cats around here. And you said he'd already had a go at Topsy.'

'Yes. But we've got no way of knowing it was definitely him this time,' I pointed out. 'I don't want to start rumours and accusations flying.'

'Huh!' Hazel said, giving me a look. 'We might not have any proof, but it's what everyone's saying.'

*

'You don't really believe there's any doubt about it, do you?' Sally said when we were back indoors. I'd put the kettle on and then collapsed on the sofa, exhausted from the stress and worry of our rush to the vet's. 'I mean, it seems pretty obvious, from what you say happened before—'

'Yes, I agree,' I said. 'But what difference does it make now? Cats will fight, unfortunately, and I can't keep her locked up indoors. It's not as if she's even mine!'

'True, I suppose.'

'I will definitely keep a lookout for that Archie though, in future,' I added. 'I'll get Sid to chase him away if he comes into the garden again.'

Sid, on hearing his name, looked up and gave an excited little bark.

'All right,' I laughed. 'I know you're overdue for a walk. Let's have a cup of tea then we'll take you out. Maybe Leo will come with us – it's nearly school finishing time.'

In fact, Leo was knocking at the door before we'd even finished our tea. Sid ran to meet him, dancing around his legs in delight, and then ran back to where I hung his lead, barking frenziedly.

'Mum said you had to rush Topsy to the vet's,' Leo said. 'Is she going to be all right? Mum said she'd been beaten up by George French's cat.'

'Well, we don't know that for sure, Leo,' I said, becoming increasingly aware that I was going to have to repeat this many times before anyone began to believe it. 'But she was hurt quite badly. She'll be all right, though. The vet will make her better.'

'Good. I hate that Archie cat.'

'Don't hate him, Leo,' I said gently. 'He's just a cat. Animals aren't spiteful, they just follow their instincts.'

We put on Sid's lead and took him along the lane and down to the river. The usual little gang of children was

273

playing on the raft, but Reggie was standing alone on the towpath, watching them. He looked lonely and crestfallen, and reminded me of Leo the first time I'd seen him here.

'Come and walk Sid with us, Reggie?' Leo called to him.

Reggie turned, his face breaking into a smile. 'Yes, please!'

Leo handed him the lead. 'Don't worry about those others,' he advised him. 'They only leave us out because they're scared of George. When George goes up to senior school, it'll be different around here – won't it, Clare? Alex said that to me at my birthday party. I don't know why. Maybe he doesn't like George either.'

'Alex is right, I think probably it will be different then,' I agreed, smiling at the boys. 'George will probably get back from school later in the afternoons, for a start, and he'll have too much homework to play out on the river so much.'

'Good,' said Reggie with feeling.

'But at least you two are friends again now,' I added. 'That's the most important thing.'

We'd only walked a few more yards when there was a shout from behind us.

'Clare! Wait up!'

I turned around to see Old Robbie, panting as he rushed to catch up with us. I walked back to meet him, followed by Sally and the two boys.

'What's this I hear about Paul Baker's cat?' he said, frowning at me anxiously. 'Some folks say she's at the vet's, some say she's dead—'

'No, she's not dead,' I said quickly. 'But it was a close call.'

'Some folks say she was in a fight,' he went on, seemingly unsure where to look now. 'Been attacked, like, by another cat.'

'Yes. She had bites that had gone septic.'

'Sorry to hear that.' He fidgeted from one foot to the other, and then went on in a rush, 'And would you say that was our Archie that's done it? That's what folks are saying.' He looked behind him now, at the sound of footsteps, as his son came out of the boathouse and strode towards us. 'Folks are saying we should have had Archie neutered to stop him fighting. Like I told you, Young Robbie. Like I've been telling you for years, we should've done.'

Young Robbie stopped in front of his father, staring at him. I waited for the outburst, but nothing happened.

'Listen,' I said eventually, as everyone was looking at me, waiting for my reaction, 'I don't really care what everyone's saying. The truth is, we don't know which cat attacked Topsy. Cats get into fights, don't they, that's the way it is. She was quite badly hurt, but she's going to be OK, that's all that matters.'

'If it *was* our Archie,' Old Robbie persisted, 'we should pay for the vet, for Paul Baker's cat. We should've had Archie neutered. He attacked someone else's cat once—'

'Don't worry about the vet bill,' I interrupted quietly. 'I haven't checked yet with Mike about whether Topsy was insured. If not, I'm happy to settle it—'

'She's not even your cat!' Old Robbie said, looking at me in surprise. 'Mike should get the money for it from Harry.'

'Well, maybe.' I shrugged. 'I know Topsy's not my cat, but I've been looking after her, so I feel responsible. And as for getting your cat neutered, I agree, for what it's worth. I'm no expert, but I've heard it can stop a lot of unpleasant male-cat behaviour. But that's up to you, of course. It might stop him fighting, it might not; maybe you should ask the vet's advice.'

'So you're not going to make a complaint about our Archie?' Old Robbie said. 'Will you tell Harry?'

'Of course not! I don't even know Harry, but why would I want to worry him about this? From what I hear, he's got troubles enough.'

Old Robbie nodded thoughtfully. 'So you're going to sort it out? That's good of you, Clare. Isn't it?' he added to his son.

Young Robbie nodded. He kept nodding for a while, looking at the ground. We all waited. I thought he probably wouldn't respond. He'd just walk away with that arrogant swagger of his, that angry toss of the head, as usual. But he didn't. He looked up at me and met my eyes.

'Yes,' he said quietly. 'It's good of you. Thank you for not making a thing of this. Let's face it, we all know it was probably our Archie that did it. He can be a nasty vicious creature, but my boy loves him. And maybe there's not enough love around here these days.' He coughed, looked around awkwardly as if he'd said too much, then added, 'I'll talk to the vet, then. About neutering him.' And he turned and walked back to the boathouse – for once, without the swagger.

The rest of us stared after him in silence. There wasn't much more we could say. Old Robbie nodded at me and turned to follow his son. Leo and Reggie began to run in front of us again with Sid, who'd been whining with anxiety to get on with his walk. And Sally linked arms with me, pulling me close as she whispered in my ear, 'Well done, mate. You've cracked it.'

'Cracked it?' I repeated, laughing at her. 'Cracked what?'

'The opposition, of course. The Frenches – the last bastion of Little Sorrel's defence against you. They'll be eating out of your hand from now on. Oh, I *am* glad I came to stay. I do like a happy ending!'

I shook my head. Happy ending? Hardly, with poor Topsy at the vet's on life-saving treatment.

'Well, I have to admit,' I said, 'it was quite gratifying to hear that little speech from Young Robbie, of all people.'

'He'll be asking to join your choir next!' Sally joked.

'Oh yes. And pigs might fly across the Sorrel River!'

Young Robbie, singing in the choir? Well, at least that had given me a laugh.

CHAPTER 29

Mike knocked on my door soon after we returned home from our walk.

'I've heard,' he said without any preamble, 'about Topsy. Will she be all right?'

'The vet says she should be.' I sighed, suddenly feeling tired from all the emotion of the day. 'Mike, do you know whether Harry had her insured?'

'No, sorry, I don't know. He didn't say anything to me about paying for it, renewing it, or anything. I'll give him a call.'

'Thanks – but can you make it sound like you're just wondering about it in case you need to pay for a renewal or something like that? There's no need to worry him, is there, if Topsy's going to make a full recovery?'

'I suppose that's true. Although …' He gave me a very direct look. 'Perhaps, as Topsy's owner, he *ought* to know what happened. We all know who was most likely to blame for this, don't we?'

'Yes, probably. But how is it going to help Harry, or anyone, if we all gang up on the Frenches about it? They might not be my most favourite family around here, but I've just had both Old Robbie and his son falling over themselves to apologise in case this was Archie's fault – and offering to pay for the vet bill and to ask the vet about getting Archie neutered!'

'My goodness, woman, you're a miracle worker,' he said, gazing at me in that way of his that made me feel uncomfortable. 'They actually admitted their cat was probably responsible?'

'In so many words, although I was careful to say it might not have been him. Well, it's true, it might not!' I said, laughing now at the look of disbelief on Mike's face. 'Cats *do* fight. Topsy might even have initiated it, for all we know.'

'I think that's pretty unlikely,' he said. 'But yes, you're right of course, it's best not to cast stones. Good news that they're going to get Archie neutered. That should calm him down. And they're paying Topsy's vet bills too? Unbelievable!'

'I said they offered. But I'm not letting them. It wouldn't be fair.'

'Oh. Well, I suppose that is the Christian way of looking at it,' he said – a bit reluctantly, I thought. 'But if Harry says Topsy isn't insured, I'll have to tell him what's happened. He'll pay the vet.'

'It's OK. I'll pay it.' I shrugged. 'I've got quite attached to Topsy.'

'But that's hardly your responsibility,' he protested.

'I'd like to,' I said firmly. 'Please, let's leave it at that.'

He frowned. 'Well, we can argue about that when you get the bill,' he said eventually. 'And when I find out about the insurance.'

*

'He's never going to agree to you paying for it,' Sally said after I'd closed the door. 'Not unless you come out as the heiress of a wealthy mad author.'

'I've got no intention of "coming out", as you put it, to anyone here,' I retorted. 'They already think I'm a stuck-up, snooty Londoner. Imagine how it would go down if they knew I could probably afford to—'

'—buy the entire village?' she joked.

'I was going to say, live somewhere a bit more upmarket. They'd have even more reason to wonder what I'm doing here.' I looked at her face and added quietly, 'Like you do. I know you wonder, too.'

She shrugged. 'No, I get it, I really do. I admit I wouldn't get it if you said you were going to stay here permanently. But I know you won't do that, because of your family.'

'Exactly,' I said, trying not to look at her. A wave of guilt washed over me. My family. They missed me, they needed me – Sally had told me that. How could I even be contemplating staying here? Because, let's face it, I *had* contemplated it. Especially recently, since I seemed to have become a little more accepted by some of the villagers. I was thinking of Little Sorrel as home, without really admitting it, even to myself, as if it was a guilty little secret.

Fortunately, we didn't have time to discuss my intentions – guilty or otherwise – because just then there was another knock at the door, Sid started barking his head off, and when I opened the door I saw why: Margaret Manners was standing on the step with her Labrador.

'Sorry to disturb,' she said briskly. 'Quiet, Brutus!' she added sharply to her dog, who had now joined in with Sid's excited barking. 'I wanted to know how the little cat got on at the vet's.'

By the time I'd filled her in with Topsy's prognosis, both dogs were straining to get at each other and play, so I suggested she came in and had a cup of tea while we let them out to chase around in the garden. I reasoned that it would probably do me more good than harm to make a friend of Mrs Manners!

'Hello again,' she said somewhat curtly to Sally, who was clearly still being regarded with even more suspicion than me. Sally treated her to a beaming smile, which seemed to take her aback slightly, and went to put the kettle on. I followed Sally into the kitchen to get out the biscuits, and when I went back into the lounge it was to find our guest staring at my photos on the sideboard.

'Did you take these?' she asked me, sounding as if she didn't quite want to believe it.

'Yes. It's – it was – my job. And Sally's. We're both professional photographers.'

'Of dogs?' she said. 'And cats?'

'Well, no, not officially. I've just taken that up, really. Since I've been away from home.'

'I see.' She managed to sound disapproving, probably at the very idea of me being here, away from home. But suddenly her tone changed as she turned to me and added, 'These are good. Very good. Can you take some of Brutus for me?'

'Your dog?' I said, in surprise. Well, why not? It might make her dislike me a little less! 'Yes, I'd be happy to, of course.'

'Not now,' she went on, raising an eyebrow at the exuberant barking going on in the garden. 'He's too excited. Come round tomorrow? I'll get him nice and calm. He'll pose for you.'

'OK. What's your address?' I asked, before correcting myself. People here didn't really refer to *addresses*. They didn't need to. 'I mean, which house is yours?'

'The yellow cottage with the thatched roof,' she said. 'White front door. I'll expect you at eleven. What are your charges?'

'Oh, I don't—' I began, and then something made me change my mind. She was treating this as a business deal. I didn't need the money, but why should she take me seriously, especially as I'd told her I was a professional, if I didn't charge her anything? I took a deep breath. 'Well, as I'm only starting with pet photography, I'll do you a special offer,' I suggested. 'Twenty pounds for the session, including a print of your choice of photo.'

'That sounds cheap,' she said.

'Well, as I say, special offer price. More if you want to choose more photos, obviously. I'll take quite a few for you to choose from.'

'Can you get them framed?'

'Yes, of course,' I said smoothly, wondering whether there was a picture framer in Sorrel-by-Sea. 'I'll price that up for you and let you know.'

'Right, you're on,' she said. 'I might get you to do one of my daughter's rabbit, too. It could be her birthday present.'

Sally had come back now with the tray of teas and I realised I was still standing in the middle of the room, cuddling the biscuit tin.

'Great!' I said cheerfully. 'Well, let's have our cuppa, shall we? Thanks, Sal.'

'D'you photograph pets too?' Margaret asked Sally as she sat down with her tea.

'No. Mostly weddings,' Sally said. 'In London.'

'Oh.' Margaret raised her eyebrows. 'I didn't think folk in London bothered with getting married these days.'

'That's true, most of them don't,' Sally agreed. 'But those who do tend to spend a small fortune on the wedding. And that includes hundreds of photographs of everything right down to close-ups of the bride's shoes and back views of her hairdo.'

'Huh! Typical,' Margaret snorted. 'More money than sense, I suppose, like most of 'em from up-country. Well, good for you, girl, give them what they ask for and let them damn well pay for it – the darn fools!'

She banged down her empty cup and stalked to the back door to call her dog. I wasn't sure whether Sally had been accepted or not. But one thing was pretty clear: I'd been right when I suspected that, if anyone around here found out I'd come into money, I'd be dismissed with the same contempt as those *darn fools* who were Sally's best clients!

*

283

The vet called me that evening to say Topsy was already looking a little better but that he might need to keep her in for at least another twenty-four hours. A little later Mike came back again with the news that Harry *hadn't* renewed the pet insurance. Paul had paid for a policy originally, but of course, since he'd passed away, renewing it had been the last thing on Harry's mind.

'He did ask why I needed to know,' Mike said, looking uncomfortable. 'But I managed to make it sound like an innocent enquiry.'

'Well done,' I said.

'I guess you're right. No point worrying him.' He turned to go, then looked back at me and asked, 'Was that Margaret Manners I saw here earlier? It was her who found Topsy, wasn't it? She's told everyone!'

'Yes. And she's now asked me to take some photos of Brutus – her Labrador.'

'Ah, that's good! I *said* you should set yourself up in business, didn't I? I hope you're going to charge her?'

'Yes, but not too much. It's a new venture for me.'

'I'll spread the word,' he said cheerfully.

'Um ... well, thank you. But of course, I probably won't be here for much longer,' I warned him. I had looked over my shoulder, lowering my voice as I said this, but Sally was watching the TV, laughing out loud at some daft comedy.

'Oh. Well, if you say so,' he said, looking at me sadly. 'I was rather hoping ... but of course ... eventually, I suppose ...' He trailed off, leaving me feeling that I should have said more, made it sound more definite. 'Well, good-night, then, Clare.'

He walked away, looking wounded.

*

The photoshoot at Margaret Manners' house the next morning went well. More to the point, I surprised myself by how much I enjoyed it. Brutus was a good subject and I enjoyed photographing him. We did some posed shots indoors – helped by promises of dog treats held aloft while he responded to 'Sit' and 'Stay' – and then went out into Margaret's surprisingly big garden, where I took lots of more natural photos of him bounding towards me, rolling on the newly cut grass, and chasing after his ball.

'I'll upload these, and you can come and look at them on my laptop and choose which you'd like to have printed,' I said.

'Haven't you got a website?' she said. 'You need a website if you want more customers.'

'Well, yes, I suppose I will need one eventually.' I still hadn't quite got used to the idea that I could take this up, seriously, as a business. In one way, the thought of it excited me, but in another, I felt too unsure of what lay ahead and where my life was going. 'I'll have to give it some thought.'

'Well, I'll pay you in cash as I don't suppose you've got a card machine or invoices or anything like that yet,' she said with a slightly disapproving tone as she rummaged in her purse.

'Oh, wait until you see the pictures. You might not like them!' I joked.

'True, I suppose.' She put her purse away. 'I'll come over and have a look at them tomorrow then, shall I? How's your choir going, by the way? I've heard everyone talking about it.'

'Yes, I think it's going well,' I said, slightly surprised by the change of subject.

'Good. I hear you're going to let people bring their dogs. Perhaps I'll come along myself next week and bring Brutus.'

I almost had to pick myself up off the floor.

'Oh, yes, please do!' I managed to say. 'I think you'd enjoy it.'

*

'So you've made another friend,' Sally said with satisfaction when I told her about the exchange. 'You might have a whole crowd of new members at your next choir meeting, especially now you're allowing dogs. I *almost* wish I could stay a bit longer and see how it goes.'

'Stay, then!'

'Some of us still have to go to work,' she reminded me.

'I know. Sorry. You're making me feel guilty now.'

'Why? Don't be daft, why should you feel guilty? If one of *my* ex-husbands was to get left a fortune by a best-selling author who'd fallen in love with him, I'd bloody well enjoy every penny of it, I can tell you! Good luck to you.'

'But seriously, Sal, there's a limit to how much leisure it's possible to enjoy. It'd be different if I was older – old enough to retire, I mean. I'd feel like I'd earned it. I can't imagine going on like this – being *on holiday* – for the rest of my life.'

'So give the pet photography a go. Take it seriously, set yourself up in business, and do as much as you want to. It'll be an interest for you, when you come home.'

She looked up at me a little sharply as she said this. *When you come home.*

'Yes,' I said quietly. 'You're right. I think I'd enjoy it.'

And she was right, too, of course, about going home. Just … perhaps not quite yet.

CHAPTER 30

The last few days of Sally's stay passed all too quickly. Once we'd collected Topsy from the vet's, we had to keep her indoors until her wounds were completely healed. She didn't like that, of course, but she seemed too weak to make much protest. She looked pathetically thin but the vet had assured me she'd soon be back to her old self, eating ravenously and running around outside. Meanwhile, it was lovely to see how Sid lay protectively beside her while she rested and recovered. I'd paid the vet bill without making any further mention of it to Mike or anyone else but despite this, the story of how I had (apparently) rescued Paul Baker's cat and taken on her care seemed to have spread round the entire village and I found myself in the most unexpected situation of being stopped in the street by people who had previously ignored me, and being thanked effusively, as if Topsy were their own. I suppose, in a way, she was. She'd become the concern of the whole village, and a symbol of their feelings for the young man they'd lost.

On the Friday, Margaret Manners came to look at my downloaded pictures of Brutus. She seemed to love them, and in fact ordered several extra prints, as well as the one included in our agreement, and wanted them all framed.

'I'll need a while to organise that,' I warned her. 'I'll order the prints straight away, though.'

'That's fine. I'd also like you to come and photograph my daughter's rabbit,' she said. 'Can you do it today?'

She duly took us to her daughter's house, where the rabbit – a pretty little thing with long ears and long grey and white fur – lived in a hutch in the garden but was allowed out into a run.

'We call him Brex,' said the daughter, Mandy, watching him lovingly as he hopped around the run, scratching at the wire netting as if he would much rather be outside it. 'It's short for Brexit.'

I laughed. 'Why?'

'Because he's desperate to get out,' she said with a grin, 'but he can't find a way to do it.'

'Silly name, if you ask me,' Margaret sniffed, but it had broken the ice and when Sally and I had stopped laughing, we were soon chatting happily to Mandy, who seemed a lot more relaxed than her mother.

I took photos of Brex inside his run, and several of Mandy holding him in her arms.

'You'll be pleased with the pictures,' Margaret told her. 'You can choose the one you like best. I'm doing this for your birthday, remember.'

'Thanks, Mum,' Mandy said, giving me a smile. 'I'll recommend you to some friends of mine, Clare – Annabel and Ravi. They've got a little cocker spaniel, Jet; they've mentioned getting professional photos done of him. And Ravi's mum, who lives in Sorrel-by-Sea, has two Siamese cats. I'm sure she'd be interested too. Have you got a card?'

'Sorry, I haven't, yet,' I apologised. 'But I'll give you my mobile number, and I'll have to look into getting some cards printed. I've only just started doing this.'

And I hadn't even been too sure whether I was going to do it! But it seemed it had become a *fait accompli*.

'I'm actually sorry to be leaving,' Sally said as she finished packing her case on the Saturday morning.

'Well, there's no need to sound so surprised about it!' I protested.

'Oh, you know what I mean. Obviously, I'm sorry to be leaving *you*. But I've had such a good time, and to be quite honest, I didn't expect to because of everything you'd been saying! I didn't think we'd be talking to people and making friends the way we have. I imagined I'd be spending my entire time trying to persuade you to come home.'

'Well, to be fair, *I* didn't expect people to suddenly start being more friendly, either. So, have you changed your mind now, then? About persuading me to come home?'

She looked at me for a moment, her head on one side. 'I guess so. It's pretty clear you're happy here. But you *will* come back eventually, won't you.'

It wasn't said as a question. I didn't answer. She sighed and went back to her packing.

'Well, until you do, I'll keep an eye on that daughter of yours for you, shall I?'

I'd called Rachel again twice since our conversation earlier that week and hadn't been particularly reassured by her overplayed pretence at being absolutely fine. I knew something wasn't quite right, but she plainly didn't want to talk to me about it.

'That's nice of you, but I'm pretty sure it's just … I don't know, perhaps she and Jason are going through a rough patch.'

'I'll make some excuse to pop round,' Sally insisted, straightening up from her suitcase and coming to give me a hug now. 'Don't pretend you're not worried – I know you are. And I know Rachel won't want you to be. I'll report back.'

'Thank you.' I hugged her back. 'I'm going to miss you. Drive carefully.'

She laughed. 'Carefully? There's no other way possible to drive up that bloody lane!'

*

I was busy during the next few days. Mandy came, with her mother, to look at the photos of Brex(it) the rabbit and choose their favourite. I asked Mike if he knew whether there were any picture framers in Sorrel-by-Sea, and he told me there was one Harry had always used, which was good enough for me. So while I waited for the prints for my new clients to arrive, I decided to go and meet the guy and discuss sizes and prices of frames.

Young Robbie came out of the boathouse in response to my shout, giving me a nod and something surprisingly close to a smile.

'Sorrel-by-Sea, is it, Clare?' he asked calmly.

'Yes, please.' I felt that, in the interest of this new civility between us, I should continue the conversation, so I explained that I was going to see the picture framer about framing my pet photographs, adding that Margaret and her daughter had started me off on this new venture.

He remained silent for a while, nodding to himself thoughtfully as he waited for me to settle myself in the boat.

'Maybe I should get you to photograph our Archie,' he said. This time I definitely didn't imagine it – there was a smile playing about his mouth, and a creasing around his eyes that hugely improved his appearance. 'He's more likely to sit still and behave himself now he's had his ... er ... his manhood done away with.'

I laughed at the awkward expression, and he joined in.

'You've had him done already?' I said.

'Yep. You were right. The vet said it should calm him down. Hopefully it'll stop him fighting so much, and being so smelly and all.' He dropped the smile and added quietly, 'How's the little cat doing now?'

'Oh, Topsy's much better, thank you. She has to stay indoors until the vet checks her over again, but everything seems to be healing up and she's eating well.'

'Good.' He nodded again. 'Wouldn't have wanted anything to happen to her. Especially not as she was ... Paul's cat.'

'I know. I understand.'

We both fell silent as he pulled out across the estuary and into the river. I sat back, listening to the swish of the oars, watching the water rise and fall. It was a grey, overcast day and the hues of the sky and the river were muted, like a painting where the colours had been washed over. But it was still warm, warm enough to trail my hand over the boat, enjoying the coolness of the water on my skin.

'Watch the fish don't bite you,' Robbie joked, and I smiled, while marvelling to myself that he was actually *joking* with me, smiling and laughing with me. How things had changed!

As if reading my mind, he cleared his throat and said, 'I was wrong about you, Clare, and I'm sorry for that. You're not like other incomers. You've done nothing but good for this village. I understand from the gossip around and about that you've settled the vet's bill for Paul's cat—'

I shook my head. 'That's not something anyone needs to concern themselves about—'

'People gossip, you know they do. But they respect you, that's the thing. You've fitted in here. What with your choir and the way you've stood up to people – people's rudeness. Myself included,' he added, raising his eyes to meet mine. 'So I just wanted to say I'm sorry for it.'

'I appreciate that, Robbie,' I said. 'Thank you.'

'I'm not going to ask if you're staying here permanently,' he added, looking away again. 'But if you did, well, I'd say it'd be a good thing for Little Sorrel.'

I nodded, feeling almost too choked up to respond. Perhaps Sally had been right that I had seemed to have overcome the final bastion of resistance in the form of Young Robbie French. Was he right – did people actually respect me now? And was I going to consider the thousand-dollar question, the one he couldn't bring himself to ask and which I seemed to have even more difficulty answering: would I ever decide to stay here permanently?

*

If any one thing helped me to answer that question, or rather, to make me admit I'd known the answer all along, it was the choir meeting that Tuesday evening. I'd been looking forward to our inaugural Dogs Welcome choir practice, but unsure whether to take Sid along. He was normally well behaved, but I'd be too busy leading the singing to hold his lead and keep an eye on him. Luckily, Sid had a little friend who was more than happy to take charge of him! Leo met me at the corner of Duck Lane and proudly took Sid's lead, telling him he had to be a good boy as he was going to look after him all evening.

We arrived at the school a little later than usual, and as I pushed open the door, I frowned in surprise at the hubbub coming from inside. Voices raised – lots of them – chatting, laughing, and trying out snatches of the songs we'd learned so far. Well, it was nice to know my little band of loyal members were in such an upbeat mood to begin the session! I stepped inside, letting the door swing closed behind me as I stared in shock around me. The 'little band' had swelled to at least twice its previous size. Margaret Manners was there with Brutus on his lead. Her daughter Mandy had come too, and a young couple Mandy introduced as her friends Annabel and Ravi, who had a little black spaniel with them.

'Jet loves music,' Annabel said, smiling at the little dog. 'He won't try to join in,' she added quickly. 'He just dances.'

A dancing cocker spaniel? This I could not wait to see! Julie had also persuaded Chris Oakley, the head teacher, to come along with his wife and their two collies, Punch and Judy. And Chris had got the school caretaker to come too, so that he could see for himself that the dogs would be kept under control and not do any damage to the school hall. Everybody seemed to have invited someone else – their brother, sister, friend or neighbour – and at least half of the newcomers had a dog or two with them. And there wasn't a surly or sad expression on a single face, human or canine!

'Oh!' I said, feeling quite overwhelmed. 'How lovely to see so many of you here.'

'We've heard how much the others have enjoyed it,' said Mandy.

'And how much good it's been doing, too,' added Chris, 'helping people who were feeling depressed.' He smiled around at us all, then went on in the kind of voice I suspected he used for school assemblies, 'Animals bring us pleasure, don't they – and comfort, too, when we need it? And singing does the same. So I think it's a brilliant idea to combine the two. A double dose of comfort and happiness.'

'I'm so glad you all agree,' I said. 'Welcome, everyone – people *and* dogs.' I smiled at Julie. 'Shall we get started straight away?'

'Can we do "If You're Happy and You Know It" first, like before?' Reggie called out, and I laughed and agreed. None of the adults seemed to mind in the slightest and the men in particular joined in with gusto.

By the time the session was finished, I felt like I was floating on cloud nine. Everyone had been keen, cheerful and enthusiastic, and some of their voices were superb, including those I had previously thought sounded weak. Some of the dogs were startled, and in some cases even a bit alarmed when we first all broke into song together, and there had been a round of woofing and a few whines to begin with, as well as some of them pulling on their leads, wanting to sniff or play with the other dogs. But they'd gradually all settled surprisingly well, perhaps reassured by the calmer, older ones who just twitched their ears from time to time as they lay dozing by their owners' feet. Neil and Lucy had to take their puppy Cuddles outside a couple of times but it was nice to see how much happier they seemed, to have their little dog with them. Everyone appeared to enjoy the presence of the dogs, even those who didn't have pets of their own.

In fact, it was hard to believe the change from our first meeting just a few short weeks earlier. I walked home with Julie, both of us excited and happy, and couldn't keep the smile off my face as I went into the cottage and put on the kettle.

I'm going to stay here, I was thinking. This has made up my mind. The family would understand, they'd want me to be happy. I'd visit them, of course – all the time – and they'd come here too, for holidays as often as possible. Other people did this, after all – lots of people moved away from their families and managed to make it work. We'd still talk to each other, still see each other – that's what Skype was for! I was still smiling as I turned on my phone – I'd had it on silent for the duration of the choir practice – and checked for messages. There was a voicemail from Rachel. Ah, I thought. Hopefully Sally has called on her and she's ringing me to reassure me that everything's fine. Perhaps I'll tell her now ... or perhaps I'll leave it a little longer. Maybe I'll tell Daniel first.

Then I listened to the voicemail message. And everything changed in an instant.

CHAPTER 31

'I'm sorry, Mum.' I'd called Rachel straight back, and she was crying. Gasping, sobbing, in a way that made my heart race and my skin prickle with fear. 'I didn't want to tell you but Sally came round and she knew – she guessed – she could see from the state I was in—'

'State?' I'd jumped to my feet, as if in readiness, I didn't know for what. 'What do you mean, what state? What's happened?' The most alarming scenarios were playing out in my mind. What didn't she want to tell me, and why not?

'I feel so ill! I'm so sick, all the time, I just keep being sick, it won't stop, and I can't even go to work—'

Ill? Sick? Ill, and she didn't want to tell me? By now, my heart felt as if it was about to stop beating. I could hardly breathe.

'What's wrong?' I heard myself ask. It didn't sound like my voice. 'Why are you ill – what is it? Have you been to the doctor? Why didn't you tell me? I'd have come home! I'll come home now.'

'Oh, Mum, that's why I didn't want to tell you. I don't want you to cut your holiday short. I'd have told you eventually, of course I would, but Sally guessed and she said I must tell you, you'd be upset if I didn't.'

'Rachel, of course you should have told me! Never mind about my holiday.'

Holiday. That's what it was, of course. In a tiny part of the back of my mind, the tiny space beyond the anxiety about my daughter, I almost laughed at myself for ever thinking it was anything other than a holiday. This wasn't my real life. My children were. Rachel was, with her illness. Oh God, I'd never forgive myself for this. For not being with her when she needed me. 'I've been *asking* you whether you were really all right. I knew something was wrong.'

'Wrong?' She sniffed, and gave a short little laugh. 'Well, it depends how you look at it, I suppose. It was what we wanted, obviously. But not like this.'

'What you wanted?' The spinning, the turmoil, in my head slowed to a stop for a moment. 'Hang on, what do you mean? What was what you wanted? What *is* wrong with you?'

'Well, obviously it's, you know, what they used to call morning sickness, but I've got the type that's not just mornings, it's non-stop, and the doctor said it might go on till at least halfway through the pregnancy, and I might end up in hospital because sometimes I can't even keep water down, and the baby might—'

'*Pregnancy*?' I heard my strange new voice yell. I sat down again. 'Baby?'

'Didn't I say?' Her voice sounded tired and weak. No wonder. 'Sorry.'

'Oh my God, Rachel!' Now I was the one crying. 'Oh, that's *wonderful* news. I mean, obviously, it *would* be wonderful if it wasn't for the sickness – wouldn't it?'

'Of course it would. We were over the moon when the test was positive. It's what we both wanted. And even when I started being sick, I knew it was normal, I thought it would pass. And Jason's been so good, looking after me, taking as much time off as he could, but I feel so terrible, Mum! It's not fair, I wanted to enjoy it, and I can't, I just want this awful sickness to end!'

'Right. I'm coming home.' I got up again, ridiculously looking for my shoes, my coat. 'I'm leaving right now. I'll be with you by—'

'Don't be silly. It's late, I don't want you to drive all this way in the dark.'

'I'll come first thing in the morning, then.' That'd give me time to pack, at least.

She didn't argue. She just sighed, a long exhale of exhaustion.

'I'm sorry,' she said eventually, her voice sounding full of tears again. 'I didn't want to ask you. But Sally said you'd *want* to come home if you knew, and you'd *want* to know about the baby—'

'Of course I did. I mean I do. I'll come and look after you. Jason has to go to work, and you don't want to end up in hospital.' I smiled, the reality of it suddenly hitting me. Needless to say, I hated to think of Rachel feeling so ill, but at the end of it all, there was going to be a baby! I was going to be a grandma! 'When's the baby due?' I asked gently.

'The beginning of February,' she said. 'If I survive that long.'

'You will, sweetheart.' I tried to do the maths. She must already be about three months along. She might even have known – or have suspected – that she was pregnant when she came to visit me here at the end of May. Or soon after, anyway. I felt a renewed stab of pain at the thought that she'd kept this from me, not wanting to worry me, not wanting me to rush home. 'You'll be fine. I'm packing my bag right now.'

'Thank you, Mum,' she said weakly. 'I must admit … it'll be lovely to have you back.'

I couldn't think straight. I packed, tidied up the kitchen – as if it mattered – and went to bed, but tossed and turned, unable to sleep. I was up early in the morning, and after dishing up Topsy's food, I stood looking down at her while she ate. She still wasn't allowed outside. What was I going to do about her? I'd have to tell Mike, obviously. I rushed round to knock on his door but there was no response. I didn't even have his phone number – or Julie's – or anyone else's here. There hadn't ever been any need, the village being so small: everyone was within a couple of minutes' walk. I went back into the cottage and started to write a note. I'd have to put it through his letterbox with the keys to the cottage. I had no idea how long I'd be gone. I took a deep breath, looking up from writing my note, staring out at the little garden. I had no idea whether I'd ever come back. The holiday was over.

As it happened, I'd just dropped the note and the keys through Mike's letterbox when he appeared down the lane, carrying his newspapers. He always liked to go for an early morning walk and bring them back to read with his breakfast. He gave me a cheery wave when he saw me on his doorstep but frowned in concern as he came closer.

'Are you all right, Clare? You don't look well.'

'I'm fine. I just didn't sleep much. Look, I'm sorry, Mike, but I've got to go. I've put the keys through your letterbox with a note. I've asked you to look after Topsy – please. She's finished the antibiotics but she has to see the vet again for a check-up before she can be allowed out.' I was aware that I was reciting exactly what was in the note and being a little abrupt about it too. I couldn't help it. I wanted to get going. 'And please say goodbye to Julie. And everyone. And ...' Here I faltered slightly. 'Especially Leo. I can't ... I'd go and say goodbye myself, but he'll be at school by now, and I ... I ... ' I swallowed. I couldn't afford to get emotional about this.

'What's happened?' Mike said, his face etched with anxiety. 'Is something wrong? Where are you going? Can I do anything to help?'

'Just the cat, please, Mike. Oh, and I've left some pictures with the framer in Sorrel-by-Sea. I've explained in the note. If someone could pick them up – they've been paid for. I'm sorry. I have to go home. My daughter's ill. I mean, she's pregnant but she's very poorly. She needs me. I don't know when … or if …' I stopped, shook my head, and gave a shrug, as if it didn't matter.

'I see. Of course you must go to your daughter.' His eyes were full of compassion. 'I understand. But please take your time and drive carefully, Clare.'

'I will. Tell Julie I hope the choir keeps going. And tell Kerry I'm sorry. Sorry for letting Leo down.' The school summer holidays were about to begin. He'd been looking forward to spending more time with Sid. 'Thank you, Mike. For … well, for everything.' I wanted to say, *for being my friend, when nobody else was.* But I couldn't get the words out.

To my surprise, he dropped his newspapers on the ground and enfolded me in his arms.

'I'll miss you, Clare,' he said. 'We all will. I won't ask if you're going to come back. I don't want to put that kind of pressure on you. But I hope things will work out in a way that allows you to do so – without letting your family down. Even if it's just for a visit. You know you'll always be welcome here.'

'Thanks,' I muttered. Even in my hyped-up state of anxiety, the irony wasn't lost on me. What I'd have given, a few weeks earlier, to be told I'd always be welcomed back in Little Sorrel. 'OK, well, hopefully one day …' I turned to go. 'Sorry. I've got to just put out the rubbish and strip the bed. I'll put the sheets in the washing-machine but would you mind—'

'Leave everything,' he said calmly. 'I'll do it. Get Sid in the car and get yourself on the road.'

I nodded my thanks, beyond bothering to argue. He stood on his doorstep watching as I brought out my bag, my laptop and camera bag, Sid's bed, and then Sid himself. We'd come without much luggage and we were leaving without much.

'Bye then,' I said, giving a little wave as I started the engine.

He mouthed something back. It could have been 'God go with you'.

And two minutes later I was heading back up 'that bloody lane', as Sally called it. Without a backward glance. Going home.

CHAPTER 32
TEN MONTHS LATER

It was hot, the kind of hot day we don't see often enough in the UK to learn how to cope with it. Heat seemed to be bouncing off the road, shimmering in the sky outside the car. I had the air conditioning belting out as well as the radio – playing gentle music to calm my racing heart – as I slowed down to turn off the main road and begin the last stage of my journey. The long, narrow, familiar lane that eventually became Steep Hill and took me back, at last, to Little Sorrel.

*

Until only a few weeks earlier, I'd doubted whether this day would ever come. I'd tried so hard to put Little Sorrel out of my mind, told myself it had been a lovely holiday with fond memories to sustain me as I settled back into my old life in London. Of course, I'd thought often, as I nursed poor Rachel through a couple of horrendous months of sickness, about the friends I'd made during my months in

Devon. I wondered whether the choir was still meeting – with or without the addition of the dogs – whether there were any new members, and whether the music was still helping them. I wondered about Mike and Julie – whether they'd set a date for their wedding yet. Whether Topsy was fully recovered. Whether Margaret Manners and Mandy were happy with their framed pet portraits. And, most of all, whether young Leo was OK. Whether he missed Sid, and whether he'd forgiven me for going without saying goodbye.

I had no phone numbers or email addresses for any of them. I know I could have tried; perhaps I could have found some of them on social media – apparently nobody is uncontactable these days. But I didn't try. I thought a clean break might heal faster.

For those difficult early weeks, my time was completely given over to Rachel: giving her tiny sips of fluids, tiny meals whenever she felt a little less nauseous, and encouraging her to rest and to try not to worry. At one point, her doctor was determined to book her into hospital to have fluids and nourishment administered intravenously, but as if the threat of this were enough on its own to settle things, she suddenly began to feel slightly better, day by day, until at exactly twenty weeks of pregnancy she had a full day with no sickness. Within another week or two she was eating and drinking normally, had started to put on weight and was blooming with health and happiness.

I'd been staying in the house with Rachel and Jason since I'd arrived back, and during that time I'd seen a completely different side to my son-in-law. His allergies seemed to have disappeared overnight. He explained this in an almost convincing way – something about the stress of Rachel's illness causing his immune system to reverse itself – which I decided to accept, rather than taking my usual cynical approach. All that mattered was keeping Rachel and the baby well. I couldn't have cared less whether Jason coughed, wheezed or collapsed at the sight or smell of his poor wife's vomit or anything else, but in fact he was the epitome of tender loving care, and if he hadn't needed to hang onto his job in the face of approaching fatherhood, I think he'd have given up work to become her full-time carer. Every evening, he took over the nursing duties from me while I cooked dinner, and I saw for the first time that their relationship was as strong and loving as I could have wished. If they'd argued from time to time before the pregnancy, then the coming baby was bringing them closer together, and I couldn't have been happier.

Once her condition had completely stabilised, Rachel started work again, and I had time on my hands. I'd gone back to my flat, but it didn't feel like home any more.

'Find yourself a new place,' Sally advised me. 'A new-build. Something swanky.'

'I'm not sure that's what I want,' I said. I didn't know *what* I wanted. 'And anyway, I don't want to spend money. The children's money. It's for them, for their future.'

Dan and Prisha were getting married in the spring. The wedding was booked for a month after Rachel's baby was due. She'd insisted she'd still be up for being one of the bridesmaids, along with Prisha's sister and cousin. It was going to be a big affair, and why not? They could afford it now. Rachel could afford to work part-time after her maternity leave. I wanted them to be able to enjoy their lives, to enjoy the things they hadn't ever expected to have.

'But surely there'll still be enough for *you* to enjoy as well?' Sally had protested.

It felt as if that was all I'd heard from everyone, ever since I'd come into the money. The money I hadn't even wanted. But I still had no idea what to do with the rest of my life. I'd thought, at one time, I might have found the answer, but now I realised it had just been a foolish dream.

'Well, I'll look on Rightmove,' I said, mostly to satisfy Sally. 'But I don't want anything big or grand.'

The legacy from the mad author might have been big, but it surely wouldn't last forever. Big flashy new-build apartments don't come cheap, nor do the bills they attract. So I spent my days idly scrolling through property websites. I thought about taking up the pet photography again. Sid was always ready to pose, and perhaps I could advertise locally to find some clients who'd like their pets photographed. Get some business cards printed. Find a friendly local picture framer. But the idea didn't grab me quite the way it had back in Little Sorrel. I couldn't get motivated.

My baby granddaughter Myla was born on the second of February, perfectly timed just one day ahead of her due date. She came into the world peacefully, without a struggle, almost as if she knew she'd caused enough trouble already. In fact, if it wasn't tempting fate to say so, she seemed to be the perfect baby: she slept like an angel, fed hungrily but nicely, as if she'd read the manual, and was giving us beautiful smiles from the age of six weeks. After Jason had gone back to work, I went to help Rachel every day, doing a few chores or taking Myla out in her pram so that her mummy could get some rest, but it wasn't long before I began to feel redundant. My daughter seemed newly energised by the pleasure of caring for her baby, and soon had everything organised and under control. It was hard to remember, looking at this happy, healthy new mum, that she'd been feeling so terrible just a few short months earlier.

'It's lovely to see you, Mum,' she said eventually, trying to be tactful. 'You're welcome any time, obviously, and it's plain to see how much Myla already loves you, but you mustn't feel like you *need* to come every day. We're fine. I'm joining a parent-and-baby group this week to meet some other mums. So if you've got other things to do ...'

I didn't, of course. I had nothing whatsoever to do, apart from walking Sid and the endless and pointless scrolling through property websites. Daniel and Prisha had settled into married life after their amazing wedding and a honeymoon in Cyprus, and were now looking at property websites themselves, with a view to moving from their flat into a house.

'We don't want anything too big,' Daniel told me, 'or too flashy. We don't want to become those kind of people, just because we're a bit more comfortably off now.'

'What kind of people?' I asked him, even though I knew exactly what he meant. I didn't want to become that kind of person either. Perhaps that was why I still hadn't touched much of the money.

Looking back, I think Rachel had probably seen through me all along.

'Mum,' she said gently one day in May when Myla was about three months old and I'd gone round to her house to play with the baby again and 'help' her with things she no longer needed help with, 'I think you're bored, aren't you?'

'Bored?' I retorted. 'Of course I'm not bored!' I'd been brought up with the mantra that only boring people get bored. And anyway, if I'd complained of being bored when I was younger, my mother would have quickly found me some cleaning or tidying around the house to occupy me.

'Well, OK, perhaps *bored* is the wrong word. But you're unsettled.'

I shrugged. 'I just can't quite get myself motivated, but I will, eventually.'

'To do what? The pet photography? That sounds like a great idea. Or ...' She looked at me carefully. 'To go back?'

'Back?' I said, trying to ignore the sudden quickening of my heartbeat. 'Back where?'

'You know quite well what I mean. Back to Little Sorrel. Mum, you know how much I appreciated you rushing back here to be with me when I was ill. I love you for putting me – us – first—'

'But of course I do – I will – always! That goes without saying.'

'—for putting us first when I needed you so much,' she finished. 'But now – well, it's lovely having you near, being able to see you whenever we want, but Mum, I *know*, perfectly well, you're not happy. You kind of found yourself, didn't you, when you were living in that village. I was worried about it at first, when you seemed so reluctant to leave, but I understand now: it was right for you. Don't get me wrong, we'll miss you if you go back, but we're only a few hours' drive away. Please don't stay here just for us – for me and Jason and Myla or for Dan and Prisha. We'll come and see you all the time. It'll be lovely. And you'll be happy – that's what we all want, honestly.'

I didn't answer. I wanted to protest that my place was here in London, that I wanted to be with my family, and be a hands-on granny, not one who lived at a distance and only got visited from time to time. But I knew she was right. Despite my instant and overwhelming love for my little granddaughter, and despite my constant and profound love for my children, I wasn't happy. I was living a false life, pretending to myself that this was what I wanted, and that it would be enough for me for the rest of my life, when all the time my heart had been left behind in that ridiculous, tiny, quiet, cut-off, inward-looking village nobody had ever heard of. Perhaps there was something wrong with me.

'I give up,' Sally said, sadly, when I told her what Rachel had been saying. 'I know when I'm beaten.' Then she smiled, hugged me, and said, 'I'm teasing you. I always knew, in my heart of hearts, that you'd want to go back. Just do one thing for me, though? See if you can get that second bedroom unlocked so I can have a bit more space for my stuff next time I come and stay.'

'Sally, I might not even be able to go back to the cottage. I have no idea whether it's still empty. Someone else might be renting it by now.'

'So where are you planning to live? *If* you go back,' she added with a mischievous grin.

'I've no idea. I suppose I'll have to start off staying in the pub. Like before,' I added, smiling to myself at the memory. 'And find out what's available.'

'So the sooner you get going the better, I suppose,' she said. 'I want you settled in somewhere before the summer, so I can book my Devon holiday.'

'Cheeky!' I laughed, hugging her back. 'You know I'll be desperate to see you by then.'

I put my flat on the market. It was the first thing I'd done that made me feel really alive and motivated. I had a few viewings, but at the end of May I suddenly decided to leave it in the hands of the estate agents. I'd waited long enough. Now that I'd made up my mind – or, it seemed, everyone had made it up for me – I wasn't going to wait around any longer. And so it was that I found myself, on a Sunday, the first day of an unusually early and intense heatwave, packing up the car again and setting off with Sid on a repeat of our previous year's adventure. Except that this year, I knew exactly where we were going, and why.

CHAPTER 33

'Oh. It's you.' Jack stared at me across the bar. 'You're back.'

'It would seem so, yes.' I smiled at him. 'I'd like a coffee, please.'

'Right.' He continued to stare at me as he made the coffee. 'So, are you back to stay? Want a room again, do you?'

'I'm not sure yet,' I said. To be honest, I was quite amazed that he was talking to me. 'Any chance of a ham sandwich or have you finished serving lunches?'

'I'll see what I can rustle up,' he said. I blinked in surprise. I'd arrived halfway through the afternoon and felt in need of some sustenance before going to see whether the cottage might still be unoccupied. Perhaps I was putting off the moment. But I'd been fully expecting the probability of Jack's usual lack of civility and the possibility of needing to buy a snack from the shop instead. 'I'll bring it over to you,' he added. 'Want a bowl of water for the dog?'

'Oh. Thank you, yes.' He must have had some kind of personality makeover. Perhaps he'd found love since I last saw him. Well, whoever she was, good luck to her! She seemed to have worked a miracle.

'I've been going to that choir of yours,' he said a few minutes later when he brought me my sandwich.

'Oh!' I tried to hide my amazement. 'It's still going, then. I'm glad to hear that.'

'Going strong,' he nodded. 'Lots of us have joined. It's cheered everyone up around here. Good that people can bring their dogs along too. Makes a nice atmosphere. Friendly. Fun.'

How pleasing to think that it was the choir, rather than a woman, that had had such an effect on him!

'That's really good news.'

'The headmaster's running it now, you know,' he went on. 'With the vicar's wife, of course.'

'The vicar's *wife*?' I repeated, my sandwich halfway to my mouth. 'Julie? Are they married now, then?'

'Yes. Last month. Thought you'd have come to the wedding, to be honest, what with them being your friends.'

'I didn't know. I didn't leave any contact details.' I don't know why I felt I had to explain to Jack, of all people, but I added quickly, 'I had to go home because of a family emergency. There was no time for … anything, really. But I'm glad to hear they're married. I did wonder whether they'd ever get around to it!'

'He had to wait to get agreement from the Bishop or something, what with Julie being divorced.' He gave me a puzzled look. 'Anyway, I expect they'll tell you all about it, now you're back.'

'Yes. Thank you.'

He left me in peace to digest this news, along with my sandwich. Although I was happy, of course, for Mike and Julie, I felt sad, and guilty, for not being at the wedding or even knowing about it. I should have tried to stay in touch. What would they think of me? I was glad I'd found out about it from this unexpectedly changed version of Jack before I met up with either of the newly-weds. At least I'd be able to congratulate them properly when I saw them, without the surprise of it, or my own disappointment about missing the wedding, taking over. It was lovely news, after all, and I mustn't make it be all about me.

Sid and I went back to the car as soon as I'd settled up with Jack, and I drove slowly up the road and into Duck Lane, pulling up outside Riverside Cottage. I turned off the engine and sat staring out of the window, feeling jittery with a mixture of anticipation and nerves. Sid was giving little yaps of excitement. He'd obviously recognised his one-time home. Was it still empty? It was impossible to tell from the outside. I'd have to see whether Mike was home to find out. But just as I was about to open the car door, there was a roar of an engine and a squeal of brakes from behind us, setting Sid off into a frenzy of barking and jumping. A black Mazda had pulled up directly behind us, its bonnet almost touching my rear bumper. Before I'd even had time to react, a large, cross-looking man had jumped out of the Mazda, slamming the driver's door and marching towards me. I wound down the window, wondering if he was lost and wanted to ask for directions.

To my surprise, he merely barked at me, 'Is there something I can help you with?'

'What?' I said, lost for words and having no idea what he was talking about.

'If you don't need to be here, maybe you'd like to move?' He waved his arm as if to shoo me away. 'You're in my parking space.'

Upset by his attitude, I opened the car door, almost hitting him with it, and squared up to him with my hands on my hips.

'Excuse *me*!' I said. 'There aren't any yellow lines in this village – or lines of any description, come to that – and there definitely aren't any marked-out parking spaces, yours or anyone else's. So I'm parking here while I call on my friend Mike at the vicarage.'

'Your friend Mike?' he said, sounding only slightly less sure of himself. 'Well, if that's the case, perhaps you'd like to park outside your *friend*'s house instead of blocking the space outside *my* house, preventing me from parking here myself.'

'No, I wouldn't *like* to!' I retorted. 'I don't see why I should move two yards down the lane just so you can—' I stopped, staring at him. 'Did you say *your* house?'

'I live here,' he said, waving behind him. 'In Riverside Cottage.'

'You've moved in?' My heart sank. 'You're the new tenant?' I should have guessed it wouldn't have remained empty, just waiting for me to decide to come back.

But then I looked at his face more closely. He looked … familiar. Like someone I knew …

'Tenant?' he was saying. 'No. It's my home!'

There was another moment of silence. We both stared at each other. The penny seemed to drop for us both at the same time.

'You're Harry,' I said. I'd have recognised him more quickly from his self-portrait if he didn't now look considerably older – with grey streaks in his dark hair – and considerably crosser. But I'd also suddenly seen his resemblance to my young friend Leo. When he was sad or upset, Leo looked just like his grandad.

'You're back from America.'

'You stayed in my cottage.'

'I heard about your son,' I said. 'I'm so sorry.'

'You're from London.' He said it like an accusation, completely ignoring my condolences. 'You managed to get my cat injured.'

'Er ... no! In fact, I—'

'You left things behind in my cottage,' he went on. 'Some pictures. Photographs. And ...' He looked away now. 'Some underwear, in the washing bin.'

'Oh!' I flushed. 'I didn't realise—'

'I threw it away. I assumed you wouldn't be coming back.'

'Right. Well ...' I gave an awkward laugh. The embarrassment of him finding my dirty knickers had slightly diffused my annoyance. 'Nevertheless, I *am* back. I'm here to see Mike – and Julie. I'll move the car when I've finished there, if that's OK?' Not that I had any idea where I'd be going.

'Well, I suppose it'll have to be OK, won't it?'

He turned to walk away, towards the front door of the cottage, but just then Topsy appeared, jumping up onto the wall between the cottage and the vicarage, and Sid, who was still in the car, immediately spotted her and began to bark with excitement.

Harry turned back. 'Please don't let your dog harass my cat.'

'Harass her?' I gasped. 'He's not harassing her, he's just saying hello! They were great friends when I was staying here. They used to snuggle up together.'

'Yes, well, I'd appreciate you keeping him away from her now. I don't want her getting injured again.'

I was almost too flabbergasted to respond. But just at that moment, there was a polite cough from behind me. Harry and I both looked round to see Mike standing on his doorstep, a shocked expression on his face. Of course, he hadn't expected to see me, and this wasn't exactly the way I'd planned our reunion.

'Harry,' he said quietly, 'sorry to interrupt, but you ought to know that Clare looked after Topsy all the time she was here. She rushed her to the vet's when she got hurt – *and* insisted on paying the bill.'

'That's not really the point, Mike,' I said. 'The point is, I loved Topsy and so did Sid.' Sid was still barking with excitement, and Topsy, as if to prove my point, was simply sitting on the wall looking calmly back at him. 'But, fair enough, Harry is her owner and he's back now.'

'Yes, I am,' Harry said with a nod. 'I didn't know you paid the vet bill. Let me know how much it was and I'll reimburse you, obviously.'

'There's no need for that,' I said. But he was already walking away.

'Sorry, Clare,' Mike began, sounding wretched as the cottage door closed behind Harry.

'Don't be silly – it's not your fault.' I felt, ridiculously, like crying. My much-anticipated return to the village felt spoiled. 'I should have tried to let you know I was coming, then you could have warned me—'

'Come here.' He walked over to me, holding out his arms for a hug. 'Please don't be upset. Harry's ... still not himself.' He held me out at arm's length now, smiling. 'But it's so good to see you! Are you ... dare I hope ... back to stay?'

'Well, I ... rather stupidly, really ... hoped so, yes. I didn't have your phone number or email or anything, but I should have tried – I'm such an idiot. I didn't even try to keep in touch. I thought it would just make it harder to settle in back at home.'

'And we felt the same way. We wanted to invite you to the wedding, obviously, but—'

'Oh yes!' I pulled him into another hug. 'Jack told me! Congratulations! I wish I'd been here, of course – but that was my fault. I ran away—'

'Your family needed you,' he corrected me. 'But look, we've got so much to catch up on, and meanwhile you need somewhere to stay. Julie's out at the moment but I know she'll agree with me: you must use her bungalow, for as long as you want. She's obviously living here with me in the vicarage now, so it's empty—'

'But surely she'll need to sell it.'

'We haven't got around to doing anything about that yet.' He shook his head as if exasperated at himself. 'But what am I doing, keeping you talking out here? You've had a long drive, you must be tired and hungry. For heaven's sake, come inside, bring Sid in, and let me make you something to eat.'

'I had a sandwich at the pub. But thank you – I'd love another coffee, and some water for Sid.'

*

By the time Julie came home, I'd filled Mike in on all my news regarding baby Myla, Daniel and Prisha's wedding, and how I'd finally decided to take the plunge, put my flat on the market and come back to Devon. After Julie and I had squealed and hugged together, Mike then had to put the kettle back on while I went through the whole story again.

'Now tell me about *your* wedding,' I insisted. 'I want to see photos! I can't believe I missed it. But I'm so happy for you both.'

We chatted for so long that eventually they insisted I stayed for a meal.

'Are you sure I'm not holding you up – you don't have to be doing anything at the church?' I said.

'No. We don't hold Evensong these days. One Sunday service is enough for such a small congregation,' Mike said, laughing.

After dinner, Julie said she'd come with me to her bungalow, where she and Mike were adamant I should stay until I had time to make some permanent arrangements. I'd obviously insisted that I'd pay her rent, and we'd agreed to argue, in the nicest sense of the word, about the amount later.

'Harry will no doubt be watching from the window,' I commented as we got into my car, 'and will be straight out here to move his car up. Honestly, what a fuss about a couple of yards.'

Mike had already told Julie about the earlier argument.

'Harry's been a bit grumpy and prickly ever since he came back,' Julie said sadly. 'We're beginning to wonder whether it was such a good idea for him to be back here. With all the memories.'

'I do understand. But surely there are happy memories here, too – of his son, growing up.'

'None of us really knows how we'd feel in similar circumstances, do we?' she said, and I felt slightly rebuked. It was true, of course, and I had to remember that Harry had been everyone's friend here. He and I had perhaps started off on the wrong foot, and I hadn't really given him a chance. Hopefully he'd be in a better mood the next time I met him!

CHAPTER 34

I couldn't admit to Julie how disappointed I'd been that I wasn't able to move back into Riverside Cottage. But the tiny bungalow where she'd lived up until her wedding to Mike was nice, and I was grateful that she was so keen for me to stay there.

'Mike and I haven't had time to talk about putting it on the market yet,' she said as she unlocked the front door. 'I'm sorry, you'll find it quite poky—'

'You haven't seen my flat in London!' I laughed. I looked around the little living room. 'This is lovely, Julie.'

Because it had been built immediately next to the shingle beach at the bend in the river, the bungalow was raised slightly above ground level, with steps to the front door and a wide veranda at the back, looking over the water.

'I've been told off by half the kids in the village for getting married and moving out,' she said, laughing. 'They all used to love coming here whenever I was looking after them.'

'Your grandson – and all your nieces and nephews,' I remembered. 'Well, I'm sure Sid's going to enjoy having the beach as his back garden too!'

'I hope it's suitable for you, at least while you decide what to do. Please make use of whatever you need to, Clare. As you can see, we haven't even moved out many of my things yet. There's plenty of furniture and crockery in the vicarage already, of course, so luckily for us there was no rush to empty this place.'

'Luckily for me, too, then. I have brought more with me this time, though – bedding and towels and some of my kitchen stuff – as my flat's up for sale now.' I gave her another hug. 'Thank you so much. How ridiculous of me to just turn up here like this, expecting to move straight into somewhere.'

'I hope you weren't too upset about Riverside Cottage.'

'Well, I did wonder if someone else might have moved in. But it hadn't occurred to me that Harry might have come back.'

'We were surprised too. But we're all – everyone in the village – doing our best to help him settle down again.' She smiled at me. 'You'll notice a change in a lot of the people here.'

'I have already.' I told her about Jack. 'He said he's joined the choir!'

'The choir has been an absolute lifeline for us all. We haven't forgotten how you helped to get it started, Clare. I hope you'll come along to the meeting on Tuesday.'

'Of course I will! And I hear people are still bringing their dogs along.'

'Absolutely.' She smiled. 'In fact, the village has become famous for it! We got a write-up in the *South Devon Gazette*: the first Devon village to have a dog-friendly community choir. We sent them a photo of us all together singing with all the dogs. It was a nice article. I'll show you a copy. They headed it "Little Sorrel Choir Members Take a Bow(-wow)",' she added, wincing at the pun.

'How funny!' I chuckled. 'Yes, I'd love to see that.'

Julie told me about Annabel's cocker spaniel, Jet, who – true to her description of him – had always done a funny little jig to the music during our sessions, but one day he'd danced so energetically he'd got tangled up in his own lead and nearly pulled Annabel out of her seat.

'That's really the only incident we've had with any of the dogs,' she said. 'Unless you count the time one of the head teacher, Chris's, dogs tried to get too … um … amorous, with little Cuddles. We had to stop singing to separate them. I think they've both been neutered now!'

I laughed, pleased to hear that neither of these little incidents had stopped anyone's pleasure at having the dogs at the rehearsals with them. Then I tried to stifle a yawn.

'Oh, sorry. I think all the excitement has finally caught up with me! I'd better bring my bags in and start unpacking.'

'Let me help. Then I'll leave you to get an early night.'

The next day was hot and sunny again. I let Sid out to run on the beach, and took my breakfast tray out onto the veranda, where I sat on the little bench seat looking out across the river. My disappointment about Riverside Cottage was slowly dissipating. This place would work perfectly well for me. Why would I need anything bigger? I could talk to Julie about buying it, once she was ready to sell. But there was no need to rush into anything.

I'd called Rachel and Daniel the previous evening before going to bed, to let them know I'd arrived safely and had, at least, a temporary home. After I'd finished breakfast, I messaged Sally.

I'm staying in Julie's bungalow. She & Mike are married! Can't live in the cottage – the owner Harry is back. Tell you more later.

I smiled to myself, imagining her take on this news, looking forward to gossiping with her about it that evening. Then I called Sid and went out for our walk. It was a Monday morning and there were quite a few people about, walking their dogs, going to the shop or just enjoying the sunshine. It couldn't have been more different from how I remembered my first experiences of walking around this village the previous year when nobody even smiled at me, let alone said hello. Now, nearly everyone recognised me, and I was greeted with surprised smiles and gasps of genuine pleasure – even hugs from some.

'How lovely to see you!' said Margaret Manners, as Sid and Brutus wagged their tails joyfully together. 'Are you back to stay?'

'Welcome back, Clare,' said Hazel in the shop. 'Really nice to have you back. I hope you'll come and help with the choir again.'

'Mum told me you're back!' said Kerry, who'd come into the shop for some provisions too. 'I'm *so* pleased. Leo will be really excited!'

'How is he?' I asked. 'I've thought about him so often.'

'He's ... doing better,' she said. I thought I detected something in her tone that I couldn't quite work out.

'Good,' I said. 'Well, tell him to come and see me – and Sid – won't you? I'm in your mum's bungalow, as I'm sure she's told you.'

'I will, of course. I'm sure he'll want to walk Sid with you.'

I said goodbye and walked back to my new home along the towpath. Young Robbie was working outside the boat-house, painting one of the little rowing boats, and he straightened up and smiled as I approached.

'I heard a rumour you were back,' he said, wiping his hands and holding one of them out to shake mine. 'I'm glad. Dad will be, too. He's across at Sorrel-by-Sea, picking up the vicar's wife from shopping. Is that right you've moved into her place along the beach?'

'Temporarily, yes,' I said. Despite the fact that he'd become more friendly to me just before my sudden departure, I still found it hard to reconcile this new, polite version of Robbie with the surly, hostile man I'd first encountered the previous year. 'How is your dad?'

'OK,' he said, nodding. 'We're all pleased Harry's back. We needed him to be back here in the village, to make our peace with what happened. Although, to be honest, I think it's going to take a lot longer for Harry himself.'

'Yes. Understandably,' I said, trying to block the image from my mind of Harry, raging at me the day before, in that ridiculous row about parking and about Topsy. 'And how is George?' I added.

'He's doing well, thanks. Moving up to senior school has been good for him. Hard at first, being one of the youngest, you know. But he's taken to the harder work, and the new subjects. It's what he needed. I reckon he was bored here at the village school. He's grown up a lot, this past year.' He gave me a look. 'He's behaving a lot better.'

'I'm glad he's more settled.' And I hoped that meant he was now leaving the younger kids like Leo and Reggie alone. 'Well, I'll see you soon, no doubt.'

'Yep. At the choir meeting, I reckon, if not before?'

'You've joined the choir?' I stared at him in amazement.

'Really enjoying it, I am. Trying to get Dad to come along. It's done everyone no end of good to sing our hearts out together every week. Never thought I'd say so, but it was just what we all needed.'

'That's great,' I said warmly. 'I'm really pleased. And yes, of course I'll be there on Tuesday! See you later, Robbie.'

If Jack, and Young Robbie, had joined the choir – the two most unlikely people in the village – I was beginning to wonder whether there were many people left here who *hadn't* joined!

*

Leo arrived as soon as school finished. I was sitting on the veranda again, reading, while Sid scampered ecstatically on the beach below, investigating all the scents at the water's edge. I looked down and saw my young friend approaching along the beach, his shoulders hunched, hands in his pockets, kicking stones, just as I remembered him – except that he'd grown noticeably taller in the space of a year and was wearing his hair slightly differently, combed into a kind of quiff at the front. Trying to look more grown-up or fashionable. I smiled, and was about to call down to him when he caught sight of Sid and ran towards him, flinging his school bag on the ground and sitting down on the damp shingle to give the dog a hug. Instead of calling out, I watched the boy and the dog playing together for a while, the pleasure they had in each other's company bringing a tear to my eye. Finally he looked up and saw me, giving me a little wave.

'Hi, Leo. Come on up. I'll get you some lemonade.'

He ran up the steps followed by Sid, who, panting, headed straight inside to his water bowl.

'How are you?' I asked Leo as I put a glass of lemonade and a couple of biscuits on the table in front of him. I ruffled his hair. 'You seem to have grown up since I was here before.'

To my surprise, he didn't smile.

'Are you all right?' I asked him gently.

He shrugged. 'Yes. I missed Sid when you went away. Are you going to stay here now or go away again?' He paused, then added more quietly, 'You didn't say goodbye.'

'I know. I'm so sorry, Leo. One of my children – my daughter – was quite ill, and I needed to go back to London in a hurry to look after her. Otherwise she could have ended up in hospital.'

'Is she all right now?' he asked.

I smiled. 'Yes. She's had a baby, a little girl. So I'm a grandma now.' I paused. I hadn't answered his question. 'I'm planning to stay here, this time. All being well.'

We sat in silence for a few minutes. He sipped his lemonade and watched as Sid galloped back down the steps to the beach.

'But things are better here for you now, aren't they?' I said eventually, as he was still silent. 'Now George has moved on to secondary school, and you and Reggie are good friends again – isn't that right?'

He nodded. 'Yes. It's better. George doesn't bother us any more. He gets a lot of homework now so he doesn't play down at the river so much anyway.'

'And it must be lovely for you, having your grandad back in the village,' I added.

He took a while to answer this time. He swung his legs, sipped his lemonade and watched Sid running along the beach below us. 'I'm glad he's back,' he said finally. 'But I liked it better when you and Sid were living in the cottage instead of him. He's grumpy all the time, and doesn't want me round there.'

'Well, yes, he might be feeling grumpy,' I conceded. 'But I'm sure that's not true.'

'It is!' he asserted. 'He told my mum I shouldn't be going round there.'

I had no idea what to say to this. I put a hand out to pat him on his shoulder, as if that was going to help. How horrible for a boy to be told to stay away from his own grandad!

'Well,' I said, 'you can come and see me and Sid whenever you like, Leo. Would you like to take Sid for a walk now? Shall we call for Reggie and see if he wants to come too?' I hesitated, and then added, 'D'you know what? I think you and Reggie are probably just about old enough now to take Sid for short walks together on your own. As long as your parents agree,' I went on quickly, 'and as long as you keep him on his lead.'

'Really?' He looked up at me, the spark back in his eyes. 'Do you think Mum will let me? I *am* nearly ten now.'

'Well, we can ask her, can't we?' I called Sid, fastened his lead and we set off together to talk to Kerry. As I expected, she was a little dubious at first until I promised her that I'd always insist on Leo and Reggie being together, that they stayed away from the water's edge and never let Sid off his lead.

'I could start with just letting them walk him up and down the lane for a few minutes while I watch from the end of the lane,' I suggested, 'and build up slowly from there.'

'OK,' she agreed, with a smile. Leo whooped with delight and wanted to go and tell Reggie the news immediately. 'It's good to see him looking more cheerful,' she told me when he was out of earshot. 'It's been … a difficult time.'

'So I hear. I'm sorry. I wish I hadn't had to leave without saying goodbye. I should have kept in touch, but I wasn't sure if I'd ever be coming back.'

'I'm glad you have,' she said simply. 'So is Leo, obviously.'

*

On the way back to the bungalow with Sid, I made a detour into Duck Lane. As I walked past Riverside Cottage, I found myself imagining – as I used to when I was living there – Harry sitting inside on his own, perhaps in the little conservatory at the back where the light was so good, maybe with Topsy on his lap or even working at his easel. I remembered how, when I'd been staying there, I'd pictured him as an older version of his self-portrait, hoping he'd look happier in the flesh. The irony, now I'd met him, wasn't lost on me. What a grump! But still, the sense I'd had of him while I used to potter about his cottage, picturing him – the artist – working on that wonderful painting in his lounge, refused to dissipate completely. Perhaps he'd had an off day when he'd confronted me, or just been surprised to find a stranger parked outside his cottage. And, of course, he was still grieving. I couldn't get that haunted expression on his face out of my mind. To cheer myself up, I walked on to the end of Duck Lane and was delighted to see another brood of spring ducklings on the pond.

'Ah, look at them, Sid!' I said, as he sat at the edge of the pond, whining softly as he watched the babies hurrying to hide themselves under their mother's protective wings.

It was somehow reassuring to see nature carrying on its business, season by season, generation by generation, nothing too much changing about that here in the countryside, regardless of what happened in our complicated human lives.

But as I cooked my meal that evening in the tiny kitchen alcove off the one living room of Julie's bungalow, I was still thinking about Harry, alone in Riverside Cottage with his grief and his memories. I'd have felt sorry for anyone in his circumstances, but how could he not want to have anything to do with his little grandson? Surely it would help him to develop a relationship with the boy. It would be good for them both, wouldn't it? His brooding dark looks were so similar to Leo's. I wondered, if the familial resemblance from grandparent to grandchild was so strong, how similar must Leo have looked to his father, Harry's lost son? Perhaps that was part of the problem.

CHAPTER 35

Having heard so much about how many people had now joined the choir, I'd been looking forward to the meeting that first Tuesday evening. As soon as I pushed open the door to the school hall, I realised reports had not been exaggerated. The room was packed, with both adults and children filling rows of chairs – various dogs of all shapes and sizes lying on the floor or being walked around the edge of the hall – and the buzz of conversation sounded happy and animated, so different from the gloom that had emanated from those few who'd been at that first church choir practice I'd attended the previous summer. Suddenly, the chatter died down as a few people began to nudge each other and I overheard mutters of 'She's here!' And with a scraping of chairs on the floor, everybody was on their feet, and there was a resounding cheer, cries of 'Welcome back!' and a few of them burst into a rendition of 'For She's a Jolly Good Fellow'.

'Oh!' I covered my face, embarrassed. 'Well, um, thank you! It's good to be back, and so lovely to see so many of you here. I'll just take a seat here at the back, I think, and listen to what you've been practising recently—'

'Are you sure you don't want to take over again, Clare?' Chris Oakley, the head teacher, was at the front of the hall beside Julie at the piano, while his two collies were sitting with his wife near the back. He beckoned me to join them, but I shook my head.

'No, I'm much happier being back here with everyone else. I only took the lead before because someone needed to get the choir started. I never did feel qualified for the job!'

'Well, as you can see, we're all eternally grateful that you did get it started,' he said. 'It's been the best thing to happen in this village for a very long time. Did Julie tell you we're considering entering for a South Devon competition for community choirs?'

'That's fantastic. You've definitely come a long way since I was here.'

'Yes. And everyone's feeling better because of it.' Chris smiled. 'We've got our community spirit back, haven't we?' he added to the group, and there was a chorus of agreement.

'The competition isn't till December,' Julie explained. 'So we've got time to decide whether we're good enough – ready enough – to enter. But anyway, shall we get started, everyone?'

I was amused to learn that the choir was still warming up with a couple of verses of 'If You're Happy and You

Know It', enthusiastically led by the children, including Leo and Reggie. And 'Lean on Me' was still a favourite, too. In fact, some of the people I would have least expected to enjoy such sentimental lyrics, like Young Robbie and Jack the pub landlord, were joining in loudly and enthusiastically. We also sang 'You've Got a Friend', which I realised must have been chosen for the same reason, extending the theme of people pulling together in difficult times. It was heart-warming to look around the hall and see the smiles exchanged among my friends as they gave their all to the song. They were taking the meaning of the lyrics on board, I was sure, and hopefully bringing those sentiments into play in their lives together as well as within the choir. After practising some interesting part-singing, including some solo verses for the strongest voices, we finished with 'Good Night, Sleep Tight'.

At the end of the meeting, I was surrounded by people who hadn't yet had a chance to chat to me since my return, all of them wanting to tell me how they hoped I'd stay this time, that they'd heard on the village grapevine about my new granddaughter, and wanted to congratulate me, and to my surprise, some even suggested that my family would be very welcome in Little Sorrel if they came to visit.

'Surely things haven't changed *that* much?' I asked Julie as I helped her and Chris stack the chairs away afterwards. 'Visitors being welcomed here?'

'Only because they're your family, I reckon,' she laughed. 'But I do think people's mindsets are gradually changing, you know. Attitudes are softening. I did hear a rumour that Margaret Manners was thinking about doing bed and breakfast again this season. She's got two spare bedrooms and always used to take visitors during the summer, until the accident.'

'Really?' I raised my eyebrows. That would be a step in the right direction, a sign that people were finally beginning to accept that they couldn't go on blaming all tourists for 'the accident', as it was always referred to. But there was one person who, I guessed, wouldn't be ready to accept this yet, if ever. And I wondered how much his feelings on the matter were going to influence the other residents.

*

The weather changed abruptly the next afternoon with a thunderstorm, and it continued to rain heavily all night and into the next day. I'd been invited to the vicarage to have a cup of tea with Julie that afternoon. I left Sid in the bungalow and ran round to Duck Lane with just a light hooded jacket over my T-shirt, the wind blowing rain horizontally across the river and soaking the legs of my jeans. As I passed Riverside Cottage, I heard a door opening, and looked up through the rain dripping from my hood to see Harry coming out of the cottage.

I'd already bumped into him a couple of times since that first meeting. It was, of course, difficult to avoid bumping into anyone in the handful of streets and single shop of Little Sorrel, but I felt acutely that I'd have preferred *not* to bump into this particular person. Now that everyone else in the village seemed to have accepted me, it felt worse – more personal – that one single resident seemed to have taken an instant dislike to me. Especially the very one who, during those weeks I'd lived in his cottage, I'd spent so much time thinking and wondering about, admiring his paintings, staring at his self-portrait and beginning to feel as if I knew him. It had been a shock to meet him in person and find him just as attractive, but considerably less pleasant, than the man I'd fantasised about. However, there was something I needed to broach, and probably the sooner the better.

'Hello,' I said, trying for a tone somewhere between too cheerful and too unfriendly. 'Um, I wonder, if you've got a minute, could I possibly pick up those photos you mentioned that I'd left behind?'

I remembered the knickers again, and tried not to think about him picking them up out of the washing bin and throwing them away. But I did want the photos back. I knew which ones they were: two framed black-and-white portraits of Topsy that I'd left on the chest of drawers in the bedroom in my haste to pack up and leave. I'd be pleased to see them again, especially now I wasn't likely to see much of my favourite little cat in the flesh, as it were.

'I'm on my way out,' he said, shortly. 'But I suppose you're going to want them back at some point so it might as well be now. Wait there.'

He turned and went back inside. Despite his curt instruction to 'wait there', I walked up the path to the front door of the cottage, brushing rain from my face, and stood on the step, sheltering under the porch. He'd left the door open, and I heard him stomp up the wooden staircase as my gaze strayed into the little living room I remembered so well. There were some pictures on the wall immediately inside the front door – pictures I didn't recall seeing when I was staying there. I leaned my head into the room slightly to get a better look, and recoiled straight away as I heard Harry returning down the stairs. But that quick glance had been enough to tell me exactly what I was looking at. It was a series of photographs: one of a baby propped up against cushions, with a wide toothless grin and a chin covered in chocolate. Another showed a young man of perhaps twenty or twenty-five, wearing football kit, with a shock of dark hair hanging into his eyes, and a slightly arrogant look on his face as if he'd just scored half a dozen goals for his side. But it was the middle of the three photos that confirmed without a doubt who I was looking at. It was a school photograph of a boy of about Leo's age. If I didn't know better, I'd have thought it *was* Leo. That same thick dark hair was combed forwards, so similar to the way Leo was now wearing his own. The boy's deep brown eyes betrayed a hint of shyness, and his mouth was set in a little pout, as if he'd been warned of the seriousness of the occasion. These photos were, without a doubt, of Harry's son, Paul. And I knew immediately that I'd been right: Harry couldn't face his grandson because he was almost a clone of the son he was still mourning.

Harry was walking across the living room now, and I turned away, feeling guilty, as if I'd been caught looking at something deeply private.

'Here you are, then,' he said.

I turned back to see him glancing at my photos as he handed them back to me.

'Thank you,' I said.

'They're actually quite good,' he said, in a slightly softer voice, making me lift my eyebrows in surprise. 'You've caught something ... something intrinsically Topsy.'

'I did love her,' I reminded him, 'while I was looking after her.'

'Yes.' He met my gaze now, and I felt my reservations about him waver slightly as I took in the sheer hopeless misery in those deep brown eyes, so like his grandson's. 'She was my son's cat. I never cared much about her before. But now ...' He shrugged. 'I guess she's all ... all I've—' He looked away again, shaking his head.

'I understand,' I said gently. I passed the photos of Topsy from one hand to the other. Did I really need them back? I could always print off more copies. 'Here,' I said, giving them back to him. 'I'm sorry. Keep them, please. They should stay with you.'

I didn't wait to hear his response – he seemed to be struggling to give me one – and I didn't want to embarrass him. I turned back into the rain and ran next door for my tea with Julie, feeling slightly shaken by the whole episode. I'd seen an unexpectedly different side to Harry. I still found it inexplicable that he couldn't put his own feelings to one side a little, for the sake of his grandson. But even more inexplicable were the feelings that had consumed *me*, standing there under his porch, dripping rain on his step, looking into those brown eyes, feeling as if I were sinking into his very soul.

I felt quite odd for the rest of the day. I'd probably caught a chill from my soaking in the rain. Or something.

CHAPTER 36

I think I'd already decided I was going to go back to doing the pet photography, but Harry's grudging comment about my pictures of Topsy being 'quite good' had spurred me on. I don't know why I cared about the opinion of someone who evidently didn't like me, and had more or less admitted to only liking Topsy herself because she was all he had left of his son. This, incidentally, although it had been quite moving to hear at the time, irritated me now whenever I thought about it, because if the stupid, stubborn man would only take a deep breath and open his heart, he still had a lovely little grandson whose love and company he could enjoy. So why *did* I care what he thought? I suppose because he was an artist himself, someone whose paintings I had admired long before I even knew who he was, and whose impeccable taste had made Riverside Cottage such a charming home.

Anyway, I was also getting encouragement about the pet photography from quite a few other people in the village.

'You *must* do some more pictures of Brutus for me,' Margaret Manners had said at the end of the choir meeting, giving the big friendly dog a pat on his head. 'I've got my favourite of the ones you had framed for me hanging over my fireplace and no end of people have said how much they like it. If you get some business cards printed, I'll pass them on to people for you.'

'All my friends love the picture you did of Brex, too,' Margaret's daughter, the rabbit owner, said, and as if on cue, her friends Annabelle and Ravi began to ask me about prices for photographing their spaniel, Jet, and Ravi's mother's two Siamese cats.

'What have I been telling you?' Sally said with some satisfaction when I told her about it the next time we chatted on the phone. 'You have a definite gift for photographing animals. And if there's one thing people are always ready to spend their money on, it's their pets. Before you say anything, I *know* you're not hard up any more, but you need an interest in life, and you can't do it for nothing or nobody will take you seriously. Besides, it wouldn't be fair to undercut other photographers in the area who need to make a living.'

'Oh. I hadn't thought of it like that.'

'So, get yourself set up properly. Think of a catchy name for your business. Pawtraits or something like that – nobody will care if it's gimmicky as long as it's easy to remember. Then advertise, with sensible charges. Give a discount to returning customers, or cheap rates for OAPs, or whatever, if you want. Or give the money to charity if you don't want it. The retired wedding photographers' benevolent fund, perhaps,' she added, laughing.

341

'Are you retiring?' I squawked.

'No, don't be daft. But I would if there was a benevolent fund!'

*

So I designed my business cards with an online printing website, and yes, I did call myself Pet Pawtraits by Clare. Sally was right: it was gimmicky, but who cared? As soon as they were delivered, I started handing them out to my friends in the village. Hazel put one in the shop window for me, and suggested it would be even better if I made a poster of one of my best prints of Sid, with my name and contact details on it. After I'd done this, Mike asked if I'd like to put an advert in the church newsletter, apologising for the fact that it was usual to make a small charge for this, which went towards such things as the pensioners' Christmas lunch.

'In fact,' he mused, 'there's a noticeboard on the village green. It hasn't been used for years – certainly not since I've been here, anyway. It might be a good idea, now people around here are feeling more community-minded again, to give it a clean-up and a coat of paint and put it to use. We can put notices on there about the choir, as well as church events. And if you want to put up one of your cards—'

'And anyone else in the village who has a business can use it,' I said quickly. 'That's a good idea, Mike. I'll help you clean it and paint it.'

That weekend, when the rain had stopped and the forecast looked good for a few days, Julie, Mike and I duly scrubbed the frame of the mildew-covered noticeboard, rubbed it down and gave it a coat of paint, before cleaning the glass and putting in a new notice about the choir meetings. Chris the head teacher wandered past with his dogs, and complimented us on our work, adding that he'd like to put a notice up about the school summer concert which was happening at the end of term. And just as we were finishing, Margaret Manners approached us in an uncharacteristically diffident way, asking whether it would be acceptable to put up a card advertising her intention to offer bed and breakfast accommodation during the summer season.

'I thought perhaps, if I advertise it here, people can tell their friends and relatives up-country about it. The fact is, nobody has had anywhere for friends to come and stay – since we, well, since we all stopped welcoming visitors.'

'Good idea,' Mike agreed. 'I'm glad you've decided to take in guests again, Margaret.'

'Thank you.' She looked very unsure of herself, for once. 'I don't suppose *everyone* will agree with you, though, Michael.'

We all knew exactly who she was referring to. The rest of the village might be coming round to the idea that visitors were welcome here again, but it was unlikely that Harry would be changing his mind any time soon.

*

As May turned into June, my new life in Little Sorrel settled into a kind of quiet routine. I walked Sid, chatted to the people I met along the lane, shopped for each day's essentials like a true countrywoman, practised the choir's songs as I sang to myself around my tiny new abode, and worked on promoting my new business, delivering leaflets through doors and photographing pets for people from both Little Sorrel and Sorrel-by-Sea, and occasionally further afield as recommendations began to spread. Rachel and I had regular catch-ups on Skype so that I could wave to baby Myla, see how she was growing, and hear her first gurgling laughs. On schooldays, as soon as the children came out at three thirty, Leo and Reggie came straight to the bungalow to have a glass of lemonade before putting Sid's lead on him and taking him for his second walk of the day. Kerry and I had gradually built up our confidence in them, and I no longer needed to watch them from the end of the lane or remind them of the rules; they kept Sid on his lead and stayed away from the water's edge but were otherwise given free rein. At the end of each week I gave them a little bit of cash each as 'payment' for their dog walking. The responsibility was good for them both, as was the envy of some of the other children.

'Even George French thinks it's cool that we've got a pocket-money job,' Leo told me. 'His dad pays him to help out in the boatyard at weekends and he thought he was the only kid around here with a job.' He put his head on one side and added, 'He's not so bad now. I don't know why I let him bully me before.'

'You've both grown up a bit, that's all,' I said, smiling at him. 'Things usually pass, eventually. Even if they're really hard at the time.'

'Like when my dad died,' he said, quite matter-of-factly. 'I mean, it's still horrible to think about it. But I don't think about it so often now. Is that bad?' he added, with a sudden worried look.

'No, Leo, it isn't. It's normal.'

And it's not as if you had a real relationship with your father anyway, from what I hear, I thought, sadly. But you could have one now with your grandad, if he weren't such an idiot.

*

The 'idiot' in question continued to walk around the village with a closed-off expression on his face that deterred most people from trying to interact with him. I felt for him, as much as everyone else did, and privately wished there was something I could do to see a smile on that handsome face. But at the same time, I felt a little exasperated, both by his moody silence and the other villagers' collaboration with it. He seemed to have no interest in being neighbourly, so everyone edged around him, excusing him for his occasional outbursts, telling each other it was understandable and he couldn't be blamed for it.

'But how long does that go on for?' I asked Julie. 'I mean, sorry, I know he's grieving, don't get me wrong.' I swallowed. I could still hardly bear to imagine how it must feel to lose a son – his only child – and at times, when I thought about him alone in Riverside Cottage with his memories and those photos on the wall, I almost felt like crying myself. 'I get that he's unhappy, that it won't ever go away or feel any better, but it's not Margaret's fault, is it?'

Harry's latest eruption had been directed at Margaret, on seeing her new 'Bed and Breakfast' sign in her window. He'd stopped her in the street, in front of several of her neighbours – who didn't have the courage to challenge him – and told her off for 'encouraging drunks and murderers back to the village again'. I, along with everyone else, had heard about the incident afterwards and there was much talk about supporting Harry in his grief and understanding how hard it was for him to cope with his loss, but not enough sympathy, in my opinion, given to the poor woman who simply wanted to supplement her pension a little by taking in some guests, now that everyone in the village, bar one, had got over their hostility towards visitors.

'I'm not being unsympathetic,' I went on – but Julie interrupted me with a sad smile.

'I know you're not, Clare. I think everyone here would agree with you, if they were honest. Well, they would now things have settled down so much and they're all being reasonable again. But Harry was always going to take longer to come round. Illogical though it is, he still blames all outsiders for what happened.'

'Including me.'

'You're not an outsider any more,' she laughed. 'He'll realise that eventually. Give him time.'

'You've got more patience than me.' I shook my head. 'And if I were Margaret Manners, I'd have answered him back, I'm afraid.'

'It's quite surprising that she hasn't. She's normally someone who speaks her mind. But at least she hasn't given in,' Julie pointed out. 'She's still taking bookings for the summer holidays.'

'Good for her.'

'Yes. Personally, I think it'll be nice to see some visitors here again. But there are a few mutterings about whether they'll be allowed on the river. I suppose it has to be up to the Frenches whether they hire out boats or not. I wouldn't like to have to make that decision, to be honest.'

'Yes, I can see your point.' I thought for a moment and then added, 'Would some kind of safety campaign help? Could the Frenches put together a leaflet about water safety, telling people about the tides, the sandbanks, the need to be competent – and sober – if they take a boat out—'

'Do you know what, that sounds like a really good idea,' Julie said thoughtfully. 'The leaflet could be handed out in the shop, as well as by the Frenches, to anyone who enquires about boats. And now we've got the noticeboard up and running again – there's loads of space on it – we could have a big poster up there too. I think I'll ask Mike to have a word with Young Robbie about it. He'll listen to Mike.'

*

A few days later I bumped into Young Robbie as I was walking Sid. We got along surprisingly well now, and I always stopped for a chat with him.

'The vicar told me about your idea for a safety campaign – for visitors, like,' he said.

'I hope I wasn't speaking out of turn,' I said. 'As a newcomer. I realise—'

'You're not a newcomer any more,' he said with a smile, echoing Julie's words. 'And, as always, you're talking a lot of sense. A year ago, mind you, you'd have had plenty of opposition. And Margaret Manners would have had a lot of opposition herself – in fact, she'd never even have considered the idea of taking in visitors again. But things have changed. We've all moved on, and it's time to start looking forward, thinking what's best for the village now.'

'I must admit I'd never have expected to hear you say that,' I said gently. 'And I did understand, of course. The accident—'

'The accident itself was partly my fault,' he said, looking me squarely in the eye. 'I've got to live with that. But I've finally come to realise Paul's death *wasn't* my fault – or anybody's.' He sighed. 'Sadly, his heart condition meant that he could have gone at any time.'

We were both silent for a moment. Then he shook his head and added, 'But it's probably too much to expect his father to accept that.'

'I don't think Harry blames you, though,' I said. 'No more than he blames anyone else, anyway. He's just angry, Robbie. Angry with the whole world. It's understandable, but—'

'But anger doesn't heal anything, does it? It took *me* a long time to realise that, even though in my case it was myself I was most angry with.' He gave me a sideways look. 'Not everyone knows this, Clare, but Justine threatened to leave me because of my temper and take George with her. She said it was affecting the boy, making *him* bad-tempered. It brought me to my senses. That was what prompted me to join the choir. I thought it might help calm me down.' He smiled. 'It did.'

I'd finally met Robbie's wife Justine – she'd been in the village shop with George that Saturday morning when I was there. She seemed a quiet, sensible sort of woman. She was telling me she'd managed to reduce her working hours so that she could spend more time with her son, and was even considering applying for a job as practice nurse at the doctors' surgery in Sorrel-by-Sea to spare herself the gruelling journey to Plymouth and back. I was glad she'd made Robbie see sense, but even more glad they'd managed to salvage their relationship and their family.

Young Robbie and I parted company and I continued my walk with Sid, all the while mulling over everything he had said. It was amazing and inspiring to hear that getting together with friends to sing some simple songs had had such an impact on this man whose black moods had been so awful. He was really a decent, likeable guy after all. Unfortunately, I couldn't imagine the choir working the same magic on Harry Baker, even in the unlikely event that he could ever be persuaded to join!

CHAPTER 37

Demand for my animal photography continued to increase. I was even selling some of the wildlife photographs I enjoyed taking so much. A couple of pictures of fox cubs playing together had attracted a lot of attention, as had my photo of the Frenches' big cat Archie, standing stock-still in surprise at the edge of the village green, having been confronted with a hedgehog, which had promptly rolled itself into a prickly ball in front of him. I'd been lucky, then, to be in the right place at the right time, with Sid – who'd had to be restrained from getting involved! I'd managed to get one of the 'touristy' gift shops in Sorrel-by-Sea interested in these, too, and they were displaying some of my prints, and already reporting some sales.

With the increase in business came the need for more space. You wouldn't think a few photographs took up much room, but I'd decided to buy a small stock of picture frames and mounts, as it was always easier for people to choose a frame if they could see their photo *in* a couple of them, and decide which looked best. Previously, I'd been using a programme on my computer to show them what various styles and colours of framing would look like, but I got the impression most people found it hard to imagine these images translated into reality. I'd also been considering buying a printer – a really good one, so that I could print the pictures myself instead of relying on online printing – but there wasn't anywhere I could put one, or the necessary stocks of paper and printing ink. There was no room for a table in Julie's little bungalow, apart from a small coffee table in front of the sofa, and even the work surface space in the kitchen was very limited.

'I'm going to have to move,' I told Julie reluctantly when she popped in to look at my latest pictures. 'It's been really kind of you to let me stay here but as you can see, I'm going to need more space.'

'I'm not being kind, you've insisted on paying me rent! But I guess it was only ever going to be a temporary solution for you,' she said. 'Not that we're in any hurry to sell.'

'Maybe not, but I expect you'll be glad to put it on the market anyway. Trouble is, I don't think there's any other vacant property here, is there?' I sighed. 'I might have to find somewhere to rent in Sorrel-by-Sea, temporarily.'

'Oh, that would be a shame.' She looked at me with her head on one side. 'I don't suppose you'd want to consider the extension. I don't blame you – much nicer to move to a newer, bigger place—'

'Hang on, what do you mean, the extension? What extension?'

Julie stared at me. 'I did tell you, didn't I? I thought I did. There are plans approved for an extension to this place. There's plenty of room at the side. I had them drawn up when I first bought it after my divorce, but in the end I got used to it being, well, small and cosy. And then Mike and I decided to get married, so I knew eventually I'd move into the vicarage, and I didn't bother about it. But it would make a huge difference. You could use the extra room as a dining room, or a study – a studio!'

'Oh!' I sat down, taking a while to digest this news. 'Well, I must admit, I do like it here – being right on the beach with the veranda – it's lovely, but just too small. So that could work for me, couldn't it?'

'I'll bring the plans round to show you,' she said, sounding excited. 'I promise I won't try to talk you into it, though. If you'd still prefer to move out, we'll get on with selling it anyway. The planning permission was always going to help with the sale. I can't believe I forgot to tell you.'

*

I gave a lot of thought to the idea of the extension during the next few days. Of course, I could afford to buy the little bungalow – and have the building work done. I could afford to do it several times over if I wanted to, but I still felt the same reluctance I'd felt from the beginning, about spending what I thought of as the children's money.

'Why is it any different from spending it on rent as you are now?' Sally challenged me. 'In fact, you'll end up spending far more of the money eventually, if you keep on renting. Go for it, for God's sake! You've already got a buyer for your flat here in London, haven't you?'

'Apparently, although of course, nothing's ever final until contracts are exchanged, and that takes forever.'

'But what I'm saying is, the flat might be small but it's on the market for loads more, surely, than you'll be paying for that little bungalow, from what you've told me about it. London prices being what they are, and Little Sorrel prices no doubt being abysmal. So once the sale goes through, you'll be back in profit, and the profit will pay for the extension.'

'You make it sound so easy and logical.'

She sighed. 'Because it *is* easy, and it is logical. You're a wealthy woman, Clare. What's not to like about being wealthy?'

'Correction: my children are wealthy, most of the money is for them. And you know quite well why I don't like the idea of being wealthy. I didn't do anything to earn it. It's come from some weird woman I never met, who had a bizarre crush on my husband. I've never liked the feel of her money in my hands or in my bank account.'

'You're the one who's weird,' she said emphatically. 'Come on, Clare, we can all see that you're not greedy or grasping, you're happy to live in the back of beyond, working at your own little business – yes, good for you! – and hardly spending anything on yourself. You've made your point. But for God's sake, do this one thing for yourself, can't you, so that your kids don't have to worry about you, or keep feeling guilty?'

'They haven't said they feel guilty, have they?' I said, alarmed.

'No,' she admitted. 'But they will, won't they, if they think you're condemning yourself to rent a tiny little shed—'

'It's not a shed!' I protested.

'—a tiny little *bungalow*, then, with no table and no proper kitchen, while they enjoy the luxury of their new mortgage-free four-bedroom homes in nice areas, ponies and private schools for the children and—'

I was laughing now. 'It'll be a while before Myla's old enough for school, never mind a pony! And as you well know, Daniel and Prisha haven't even *got* any children. I hope I haven't missed the news of another pregnancy?'

'No, I'm teasing you. But you get my point, don't you?'

'I suppose so. OK. I'll think about it. I'll chase up the estate agent and find out how the sale of the flat's progressing. But it's early days.'

'And you don't need to wait for that,' she reminded me gently. 'Life's too short, love. You should know that. Brian—'

'– should have enjoyed his own wealth,' I finished for her, suddenly feeling tearful. 'I wish he had, Sal. I wished we'd enjoyed it together.'

'Don't get all sloppy and sentimental on me,' she said. 'You didn't even love each other in the end. You'd have been no happier together with the money than you were without it. He had the sense to realise that, didn't he?' She paused. 'I suppose he must have still loved you a bit, in a way, though. He wanted you to enjoy the money.'

'I thought you were trying to stop me feeling sloppy and sentimental!' I wiped my eyes. 'Poor Brian. I wonder what he'd have thought if he could see me now.'

'He'd have thought you were as nutty as his fruitcake author,' she laughed. 'And that would've made two of us!'

*

I spoke to my London estate agents the next day, but the news wasn't good. The potential buyers of the flat had changed their minds but, according to Howard, at Howard Harrison Homes, there were plenty more *interested parties*.

'Let me know when an interested party actually *comes* to the party, then,' I said. 'I won't get my hopes up until they've signed contracts.'

But when Julie brought the plans for the extension to the bungalow round to show me, I did have a look, and I couldn't help feeling interested.

'Perhaps I'll talk to some builders,' I said. 'Get some quotes for doing the work.'

'OK.' Julie smiled at me. 'Honestly, Clare, we're happy for you to stay here as long as you want. While you're paying rent, it's saving me from having to start the whole palaver of putting the place on the market. If you decide to stay, and go for the extension, so much the better, but there's no rush.'

I asked around the village for recommendations of local builders, and was given a couple of names and phone numbers, but I kept putting off doing anything about it. I liked the idea of staying in the bungalow – of making more room there, and carrying on with my business. But idyllic though the setting was, right on the beach there, and much as I liked the place, it didn't quite feel like *mine*, didn't feel quite like my own home in the way Riverside Cottage had done. I told myself that it would probably feel different if I bought the place. But I wasn't sure enough about that to lay out a considerable sum of money on both the bungalow and an extension, even if, as Sally said, I could easily afford it.

*

The weeks passed, quietly and easily, with the weather warming up as June progressed, and suddenly a couple more B&B signs appeared in other cottage windows in the village.

'They're the same people who took in visitors before,' Julie told me. 'Before it all stopped, after the accident.'

'Well, it's nice that they feel it's time to move on and get back to normal, isn't it?' I said.

'Yes. And the idea of the water safety campaign is helping. I think it's reassuring people that there's no need for history to repeat itself,' she said firmly.

The Frenches had written the text for a leaflet now, and I'd helped Young Robbie with the design on the computer and got Mike to print out a batch of copies. I'd just delivered a stock of them to the shop, and I was on my way to put one on the village noticeboard, when Julie had caught up with me on her way to a meeting at the church, and walked with me.

'It could be a good idea for the people doing B&B to keep some of these leaflets too,' she said. 'Their guests would have no excuse for not reading them, then.'

'Brilliant idea,' I agreed. 'And Young Robbie says he'd be happy to talk to any visitors who are interested, about the river, the estuary, the country code, and, you know, history of the village and stuff—'

'He's *happy* to do that, is he?' said a voice at my shoulder. I hadn't noticed Harry walking up behind me. 'Happy to tell the *history* – about what happened last time visitors were encouraged to this village?'

His tone was deceptively mild, although there was a scornful edge to it. But when I turned to face him, the sheer pain in those dark eyes made me almost take a step back. Julie had been right when she'd defended him to me: his heartbreak was so understandable, so palpable, it would be wrong to react with annoyance.

'Harry,' I said quietly, 'I can't begin to imagine how awful it was for you. But it was an *accident*.'

'I wouldn't expect you to know anything about it,' he said, 'being an incomer. But everyone else here understands – or they used to,' he added, and a look of confusion clouded his eyes as he turned to Julie and added, 'You all seem to have forgotten him already. My son. Everyone loved him in this village, but now it seems I'm the only one who still cares about his memory.'

'Harry, that's just not true at all!' Julie said, taking hold of his arm and trying to give him a hug. I hung back, looking at the misery on his face and wishing I could hug him myself; to take him in my arms and hold him and soothe him. But to him, I was just an incomer, someone who'd never understand. 'Of course we all still care,' Julie was saying softly. 'We all miss Paul, we all wish we could turn back the clock, and that the accident had never happened. But don't we owe it to his memory, to pull together, to help each other heal—'

'With silly notices like this? And a *choir*?' he muttered, glancing at me. 'How's that supposed to help?'

'Actually, it's helped tremendously,' she said. 'And we're grateful to Clare for getting it started. But it's Chris Oakley who's running it now.'

'I couldn't care less if the prime minister himself was running it,' he said, more vehemently now, shaking off Julie's consoling arm. 'All I can see is, suddenly you're all encouraging visitors back again, and you seem to think all it takes is to get everyone singing silly little songs about being happy, and we'll all forget what they did.'

Julie glanced at me, looking embarrassed, shaking her head as if to tell me not to take this personally. But I hadn't, anyway. He wasn't being fair, but how could I feel offended? His face was etched with the kind of pain I hoped never to experience as long as I lived. It was lined with exhaustion, his eyes dull with the lack of sleep I could only imagine comes with such horrific grief. I found myself simply wanting to hold him in my arms and comfort him. To stroke his hair, his face, as if he were a child, and tell him I understood.

What the hell was I thinking? I shook myself, blinking myself out of whatever had overcome me, and said, far more abruptly than I meant to, that I needed to get on with what I was doing. Clutching my water safety leaflet, I walked off towards the noticeboard on the village green, where with shaking hands I unlocked the glass door and pinned the pages of the leaflet to the board.

LITTLE SORREL: HOW TO BE SAFE ON OUR WATERS read the heading. I stared at it for a moment after I'd finished and locked the noticeboard again. I'd thought it was a good idea. I'd thought I was being helpful, suggesting this as a positive step, encouraging future visitors to learn how to prevent any more accidents. But was I, in fact, just being insensitive? Had I encouraged the villagers, as Harry implied, to forget his personal tragedy and move on as if nothing had happened? Perhaps he was right. I was an incomer, no matter how hard I tried to fit in, and I still didn't really know how it felt to have lived here all my life, or even to have lived through the horrible time of the accident.

I took a deep breath and squared my shoulders. If I was going to make my home here, I needed, however hard it was, to talk properly to Harry – and preferably without being overcome by those inappropriate feelings I'd experienced earlier.

CHAPTER 38

Harry might have sneered at the silly songs we were singing in the Tuesday evening choir but he seemed to be the only person in the village now who did. Even those who weren't interested in joining often stopped me, Julie or Chris Oakley in the street to ask how it was going, appearing to be genuinely pleased to hear how successful it was, as if they were proud of their friends and neighbours who were taking part. We'd made the decision to enter the South Devon community choir contest in December. Chris warned everyone that, as a new group of complete amateurs, we probably wouldn't be anywhere near good enough to be placed among the winners, but it would be a good experience for us and something to work towards. We'd started practising the Coldplay song 'Fix You', which Harry's sisters, Audrey and Hazel, had suggested. I did wonder whether yet another song about helping each other over hard times was really a good idea, but once again our group of friends and neighbours seemed to find inspiration and personal strength from the lyrics, turning to look at each other and smiling as they sang.

'I think our best song so far is "Memory",' Chris announced at the end of the following week's session. 'We need two of our strongest ones for the contest, but I don't want them to be over-practised to the point where we're bored with them. So let's enjoy a few others in the meantime, and we'll really ratchet up the work on our best songs during the final couple of months.'

Everyone seemed quite excited by the idea of entering the contest. I just hoped they weren't going to be put off or demoralised by the level of talent we'd probably face from other, more experienced choirs, but when we chatted among ourselves the general opinion seemed to be that we'd treat it as a bit of fun. Sadly, though, there would be one element of our sessions missing from the performance at the contest: Chris had asked the organisers, but we weren't surprised to be told that the dogs wouldn't be allowed to come with us.

'It would be too much for them, anyway – all those people in the audience,' Lucy said, hugging Cuddles protectively.

'It might be too much for me, too!' Young Robbie joked.

At the end of the practice that evening, I was talking to Julie when Leo came over to us to remind me that it was nearly his tenth birthday. It was hard to believe a year had passed since the little party I'd held for him at Riverside Cottage for his ninth.

'I'm having a barbecue party in my garden this time,' he confided. 'We're having sausages and burgers.'

'Wow, that sounds like a lot of fun!' I said, smiling. As he turned to run off back to Reggie, I added to Julie, 'I wonder if Kerry would like some help with that?'

'But you'll be invited, obviously!' Julie laughed. 'As one of Leo's very best friends.' She caught the look on my face and went on, 'Don't worry, I'm paying for the party. Kerry's got enough expenses coming up without the extra cost of feeding a gang of hungry boys.'

I didn't like to ask what she meant by this, but said I hoped she would let me know if there was anything at all I could do to help.

'And what can I buy him this year for a present?' I wondered.

'Well, your framed picture of Sid is still his most treasured possession,' Julie said. 'I honestly can't think of anything he'd like more than another photo. But wait until after his birthday. You'll see why.'

I puzzled over this, of course, during the coming days. There was obviously a surprise being planned and I didn't want to spoil it by asking questions. But I had a funny little feeling I might know what it could be. I hoped I wasn't wrong!

*

Meanwhile, my determination to have a proper heart-to-heart talk with Harry, to clear the air and try to make my peace with him, wavered a little every time I saw him. I always gave him a smile and said hello, in return for which I usually merely received a nod. What I needed, I decided, was a topic of conversation that would engage his interest and keep him from marching off with that set expression on his face whenever our paths crossed.

'Hello, Harry,' I tried, when we both happened to be waiting to be served in the shop. At least he couldn't walk away from me now – not without putting all his shopping back on the shelves.

He looked down at his feet and muttered something indecipherable in response.

'I've been meaning to say,' I ploughed on brightly, 'how much I admired your work. Your paintings, I mean. When I was staying in your cottage.'

'Really?' he said in a slightly weary tone.

'Yes, really. I particularly loved the big one in the lounge of the yacht and the sunset sky.'

'Thank you.'

'Do you sell your work?' I persisted. 'I mean, is it your profession, or just a hobby?' Too late, I realised I was insulting him. Of course it wasn't just a hobby! He was far too good.

'I used to sell them,' he said. 'Not any more.'

'Right. I just wondered, you see, because you might have heard, I've recently begun to sell my own work. I'm a photographer—'

'I know. Cute little pictures of dogs and cats.'

I almost gave up at that point. He quite clearly didn't want to talk to me. But then I glanced at his face again and was struck, once more, by the sheer misery in those sombre dark eyes.

'But those cats and dogs make people happy, as you should know,' I said softly. 'You obviously love little Topsy.'

'My son loved her,' he replied just as quietly, without looking at me. 'That's all that matters to me.'

'Of course.' How much difference might it make to his face if he ever smiled? 'But she's beautiful, and so affectionate. She must help to lift your spirits.'

'Perhaps,' he said with a little shrug.

The woman in front of me in the queue turned to give me a sympathetic look. I wondered if *anyone* in the village was managing to have a proper, pleasant conversation with Harry.

'OK,' I said, suddenly determined to go on, and tell it like it was. 'I'm sorry, I do understand you're in a dark place, and perhaps nothing *does* help. But anyway, Topsy's a lovely little cat. And as I said, your paintings are beautiful.'

He blinked, and looked back down at the floor again. The woman in front was served and I moved forwards, turning away from him.

'Your photos of the cat are beautiful too,' he said suddenly to the back of my head. 'I'm grateful for them.'

'Oh. Well, you're very welcome.' I smiled to myself, but didn't turn back – I sensed he hadn't wanted to face me while saying that. I lifted my wire basket onto the counter and began to chat, instead, to Hazel as she scanned my apples, carrots and butter and I loaded them into my shopping bag. But all the time, I was conscious of Harry's presence in the queue behind me. We still hadn't had the kind of meaningful conversation I wanted to have with him, but it could have been worse. Perhaps it was a tiny step in the right direction.

*

Leo's birthday party was on the last Saturday of June. I was relieved to wake to a fine, sunny morning with just a gentle breeze – perfect for a barbecue. Conscious of Julie's advice about giving him another framed photo for his present – but with the intriguing warning about waiting until after his birthday, which was the following day, I felt awkward about turning up empty-handed, so I'd asked if I could buy the birthday cake. Julie had seemed quite relieved to accept this offer, saying she normally made them herself – for Leo and often some of the nieces and nephews too – but was running out of time this year. I'd found the name, on the internet, of a specialist cake baker called Dawn who was based in Sorrel-by-Sea, and I ordered an iced chocolate sponge from her in the shape of a dog. I'd shown Dawn a photo of Sid and she'd asked me to leave it with her, promising to make the cake look just like him. When I returned on the morning of the barbecue to collect the cake, I was stunned to see how realistic she'd made it. The cake-dog was sitting on a cake-cushion, inscribed with the words HAPPY BIRTHDAY LEO: 10, and dotted with the all-important ten candles. I couldn't have been more pleased, and promised to recommend Dawn's business around Little Sorrel. In return, she asked me for some of my business cards to distribute to her own customers.

'Small businesses like ours have to help each other,' she said firmly.

When I took the cake to Kerry's house that afternoon for the barbecue, there were a lot of squeals of approval.

'It looks just like Sid!' Leo said in amazement. I laughed, explained about the photo, and looked up to see Kerry and Julie smiling and winking at each other. I wondered again if I'd guessed right about the secret. But surely, Kerry had always said no to the idea … hadn't she? There really wasn't time to think too much about it then, as the kids wanted to play some team games, which took a bit of organisation and I was happy to help out. And I was almost too scared, for Leo's sake, to hope I was right.

I stayed behind at the end of the party to help clear up in the kitchen. Leo was in the living room, looking at the early birthday presents he'd had from his friends.

'It went well, didn't it?' I said. 'I think the birthday boy enjoyed himself?'

'Yes, he really did,' Kerry agreed. Then she sighed. 'But of course, there was just one thing missing. Well, one *person*.'

I caught the look Julie gave her, and guessed. 'You asked his grandad to come?'

'I did,' Kerry said, with a shrug. 'Mum thinks I should just leave it alone and not waste my time or get Leo's hopes up. But it would mean so much to him if Harry made an effort once in a while. I mean – for his birthday, you'd think, wouldn't you, that he'd put himself out, even if he just called round for ten minutes?'

'Yes. I agree, it wouldn't have killed him,' I said. 'But perhaps your mum's right, you're wasting your time.' I thought about the picture of Paul on Harry's wall. That face, those eyes, so like Leo's it was uncanny. 'He's grieving, of course,' I conceded, 'but surely he could have put Leo before his own feelings just for one afternoon.'

Julie tutted with exasperation. 'The point is, Clare, he never showed very much interest in Leo even before Paul died. Paul never showed much himself, so why would his father? Leo used to go round to Riverside Cottage on Saturdays but he was never encouraged to stay for long. I'm afraid, as I told Kerry at the time, they were both as determined as each other not to get involved.'

Kerry turned away from us both, running water into the sink and splashing plates in the bowl noisily.

'I'm sorry, love,' Julie said more gently, touching her daughter's arm. 'But you know it's true. Nothing's changed. Don't let Leo see it rattles you.'

'It doesn't *rattle* me, Mum. It's just so sad, and such a waste. They could be enjoying each other's company. It would have helped them both to get over Paul.'

She choked slightly over Paul's name, and I felt a rush of sympathy for her. I suspected she'd never got over him herself, perhaps never had another serious relationship since their break-up. She was right: it was all such a waste – a wasted opportunity for Leo's little family to come together and heal. No wonder his mum and grandma felt so frustrated.

*

The following afternoon, the silly tune of my phone interrupted my reading in the sunshine on the veranda, and I was surprised to see Kerry's name flash up on the screen. Since being back in Little Sorrel I'd made sure I had all my new friends' numbers. If any future emergency took me away from the village again, I wouldn't risk losing touch!

'Hi, Kerry,' I said. 'Is everything all right?'

'Clare, it's me!' said an excited little voice. I sat up straight in surprise to hear Leo, evidently using his mum's phone. 'I couldn't wait to tell you what I got for my birthday from my mum and my nan. It's a puppy! Like, an actual, real puppy!'

As his voice had risen to fever pitch, I'd heard a little yapping sound in the background, so I was a step ahead of him. And I'd guessed right! His secret birthday present was the one thing he'd always longed for. I was so pleased for him.

'Leo, that's wonderful!' I said as he went on, excitedly telling me all about the little dog, which was a crossbreed they'd collected from a rehoming centre near Plymouth that morning, and which Julie and Kerry had chosen secretly one day while he was at school.

'He's little and cute, like Sid,' Leo said. 'But he's black, with white splodges, so I'm going to call him Splodge. He's almost a year old, so he's not, like, an actual *baby*, but Mum says he's still a puppy.'

'And at least he's already toilet trained!' I heard Kerry call out in the background, and I laughed. That was certainly a bonus.

'Will you come round and see him, Clare? We're not supposed to take him out for a few days, until he's got used to our house and our garden. They said at the centre, we have to get him *settled*.'

'That's good advice, Leo. Of course I'm coming. I'm getting my shoes on right now!'

'I'll still walk Sid every day, by the way,' he said quickly, just as I was about to hang up. 'When Splodge is OK with me walking him, I can take them out together.'

I laughed and said it didn't matter if his new puppy meant that he had less time for Sid, but he went on to say, earnestly, that he and Reggie would walk the dogs together so they could lead one each.

'And Mum says I can bring Splodge to the choir practices when he's settled down enough, too!' he said happily.

When I arrived at their house, and after I'd greeted this new bundle of fur enthusiastically as he leapt up at me, tail wagging as if he'd known me all his life, Kerry took me to one side and explained why she'd eventually changed her mind about getting a dog.

'It was a few things, really,' she admitted. 'Well, I suppose what clinched it was Mum offering to help out with the cost. It's not just what we had to pay the rehoming centre for him, it's things like pet insurance and so on—'

'Tell me about it!' I agreed.

'But I've been feeling bad about denying Leo this one thing he wanted so much. He'd always promised he'd be responsible for the dog himself if we got one, and I felt he'd proved how responsible he *can* be, by the way he's walked Sid every day with Reggie. Then a few weeks ago, he counted up all the pocket money he's been earning – thank you for that, Clare! – and presented me with this handful of pound coins and asked if he'd got enough to buy himself a dog.' She smiled at me sadly. 'He's got no brothers or sisters, no dad, no grandad worth having. No family apart from me and Mum, and all he wants is someone else to love. How could I go on refusing?'

It was obvious now, what Julie had been hinting at for *my* birthday present to Leo. I'd brought my camera with me anyway to take pictures of the puppy, so I spent a happy half hour or so taking shots of Leo posing and playing with Splodge, and I promised him a large framed portrait to remind him of their very first day together.

Someone to love. It wasn't too much to ask, was it, to make a boy happy?

CHAPTER 39

Leo was true to his word: as soon as Splodge had settled down in his new home and was ready to be taken out on his lead to explore the village, he brought the puppy round to the bungalow to make Sid's acquaintance. Anyone watching that first meeting would have thought the two little dogs had been old friends being reintroduced at a party. Within minutes of their first tentative circling of each other, sniffing each other's behinds and wagging their tails, they were bounding excitedly around the house, sending papers and cushions flying. Sid kept charging towards the door, expecting to be let out onto the beach with his new companion.

'I'm not allowed to let Splodge off the lead outside,' Leo said, stroking his puppy tenderly. Splodge really was a cute little dog, with his funny pointy ears and his fluffy black coat, patterned with spots and splashes of white.

'No, of course not. Come on then, let's put both their leads on and take them out for a walk together.'

Sheila Norton

This first occasion was then followed by the regular appearance of Leo and Reggie together at my door as before, except that now they had a dog each to walk. I continued to pay them pocket money for walking Sid, and the two boys took their duty very seriously. Watching them from my window one afternoon as they walked off along the lane with the dogs tugging at their leads, I noticed other children from the village tagging along with them. My young friends' popularity seemed to have doubled along with their responsibilities. I smiled as I saw Leo allowing little Evie to pat Splodge's head, and Reggie stopping to let George French give Sid a stroke. It was hard now to believe Leo was the same little boy who I'd found sitting, alone and miserable, by the river the previous summer.

*

By the middle of July there was a steady trickle of visitors arriving in Little Sorrel. Nobody seemed sure how it had come about that people from other parts of the country knew the village was once again open for tourists, but Julie and I both suspected that Margaret and the others who were offering bed and breakfast had quietly been advertising on the internet or in Devon tourist guides – and who could blame them? Well, of course, there was still one person who very much *did* blame them – looking away pointedly whenever he happened to pass one of the holidaying families in the street or coming out of their accommodation.

Perhaps because he now had new incomers to focus his disapproval on, Harry seemed to have become a little less antagonistic towards me. I sensed there was a kind of

372

reluctant acceptance of the fact that I wasn't going to give up and go away. What he certainly didn't know, and what I wasn't ready to admit to myself either at that point, was that even if I'd had no other reason to want to stay in Little Sorrel forever, meeting Harry had given me one.

I'd found myself, approaching the grand old age of fifty-nine, when I'd been happy to presume such stuff was behind me for good, thinking constantly of a brooding face, a pair of dark eyes that were heavy with pain, a mouth turned down in sadness, where it should have been forming smile-creases in his cheeks, and a harsh gravelly voice that could have sounded smooth and deep in laughter or in song. I told myself it was just because I wished he'd cheer the hell up, and that I wanted to see him smile because I was fed up with his moods, not for any other reason. Or perhaps I wanted to hear that lift in his voice because he'd probably make a useful addition to the choir; and I stared into those eyes when we chanced to meet and exchange a few polite words, because the misery in them made me feel sadness and pity. I wasn't admitting to anything else!

And so the summer was progressing, with the atmosphere in the village improving day by day, new visitors being welcomed by all bar one, the water safety advice being taught, studied, and gratefully followed, and nobody noticeably being hurt. I was busy with my animal photography, but not so busy that I didn't think often, and with increasing longing, of the people I loved back in London. I missed my kids. I missed my little granddaughter. I missed Sally with her irreverent wisdom and humour. I got to the point, at the end of July, where I stopped asking them all nicely, and instead demanded, that they came down to visit me.

'But you haven't got room to put us up,' they all replied, having had the size and limitations of my new abode described to them in great detail. 'You need to get on with doing that extension.'

I still hadn't made up my mind about that. But that was no excuse!

'There are *three* people here doing bed and breakfast now,' I said sternly. 'And there are still a few vacancies. But if you leave it too long—'

Within days, I'd had promises from them all, and made accommodation bookings for them during August. With this to look forward to, I settled back again into my peaceful existence, using my new career, new friends and the fun of belonging to the choir to try to drown out those ridiculous and increasingly obsessive thoughts about a certain person.

*

I'd often seen little Topsy around the village since I'd been back, and always stopped to bend down and make a fuss of her. I missed her company, having her snuggling down on the sofa with me in the evenings, the way she used to when I was staying in Riverside Cottage. Sometimes she followed me along the road, meowing as if to say she missed me too. But I was surprised, one morning a couple of weeks after Leo's birthday, to find her sitting on the doorstep of the bungalow when I opened the door. In fact, she walked straight into the house, meowing happily, and within minutes she'd come nose to nose with Sid, who'd come running as soon as he heard her. The dog and the little cat then had a joyful reunion, chasing each other around until both flopped down on the rug together. I watched all this, of course, with a smile on my face, but I knew I'd better not do anything to encourage Topsy to stay.

'Off you go, now,' I said, opening the door again. 'Back home, little one.'

She looked at me in surprise, as if she couldn't believe I was throwing her out after she'd finally managed to find us. Eventually I had to pick her up and put her outside, which made me feel mean – and I felt even worse when she then proceeded to sit on the doorstep crying. After a while I presumed she'd given up and gone, but it turned out she'd simply found her way round to the back of the house and was sitting on the beach, meowing up at Sid, who was on the veranda. Within seconds, she'd worked out that all she had to do was climb the steps, jump over the gate in the veranda's rail, and she was back with us.

'Oh dear,' I said, laughing as I picked her up and listened to her purring in my arms. 'What are we going to do with you? Come on, Sid, let's go for a walk. Topsy won't stay here on her own.'

I was right: she didn't. Instead, she followed us down the lane and round to the shop, where she waited patiently outside with Sid, then up to the church, past the green and down to the river.

'I think I'd better take you home,' I said. 'Come on.'

With Topsy still following us, showing no sign of tiring of this new game, we headed into Duck Lane and I knocked on the door of the cottage, my heart suddenly thudding painfully as I waited for Harry to come to the door.

'Hello?' he said a little shortly when he saw us there. He was casually dressed in jeans and a T-shirt that had splashes of paint on it.

'I've brought Topsy back,' I said, picking her up from behind me to show him.

If I'd been expecting him to thank me for finding her straying far from home, I had overestimated his idea of politeness.

'Why have you got her?' he said.

'She turned up at my place. Walked in and wanted to stay!' I gave a little laugh, still stupidly imagining he might see the funny side of it. 'And she really didn't want to leave. So I thought—'

He took Topsy out of my arms, sighing in exasperation.

'I wish you wouldn't encourage her to stray,' he said, and went to close the door on me.

I held onto the door. 'Hang on a minute. I told you, she just walked in. She's followed me all round the village. I haven't encouraged her. Perhaps she just likes my company!' I turned to go, but he put a hand on my arm to stop me.

'I'm sorry,' he said, to my surprise. 'I didn't mean ... well, I shouldn't have said that. It's just that I worry about her, after what happened before, when I was away.' He cleared his throat, as if it had hurt him to talk so candidly. 'Thank you. I know you looked after her when you were staying here, and took her to the vet's and everything. Fair enough, I guess she does like seeing you.'

His eyes met mine, finally, and for a moment we just stared at each other. It seemed neither of us knew quite how to cope with him suddenly being nicer to me.

'Well, it's going to be quite hard to keep her away, now she knows where I am,' I said. 'I do understand you worrying about her, but cats will wander, whether we like it or not.'

'Yes, you're quite right, of course. It was good of you to bring her back.'

There was still no smile, just a kind of weary acceptance. He nodded, as if to dismiss me, but before he turned away I found myself, inexplicably, blurting out, 'Are you painting again now?' with a nod at the stains on his T-shirt.

'Yes,' he said. 'I am.'

'Another landscape?' God knows why I was persisting. Something in me just didn't want him to close the door on me yet – literally or metaphorically.

'No.' He stared at me. 'Why are you so interested?' He said it as if he were merely puzzled, rather than annoyed, by my interest. In fact – perhaps I imagined it – but I thought I saw a fleeting glimmer of amusement in his eyes. 'Or are you just nosy?' he added, with – definitely – a slight twitch of his mouth.

'Both,' I said. I could outstare him, I decided. I felt strangely exhilarated by the challenge of it. 'I'm interested because I loved what I saw of your work. And I suppose I'm nosy because I'm just interested in ... people.' I trailed off now, awkwardly, because it had been on the tip of my tongue to say *in you*. But I continued to stare back at him. If he shut the door on me again now, well, so be it.

'Are you, indeed?' And there it was again – just for a second, that glimmer of amusement in his tone, and – yes, in his eyes, too. 'Well, as you rightly guessed from the state of my attire, I'm in the middle of a painting right now and it's going to be ruined if I don't get back to it. And your dog looks as if he's getting impatient. So I'm afraid we'll have to continue this *very* fascinating conversation about your interest in people another time.'

'I'll look forward to that,' I said. I gave him a smile, and he looked away. I'd won!

I was halfway home before I realised I was singing to myself. And still smiling.

*

'Are you coming to the concert, Clare?' Leo asked me excitedly when he, Reggie and Splodge came for Sid as usual the next day.

'Oh, the school concert?' I smiled at them both. It was being held on the last day before school broke up. 'Are you two in it?'

'Everyone's in it!' Leo laughed.

Of course, with such a small number of children, it was hardly possible to leave anyone out. How nice!

'Me and Leo are both singing solos,' Reggie told me, beaming with pride. 'That's cos we're in the choir, you see. We're the best singers.'

'Wow, that *is* exciting! Of course I'm coming,' I said. 'I wouldn't miss it for the world.'

*

'I'm glad to hear *you're* coming to the school concert, Clare,' Kerry said when I happened to see her in the street the next day. 'Needless to say, Harry has refused point-blank. I did warn Leo not to bother mentioning it to him. What's the point of getting his hopes up and being disappointed all over again? But, apparently, when the boys were walking the dogs yesterday, they ran into him outside the shop – did they tell you?'

'No, they didn't.' I thought back to the previous afternoon when the two boys returned Sid to me after their walk. They'd seemed quiet, I realised now, but I was talking on the phone to Rachel at the time so I hadn't taken too much notice. 'I hope that isn't going to spoil the occasion for him. He seemed so thrilled about his solo.'

'Yes, he is. I think he's still looking forward to it, but every rejection from that miserable old so-and-so still has the power to hurt him, you know. I guess he'll learn to harden his heart eventually.'

Harden his heart. I thought about this, on and off, during the rest of the day. For a ten-year-old boy to have to become hard-hearted because of his grandfather's rejection seemed so sad and unfair. I just hoped the build-up of excitement surrounding the end-of-term concert and the start of the school holiday would be enough to soften the blow.

CHAPTER 40

That Tuesday night after choir practice, Julie suggested I went back to the vicarage for a nightcap with her and Mike.

'It's his birthday,' she explained.

'Oh, I didn't know!' I said. 'You could have missed tonight's practice and gone out together instead.'

'But we're not really going-out types,' she laughed. 'There's nowhere to go here anyway, apart from the pub. Much nicer to have a little drink at home. I've got some sausage rolls to put in the oven, and some cheese in the fridge. Please join us.'

'I'd love to. Thank you.'

Mike greeted me with his usual hug, and when I apologised for not knowing about his birthday, he brushed it aside, saying he never bothered making a fuss about it.

'But at the same time, it's nice to raise a glass in the company of a couple of good friends,' he added.

'A couple?' I queried, looking around the room as if there might be someone hiding behind the curtains.

'I hope you won't mind,' he said, giving me a look as he poured our drinks, 'but I've asked Harry to join us too. I know you find him difficult, Clare,' he went on before I'd even had a chance to respond, 'and you're not alone there, of course. But Julie and I are trying to encourage him to socialise a little more. He could hardly say no to a drink on my birthday.'

Actually, I wouldn't have put it past Harry to say no to anything. But with the memory of our recent conversation on his doorstep still fresh in my mind – still playing in my head every night when I tried to sleep, if I were completely honest – I felt myself flush slightly as I agreed that of course, it was only right for Harry to be invited to his neighbour's birthday celebration.

'Look, Clare,' Julie said, coming into the room with a plate of cheese and biscuits, 'I've framed that picture.'

She'd bought a copy of one of my photos of Leo with Splodge, a different one from that which I'd framed for Leo's birthday present. Julie had fallen in love with this particular one because it was such a nice shot of her grandson. He was looking up at the camera, his smile so wide, his eyes gleaming with happiness. She'd insisted, despite my arguments, on paying me for the print, but said she'd already got a suitable frame. Looking at it now, in pride of place on the sideboard, I had to agree the plain black frame set off the picture perfectly.

We went on to talk briefly to Mike about the songs we'd been singing at the choir practice, and just as Julie went back to the kitchen to get the sausage rolls out of the oven, there was a knock at the door and Mike went to let Harry in.

'Oh, you're here too,' he said to me without any apparent enthusiasm as he came into the lounge. 'Sorry. Hello, Clare,' he amended hurriedly as Julie, carrying in the sausage rolls, gave him a sharp look.

'Hello,' I said back, then lapsed into an awkward silence, fidgeting with my glass, feeling like a schoolgirl at her first party.

'Sit down, Harry, for heaven's sake,' Julie said. 'Mike, get Harry a drink.'

Harry hesitated, looking uneasily at the only free seat – next to me on the sofa. I moved up, so that we didn't need to be too close to each other, and with a little cough he lowered himself down at the other end, without looking at me.

'Here you are, mate,' Mike said, bringing him a glass of wine.

'Right. Well, let's have a toast, shall we?' Julie said brightly, raising her own glass and smiling around at us. 'Happy birthday, darling!' she added to Mike.

'Happy birthday, Mike!' I echoed, raising my own glass.

We all looked at Harry. But Harry had put his glass down. He was staring across the room, staring at the framed photo of Leo with the puppy. His face had gone a strange colour.

'Harry?' Julie prompted him. 'We're having a toast to—'

Ignoring her, Harry turned to me. 'Did *you* put that there?' he demanded.

Julie swung around to see what it was he'd been looking at. 'The photo?' she said. 'No, Harry. I bought it from Clare and put it in a frame. It's a lovely picture, isn't it?'

He looked at it again, and then swung back to me. 'You've been taking photos of my grandson?'

'Your grandson?' I said, my voice wobbling. I was upset for Mike and Julie – to be arguing in their house, when they'd been kind enough to invite us for Mike's birthday. 'I didn't think you even—'

'It's all right, Clare,' Julie stopped me in her calm, no-nonsense way. 'I'll put the picture upstairs if it's upsetting you, Harry. Please don't be cross with Clare. She took some pictures for Leo's birthday. She gave him one as a present, and I wanted to buy one too.'

'His birthday, which you couldn't even be bothered to acknowledge!' I said, too annoyed to take on board the frantic head-shaking signal from Mike or the worried look on Julie's face. 'Why shouldn't Julie have a picture of Leo on display? He's her grandson too! And she's helped his mum bring him up!'

Harry got to his feet, breathing fast as if he'd had a shock, almost kicking over his glass of wine.

'I'm sorry – I can't – I'll have to go – it's just – all too much—' he gasped as he stumbled out of the lounge.

Mike went after him, trying to placate him, but the front door closed with a thud and he returned to the room, sighing. 'I'm so sorry,' he said. 'Perhaps it was a mistake to invite him. He's obviously not ready to—'

'It wasn't your fault,' I said wretchedly. 'It was mine, if anything. I know I shouldn't have reacted, and now I've spoiled your birthday. But honestly, he just makes me cross sometimes!'

And at other times he just makes me want to hug him, I thought miserably, aware that this stupid little fantasy was even less likely now than ever to become a reality!

Mike sat down on the sofa next to me and put his arm around me. 'You haven't spoiled my birthday at all,' he said gently. 'You're our dear friend and you could never spoil anything for us. You were only trying to defend Julie. Come on, drink up and have a sausage roll.'

I laughed, despite myself. 'They do look lovely. I'm sorry, Julie,' I added, as she passed me the plate. 'I'm afraid I didn't help matters at all.'

'I'm beginning to think nobody can,' she said sadly. She grabbed a sausage roll for herself and took a bite before going on, through a mouthful of crumbs, 'I just hope, for Harry's sake, time will eventually heal.'

'You wouldn't know, of course,' Mike went on. 'But Leo looks the spit of his dad Paul. Particularly in that photo, unfortunately.'

'I did know, in fact. I saw some pictures of Paul on the wall of the cottage.' I sighed. 'But I still don't think Julie should have had to hide Leo's photo just because—'

'I don't know, Clare,' Julie said with a sigh. 'OK, Harry obviously sees Leo around the village, but in that particular photo – well, it could *be* Paul, at that age. It wouldn't have hurt to put it out of sight for tonight. It was insensitive of me not to think of it.'

'You're a much nicer person than me, Julie!' I said with a rueful laugh as I bit into my sausage roll. 'And a much better cook, too. These are delicious!'

I stayed long enough to enjoy a second drink, some cheese and another sausage roll, and reassure myself that the incident with Harry really didn't seem to have spoiled Mike's birthday celebration for my sweet-natured, caring friends. I admired them both for their Christian understanding and tolerance. I envied them their ability to remain so calm and sympathetic. But as for me – I was only pretending to be calm. I'm not saying I was right. I'm not saying it was a sensible thing to do. It might not even have happened if I hadn't had that second drink. But the minute the vicarage door was closed after me, I marched straight up the path of the cottage next door and rattled the door knocker.

At first there was no response. If, at that point, I'd given up and walked away, everything might have turned out very differently. But I knocked again, just as a light went on inside, footsteps sounded, coming down the stairs, and the door was flung open, to reveal Harry in a pair of boxer shorts, with a towelling robe flung loosely over his shoulders. Trust me not to even give a thought to the fact that it was nearly eleven o'clock.

'Oh,' I muttered, staring at his face, to avoid looking anywhere else. My embarrassment had, for just a moment, made me forget why I'd come. 'You were in bed.'

'And not expecting visitors,' he said. I sensed, rather than actually saw, him pulling the robe around himself and tying it. 'What is it now?'

'*Now*?' I said, my annoyance resurfacing. Anyone would think I knocked on his door in the middle of the night on a regular basis. 'I just wanted a word with you, that's all.'

He sighed. 'A word? Well, if it's urgent enough to get me out of bed, I suppose you'd better come in.'

I followed him into the living room, where he sat down on one of the sofas and looked at me expectantly. I stayed standing. I felt it at least gave me a slight advantage, although my courage was beginning to fail me now. What good was this actually going to do? He'd made it quite clear how he felt, and nothing I said would make any difference. But nevertheless ...

'I'm sorry, but I just had to say this while I'm still cross enough to say it,' I began.

'Go on then.' He looked, and sounded, tired and defeated.

'Mike and Julie are your friends. They're lovely, kind people—'

'I know.'

'But you were so rude to them this evening!' I stared at him. 'You were invited for a drink, to celebrate Mike's birthday, and you walked out in a temper—'

'Not in a temper, actually. I was, in case you're incapable of understanding such things, extremely upset. The picture—'

'—reminded you of your son! I know! I get that, and I'm sorry; how can I, or anyone, ever tell you enough how sorry we are for your loss? But Leo's your grandson, and he can't help looking exactly like his father! Are you really going to keep on punishing that child because of the way he looks?'

'Punishing him?' He glared back at me now, all pretence of indifference evaporating. 'I'm not *punishing* him. I never had much to do with him. Not even before ... what happened. As you so kindly reminded us, his mother and grandmother brought him up, not me, or my son.'

'So I've heard. And I can't comment on that because it was all before I came here—'

'Exactly. You know nothing about it!' he retorted.

'But what I do know, is: yes, sadly you lost your son, but Leo also lost his father. Whether he chose to have anything to do with the boy or not, Paul *was* his father, and Leo looked up to him, and grieves for him. You might never have another son, and he'll definitely never have another father, but he's still got a grandad! And you could choose to build a relationship with him if you wanted to, if you could just be the adult here and put your feelings – your distress about how much he looks like Paul – to one side and give that kid a chance.'

Harry had got to his feet, his face stony, looking like he couldn't even speak. I instinctively took a step back. I'd gone too far. But it was too late to stop now.

'He's a fantastic little boy,' I said more quietly. 'He was one of my only friends when I first came to this village. He was lonely, and unhappy – despite his lovely mum and nan. The other kids were being mean to him. I bet you didn't even know that, did you? And I was lonely too, being a newcomer here, everyone still too upset about … what happened to Paul … to want me around. Leo and I were company for each other and I got to know him well.' I paused, meeting Harry's eyes now. 'You don't know what you're missing.'

'I don't need a relationship with a child to tell me what I'm missing.' His voice was hoarse with grief. 'I *know* what I'm missing. My son.'

I swallowed. I'd done this all wrong. I should just leave it there, go now, before I did any further damage.

'I know, I do know that,' I said. 'And I'm sorry if I've upset you, but I just had to say—'

'*Why* did you *just have to say* it?' he demanded. It came out almost as a howl of anguish. 'I *know* it. But you have no idea how I feel, how much pain I'm in, it never goes away! And every time I see that child, I want to cry – I want to cry my bloody eyes out, don't you understand?'

'Oh, Harry, I'm so sorry,' I said. Without any further thought – without even consciously remembering that this was what I'd wanted to do for so long – I stepped closer, putting my arms around him and holding him close. He didn't resist. It was as if all the strength had gone out of him, together with all the anger.

'I thought I was ready to come home,' he said in a quiet, broken voice. 'I *wanted* to come home. But it's so hard being here, opening Paul's bedroom door again, seeing his things, walking around the places he used to go, seeing the people he used to love—'

'Of course it is. I shouldn't have said anything,' I said, stroking his back, shushing him as if he were a baby.

'No, you're probably right.' He swallowed hard and seemed to pull himself together slightly. 'I'm being selfish. That kid – my *grandson* – I honestly didn't know he wanted me around. I didn't know he'd been lonely. I thought because he'd got his mum and his nan, he didn't need anyone else, but of course he does. I need to make an effort, don't I? Seeing him, looking so like …'

He trailed off, shaking his head.

'It might even *help* you,' I suggested gently. 'In the long run.'

'Do you think so?' He wiped his eyes, gave a little laugh and looked down at me, a puzzled expression on his face now. 'What makes you so wise?'

In fact, I wasn't feeling particularly wise right at that moment. I was feeling pretty stupid. I'd got hold of this man – this man I'd been unable to get out of my mind ever since I first clapped eyes on him – in a kind of bear hug, and despite the distressing circumstances, it felt so right, I hadn't wanted to let go of him. And now I wasn't sure how to, because he'd followed up by putting his own arms around my waist, and there we were, in each other's arms, looking into each other's eyes, every bit as if he was going to …

… but of course, he didn't. The kiss that I'd imagined so often was, of course, out of the question. I knew that. The poor man was upset, grieving, holding onto my waist only for support, looking at me in that strange hungry way simply because of the pain he was feeling. So I couldn't really explain why I felt almost weak with disappointment as he straightened up, blinking, letting go of me and looking around the room as if he'd almost forgotten where he was.

'I'm sorry,' he muttered, stepping back from me. 'I didn't mean to grab you like that. I don't know what came over me.'

'Don't be silly. Everyone needs a hug now and then,' I said lightly.

'Yes.' He looked down at the floor. 'Well, I guess I should say thank you, anyway. For the advice. You're right about

389

spending time with my grandson. And about me being rude to my good friends next door. You're probably always right, which I suppose is why I've found you so bloody annoying—'

'Well, thanks.' But I laughed, anyway, and finally he gave an awkward little chuckle too.

'Perhaps we should call a truce,' he said, turning his gaze back on me now, so that my heart began to race all over again. 'I'll try not to call you an incomer any more—'

'Thank you. And I'll try to be less *bloody annoying*.' I paused, and then added in a tentative voice that came out almost as a whisper, 'So ... are we friends now?'

'I think so.' He looked at me questioningly. 'If I'm forgiven?'

In response, I took a deep breath for courage, stood on tiptoe to reach him, and gave him a quick kiss on the cheek.

'See you around, then,' I said, turning away, suddenly awkward, as he was still looking at me with his solemn brown gaze. 'I'd better get back to Sid. He'll need to be let out – he'll have his paws crossed by now. And, um, let you go back to bed ...'

He smiled at this, and I smiled back, and the awkward moment seemed to be diffused. I had a grin on my face and a spring in my step as I walked home. We were friends. He'd hugged me – apparently by mistake, but still, he hadn't looked particularly revolted by it. Could it be .. could it actually be that, despite his grieving, and behind his miserable façade, he'd really liked me just a little bit all along?

It was true I hadn't slept particularly well at night ever since I'd met him, but that night I didn't sleep at all. I remembered a night when I was about fifteen, desperately in love with my first boyfriend, when I'd stayed awake all night because I was so afraid that if I fell asleep, I'd wake up to find it had all been a dream. How ridiculous that I was having almost the same kind of crazy night-time thoughts now, at nearly fifty-nine. And … not even minding.

CHAPTER 41

The school concert was the following afternoon, and when I look back on it, I remember it as the turning point for Harry and Leo. When I'd arrived at the school hall, there were already quite a few people in the audience, and there in the front row, right in the centre, as if he'd got there an hour early and reserved his place, was the one person who would make the day completely perfect for my little friend: his grandad. In fact, my only concern was that Leo would be so surprised to see him there, it might put him off his words and spoil his solo performance. But I needn't have worried. Having now had months of training with our choir, our young protégé simply gave one beaming smile of recognition on seeing Harry there, and then regained his professionalism and sang like an angel.

'He was amazing!' Julie said, wiping a tear from her eye as she, Kerry and I hugged each other afterwards. 'They all were, of course, but Leo – well, he used to be so shy. It's such a transformation.'

'And did you see who was in the front row?' Kerry demanded of her mum. 'I couldn't believe it! He'd refused outright to come. I wonder what on earth happened to change his mind.'

'So do I,' said Julie, and she looked sideways at me for a moment, her eyebrows raised, while I pretended to be ever so interested in a speck of dirt on my shoe.

'I couldn't help hearing some loud knocking on the cottage door last night,' she said later, after Kerry had rushed off to get on with her work. 'Late. Just after you'd left us, actually. And some raised voices. I hope everything was all right?'

'I'd say everything was absolutely fine,' I said, trying, and failing, to hide my smile.

She put her arm through mine and squeezed my hand. 'Good,' she said. 'I'm glad.'

Harry slipped away at the end of the concert, having noticed the three of us huddled together chatting, and simply gave me a nod and a smile. I hoped he didn't think I was gossiping about him and the previous evening. I was trying to talk myself out of giving it too much importance in my mind, but it wasn't easy.

As soon as school had finished, Leo and Reggie came round as usual to walk the dogs. They were both in an overexcited mood about the success of the concert, but Leo in particular was beaming from ear to ear, full of the fact that his *grandad* had come, had sat in the very front row and clapped and cheered louder than anyone.

That evening, there was a knock at the bungalow door, and I was surprised and a little flustered to see Harry there, looking strangely shy, but more handsome than ever in smart jeans and a blue shirt, and holding a bottle of wine.

'I just wanted to say thank you again,' he said as I let him in. 'For encouraging me to do the right thing. As you said, Leo's obviously a very special boy. I've spoken to his mum, and I'm going to be seeing him regularly now. And helping her, too. She shouldn't have to struggle, she should have support from – his father's side – and, well, she should have had that all along, of course. That's for me to put right now.'

And before I could even reply, he'd bent down and given me a quick hug. Just a thank you hug from a friend, I told my racing heart firmly as I poured out the wine. Don't go reading too much into it. After all, it had been me who'd told him we all needed to hug someone.

But over the next week or so, we managed to find an excuse to call on each other every day. The friendly hugs lasted a little longer each time; the occasional friendly kisses on the cheek started to linger. Harry still had his sad times, his quiet moments when it was harder to reach him, and of course I respected this and gave him space – but he seemed to be managing his feelings a little better, day by day, week by week. People around the village were noticing and commenting on his improved temperament, and of course it wasn't long before they were also noticing – and raising their eyebrows at – us being out and about together.

Slowly, quietly, we became a couple, in a gentle and gradual way, as if it were happening without either of us really doing anything. We were, I suppose, *courting*, in the old-fashioned way. We'd sometimes walk the dogs with Leo and Reggie. Harry would come to the bungalow and I'd cook him a meal while he looked through my photos, holding prints up to the light and approving them with his artist's eye. Or I'd go to the cottage and spend quiet afternoons watching him paint, helping him in the garden, sharing a pot of tea and a cake I'd baked. He'd thrown himself back into his painting with enthusiasm and was keen to start selling his pictures again. We discussed mounts and frames together and talked about hiring the school hall one day and having a joint exhibition. I loved his company; it felt oddly as if we'd known each other for ever. And of course, I'd been wildly attracted to him from the moment I first saw his face. It took a little longer for him to admit he'd felt the same about me – and for us to, finally, spend a whole night together in the cottage, waking up to the sun streaming in through the window of that bedroom I'd always loved so much.

When Sally came for her week's holiday, staying with Margaret Manners, it took all of ten minutes for her to find out what I'd resisted telling her in our phone conversations before her arrival.

'You're seeing someone, aren't you?' she said, holding me at arm's length and looking me up and down. 'It's written all over your face, you crafty moo! Who is it? Not the grumpy ferryman, is it? – the young one, I mean – or .. surely not the old one?'

'No!' I laughed. 'And Young Robbie's not grumpy any more, we're good friends these days. And anyway, his marriage is back on track now.'

'So …' Her eyes suddenly widened. 'Not … oh my God, it *is*, isn't it? You've gone all red, Clare! It's the guy who owned the cottage, the miserable one, the one who—'

'Harry,' I said, the smile spreading across my face just from the pleasure of saying his name. 'Yes. We're seeing each other. And he's not miserable; he was grieving. It's …' I shrugged, unsure how to put it into words, 'It's all such a surprise, Sal. At our age.'

'Our age?' she retorted. 'We're not exactly over the hill yet, old girl! I've been known to have a few little flings myself over the years – between marriages.'

'Yes, and good for you!' I hugged her, laughing again. 'But … I know it's early days, but I have a feeling this isn't just a fling.'

'Well, in that case, my love,' she said more gently, looking at me quite seriously now, 'I hope he treats you well. Because if he doesn't, he'll have me to answer to.'

'I'll tell him that,' I assured her. 'Or if you like, you can tell him yourself. He's coming round after dinner.'

*

A couple of weeks later, my family came for their holiday. Daniel and Prisha were staying with Margaret Manners, while Rachel, Jason and Myla stayed with Margaret's daughter Mandy – owner of Brex the rabbit. Mandy was now taking in guests herself, and was delighted to offer to babysit if needed. I prepared myself to go through the whole thing again of telling the family about Harry. But I'd reckoned without the superior detective skills of my daughter, who hadn't even needed to see my blushing face or the look in my eyes which Sally reckoned had given the game away, to guess I had 'a new love interest' as she delicately put it.

'And we're pleased to hear about it, Mum,' she assured me when, having lunch together in the pub on the first day of their holiday, I explained who it was and how it had come about. 'As long as he's good to you, that's all we care about.'

'I'll sort him out if he's not,' Daniel asserted fiercely, and I laughed, and told him he'd have to get behind Sally in the queue for that!

*

It was just as we were finishing lunch that day that Rachel suddenly remembered, 'Oh, I've got something here for you, Mum.' She pulled a rather official-looking envelope out of her pocket. 'It must have slipped through the redirection system.' She or Daniel had still been going back to my old flat every couple of weeks, although we were now keeping our fingers crossed that a potential new buyer was going to sign contracts soon.

I turned the envelope over in my hands. 'It's probably just some kind of junk mail,' I said. 'Unless I'm being chased for an old speeding offence or something. Thanks, anyway.' I put it in my handbag. 'I'll open it later. Now, come on, tell me all about these new friends you and Myla have made at the parent-and-baby group—'

'Not till you've told us some more about the new boyfriend,' Rachel laughed. 'Like, when are we going to meet him?'

Of course, they met him several times throughout that week, and were charmed. Harry was a different person these days from the scowling, taciturn man who'd stalked the village, taking his grief out on everyone else. His ready smile lit up his whole face, his eyes sparkling exactly as I'd always imagined, even when I used to look at his self-portrait in Riverside Cottage before I met him. People around the village had remarked on his nicer nature, his readiness to smile politely and stop for a chat. Of course, I wasn't claiming responsibility for these improvements – not all of them, anyway! It was mostly his own determination, now that he'd made the decision to get to know his grandson and try to move on with his life, to put on a brave face for the world and wait for his heart to gradually catch up.

*

It wasn't until the last day of the family's holiday that I rediscovered the letter in my handbag as I fumbled for my purse to pay for some groceries in the village shop. I'd asked the family to come to the bungalow for our final meal together that evening. I realised I'd have to cook something easy, like a chilli, that we could eat off trays on our laps, and someone might have to sit on the floor, and that had got me, once again, wondering about the idea of the extension. Or moving, if a bigger house were to come on the market.

I opened the letter when I got back from shopping, slitting the envelope open while I waited for the kettle to boil, and skimmed the contents quickly, expecting to be consigning it to the recycling bin within a matter of minutes. And then I sat down. And forgot to make the coffee. And I was still in a daze when the family arrived for that chilli.

*

'So anyway,' I said as we finally polished off our meal, 'I've got some news.' I waved the letter in the air. 'It's from the literary agent – Sarah Matheson – who looks after your dad's crazy author's business.'

I read out the letter. And looking at their faces afterwards, I then read it out again, more slowly. I was still struggling to take it in myself, so I couldn't blame them for looking shell-shocked.

'Film rights?' said Daniel eventually. 'But didn't you tell us one of the books had already been made into a film?'

'Yep. That was her – Jacqueline Bright's – first novel. This is, apparently, a sudden interest from a film producer in the second book. The producer wants to option the rights. We'll get a fee just for that. And if they go ahead and produce the film – which apparently looks very likely – there will be lots more money coming in.' I paused. 'If I agree, of course. As I'm now the author's *estate*, the rights belong to me, and it's up to me to say yes or—'

'But of course you'll say yes, won't you?' Rachel said. 'I mean, why wouldn't you?'

'I don't know.' I sat back, shaking my head. 'I suppose it's all just a bit overwhelming. I feel out of my depth.'

'Then give her a call – the literary agent,' Rachel said. 'She's probably wondering why you haven't already replied. That letter was lying on the doormat of your flat—'

'And then in my handbag all this week,' I admitted. 'I thought it was junk mail.'

I'd had post from Sarah Matheson before; she'd obviously been in touch after Brian died, and now I just received biannual statements showing me a trickle of royalties still coming through from the mad author's book sales. After so long, these were almost negligible, which was why the whole idea of someone suddenly deciding that another film might be a nifty idea was such a shock. But really, as Rachel had said, what was the point of saying anything other than a big fat yes? Thanks to the legacy, we weren't exactly short of money, but the kids had made a dent in their shares already. There'd been Daniel and Prisha's wedding and the new house they were buying, new cars for Rachel and Jason, the pram, cot, and never-ending stream of things necessary for baby Myla, to say nothing of new furniture, fitted kitchens, new carpets and new wardrobes – and why not? That was exactly what I'd wanted for them – not to have to struggle any more. But eventually the rest of the money would run out, however carefully they invested it. I had no idea what sort of remuneration to expect from film rights being sold, but the kids seemed to think it wasn't to be sniffed at.

'OK,' I said, 'I'll call her tomorrow.'

*

The family were on their way home the next day by the time I'd finished the call and had a chance to calm down. I forced myself to wait until the evening, meanwhile working out how to make a group call on WhatsApp. There was a lot of excitement and squealing going on when I finally told them the sort of deal Sarah Matheson was hoping to get with the film producer. Apparently, the type of book Jacqueline Bright wrote was now hugely back in fashion and the producer already had ideas for celebrity leads in the film.

'Right, Mum,' Daniel said when they'd all quietened down. He sounded quite severe, 'We want *you* to use some of the money now.'

'Yes,' Rachel agreed. 'Stop making excuses about us needing it. We've all got what we need now—'

'But you and Jason were talking about moving. You can get a bigger house – more space, in case you have another child—'

There was a beat of silence, and then she laughed. 'Yes, we were talking about moving. But not to a bigger house. We weren't going to tell you this yet, Mum, but we're actually thinking of moving to Devon.'

'*What*?'

'Don't sound so shocked. We've both fallen in love with Little Sorrel now – you of all people should understand how that happens!'

'You want to move *here*? To Little Sorrel?' I yelled. The thought of having my beloved daughter and granddaughter living close to me again was even more overwhelming than the shock of the potential film deal. The pain of saying goodbye to them all the previous night had even started me wondering, all over again, whether I really should have stayed in London. I missed them all so much. Maybe Daniel and Prisha might even be tempted, eventually, to move down too?

'We won't necessarily be living in Little Sorrel,' Rachel said. 'I doubt we'd find anywhere there – there are so few houses in the village. But somewhere in the area.'

'And you needn't start thinking we'll be joining you,' Daniel put in, as if I'd spoken my thoughts aloud. 'Well, not in the foreseeable future anyway. Sorry.'

'But even so, it would be wonderful if you and Jason moved down, Rach. I'll start looking out for properties—'

'Look for your own, first!' she laughed. 'Mum, you really have to move from that tiny bungalow now. It's ridiculous. At least buy it and get the extension done, if nothing else.'

She was right: it made absolute sense, I thought to myself after I'd hung up. But I still didn't do anything about it. I didn't talk to Julie about buying the bungalow. I didn't look at the quotes from the builders. I decided I should wait until we knew for sure about the film deal. And eventually I wondered if somehow, in the back of my mind, I'd known there was going to be a much better solution just around the corner. Quite literally.

CHAPTER 42
TWO MONTHS LATER

'This is getting ridiculous,' Harry said, shifting the printer from where I'd got it balanced on one of the chairs. 'You need a table.'

'I know. But there isn't room.' I gave him an apologetic look. 'I know, I know, I should have made a decision about buying the place, and having the extension built, but—'

'But you've been so busy.' He put his arms round me. 'And it's great, isn't it? Great that so many people want photographs of their pets that they travel so far to come here because your pictures are so good.'

'To be honest, it's because of the summer visitors.' I gave him a careful look, but he was nodding agreement. It had taken a while, but he'd pretty much got used to seeing holidaymakers in the village again, and even now, in October, we had a steady trickle of visitors staying, and day-trippers coming down from Plymouth or Exeter, strolling around the streets, remarking on the peace and quiet and seeing my cards and sample photos displayed in the window of the shop.

'Yes. And I'm pleased for you,' he said, kissing the top of my head.

'It hasn't done you any harm, either,' I pointed out.

He'd got his own cards on display now too, and it was amazing how many of the holidaymakers during the summer had been eager to go home with one of his beautiful landscape paintings parcelled up in the backs of their cars.

'I know.' He held me out at arm's length and gave me a serious look. 'Clare, we both need more space. Not for ourselves so much but for our work. Ideally, we need a little studio, where I can paint, you can print your pictures, and we can display our work, so that people can walk around and look at them on the walls. Selling from our homes, the way we've been doing, isn't ideal.'

'No, I agree, it's not.' I smiled. I liked the idea of combining our two businesses, working as a team, perhaps as a joint enterprise. Spending our days together peacefully in a little studio somewhere, both immersed in our work but in each other's company. 'But there isn't anywhere suitable,' I said with a shrug.

'There could be.' He looked around the room. 'This would be perfect, in fact, if we were to buy it from Julie.'

I frowned. 'Well, maybe, if I got the extension built. But would that work? Would the extension give us both enough space?'

'There'd be plenty of room, even without an extension, if you weren't living here.' He grinned and pulled me close to him. 'Move in with me, Clare. Please? We don't need to wait any longer, do we? We're both adults. Well, old people! And we're good together – aren't we?'

I laughed. 'Not so much of the *old*! But yes, of course we're good together, and of course I'd love to move in with you.' Needless to say, I'd been hoping we'd agree to do this, sooner or later. Perhaps subconsciously that was why I'd put off making any decisions. 'And you're right, as just a studio, this place would be perfect. And there's plenty of room in Riverside Cottage. I've always loved it there—'

'Actually, I wasn't thinking of us living there. Not long-term, anyway.'

'Oh!' I stared at him. 'Why not?'

'I love the cottage too. But I'd quite like somewhere with a bit more space. Room for Leo to stay overnight sometimes. I still find it hard to use the second bedroom,' he added quietly.

'Of course. It's lovely that Leo spends so much more time with you now, but I can imagine how you feel, about Paul's room.'

'Being with Leo is helping, just as you said it would.' He smiled. 'So I'd like a bigger garden, too. Room for him and Reggie to play out there with the dogs, and – well, for games of cricket and stuff like that, in the summer.'

'That all sounds wonderful, Harry, but there's nowhere available.'

'Yes, there is. Sorrel House.'

'You're joking.' Sorrel House – the biggest old house in the village – had been empty for years and was in a state of disrepair. The locals were in the habit of saying that it would fall down before anyone came along who was daft enough to buy it.

'I'm not joking at all.' Harry's eyes were gleaming with excitement. 'I've had a surveyor's report done on it, Clare. It's a good, solid house – apparently, most of the damage is cosmetic rather than structural. It'll take time, of course, but by the time we've bought this place from Julie and done it up as our studio—'

'And we'll live in the cottage in the meantime?'

'Of course.' He smiled. 'And from what you've told me about Rachel and Jason, I don't think we'll have any trouble selling that, either, when we're ready.'

'Oh!' I squealed. 'That would be *perfect*, wouldn't it? It would be lovely for them to move into the cottage – if they want it, of course. Unless they'd prefer somewhere bigger.'

'Yes, they might do, eventually. But it could work for them to begin with, couldn't it? At least it'd get them down here.' He smiled at me. 'I know how much you miss them.'

I closed my eyes for a moment and tried to visualise the future. Could it really work? It seemed too perfect. That lovely old house, renovated and restored to its former splendour. Room in those grounds for Leo to run and play with Reggie and the dogs – and for Topsy to curl up in the sunshine on a windowsill. This little bungalow converted into our studio. Rachel, Jason and Myla living in Riverside Cottage.

'It just sounds too good to be true,' I said. 'Like a dream.'

'A dream that can come true,' he corrected me, stroking my hair away from my face. 'And why not? We've both had our share of struggles and sadness and loss, haven't we, and now we're both comfortably off—'

I frowned at this, and he laughed. 'Come on, Clare – I *know* you never wanted to splash your money around. You've only just got around to telling anyone here – even Julie and Mike, even me! – about your inheritance. I respect you for wanting to live the same as everyone else, determined not to show off about the wealth you didn't even want. But *I'm* pretty well off too, as I've explained to you. I didn't want the life insurance pay-out on my son's death. It felt all wrong, like I was benefiting from the worst thing that could possibly happen. But now I realise I can use it in the best possible way by helping my grandson – Paul's son – just as you've been helping your own children. And anyway, wouldn't your ex-husband have been happy to know you were enjoying life?' He swallowed quickly and added, 'Wouldn't Paul have wanted to know I was, too?'

'Yes, he would. You're right.' I kissed him. 'OK, you've convinced me.'

'You don't want to think it over? You haven't even seen inside Sorrel House yet!'

'No, but let's do that tomorrow. Let's call the estate agents now! I want to get on with it, before I change my mind.' I paused. 'You *knew* I'd agree, didn't you?'

'Yes, I did. Well, I hoped! I remember you telling me how you arrived in Little Sorrel that very first day, not knowing where you were or why you wanted to stay.'

'Yes. I felt, strangely, as if I knew my future was going to be here. Despite being made to feel so unwelcome!'

'And as soon as I saw you,' he said more softly, 'parked outside the cottage that day, squaring up to me with your hands on your hips, refusing to back down, refusing to pander to my bad mood – I knew you were *my* future. Knew it, but couldn't understand it. I didn't think I'd ever be this happy again.'

'I felt the same,' I admitted. 'So maybe dreams *can* come true. Even at our ancient age!'

'Do you know what?' he said. 'I don't think there's any *better* time for them to come true.'

EPILOGUE

It's a cold day, just before Christmas. I'm on my way back to Little Sorrel from a Christmas tree plantation on the outskirts of Dartmoor with a six-foot tree poking out of the back of my car and the radio belting out 'Driving Home for Christmas'. Perfect. I've turned up the volume, and I'm singing along, when I have to slow down for a tractor in front of me and suddenly I'm having a flashback to that day, two and a half years ago, the very first time I ever drove down this godforsaken lane with no idea where it ended up. The tractor signals to pull into the layby at the top of the hill and I wave my thanks to him as I pass. I'm not stopping to look at the view this time. But I do look out at all the familiar sights in a slightly different way, as I drive back down the hill and into the village, remembering how I felt that day.

Here's the Ferryboat Inn, looking very pretty and festive now with Christmas lights draped around the doors and windows. Here's Saint Peter's church, where everyone

– even non-believers like Harry and me – will be crowding together on Christmas Eve for Mike's favourite service of the year. Here's the little village school. The children have broken up for the holiday now, but a few younger ones are playing at the side of the school building, on the steps down to the river, while some of the older boys are standing in a group together chatting. I beep my horn and wave at Leo and Reggie, who have Sid and Splodge with them on their leads, and George French, who at twelve now towers over the others and has been seen around the village recently holding the hand of a girl from his class at the high school.

Outside the village shop, Audrey is choosing apples from the fruit and veg display, while her sister Hazel watches her from inside. They both look up as I drive past. So few cars travel through the village, especially at this time of year, that people always look. They wave, making thumbs-up signs when they see the tree sticking out of my boot.

Chris Oakley comes out of the shop just then, and I pull over and wind down my window.

'Recovered from last night yet?' I say with a smile, and he laughs, shaking his head.

'Wasn't it great, Clare?' he enthuses. 'I mean, I know our choir didn't win any prizes—'

'We didn't expect to,' I remind him.

'No, but to get a special commendation for doing so well considering we were a gang of complete novices – that was nice. Especially for the kids,' he adds.

'Yes. They were over the moon. They'd worked so hard. Well, we all had! It was a lovely evening.'

We'll be entering the contest again next year. Who knows, by then we might even be good enough to be placed somewhere. The choir has grown to the extent where about half the human population of the village – and virtually every dog – comes along to our practice sessions. We'll be having mulled wine and mince pies at the next one, with bowls of dog treats all round.

I say goodbye and carry on into Duck Lane, parking outside the cottage and chatting for a while to Julie and Mike, who are putting up a Christmas wreath on the vicarage door. Harry's heard my voice and comes out to greet me with a hug.

'Well done,' he says, nodding at the tree. 'I'll take it inside.'

'Are they here yet?' I ask him breathlessly.

'No – it's only half past eleven!' he laughs. 'They'll probably not be here till after lunch.'

Rachel, Jason and Myla are on their way to spend Christmas with us. Harry's spent the past week clearing the second bedroom. I offered to help him, but he wanted to do it himself, slowly going through Paul's things and packing them up for the charity shop in Sorrel-by-Sea.

'It had to be done. I just needed a reason to do it,' he said when I protested that it would be too upsetting for him.

We're hoping to be moving into Sorrel House in February. The most essential work should be finished by then, and we can take our time over internal redecoration. Rachel and Jason have a potential buyer for their house and they're so looking forward to moving down here. Rachel told me on the phone the other day that the excitement has brought Jason out in hives.

'I thought his allergies were all in his mind!' I said, and felt quite guilty when she refuted this.

'But he's learnt to cope with them better,' she added. 'I think becoming a father has given him other things to worry about.'

*

'Come in out of the cold,' Harry says to me now. 'I'll make you a coffee before I start on the Christmas tree.'

We sit in the kitchen to drink our coffee, little Topsy curled up on my lap, purring, and we talk again about the choir contest the previous evening. We'd hired a coach to take us all to Plymouth. Harry was in the audience. It was the first time he'd heard us perform; he'd never wanted to come along to a practice.

'I wasn't interested in joining. I'm a rotten singer anyway,' he admits now. 'But I was being a coward, too. When you told me about some of the songs you were rehearsing, I thought I might find it too emotional.'

'But you were OK last night? When we sang "Lean on Me"?'

He smiles ruefully. 'Actually, I had tears pouring down my face. But not because I was upset – because it was so absolutely beautiful.'

I take hold of his hand across the table and squeeze it.

'And the words,' he goes on quietly, 'they're so true. When I think about how much more I suffered, earlier on, because I didn't reach out to my friends and neighbours for support – I just alienated everyone instead – I feel such

412

an idiot. I can't imagine what you saw in me, when I was such a horrendous grump.'

'Nor can I,' I tease him. 'I must have had a screw loose. I was just thinking, driving back here today, about the very first time I drove into this village. I fell in love with it instantly, without knowing why. I suppose it was the same thing with you. I even fell in love with your self-portrait – on that wall!' I pointed and laughed. 'Before I even met you!'

'Definitely a screw loose,' he teases back.

We don't tend to overdo the mushy stuff. We both know how we feel, and that's good enough.

He gets up to go back outside for the Christmas tree.

'I had a text from Daniel earlier, by the way,' I remember to tell him as I follow him to the door. 'Prisha's had her scan. Everything looks fine. The baby's due in July.'

'Oh, that's great! How exciting!' He gives me a thoughtful look. 'I wonder if she'll manage to talk Daniel into it.'

'Moving down here? I don't know. The problem's his job, obviously, but he has said he's been thinking about a change. Perhaps now Prisha's decided it's what she'd like ... I know he'd do anything for her.'

'Even if they were to move to Plymouth, or Exeter – much easier for work, and housing, than here – it'd be nice for you, to have them closer, wouldn't it? And nice for Rachel and Jason too.'

'And the grandkids, growing up together. But at the end of the day, it has to be their decision.'

I smile, thinking about little Myla growing up here, and one day being old enough to go to the village school. Leo already adores her. Whenever they've been visiting, he's played with her almost as much as he plays with Splodge and Sid.

*

I know there's one person, though, who's never likely to move down to Devon, and I'm thinking about her now as I help Harry lift the Christmas tree into its bucket, and we start decorating it with the baubles and lights he found in a box at the bottom of Paul's wardrobe.

'I haven't called Sally about last night yet,' I say. 'She asked me to let her know how we got on in the choir contest.'

'So you haven't told her the news?' He raises an eyebrow at me.

'About the choir? The commendation?' I'm teasing him again, and he knows it. 'Or was there something else?'

'Go on, call her now,' he says with a smile. 'Turn your phone volume down – you know how she's going to squeal!'

Sally answers almost immediately. 'So, did you win?' she demands.

'Don't be daft, of course not. But we got a special commendation for putting on "the highest standard of performance from an inexperienced choir".'

'Ooh, get you! Seriously, that's great, Clare. I bet you're all chuffed.'

'Yes, we are.'

'Family arrived yet?'

'No – any time now. We're just decorating the Christmas tree.'

'Nice. Have a good time, then—'

'Sal, there's something else,' I say quickly. I'm having trouble keeping the smile out of my voice. She's going to guess. She knows me too well.

'Go on,' she says. 'Daniel's moving down?'

'No. At least, he might, one day, but—'

'Well, that's all very nice, but I hope you don't think *I'm* going to join this mass exodus to the countryside. I miss you like crazy, but you need to have at least one sane friend left who still knows one end of the Central Line from the other in case you need to visit the metropolis.'

I laugh. 'I know you're never going to leave London—'

'Apart from anything else, some of us still have to work for a living,' she ploughs on, 'and there's nothing in your neck of the woods for a poor struggling wedding photographer to earn her crust from. Hardly anyone lives there, and those who do get married are too poor to pay for flashy weddings with creatively designed photographic souvenirs. They probably just get your vicar friend to say a few words after morning service and pop back to their cottages for tea and biscuits—'

'Our village is *not* poor and downtrodden,' I protest, laughing. 'I'll have you know we're a popular tourist destination these days! And anyway ...' I pause, partly for effect and partly to prepare myself for the squealing that's bound to come, '... there's going to be one very big, suitably flashy wedding in the spring that you might want to come to. I might even hire you to do the photographs – unless you'd rather be my bridesmaid.'

There's a deathly silence for a moment. Has she fainted? Have we lost the connection? But no – it's just a delayed reaction. I hold the phone away from my ear, grinning across the room at Harry, who can hear the squeals from the other side of the Christmas tree.

'Oh my God!' she screams. 'You're getting bloody married! When did you decide this? Have you told anyone else? What's the date – quick, I need to clear my diary! What are you wearing? Is your vicar making you do it in church? Who's coming? Where are you having the reception – in your huge new manor house? Who's doing the catering? What about a cake?' She stops for breath, but I can't speak for laughing. And then, in a quieter voice, a small, solemn voice that stops the laughter in my throat and brings a tear to my eye instead, she adds, 'You *are* quite sure he really loves you, aren't you, Clare? I hope you've warned him that I'll murder him if he ever hurts you.'

'Don't worry, love.' I look across at Harry again. He's stopped in the middle of putting a star on top of the Christmas tree, watching me talk to my oldest friend, and he's smiling at me with a tenderness that makes me feel like my heart might burst. 'You won't need to be committing any murders.'

*

'What was all that about murder?' Harry asks me a little later, as we stand back to admire the finished tree. 'Was she asking about the film?'

The film producer has recently been in touch with the literary agent. From what she's told me, the movie's going to be a lot gorier than the book was. People like a lot of blood and guts in their films these days, apparently.

'Yes,' I fib, smiling at him. 'She was wondering what Brian's crazy author would say if she knew how things had worked out.'

'Mm.' He nods thoughtfully. 'I reckon Jacqueline Bright was of the generation of authors who'd have wanted a happy ending. Despite whatever's gone before.'

'Yes, I think you're probably right. She must have wanted, in her own warped way, to make Brian happy. I hope she'd have been satisfied with our own happy ending instead.'

'Well, to have harboured those feelings about Brian for all those years, she must have been a romantic at heart,' he muses.

And to my own surprise, I actually find myself thinking … well, maybe she wasn't quite so mad after all.

ACKNOWLEDGEMENTS

Thanks again to my agent Juliet, and to everyone at Ebury (past and present) who's contributed to making this book, and its predecessors, even better than I'd hoped.

If you enjoyed

Escape to Riverside Cottage

Leave a review online

Follow Sheila on Facebook/SheilaNortonAuthor and on
Twitter @NortonSheilaann

Keep up to date with Sheila's latest news on her website
www.sheilanorton.com

Make sure you've read Sheila's other novels …

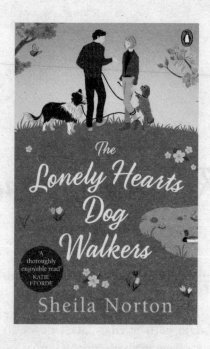

The
Lonely Hearts
Dog
Walkers

'A thoroughly enjoyable read' KATIE FFORDE

Sheila Norton

Could this be the perfect place to start over…?

When Nicola's marriage falls apart and she's left broken-hearted, she decides to move back home to the idyllic village of Furzewell. But her fresh start isn't everything she hoped it would be – daughter Mia is struggling to fit in at school and she's finding it challenging living with her overbearing mother.

But when she joins the local dog-walkers group, Nicky finds the support she's been looking for – The Lonely Hearts Dog Walkers never fail to be there for each other in a crisis. When their local park is threatened by developers, they are determined to rally together to save it.

Can Nicky fight to protect her new community and find her happy furever after…?

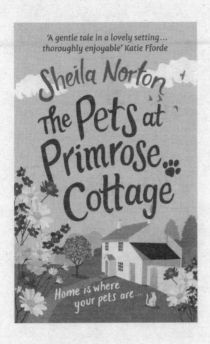

'A gentle tale in a lovely setting...
thoroughly enjoyable' Katie Fforde

Sheila Norton

The Pets at Primrose Cottage

Home is where
your pets are...

Emma Nightingale needs a place to hide away...

Fresh from the heartbreak of a failed relationship, she takes refuge in quiet Crickleford. And not before long – and quite accidentally too – Emma finds herself the town's favourite pet-sitter, a role she isn't certain of at first, but soon her heart is warmed by the animals; they expect nothing more of her than she is able to give.

The last thing Emma wants is for people to discover the *real* reason she is lying low, but then the handsome reporter from the local paper takes an interest in her story. Can Emma keep her secret *and* follow her heart's desire...?

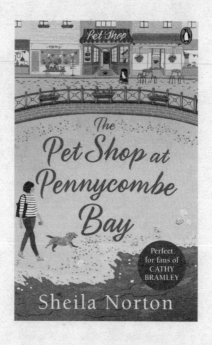

When the going gets ruff, it's time to make a change…

In need of a fresh start, Jess has moved to the beautiful Devon seaside town of Pennycombe Bay. However, it isn't the new beginning she was hoping for – she enjoys her new job at the local pet shop but feels like she's treading on eggshells living with her moody cousin Ruth.

When she meets handsome stranger, Nick, on the beach, she thinks she's made a new friend or something more. Although her hopes of romance are quickly dashed when she finds out he's seeing another woman …

Can Jess make Pennycombe feel like home?